Andrea Laurence is an award-winning author of contemporary romances filled with seduction and sass. She has been a lover of reading and writing stories since she was young. A dedicated West Coast girl transplanted into the Deep South, she is thrilled to share her special blend of sensuality and dry, sarcastic humour with readers.

Kimberley Troutte is a RITA® Award-nominated, *New York Times*, *USA TODAY* and Amazon top 100 bestselling author. She lives in Southern California with her husband, two sons, a wild cat, an old snake, a beautiful red iguana and various creatures Hubby and the boys rescue.

To learn more about her books and sign up for her newsletter, go to kimberleytroutte.com

Also by Andrea Laurence

What Lies Beneath
More Than He Expected
His Lover's Little Secret
The CEO's Unexpected Child
Little Secrets: Secretly Pregnant
Rags to Riches Baby
One Unforgettable Weekend
The Boyfriend Arrangement

Also by Kimberley Troutte

Forbidden Lovers
A Convenient Scandal

Discover more at millsandboon.co.uk

FROM MISTAKE TO MILLIONS

ANDREA LAURENCE

STAR-CROSSED SCANDAL

KIMBERLEY TROUTTE

MILLS & BOON

First Published in Great Britain 2019
by Mills & Boon, an imprint of HarperCollinsPublishers,
1 London Bridge Street, London, SE1 9GF

From Mistake to Millions © 2019 Andrea Laurence
Star-Crossed Scandal © 2019 Kimberley Troutte

ISBN: 978-0-263-27184-3

0619

MIX
Paper from
responsible sources
FSC™ C007454

This book is produced from independently certified FSC™ paper to ensure responsible forest management.

For more information visit: www.harpercollins.co.uk/green

Printed and bound in Spain
by CPI, Barcelona

FROM MISTAKE TO MILLIONS

ANDREA LAURENCE

Prologue

This couldn't be right.

Jade Nolan studied the genetic test report she'd just received in the mail. The DNA kit had been a Christmas gift from her younger brother, Dean. He'd gotten it for everyone in the family this year. He thought it would be fun to see what parts of the world they'd come from. They were fairly certain of the family's Irish and German heritage, so there weren't going to be many surprises.

But the words Jade was looking at were a surprise and then some. They were actually a shock.

"Jade? Are you okay?"

She looked up from the paper in her hand and stared blankly at her best friend, Sophie Kane. They were hanging out drinking wine and watching their favorite show together just like they did every Tuesday. But the minute Jade looked at the report, the evening had taken a sharp, unexpected turn.

"No," she said with a shake of her head. "I'm not okay."

How could she be okay? According to the report, she wasn't closely related to any other users in the company's database. Considering that she'd been the last of her family to mail in her DNA sample, that wasn't possible. Both her parents and her brother had submitted their DNA weeks before she had. They should be showing under the family section of her report. And yet they weren't.

Never mind the fact that her DNA showed she wasn't Irish and German. She was coming up English, Swedish and Dutch. She'd seen her brother's report and they didn't align at all.

"What does it say?" Sophie pressed. She set down her wine and leaned in to lay a comforting hand on Jade's shoulder. "Tell me, honey."

Jade swallowed hard, trying to dislodge the lump that had suddenly formed in her throat. She couldn't speak. In an instant, a lifetime of unfounded doubts had rushed into her mind. Years of being the family misfit. Insecurity about her physical differences. Jokes about being the milkman's daughter, since she was blonde with dark brown eyes, and the rest of her family had dark, almost black hair and green eyes. The jokes were all too real now.

No matter how many times her mother had assured her that her grandmother was a blonde, no matter how many grainy old pictures were hauled out to prove that her willow-thin frame came from her father's family, it didn't help. Her grandmother's hair had been a dishwater blond in her youth, not Jade's pale, almost platinum color. The family in the old pictures were poor and undernourished, not naturally slim like Jade, with her ballerina's body.

Jade had always felt like the odd one out. Now she had the cold, hard evidence to prove what she'd known all along. She was not a Nolan.

She stood up suddenly and the report slipped from her fingers, falling to the floor. Jade didn't notice.

"I think I'm…*adopted*." She was finally able to say the words aloud, but they sounded foreign to her ears.

Adopted. The reality of it was like a fist to the gut. Why had her parents kept this from her? She was almost thirty years old. She had married and divorced. When she and her ex-husband, Lance, were discussing children, her mother had even told her stories about her pregnancy with Jade. About how her father had fainted in the delivery room. Now Jade realized it was all a lie. An elaborate, complicated lie.

But why?

She didn't understand what was going on. But she would get to the bottom of it one way or another.

One

Being the boss was boring as hell.

Harley Dalton sat on the top floor of his Washington, DC, office building and flipped through some reports. He wasn't reading them. Managing a company wasn't really his thing. He'd started one only because he didn't want to take orders again after getting out of the navy.

He'd never expected it to be so successful. Dalton Security now had four offices in the US and one in London, with hundreds of employees. They were the company to call if you found yourself in a bind, or if a situation needed to be handled. Nothing outright illegal, of course, but things would be dealt with in a quick and efficient manner that sometimes fell into a fuzzy gray area.

One of the things his company had handled was the

recent abduction of a fourteen-year-old girl. She'd run away with her soccer coach, who was nearly fifty. It was on the nationwide news as people hunted for the young girl across the Midwest. It was also on the news when Dalton Security successfully tracked down, apprehended and delivered the pervert who'd kidnapped her to the front door of the police station, a little worse for wear. The girl was returned home safely. Dalton's stock prices had shot through the roof. All ended well.

At least well enough, considering Harley found himself in stuffy suits sitting at big desks talking to people all day. He wasn't the one in the field anymore and it grated on him. He wasn't toting a Glock and apprehending suspects. He was a damn paper pusher now.

He'd never imagined that being a millionaire would suck so hard.

"Mr. Dalton?" His assistant's voice chimed over the intercom on his phone.

"Yes?" he replied, trying not to growl at Faye. It wasn't her fault he was feeling strangled by his silk tie today.

"I have a Mr. Jeffries on the phone, sir."

Jeffries? The name didn't sound familiar. "Who is he?"

"He says he's the CEO of St. Francis Hospital in Charleston."

Now why would the CEO of a Charleston hospital be calling him? Harley had been born and raised in the city, but hadn't been back in a decade. His mother still lived there. He'd bought her a beautiful old plantation house that he had yet to visit. The CEO wouldn't be calling if something had happened to his mother. What could it be? Normally Harley didn't take phone calls from people he didn't know, but his curiosity was piqued.

"Put him through," he told Faye.

The phone chimed a moment later and he picked up. "This is Dalton," he said.

"Hello. This is Weston Jeffries. I'm the CEO of the St. Francis Hospital group in Charleston. I was hoping to speak with you about a…*situation* we're having here."

"Normally new cases are handled by our client intake department," Harley said. If they wanted special surveillance equipment or needed to investigate pending hires, that didn't need to come across his desk.

"I understand that," Mr. Jeffries said. "But from one CEO to another, this is a really delicate situation for us. We've already gotten more media scrutiny than we care to."

Media scrutiny? Apparently he needed to pay more attention to what was going on back home. "Well, why don't you tell me what's happening and I'll see what we can do."

"We've been contacted by a woman who claims she was switched at birth when she was born at our hospital here in 1989. She'd thought at first maybe she'd been adopted, but her parents are adamant that they delivered a daughter at St. Francis that day. She believes them, so in her mind, that only leaves the possibility that she was switched as an infant here. We are looking for someone to investigate what happened, as quietly as possible. The woman has already gone to the local news and we don't want to make the situation worse than it already is."

While someone being switched at birth was interesting and potentially damaging to the hospital, he still wasn't sure why the man insisted on speaking to him about it. Then again, Harley was bored to tears. He might as well listen. "Do you believe the hospital was at fault?"

"It's hard to say. Our technology and security weren't as good back then as they are now. The woman was also born in the middle of Hurricane Hugo, so it wasn't exactly business as usual around the hospital at that time."

Hurricane Hugo? That was an odd coincidence. His girlfriend back in high school had been born during Hurricane Hugo. His mind was suddenly flooded with memories of the willowy blonde who had headlined his teenage fantasies. She had been beautiful, smart and way out of his league. After she'd dumped him, he'd tried to put the memory of her in the past where it belonged, but he found that thoughts of her crept into his mind more often than he liked.

Like now.

He wasn't listening to a word the man was saying. "What was the woman's name?" he interrupted.

"Jade Nolan."

Upon hearing her name, Harley felt as if someone had reached out and punched him in the gut. Jade. Of all the women in Charleston, it had to be her case that dropped in his lap. Against his better judgment, he knew in that moment that his company would take the case. He also knew that for the first time in several years, he was going to handle it personally.

It might not be the healthiest thing to do, emotionally, but he had to see her again. It had been almost twelve years since she'd broken up with him and run off with that insipid little weasel, Lance Rhodes. He'd heard that she'd married him. Maybe she was still married to him. He'd seemed to be everything she wanted. Everything Harley wasn't.

Call it morbid curiosity. Call it a reason to get out of this office with the walls closing in on him like a Star Wars trash compactor. But he was driving to Charleston in the morning.

"Mr. Dalton?"

Harley again realized he'd been sitting silently on the line for too long. "I'm sorry, Mr. Jeffries. We'll take the case. Someone will be calling you back to get more details, but I will be down in Charleston within the week."

"You're going to handle it personally?"

"In this situation, yes."

"Thank you so much, Mr. Dalton. I look forward to speaking to you when you come into town."

The call ended and Harley sat back in his chair to consider the ramifications of what he'd just done. Taking the case on wasn't the problem. He had no doubt that his team would uncover the truth of what had happened, if anything had happened at all. Going down personally was another matter. He could tell himself it was a good excuse to visit his mother and see his old stomping grounds, but anyone who knew him back then would know that he was going down there to see Jade.

She wasn't the right kind of girl for him. He'd known that back in high school. He'd spent a lot of time in detention, while she was the treasurer of the National Honor Society. They ran in completely different social circles—Jade with the smart kids and him with the juvenile delinquents. And yet the first moment he'd laid eyes on her in their French class, he knew he was done for.

Maybe it was those big Bambi eyes that stood out against her pale skin and ice-blond hair. Even now, he remembered what it felt like to rub those silky strands between his fingers. She'd always looked at him with a touch of curiosity and anxiety hidden beneath thick lashes. The anxiety he was used to; he'd had quite the reputation around their high school. It was the curiosity that intrigued him.

Although he was doing fine in French, he'd pretended he wasn't and had approached her about tutoring him after school for some extra cash. He knew her family didn't have a lot of money. Neither did he, but he was willing to part with what little he had to spend some time with her.

Harley had paid her ten dollars a week for the rest of the semester to sit with him and practice French. He'd ended up getting an A in the class, which wasn't his goal, but it hadn't hurt. He'd just wanted to spend time with Jade, and he didn't think she would do it otherwise. He was wrong. One sultry summer night in Charleston, he'd worked up the nerve to kiss her, and everything had changed. Including him.

He had spent most of his youth running wild. His mother, a single mom, had worked two jobs to keep them afloat, so he'd spent most of his time without adult supervision. When he was with Jade, his usual pastimes didn't seem as exciting anymore. He'd found he much preferred the rush of kissing her, or nearly being caught by her parents when he'd sneak in through her bedroom window at night. She was everything he hadn't thought he would want. His previous romantic experiences had involved girls with too much makeup and too much time on their hands.

Jade thought about nothing but the future. She'd been so desperate to avoid the struggles of her parents that she was constantly worried about her grades, which college she might get into and what she was going to do with her life. He had no doubt that one day she would be Dr. Jade Nolan.

What Harley wasn't so sure about was how he might fit into Jade's future. Apparently, she had the same concerns. Not long after she'd started college, she broke things off with him. He knew as well as anybody that they weren't right for each other—or more accurately, that he wasn't good enough for her. So he hadn't fought to keep her. That was one of his biggest regrets, if he admitted to any at all. He preferred to look forward. And that's what he'd done.

A week later, he'd walked into the navy recruiting office and never looked back. He hadn't seen Jade since that day they broke up, despite her being on his mind all the time.

Glancing down now at the information he'd copied into his notebook during the call, he figured that was all about to change.

* * *

The doorbell rang.

Jade knew the investigator the hospital had hired was coming to interview her today, so she leaped up from the couch when she heard the chime ring through the house. Someone from St. Francis had called to make sure she would be home. She wasn't entirely sure what she would tell the investigator, since she'd been literally just born at the time the incident took place, but at the very least, she could get an idea of who this person was and how he or she would handle things.

The company had been hired by the hospital, after all. Her best friend and pro bono attorney, Sophie, had given her sound advice. She'd suggested they go to the local media when the hospital had tried to brush her off. Within twenty-four hours of her interview with the press, the hospital's legal team had phoned and told her they were hiring a third-party investigator to determine what had happened. Apparently they'd gotten a lot of flak, especially when the news station contacted them and they refused to comment.

That was a week ago. Things had changed quickly.

Jade went to answer the door, flinging it open in a rush, and then stopping short as she recognized the man standing on her porch. In an instant, her heart stuttered, her body stiffened. It was like she'd run straight into a brick wall she hadn't seen coming.

"Hello, Jade."

There was no way she could've seen *this* coming. Her mouth dropped open, the words dying on her lips. She couldn't even manage to say hello. Not with her ex-boyfriend Harley Dalton standing on her front porch.

It had been forever since she'd seen him—her first semester of college, to be precise. A lot had changed about Harley since then. He was bigger now. Brawny, almost. She'd heard that he went into the navy after they'd broken up, and it showed as his broad shoulders strained against his expensive, tailored gray suit coat. He'd dwarfed her in high school and there was an even more pronounced size difference between them now.

A lot of things were still the same, however. The dark blue eyes with the wicked glint. The broken nose. The devilish smile that promised more than she could handle, then or now…

The way he looked at her was different, though. The heat in his eyes wasn't stoked by desire today. It felt more like animosity. And close scrutiny. It was startling to see that, although Jade supposed he might still be mad at her for breaking up with him all those years ago.

"Jade?" He arched a brow, a questioning look on his face.

She clamped her jaw shut and nodded. "Hello, Harley," she finally managed to say. "Sorry."

"So you *do* remember me," he said with a smirk.

As though she was ever likely to forget. He'd been her first love. Maybe her only real love, if she was honest with herself. She wasn't about to let him know that. "Of course I remember you. What are you doing here?"

"St. Francis hired me—my company, rather—to look into your claims of staff misconduct at the hospital."

Jade hadn't kept tabs on Harley over the years, but

that type of work seemed right up his alley. Maybe if she had paid more attention, she wouldn't have been blindsided when the hospital hired him—the one man she'd managed to avoid successfully all these years. "Oh," she said, trying not to sound disappointed or concerned. There wasn't much she could do about it now. Even if she called the hospital and complained later, it wouldn't get Harley Dalton off her front porch today.

"They didn't tell me who to expect. I didn't realize… Come in," she offered, taking a step back from the door to let him inside her small rental house.

As he stepped over the threshold, the faint breeze blew in with him and brought the scent of him to her nose. The woodsy fragrance of his cologne mingled with his familiar manly musk immediately took her back to being eighteen again. To snuggling against him in his pickup truck. To fogging up the windows while he nibbled on her neck…

Whatever confidence and self-assurance she'd gained over the years faded to nothing when she looked at him. In their place was a flutter of butterflies in her stomach and a sudden awareness of parts of her body that she hadn't noticed in a very long time. Maybe since the last time she'd touched Harley. Lance had been a lot of things, but an intensely sexual creature was not one of them.

Jade had been okay with that. She'd traded that intense passion for security and stability. Or so she'd thought. Being around Harley again had just reminded her of everything she'd passed up in her quest for a better life.

It was a high price to pay. She'd been in the same

room with him for less than a minute now and was already almost overwhelmed by his presence. She needed a moment alone or wasn't sure she could get through a half hour interview without making a fool of herself.

"Would you like something to drink? Some sweet tea?" she asked.

"Sure. Thank you."

Jade gestured toward the couch. "Have a seat. I'll be right back."

She immediately turned on her heel and disappeared into the kitchen, trying to erase from her mind the image of him smiling at her. At one time, she'd lamented the closed-off floor plan of the older home she was renting, but now was relieved to have a barrier of wood and drywall between them.

Jade took her time pouring two glasses of sweet tea, and even put together a plate of cookies. She remembered that Harley had a sweet tooth, and that bought her a few more seconds to compose herself. But eventually she had to go back to the living room and face him again.

She wasn't sure what to think of his sudden appearance, or the faint scowl on his face. Questions were swirling through her mind. Did he not believe her side of the story about being switched? He had been hired by the hospital, after all. Or was it because he was still angry with her? If so, why had he taken the case? Was it because he still found her attractive? If so, did she really care? She wasn't really equipped to deal with something like that right now, what with everything else in her life spinning out of control.

"Do you need any help?"

Jade jerked her head up and saw Harley peeking around the corner. Trying not to look startled, she took the plate of cookies and handed it to him. "Here, take these. I'll carry the tea."

"Mmm, shortbread," he said, appreciation lighting his eyes.

"Those were your favorites, weren't they?" she asked, wishing immediately that she hadn't. She didn't want him to think she recalled things like that after all these years apart.

"They still are. I can't believe you remember." Harley popped a cookie into his mouth and chewed thoughtfully, drawing Jade's attention to his full lips.

A lot of time had passed, and yet it felt like almost none at all when she looked at Harley. She could almost feel those lips on hers as if it was yesterday. He might have been a bad boy, but he was a good kisser. A great one.

How long had it been since Jade had been kissed?

A real kiss. Not a peck. A long, slow, toe-curling kiss? She didn't even know. A long time. Sadly, it had been long before her husband turned away from her and had taken up drugs instead.

Deep inside, a part of her wished to experience that thrill of attraction again. To feel wanted and desired. But she knew that Harley was not the one to relight those fires. Those flames would be all consuming and that was a risk she wasn't willing to take. Not back then and not now.

Harley finished his cookie and smiled at her in a way

that made her wonder if he knew exactly what she was thinking. Jade had never been very good at hiding her emotions, but she needed to do better. Especially when he was around. He was here to interview her about her claims against the hospital, but she could just as easily be a teenager again, helping him study French over tea and cookies, and fantasizing about making it to second base.

He turned and walked into the living room, and with no other choice, she followed him. Harley sat on the end of the couch and she opted for the chair to his right. She set the tea on the table, unsure of how to start this conversation. Did they go straight to the investigation and ignore the elephant in the room? Or should they take the time to catch up after more than a decade of not seeing each other?

"So how have you been?" he asked, making the decision for her.

"Good," she said on reflex. Since her divorce, people were always asking her how she was. She found they didn't really want to hear the truth. "Most days, at least. A lot has changed since I saw you last, but I'm doing okay."

Harley glanced down at her hand and his brows knitted together in confusion. Presumably he was looking for the wedding ring she'd taken off a long time ago. "I heard you married Lance, but I don't see a ring."

"I did marry him. My junior year of college," Jade said. "It ended a couple years ago."

Harley straightened, apparently unaware of what had happened. She was surprised the investigator hadn't thoroughly looked into her past before he'd arrived. "I'm sorry to hear that," he said.

Jade could only nod. She didn't want to tell him about what had happened with Lance. It wasn't a pretty story, but it had been in the news and anyone with a desire to could look it up. He could get all the details if he wanted to know.

"What about you? Any family?"

Harley chuckled and shook his head. "Oh, no. I spent eight years in the navy, traveling all over the world. There wasn't much time for starting a family or even settling down in one spot. After I got out, I started my own business. That takes up every moment of your day for a while. Thankfully, things are running smoothly, without my constant supervision, now."

Jade hadn't been sure what Harley would do with his life. Some had bet their money he'd end up in jail. Others, that he'd accomplish nothing. She had seen more potential in him than that, and was pleased to hear he'd become an entrepreneur.

"So your company does private investigations? Like hired detectives?"

"Not entirely. Across our five locations, we do a lot of different work that falls in the security detail bucket. Personal security and protection, home security setup and monitoring, missing persons cases…lots of different things where the police can't or won't step in, for whatever reason. We specialize in government contracts and a higher end clientele who want to keep things quiet. Investigations are just one aspect of what we do at Dalton Security."

Dalton Security? Now that he'd said it, Jade realized she'd heard of the company. Maybe in reference to the recent Bennett kidnapping case. That had been on every news channel she'd seen for weeks. Dalton Security had broken the case wide open and delivered the teen back to her parents.

It had never occurred to her that it was Harley's business. It sounded like he was doing even better for himself than she had hoped. The nice suit and gold Rolex on his wrist were evidence enough of that. She was glad to hear it. Jade knew his mother had struggled to raise him on her own. The last she remembered, Harley's mom had worked as a cashier at a grocery store and cleaned houses on the side.

"This seems like a pretty puny job in the scheme of things your company handles. Why would the CEO of Dalton Security—of all people—be working a case like this?"

Harley's gaze met hers and she felt a shiver run through her whole body. When he looked at her that way, it was as though he could see straight through her, into her soul. There was nothing she could hide from him. She was an open book left out for him to read if he wanted to bother. It was unnerving and thrilling at the same time. For so long, she'd felt invisible.

Harley saw her.

"Isn't that obvious, Jade? I took the case so I could see you again."

Two

The sight of Jade was breathtaking.

Damn it.

Harley hadn't known what to expect when he walked up to her door. She had been a pretty teenager. Pretty enough to headline in every one of his high school fantasies, and a couple of his grown-up ones. A part of him had hoped that she wouldn't be as attractive as he remembered. That perhaps she'd aged poorly or had taken up chain smoking. That would make it easier for him to do his job and walk away from the whole situation as planned.

But when she opened her front door today…he had to brace himself for the impact of how stunningly beautiful a woman she'd become. She still had the kind of naturally platinum blond hair that women spent a fortune on in the salon. It was just pulled back into a sleek ponytail, but the ringlets that fell down her neck were captivating. With her pale complexion and large eyes, she was like a flawless porcelain doll.

It was an incredibly frustrating sight for Harley, making the situation infinitely more complicated. Curiosity and boredom had brought him to Jade's door. Her beauty could keep him around longer than was necessary to wrap up this case. He was painfully aware that the attraction between the two of them was just as intense as it ever was. The look in her eyes when she marched off into the kitchen told him that much.

To be honest, that was the last thing he wanted to know. Being attracted to Jade hadn't ended well for him the first time. Not because it wasn't reciprocal; he could've taken that. No, his heartburn came from the fact that even though she'd wanted Harley, she'd chosen Lance. That spoke volumes. Just because her ex wasn't in the picture any longer didn't mean anything had changed. She might still prefer a stuffed shirt over a guy like Harley. Fate had brought them back together, but it didn't mean this time would be any different for the two of them.

And yet the way that Jade had looked at him when he said he was here to see her made him realize she had no clue how beautiful she truly was, or how he could still be attracted to her after all this time. That was a damned shame. What had happened to her since the last time he saw her that she could ever doubt it? What had her suitable, respectable husband done to break Jade's spirit?

"You took the case just to see me?" she asked in

obvious confusion and doubt. Jade seemed baffled by the whole situation. In fairness, he'd had several days to prepare to see her again, and she'd been thrown a curveball without warning.

"Let me rephrase that." He backtracked, realizing the implications of his words. "I wanted to make sure your case was handled by the best guy at my company, and that means by me."

Harley didn't want Jade to think he'd come here just to profess his undying love and pick up where they'd left off. He hadn't. He'd gotten over her a long time ago, whether he'd wanted to or not. Going through navy boot camp was enough to push anything other than survival out of his mind. The quiet moments were another matter. Those were harder to get through. That's probably why he'd opted to spend most of his service overseas in the thick of things.

He couldn't help but notice there was a slight flicker of disappointment in her eyes before she smiled and nodded. The attraction seemed to be mutual, even if fleeting. She still seemed conflicted by her attraction to him. "Of course. I appreciate your help with all of this."

There was something in her tone that struck Harley as disingenuous. Did she not want him here, or was it about *why* he was here? He wasn't sure, but since he wasn't going anywhere, he decided to do what he could to quell her concerns. "The hospital hired me, but I want to assure you that I'll be an impartial third party as I investigate what happened. I'm being paid to find the truth, whether that reflects favorably on the hospital or not."

Jade let out a ragged breath and the tension seemed to ease from her shoulders. "I'm relieved to hear you say that. There's no way I could afford to hire my own investigators. And any attorneys I might hire would be more interested in suing the pants off the hospital to get a cut for themselves. I just want to find out the truth."

Harley was surprised. He looked around the house, which was okay, but nothing special. The furniture was worn, and he'd noticed when he pulled up that her car was an older model. Financial security had certainly seemed to be a priority when she'd left him for the more successful Lance, and yet her ex didn't seem to be contributing much to her way of life now. As a young divorcée, wouldn't some kind of settlement from the hospital be important to her? "You're not interested in suing the hospital?"

Jade shrugged. "If they're at fault, I wouldn't turn it down. I can put it toward buying a home or stick it in my retirement account. But what I'm really after…" She hesitated and shook her head. "The truth is that the results of my DNA tests just confirmed what I've always felt deep down inside."

Harley frowned. "And what's that?"

"That I've never belonged." Her dark gaze fixed on him and he felt her raw emotions like a vise squeezing his chest. "I've always felt like a puzzle piece that got tossed into the wrong box. I was never going to fit in and now I know why. So, I want to know where I *do* come from."

"What about Arthur and Carolyn?" Her folks hadn't been particularly fond of Harley—he wasn't the kind of boy any parents wanted dating their teenage daughter—but they'd always seemed like good people. Jade loved them dearly and he'd never suspected that they treated her like anything other than their little princess.

"The parents that raised me will always be my parents, but I want to know who my biological family really is. Where I come from. What my life should've been like, so that something about it can start to make sense."

He didn't know what to say to that. Harley had always thought that Jade had her life together. She was smart and ambitious. She made the most of her every opportunity. The framed certificate on the wall declared that she had her PhD in pharmacology. He'd always thought she was someone who knew who she was and what she wanted. To hear otherwise was unsettling. It made him want to question everything he felt was a fact. It also made him desperately want to uncover the truth for her so she could have some closure.

"Have you always felt so lost, Jade?"

She avoided his gaze for a moment, perhaps knowing instinctively that she couldn't lie to him. He'd spent many years in the navy learning interrogation techniques. Even if she could've lied to him back in high school, she couldn't now. He'd know the truth.

"Not when I was with you," she said at last. "That was probably the only time things felt right in my life."

Harley knew exactly what she meant. He'd spent most of the past decade in a tailspin, trying to right his course after their breakup. He'd lost his True North when Jade left him for Lance, and he really hadn't recovered. Sure, he'd been successful. He'd moved on with his life. But somehow he knew that there was a hole in his world where Jade belonged. He had yet to find someone or something else to fill it. None of the women he'd dated—and he used that term loosely—fit the bill. Sex was fine, but he never wanted more with any of them.

He'd never dreamed that Jade would feel lost, too.

"I will find out the truth. I intend to find out what happened to you and why. I'll find your family."

On reflex, he reached out and took her hand. It felt small and delicate in his large, rough ones, rousing a protective instinct he wasn't expecting. He'd come here today thinking he would satisfy his curiosity, scratch his itch to work in the field again and perhaps finally be able to move on where Jade was concerned. As she clutched him tightly, he felt the heat of awareness travel up his arm, warming his chest. He remembered this feeling. A feeling that happened only when he touched her.

This was all wrong. His plan had started unraveling the moment she opened the door. This was the exact opposite of what he wanted to happen. He couldn't be attracted to Jade and not end up in the same mess as last time.

Or could he? Maybe he could compartmentalize the attraction and keep it separate from any emotional attachment. It wasn't like they were kids any longer. He'd had plenty of women in his bed without strings, and it had worked fine. If Jade was open to the idea of indulging for old time's sake, it might be exactly what he needed to close the book on the two of them for good. It was a risky proposition—one she might be completely uninterested in—but he had to find a way to get through the next week or two with her constantly on his mind.

"Thank you," she whispered softly.

"I promise you that, and I'm a man of my word." Harley's attention was drawn away from her by a ring tone coming from the kitchen.

"That's my phone. Excuse me one second." Jade got up and left the room, answering the phone after a moment.

Anxious, Harley got up from his seat. He paced around the living room to burn off some of the excess energy running through his veins. Touching her, even just that little bit, had set off a chain reaction in his nervous system. He was suddenly on edge, ready to leap out at the enemy or jump from a plane. There would be no adrenaline payoff in this situation, however. At least not right now or he'd frighten her off. He needed to keep his hands to himself and get through this interview.

He turned and focused on a row of photographs that lined the fireplace mantel. The biggest was a portrait of her and Lance on their wedding day. It made Harley's chest ache to realize how beautiful she'd looked that day. The dress and flowers didn't matter to him; he focused in on her face. She was beaming with excitement, so happy for the future she was going to have with Lance. A future he didn't think she got.

Would things have been different if she had married him instead?

Harley shook away those thoughts because they weren't helpful. In reality, the teenage Harley Dalton would never have been enough for someone like Jade. He had been spinning his wheels, unsure of what he wanted to do with his life. All he knew was that he wanted to spend every waking moment with Jade. That didn't pay very well. His life took the path it had only because of the choice she'd made to be with someone else. He never would've joined the navy, built his own company or made a whole new life for himself if she hadn't walked away from him. If he hadn't felt like he needed to better himself and his situation to be worthy of a woman like her, he might never have worked so hard.

He supposed he should thank her for that, but he wouldn't. Instead, he'd just do his best to crack the case and get her the answers she deserved.

And if he was a smart man, he'd stop there.

"So that's it? He held your hand and asked you a few questions?" Sophie looked across the kitchen table at Jade and wrinkled her nose. "I was expecting more when you said your first love showed up on your doorstep to take on your case."

"That was enough," Jade said with a sigh. "I don't think my heart could've taken much more than that."

Sophie had shown up for their usual Tuesday gathering, eager for all the juicy details. She hadn't lived in Charleston back then, so she didn't know Harley, but she knew Jade had a love that predated Lance. She was eager to dig into that, even if Jade wasn't interested. For the most part, Sophie's life was wrapped up in her work. Being a lawyer took up long hours, leaving her little time for much else. As such, Sophie was always interested in exciting tales to live vicariously. She would also push Jade into situations from time to time. Like doing that news interview after the hospital sent her a letter that politely told her to get bent.

"Was he as cute as you remembered?"

Jade twisted her lips in thought as she pictured the solid wall of man standing in her doorway. "*Cute* isn't the word I'd use for Harley. Cute is for puppies and babies. He was…hot. Ripped-guy-on-the-cover-of-a-romance-novel hot."

Just thinking about him holding her hand was enough to make her face feel warm and her whole body languid. It was an innocent touch. A supportive gesture not meant to titillate or entice, but the impact on Jade had been massive. It had been a long time since a man had touched her. Even longer since a man had looked at her the way Harley had. Her body could recall the feeling instantly, making her want to turn on the fan despite it still being February.

Maybe it was the red wine on an empty stomach. Or a bad mix of alcohol and unfulfilled desires.

"I think you need to sleep with him."

Jade shot to attention in her chair. "What? You're joking, right?"

"Not at all. I think after everything, a hot tryst with some serious man candy is just what the doctor ordered."

"Harley is not the kind of guy for me to start a relationship with."

"Who said anything about a relationship? I was

just thinking about a hot tumble. You don't have to keep him."

Jade could only roll her eyes. It was a tempting thought, but a silly one. Why would someone as successful and handsome as Harley want someone like her? Even short term. He could do better and avoid dealing with the past in the process. "I wouldn't even know what to do with a man like that, to be honest. I'm out of practice and he's not rookie material."

"I need to see a picture of this guy. He doesn't sound like he could be real." Sophie picked up her phone and immediately set off to search for him on the internet. "Nothing is coming up when I hunt for Harley Dalton," she said. "No Facebook. Not even his company website has a photo of him."

"I'm not surprised. With the kind of work he does, I imagine he has a limited online presence. You'll just have to take my word for it."

"For now," Sophie said, making Jade worry that her friend would nose in where she didn't belong. "Next time I come over, I expect you to have hauled out your yearbook, if nothing else."

"What's more important is that the hospital isn't blowing me off now," she said, trying to switch the subject from her hunky ex. "Hiring an investigator is a big step."

Sophie grinned and took a sip of wine. "I told you I knew what I was doing. There's nothing quite like public shame. Now they're going to get to the bottom of the case and you don't have to pay a dime. No reason to worry."

Jade wasn't so sure about that. At this point, she almost wished that her parents had just been lying to her about being adopted. That certainly would've been easier to cope with. Instead, they'd been adamant that she was the baby they'd left the hospital with. She had a tiny birthmark on her hip that her mother had noticed before they went home. What her mom couldn't be sure of was whether or not the baby she'd delivered had had that same birthmark beneath her swaddling blankets and diapers.

"How am I not supposed to worry? This scenario can only end badly. My parents insist I wasn't adopted. The only time and place something could've happened to me was while they were still in the hospital and I was in the nursery. Someone made a huge mistake and two families have paid the price for it."

"That's not an impossible mistake to make. Especially during Hugo."

Jade shook her head and sighed. How had she gotten caught up in something like this? Being switched at birth was the stuff of television movies, but Sophie was right about the storm. It had been a Category Four when it hit Charleston. The whole town was in chaos amid power outages, massive flooding and large numbers of casualties being rushed into the hospitals for treatment.

It sounded like the perfect storm for something to go wrong in, and if something would go wrong, it would happen to Jade. She was a magnet for that sort of thing. But being switched at birth? It was a crazy thought.

The hospital agreed, dismissing the claim as nonsense. And until she'd gone on the news, they would've gladly brushed her off. Instead, they'd hired Dalton Security, a company she now knew was famous for getting the job done no matter what it took. Harley had always been a rule breaker when he felt the cause justified it. Now that seemed to be the company motto. He would do what he was hired to do and find out the truth, although she worried about how many lives would be upended in the process.

Jade set her wineglass on the kitchen table and sat back in her chair. "Maybe this whole thing is a mistake."

"What do you mean?" Sophie asked.

"I mean, maybe I'm digging into something that's better left buried. It's been almost thirty years since the switch happened. I'm looking for answers, but what… what if all I find is heartache? It's going to destroy families."

"Or unite them," Sophie countered. "Your parents know that you love them, and they love you no matter what they find. That isn't a risk. But I'm willing to bet a part of them would want to know what happened to their biological daughter, too. They have to wonder if she's safe and happy. They wouldn't trade you for the world, but this will bring them peace of mind, if nothing else. You're going to gain family, not lose them."

"You can't be so sure. Maybe my parents will realize their real daughter is so much better than I am, and they'll choose her over me."

"That is the most ridiculous thing I've ever heard. Anyone would be happy to have you for their daughter. I have no idea who you were swapped with, but your parents did not get the short end of the stick with you, Jade."

"I know," she admitted reluctantly. That was her insecurity speaking. Her parents would be shocked to hear her even suggest such a thing. "I just don't like not knowing how any of this will turn out."

Sophie crossed her arms over her chest in exasperation. "Well, you'll never know until you try. And even if you stopped the investigation now, it's too late. The genie is out of the bottle and there's no way you'd be able to pretend you don't know the truth any longer. You might as well follow the trail to see where it leads, or you're always going to wonder and harbor regrets."

Jade frowned at her friend. That's all she could do, because she knew Sophie was right. The minute she got that DNA test in the mail there was no turning back.

"Your biological parents are out there, somewhere. You've always wanted to have that connection to someone that you felt you lacked. You'll have more family now. More people to depend on. More people to love you."

"You make it sound like this is all going to end like a Disney movie. I'm not about to find out I'm a secret princess. Birds aren't going to make my clothes and a prince isn't going to sweep me off my feet. My real parents could be horrible people. And even if they aren't, this is going to end in lawsuits and tears, and maybe even someone going to jail, if we were switched on purpose."

"Maybe. But I'm an optimist. And I think this is going to be good for you. You need some good in your life after everything that happened with Lance."

Jade groaned and pushed herself up from the table. "I don't want to talk about all that tonight."

"We're not. And I didn't mean to bring it up. I'm just saying that I think you deserve some happiness. I think there are good things on the horizon for you. Even if your real family doesn't turn out to be everything you've hoped for, there can still be positives. Maybe you'll get a huge settlement from the hospital and you can buy a nice house. That would be something good."

Jade picked up the half-empty bottle of wine from the counter and carried it back to the table. She refilled both their glasses. "It would certainly help," she admitted. "Lance's addiction ate through all our savings. I'm making decent money now, but things like a house are just pipe dreams with the cost of living in Charleston."

She set the bottle on the table and sat down in the chair. "Things weren't supposed to end up like this, you know? Everyone said that Lance was the smart choice for me. He was older, established, educated... Marrying him was going to provide me with the stable, safe and loving home I wanted for myself and my future family. We wouldn't struggle with money the way my parents did. Everything was supposed to end up perfectly."

"No one could've expected what happened to Lance, honey," Sophie said. "They call it the opioid *epidemic* for a reason. A lot of people get caught up in it without meaning to. He was never the same after that car accident."

"No, he wasn't."

It had been the beginning of the end for their marriage, although Jade didn't know it then. She was too busy fighting her way through her last year of pharmacy school to see the warning signs. He'd needed the pain pills after his back surgery, but the more he took, the harder it was for him to manage things at work. The more stress he was under, the more pills he needed. As he started to fail, Jade had graduated and thrived in her new career as a pharmacist. Lance couldn't cope with the idea of her being more successful than he was, and it just fed into his existing drug problem.

The next thing she knew, the cops were at her door at 2:00 a.m. and she was being questioned about a break-in at the pharmacy where she worked. Apparently, Lance had taken her keys to steal pain pills. His doctors had recognized he had an issue, and refused to give him more pain medication, so he'd resorted to more desperate means to get it. Jade had filed for divorce before Lance could even get a public defender assigned to him. It was one thing to battle addiction, but to put her career at risk in the process seemed like a deliberate move on his part that she couldn't overlook. He couldn't stand her success and she was tired of propping up his ego.

"The irony of it all is that I broke things off with Harley because he was supposedly the bad boy who wouldn't amount to anything. Lance was the good guy with a future. Harley was trouble with an angel's smile that would lead me down the wrong path in life. I can't help but wonder sometimes," Jade said, as she fingered the rim of her wineglass, "what would have happened if I'd made a different choice. Did things work out the way they were meant to? Or did I go against my gut and make the worst mistake of my life by walking away from him all those years ago?"

And if it had been a mistake, Jade couldn't help but wonder if Harley showing up on her porch was a second chance to make things right. Did she dare take the risk?

Three

Harley felt like a stupid, insecure teenager again.

That didn't happen very often, and frankly, it was silly that he felt that way now. He was a grown man. A successful CEO of his own company. There was no reason for him to feel anything but completely confident in his skin. But walking up the driveway to the Nolans' house made him just as anxious as it had when he'd picked Jade up for dates all those years ago.

Perhaps because it was the same little house—a brick-and-vinyl rancher with a carport and neglected flower beds. It was an older home in a poorer area of town, but he knew this part of Charleston well. The apartment he'd shared with his mother was only a few blocks away, or it had been, before it was demolished and replaced with a shopping center.

The whole neighborhood seemed quieter now, as though all the children he remembered running the streets were grown and gone. Things seemed to be more in disrepair as owners aged and were unable to maintain their properties or were forced to move out and rent to people who didn't care as much for their begonias as they did.

At one time, Harley had felt like he fitted in around here. Now, with his shiny black Jaguar in the driveway instead of a beat-up old truck, and a designer suit replacing his torn jeans, it was obvious that the neighborhood wasn't the only thing that had changed.

As he faced the front door, where Arthur Nolan had greeted him dozens of times with a sour expression, he was glad he'd asked Jade to meet him here today. He'd already interviewed her, but having her there while he questioned her parents would make things easier.

Or so he thought.

The door opened and he looked up in time to see Jade step into the doorway. She must have come from work because she was wearing black dress pants, heels and a clingy red sweater that was precisely the same shade as her flawlessly applied lipstick. Her blond hair was slicked back into a bun, highlighting her delicate bone structure as she smiled at him. She looked poised, professional and absolutely stunning. He wasn't sure his heart could withstand this version of his high school sweetheart.

"Are you going to come in or just stand out there in the cold?"

"I haven't decided," he replied. "Your dad still got that shotgun?"

Jade looked to her right and nodded. "Right here by the door as always. I doubt he's keen to use it on you any longer. You're safe to come in."

Harley climbed the steps and leaned close to her, drawing in her scent before whispering into her ear. "If he knew the things I did to you back then, he'd shoot me on the spot."

Jade's eyes widened as she took a step back. Her pale skin flushed pink as her lips tightened a bit with amused disapproval. "Best you keep that to yourself," she noted. "Come on in and have a seat. I'll get them both."

Finding himself alone in the living room, he realized not much had changed inside the house, either. The furniture was the same, although the old tube television in the corner had been replaced with a new flat screen. There was also a large framed portrait over the desk of Jade on her wedding day. Unlike the one at her house, this was just her. Her back was turned, showcasing the lace and buttons that traveled down her spine into the intricate train of her dress. She glanced over her shoulder with a coy smile that made him wish she'd been gazing at him that day instead of Lance.

"Look who the cat dragged in," a man's voice boomed from behind him, distracting him from his unhelpful thoughts.

Harley turned around to find a softer, graying version of the Arthur Nolan he remembered. This one didn't glare at him with disapproval, putting Harley slightly more at ease. He smiled and reached out to shake her father's hand. "Good to see you again, sir, although I wish it were under different circumstances."

"Don't I know it," Arthur said with a serious expression. "This has been really hard on Carolyn, and Jade, too. You can't imagine something like this happening to you."

"I'll do everything I can to find the answers for your family."

Arthur nodded and patted him on the upper arm. "Good, good. Let's have a seat. Carolyn is going to be a minute. She's fussing with some coffee."

Harley sat down in a wingback chair that faced the sofa. Arthur sat there, leaving a space for Jade's mother beside him. A moment later, Jade came in with a tray of mugs, cream and sugar. She put it down on the coffee table between them and took a seat in the chair beside Harley. Carolyn followed with a carafe of hot coffee and poured everyone a cup.

"I know it's late in the day, but it's so chilly, I thought we needed something to warm us up."

"Thank you, Mrs. Nolan."

Carolyn looked up at him with a wide smile as she appraised what had become of the boy who had once graced her doorstep. "I think you can call me Carolyn now, dear. You're not a teenage boy sniffing around my daughter any longer."

Harley smiled back and nodded, but there was something in her eyes that made him question her words. There was a curious curl to her lips as she looked him over, then glanced back at her daughter. It made him wonder if perhaps Mrs. Nolan didn't think he was such a bad match for Jade, after all.

Interesting thought, but she was wrong.

"If you don't mind, I'm going to record this interview. It will allow me to focus on the discussion now instead of taking notes, and I can go back and do that later."

Her parents nodded. He started the recorder on his phone and placed it gently on the coffee table between them. "So tell me about the day you checked in to St. Francis to have your daughter."

"It was chaos," Carolyn began. "Everyone was waiting on the storm to hit. Arthur was nailing wood on the windows and sandbagging the sliding door to keep out the water. We'd stockpiled some supplies, and did everything we could do to prepare. And then I went into labor."

She shook her head. "I had another week to go. I thought for sure we'd get through the storm, but no, Jade was ready." She looked at her daughter and a pained expression came across her face. "Well, not Jade. Our biological daughter. It's so hard to come to terms with all of this. I can't think about the baby I raised and not think it was the same Jade in my belly all that time. Who would do such a thing?"

Harley noticed tears glittering in Carolyn's eyes. Tears weren't his specialty, but he could cope. He'd learned he was better at keeping interviewees focused than he was at consoling them. "I understand this is hard for you," he said. "Just go over what you remember about your time at the hospital."

Arthur put his hand over Carolyn's and squeezed it. "We made it to the hospital before the storm hit," he continued. "We had a few hours to go and were worried about a long labor, since it was our first baby, but our daughter arrived rather quickly and without a fuss if you don't count me fainting. It's hard to believe, but having a baby was the easiest thing about that day. About two hours later, the power went out. The wind picked up. All hell broke loose. Since the nursery didn't have any windows, they recommended that the babies stay there for their own safety. It broke Carolyn's heart because she'd barely gotten a chance to hold the baby before she was taken away. Maybe if we'd spent more time with her..."

Harley hated to hear the Nolans blame themselves. He didn't know what had happened, but he knew it wasn't anything they did wrong. "Don't beat yourself up about this. From what I understand, newborns all look very similar, especially in those first few hours. It takes time for their individual features and personalities to come out. You went through a lot that day and had no reason to question the staff."

Arthur nodded, but Harley could tell he still blamed himself somehow. "After the storm went through, things weren't much better. There was only emergency power. Most of the staff was downstairs in the ER. There were only maybe two or three nurses working the whole maternity ward and I'd say there were easily nine or ten mothers there at the time."

"Did any of the staff or people you saw at the hospital seem off to you? Anything at all strike you as odd?"

Carolyn furrowed her brow in thought. "Nothing other than the hurricane. The staff were stressed out but they seemed really focused on keeping everything afloat. There was even one nurse, I forget her name, who sat and chatted with me for a while. She was so sweet. I can't believe I can't remember her name now. But everyone was great. Did you notice anything, Arthur?"

He shook his head. "Everyone seemed to be coping. That's all anyone could do. If anything seemed strange, I chalked it up to that."

"How long was it until you got to really spend time with Jade?"

"The next day," Carolyn said. "By then the power was back on and things seemed to be closer to normal. I got to spend most of the day with her. That's when I first noticed that birthmark on her leg. That means the switch had already taken place, doesn't it?"

It did. Harley knew exactly which birthmark she was referring to, although he wouldn't say as much to her parents. It was crescent shaped and high on Jade's upper thigh. He'd kissed it a dozen times in his youth. "It sounds like it."

Carolyn started crying in earnest and Arthur comforted her. The conversation continued on for another half hour or so, but Harley had already gotten what he needed. The switch had happened early, during the storm itself. That at least narrowed the window in terms of hospital staff and visitors with access to the babies.

Harley knew he should be focused on the parents as they continued, but he had a hard time not watching Jade's expression as they spoke about that day. About the birth of the child that wasn't her. Speaking about the arrival of the baby they adored, but didn't come home with. It was hard for her to hear, he could tell. It was hard for them, too, but it was her pained face that drew his gaze.

He hated seeing her like this. Harley was no knight in shining armor come to save Jade; he knew that much. But perhaps he could set this situation to rights for her. He'd done his research on her since their interview and had found himself at a loss as he stared at his computer screen. She had been sold false goods with Lance and now she was paying for it. Finding out her ex was serving time was surprising to Harley, so he knew it had to have blindsided Jade. She'd put all her faith in him, and Lance had destroyed their future together.

Harley supposed that another man in his shoes might think it was her karmic retribution for spurning him all those years ago. But he had loved Jade too much to ever wish ill on her back then. He'd just wanted her to be happy. And now, he wanted to help. Not by sweeping her off her feet, as much as the idea of carrying her off to bed appealed to him.

No, all he could do was find the truth for Jade and hope that she could be happy at last, knowing where she really belonged.

Jade walked Harley to his car when the interview was over. It was dark now, with the winter evenings still coming early. She was looking forward to spring, with warmer temperatures and maybe the chance to work in the garden. To get to that, though, she first had to make it through this investigation with Harley.

"I hope my parents were helpful," she said, as they reached his car.

"They were. As helpful as they could be considering they weren't involved. If nothing else, I was able to narrow the timeline down. You were switched almost immediately after you were born. Probably during the worst of the storm, when everything was at its most frantic. It was a crime of opportunity, in my opinion."

"A crime? As in someone actually did it on purpose?" Jade had lain in bed for several nights wondering how any of this could've happened, but she'd rarely considered it might be deliberate. "I could see if it was a mistake in the chaos, but you really think someone did it on purpose?"

"I do." Harley crossed his muscled forearms over his chest and leaned back against his shiny sports car. It was so sleek and low to the ground she wondered how he even got in and out of the thing.

"To what end? What did it get them? I can't see how anyone would benefit from it."

"That I don't know yet. I'll find out one way or another. But in my gut, I know it was done intentionally. They may not have known in advance which babies and when, but they saw their chance during the storm and took it."

They. He kept saying that with an intense expression on his face that both frightened and thrilled her. Who was he talking about? Jade had a hard time imagining what kind of person would do something like that. Then again, people were surprising her a lot lately. That reminded her... She reached into her pocket and pulled out a note she'd received the day before.

"Harley, before you go, I want you to take a look at

this. It came in the mail yesterday. I thought it might factor into your investigation."

Harley took the letter from her and unfolded it carefully. His gaze went over the text again and again, with his expression darkening more each time. His jaw was clenched tight in anger when he finally looked up at her.

"Why didn't you mention this sooner?"

Jade stiffened as his wave of rage was aimed in her direction. She wasn't expecting that. Was he really upset with her? She took a step back on reflex. "I wanted you to speak with my parents first. They don't know about the letter and I don't want them to know."

Her parents were dealing with enough right now without knowing that Jade had received a threatening letter from some anonymous whack job. And to be honest, she wasn't too concerned. She'd just appeared on television. Any weirdo sitting at home watching the news could've written her that letter.

"Do you have any idea who would've sent this to you?"

Jade shook her head. The handwritten text was fairly straightforward—let it go or else. That could be from anyone. "I thought maybe someone from the hospital wanted me to back off. They were basically shamed into cooperating when I went public with my story. I'm sure there's someone there who wishes I would just go away. Or someone that saw me on TV. I wasn't taking it too seriously."

Harley narrowed his gaze at her. "You need to take it seriously, Jade. If nothing else, because whoever sent this knows your home address. That's a problem. Are you listed in the phone book or online?"

Jade's spine straightened at that thought. She'd been so preoccupied with other things that she hadn't thought about that aspect of it. A chill ran through her and she snuggled farther into her favorite sweater. She wished she'd brought a coat out here with her, but she hadn't anticipated a long conversation. "No. It's a rental so you'd think there wouldn't be anything associating my name with the house, but I suppose you can find anything on the internet for a price."

That made the corners of Harley's full mouth turn down into a frown. It made her want to reach out and rub her thumb across his bottom lip the way she had before. The dark, angry storm in his eyes, however, kept her arms firmly crossed over her chest where they belonged.

"Do you have the envelope it came in?" he asked.

She nodded and pulled it out of her pocket. "Here. What are you going to do with it?"

Harley reached into the breast pocket of his coat and pulled out a plastic specimen bag. He put both the letter and the envelope inside and sealed it up. "I'm going to send it to my lab along with the DNA swabs I took of you and your parents. I'll see if they can pull some prints or DNA off of it. I might need to get prints from you later so we can exclude yours."

"You have your own lab?" *And you keep evidence bags in your coat?* She kept the last part to herself. She got the feeling he wouldn't understand why she thought it was weird.

Harley nodded. "It's a necessity. Local police investigations are stymied by the backlog awaiting lab testing. Since I have my own state-of-the-art lab in DC, none of my investigators have to wait. Things can move forward faster. It was one of the first things I invested in when the company started to gain success."

Jade tried not to look impressed, but it was hard. The Harley she was looking at was so different from the one she remembered. At least on the outside. On the inside, she was pretty sure the rebel was still there. He might have a sports car instead of his old truck, but he probably still drove fast. And no doubt liked to bend the rules as far as he could. That had always made her nervous back when they were dating, and still did now. She could look at Harley but not touch. And definitely not keep.

"Anyway, the results might help us narrow down who might be involved. Maybe the person who was behind the switch sent the letter. Or someone else who knows something about the case." He put it away and looked at her with a softer expression on his face. "Is this the first note you've received?"

"Yes."

"Anything else unusual? Phone calls? The feeling that someone is following you?"

Jade sighed and tried to think back over the last week since she'd gone on the news and her story had spread across Charleston. It had been chaotic to be sure, but she hadn't felt like she was in danger. "Nothing I can think of. I lead a pretty quiet, boring life compared to yours, Harley."

"Good," he said with a curt nod. "That was what you wanted, after all, right? Safe, comfortable? All the things you didn't think I could give you."

She had been waiting for this moment. He'd been so professional thus far, but she knew eventually he would mention their breakup. How could he not?

"I don't know what you could've given me. We were kids and I made the best decision I could at the time. I ended up being all wrong about Lance, but I could've been wrong about you, too. But something tells me you weren't interested in a quiet life back then and you're not interested in it now."

He shrugged, confirming in her mind that it was true. "A little excitement isn't all bad, Jade." He pushed off his car to come closer to her, suddenly invading her personal space.

One moment she thought he was irritated with her over their breakup, and the next she could feel his body heat as he moved nearer. Jade looked up at his dark blue eyes, which were virtually black in the dwindling evening light. When he looked at her like that, she could feel her belly clench and her neck and shoulders tense. He could bring some excitement into her life for sure. She had sorely missed that kind of thrill. Unfortunately, with Harley there was always the promise of more than she bargained for.

"I'll, uh, take your word for it," she said. Jade forced herself to take a step back, when every nerve in her body urged her to take a step forward into his arms. The way he looked at her was practically a dare. It was a dare she wanted to take on, but that was exactly why she moved away.

The last thing she needed was her father out on the porch again with his shotgun.

Harley sighed, but she could tell he wasn't going to push the issue. Not here. Not now. But eventually she wouldn't be able to run.

"Well, listen, you're probably freezing, so I'm going to go. I plan to stop by where I'm staying for a few things and then I'll meet you back at your house."

Jade hesitated, wondering what she'd just missed in the conversation while she'd wrestled with her desires. Had she gotten lost in his big blue eyes and not heard him say he was coming to her home? "What? Why are you coming by?"

He patted his suit coat pocket and the letter he'd put inside. "Someone is threatening you, Jade. This is serious. You need someone to protect you."

"You?" He was joking with her, right?

"Of course, me. I don't have any other staff in Charleston right now. Is that a problem?" He arched his brow at her, upping the ante of the dare.

Yes, it was a problem. In a dozen different ways, yes, but she voiced the least complicated one she could come up with. "There's no way I could afford to pay you for security detail, Harley. I don't have any savings left after what happened with Lance."

His brows knitted together in a heavy frown. "You should know better than that, Jade. I'm not doing this for the money."

"But I—"

He reached up and pressed a finger to her lips to silence her argument. "Consider it pro bono work. I need all the tax deductions I can get."

She took another step back in retreat from his touch despite her desire to move closer and let him press his lips to her mouth instead of his fingertip. "Don't I get any say in this? I don't recall asking you to—"

"Nope," he interrupted. "If I know you, and I'm pretty sure I do, you're not going to take this situation seriously. I'm here to do that for you." He smiled and walked away from her. He opened the driver's side door to his car and hesitated. "I'll be there in about an hour."

Jade watched him back out of the driveway and disappear down her parents' street. Her stomach was aching with worry even as her blood still hummed hot in her veins.

Being close to Harley was dangerous. And now she was going to be around him more than she'd ever anticipated. What was she going to do? It was one thing to see him in short visits, but if he was staying with her? Sleeping feet away in her guest bedroom? Would she be able to resist the pull he had on her?

Jade prayed this investigation would be finished quickly. Her reignited libido couldn't take this for too long.

Four

"So, let me get this straight," Harley began, with an exasperated expression on his face. "You're a single woman living alone with no alarm system or means to protect yourself if something happened."

Jade had only expected Harley to show up and get settled in for the night. It was late enough when he arrived. She didn't expect him to do a full home investigation, but then again, this was what he did for a living. So far, nothing nefarious could be found, but now that he was finished, it was time for the inevitable lecture about her personal security.

Jade wasn't really listening. She was too distracted by watching him work, her gaze drawn to his clenched jaw and brow furrowed with concern. He took it all very seriously. He was very thorough, she had to admit. He'd studied her windows more closely than she ever had. She'd never even opened them before, so she couldn't tell him if they had locks or not.

"This neighborhood is pretty quiet," she argued when he looked at her with dismay. "I'm not aware of any criminal activity that would send me running after an alarm system."

She had initially been worried about having Harley's hulking presence in her house. Every room felt smaller with him in it and she had no escape from him. He was a constant reminder of her past, of her current predica-ment and of what she couldn't have in the future. That seemed less important now as he was nitpicking every aspect of her home.

Jade liked this little house. It was the first place she'd ever had by herself. She'd moved from her college dorm to Lance's house, then they bought another house to-gether when they moved to Virginia Beach with his work. This was all hers. Her life was all hers. She didn't have a husband to tell her what to do any longer and she didn't need Harley to take over the role.

Harley just shook his head. "It's all got to change, Jade. If you're not comfortable with guns, that's fine, but you've got to have something in place to keep you safe. Maybe a stun gun. The noise alone is usually enough to deter an attacker."

"An attacker?" How had they gone from a threaten-ing letter to break-ins and physical assaults? "It was one letter. And you're here now. That's all I need, right?"

"Yes, I'm here, but I won't be around all the time. You need more protection here than you've got." He whipped his smartphone from his hip and started typing with a flurry of thumbs. "That's about to change."

"What are you doing?"

"I'm emailing Isaiah with my East Coast surveillance team. I'm going to have him send down someone to secure the home and make it safe for you to be here alone."

Jade's eyes grew large. That sounded intense. And expensive. "Harley, I—"

"It's not going to cost you anything," he interrupted, holding up his palm. Apparently, he'd come to anticipate her concerns before she voiced them.

"How is that possible?" It cost someone something. Jade might not be rich, but she wasn't in a position to happily accept handouts, either. Especially from Harley.

He glared at her. "Please don't argue with me about this. It will make me feel better. This is what I do for a living, remember? Whoever wrote you that note wants to scare you into dropping your search for answers. If you're going to continue, and I think you should, you need to be smart about it."

She sighed and shook her head. It was too late to waste any more energy on this. If he wanted to put armed guards in her trees to leap down on intruders, she'd let him. It had been a long day and she was ready for bed.

While she'd been fairly nonchalant about receiving that note when she'd spoken to Harley, it was only because she'd stayed up most of the previous night convincing herself it was nothing. She'd never expected anything like this to happen, and when it had, she'd been taken aback. By the time she'd fallen asleep, it was almost time to get up. She usually opened at the pharmacy, which allowed her to get off in early afternoon, but that didn't make it any less painful when her alarm went off at five.

Jade looked over at Harley, who was still typing furiously into his phone. Part of his business was in alarms and surveillance, so she shouldn't be surprised he'd want that done here. Maybe that would make him feel comfortable enough that he wouldn't have to sleep here every night. She hoped so.

And yet she didn't.

It was confusing being around Harley again. More confusing than she'd expected it to be. She thought she'd gotten over him a long time ago, but whenever he got close to her, her body responded as though it remembered him. She felt this desperate urge to reach out and touch him. For him to touch her. It was a ridiculous and inappropriate thought about the man who'd been hired to investigate her case. She knew that. Apparently she had made a mistake going too long without male companionship after her divorce. Harley had showed up unexpectedly and here she was, ripe for the picking.

As much as the idea of being plucked by Harley was appealing to her neglected body, her head knew better. He was not the one for her. She'd overridden her body before, and she knew she could do it again. The only difference this time was that Harley was so close, and would be for who knew how long. It was easier before, when she could just break off with him and return to college, where she didn't have to see him every day.

But she could stay strong. She had to. It wasn't smart

to muddy the investigation with personal feelings. And feelings where Harley was concerned were a terrible idea. He might be attracted to her, but there were times when she got the sense he didn't want to be. If they did hook up, that would be all there was to it. Neither one of them seemed keen to make the same mistake again.

"Okay, that's done," he announced, then slipped the phone back into its holster on his belt. "They'll probably be out the day after tomorrow or so to get you set up."

Jade just nodded. It wasn't a bad idea, really. It would give her some peace of mind. "Thanks. It's getting late, so if you've got all your things, I'll let you get settled in for the night," she said. The sooner she got him settled in for the night, the sooner she could put a couple walls between the two of them.

"Great." Harley bent to pick up the small overnight bag and larger garment bag he'd brought into the house with him.

She led him down the hallway toward the bedrooms. The little bungalow had been perfect when she was looking for a place. Since it was just her, two bedrooms and a single bath were all she needed. Now, as she stood in the hallway and realized the two beds were technically only about eight feet apart, she wished her place was a little larger.

"This is the guest room." She opened the door to the small room that had yet to house any actual guests. She used it mostly for an office and storage, but she'd put a sofa sleeper in there just in case someone needed to stay. "I went ahead and unfolded the sofa bed. It has clean sheets and blankets on it, but if you get cold, there's another in the closet. You probably saw it earlier, but the bath is here at the end of the hallway. There's just the one to share."

Harley eyed the space and then turned back to her. "And you're right across the hall?"

She gestured to the closed door. "Yes. That's me."

"Okay, great." He threw his bags down on the bed and switched on the little bedside lamp.

She watched him circle the small space like a Great Dane trying to get comfortable in a tiny bed made for a Chihuahua. Finally, he sat on the edge of the bed and the metal frame and springs gave a loud squeak of protest. She closed her eyes in embarrassment and wished she'd bought a regular bed for here. It would've taken up most of the room, but would have been better for company. Especially tall, muscular company.

It occurred to her that he would be more comfortable at his nice hotel suite or wherever he was staying. Heck, he'd probably be more comfortable in a sleeping bag on the front porch. He shouldn't suffer because he felt the need to protect her. "You don't have to do this," she said.

He looked at her, his blue eyes searching her face for a moment, and then he smiled in a way that made her stomach clench. "I know I don't. Good night, Jade."

His words were a gentle dismissal to keep her from trying to talk him out of this. He was obviously too stubborn and would stay here no matter what. Jade had to appreciate his dedication, if nothing else. "Good night, Harley."

She left his room, pulling the door closed behind her and crossing the narrow hallway to her own room. Shutting the second door, she leaned back against the wood and felt her body finally starting to relax. She hadn't realized it until she was alone again, but she was strung tight as a drum when she was around Harley. It was emotionally and physically exhausting to be so close to him after all this time. The attraction between them, long-suppressed and bubbling just below the surface, was at constant odds with her sense of self-preservation. Keeping everything in check was a balancing act she wasn't sure she could keep up much longer.

Dropping onto her own bed, she stared at the door. She supposed she should be happy to feel something. After everything that had happened with Lance, she'd almost become numb. Her mother actually thought there was something wrong with her because she hadn't cried over the divorce. It was as though she was in a state of shock that didn't allow her to feel anything at all.

She'd stayed there, stuck in limbo all this time, snapping out of it only when she'd received that DNA test.

Then, suddenly, all her emotions were flipped back on like a switch and her whole body was a bundle of raw nerves. She spent all day on the verge of tears or laughter, never quite sure which one was ready to burst from her without provocation. Could she risk unleashing that kind of pent-up energy on Harley?

With a sigh, she slipped out of her heels and got ready for bed. Maybe she would be exhausted enough to fall into a deep sleep and forget that Harley was only feet away.

Somehow, she doubted it.

* * *

A loud crash snapped Harley out of a restless sleep as his tailbone whacked the ground. It was only then that he realized the springs had given way on the sofa bed and he was lying on the hard wooden floor with only the thin mattress beneath him.

A pounding of fists at the door came next. "Harley, are you okay?"

"Yes, I'm fine. The bed is another matter."

The door slowly opened and Jade stuck her head inside as she switched on the overhead light. Her face was washed clean of makeup and her long, pale hair was loose around her shoulders. For a minute, as he looked at her, it was as though she were seventeen again. Beautiful. Natural. Just the way he remembered her when he thought back on their time together.

Until she started laughing at him.

She held it in at first, but he could see the facade start to crumble as her hand went to cover her mouth. The giggles escaped from her lips, making him glance down at himself. He really did look ridiculous sprawled across the lopsided mattress, in a tangle of blankets. He had to laugh, too. He was too damn big for a bed like this and he should've known better than to even try sleeping on it. He'd tried not to move too much once he got into bed, but once he was asleep, he couldn't help it. He'd rolled over and—*BOOM.*

They both laughed for a moment, their ever-looming tension finally dissipating with the emotional release. He supposed it was worth making an ass of himself if it helped break the ice between them. It would be a long and awkward assignment if they never got past it.

He shook his head and started checking out the sofa bed. He thought perhaps he could put it back together, but the hooks of the metal springs had actually ripped through the plastic fabric that held up the mattress. This thing wasn't fixable. He would buy her a new sofa bed. A sturdier one. Maybe just an actual bed, with box springs and a steel frame.

Harley threw back the blankets with a heavy sigh and Jade's laughter abruptly silenced. He looked down at himself again and realized he wasn't wearing anything but a snug pair of black Calvin Klein boxer briefs. He wasn't much for pajamas, but hadn't thought about it until he exposed himself. When he glanced back at Jade, he realized her eyes were fixed on his chest and stomach, her mouth agape. It was probably a different sight than she remembered. His whole body had changed over the years. He'd been a scrawny kid back then. Now he was a solid man made of muscle and covered in coarse, dark brown hair.

When she finally closed her mouth, a curious smirk formed at the corners of her lips. Jade seemed to like what she saw. And he liked that she liked it. He just wasn't sure what he should do about that glassy look in her eyes. Probably nothing. Maybe everything.

He got up from the shambles of the bed, wrapped the blanket around himself and snatched his pillow from the floor. His movements seemed to jerk Jade from her intense study and make her realize what she was doing. When her eyes met his again, he couldn't help smiling with amusement. Her cheeks flushed red as she seemed to realize that he'd caught her staring at him. With any other woman, he would've walked up to her, dropped the blanket and let her look and touch her fill. He wasn't shy, especially when he wanted something. Or someone.

But not with Jade. Things were too damn complicated between them for that. If there was one lesson he'd learned in the military, it was that life went the smoothest when he was in control. His existence before that point had been a mess as he spiraled through situations he didn't have a handle on. After his service ended, he'd applied that principle to every part of his life and things were infinitely better. He had the distinct feeling that maintaining control would be more difficult with Jade in the picture.

"This bed is toast. I guess I'll just move to the couch in the living room," he said. It might not be more comfortable, but it wouldn't collapse on him. Hopefully.

"Don't be silly," Jade said with a shake of her head. "The living room furniture is okay for sitting, but it's awful for sleeping. I couldn't afford anything nicer. But I have a king-size bed in my room. There's plenty of room for you there."

Harley arched a brow at her. She wanted to share her bed? After the way she'd looked at him just now, he wasn't sure that was such a good idea. She might not admit it to him, or even to herself, but she wanted to touch him and reacquaint herself with his body. And he wanted to let her. "I don't know about that, Jade."

She stuck out her chin defiantly. "We're adults, Harley. Surely we can sleep in the same bed without an issue. If it makes you feel better, I promise to keep my hands to myself." She held up three fingers in the Girl Scout salute before opening the door the rest of the way.

Harley now got a good look at the little cotton nightgown she was wearing to bed. It was short, with the lacy trim skimming her upper thighs. The fabric was pale pink, and transparent enough for him to see the rosy shade of her nipples as they pressed against it. The light from her bedroom behind her highlighted her figure through it, showcasing her narrow waist and the slight curve of her hips.

He swallowed hard. "I promise nothing," he said in a gruff voice. He didn't like to go back on his word, so he didn't make promises he knew he couldn't keep. As it was, he was clutching his pillow in front of himself to hide his pulsating desire. How could such a sweet, innocent piece of clothing stir such a reaction in him?

Probably because Jade could wear a clown suit and he would still want her. That was the long and short of the matter. He might not like it. He might even try to convince himself that he didn't harbor such a strong attraction to Jade any longer. But it was a damned lie. She'd hurt him when she chose Lance, even if he didn't want to admit that to himself. And he could tell himself he didn't need someone in his life who didn't think he was good enough for them. But somehow all that flew out the window where she was concerned.

"Come on," she said with a laugh, and left the doorway, seemingly oblivious to the heated thoughts running through his mind.

Did she think he was being funny? He wasn't sure, but he was running out of sleeping options if he was going to stay here and keep her safe. Once the security equipment was up, he could return to his bed at his mother's house, but until then, he needed someplace to get some decent rest. Reluctantly, Harley followed her out of the guest room and glared across the hallway to Jade's bedroom. He could see the large bed with the floral quilt tossed back and half a dozen decorative pillows piled on the unoccupied side.

While he stood there, Jade leaned across the mattress to snatch the extra pillows off the bed. As she stretched for the last one, the hem of her nightie crept higher and higher, until he could see the firm cheeks of her bottom peeking out from baby blue cotton panties. Not a thong or cheeky cutouts. They were sweet. Innocent. Just like the kind he'd fantasized about peeling off of her back in high school.

He curled his hands into fists. The universe was testing him; that's what it was. There was no other explanation.

"Here you go." Jade pulled back the comforter and patted the mattress in an invitation his eighteen-year-old self would've killed to get.

Harley swallowed hard and made his way around the bed to his side. She was right. It was a big bed, and there was plenty of space. He just knew there wasn't a bed big enough for it not to be a temptation with her so close by.

"Thank you," he said, as he slipped under the blankets. Her sheets were butter-soft and smelled like lavender, just as she always did. It was almost enough to lure him into a state of comfort that would allow him to forget where he was and who was beside him.

Almost.

As it was, he lay on his back, every inch of him stiff as a board. He didn't want to relax enough that he might brush against her under the sheets. He closed his eyes and tried to will himself to sleep.

Moments later, in the dark stillness of her bedroom, he heard Jade's soft voice from beside him. "You know, I never thought I'd share a bed with you, Harley."

His eyes fluttered open, but he kept them pinned on her ceiling fan as he chuckled. "No, me, neither. If I'd kept you out past eleven your father would've had me arrested. Keeping you overnight... I'd be dead."

Jade laughed, too, the melodic sound bringing back memories of them in the back of his pickup truck, looking at the stars. He remembered lying there, gazing into those big doe eyes and feeling his heart slipping away to the smartest girl in school.

Against his better judgment he rolled onto his side now and looked at her. Even in the darkness he could see her facing him, her white-blond hair sprawled across her pillowcase. Her head was resting on her hands as she watched him with curiosity in her eyes. He longed to reach out and cup her cheek and let his thumb drag gently across her bottom lip. Instead, he balled his fists beneath his pillow.

"It was a mistake, you know."

Harley frowned at her. "What was?"

"Choosing Lance."

"I read about what happened with him, and his drug problem. I'm sorry about all that."

"That's not what I meant. I mean that I hurt you, and I never wanted to do that."

Harley wasn't expecting an apology and he wasn't sure how to accept it. "It was for the best." He said the words, but didn't believe them.

"Maybe so. Perhaps things happen the way they're intended to. But lying here next to you after all this time makes me wish I'd gotten one last kiss before I let you go. I probably regret that more than anything else."

Without thinking, Harley surged forward and pressed his lips to hers. He'd had those regrets, too, and now, having her so near, he couldn't fight it anymore. He had to touch her, taste her, even if it was just to convince himself that his memories of her were wrong. She couldn't possibly be everything he'd built her up to be in his mind. She'd become a fantasy because he couldn't have her. The reality would no doubt disappoint him. He hoped that once the kiss was done he could put aside his attraction to her and focus on the case.

He couldn't have been more wrong. Jade melted into his arms, moaning softly against his mouth. She wrapped her body around him, pulling him close to her. He could feel every inch of her curves as they pressed against him beneath the thin cotton of that nightgown. As one of his hands held her face to his, the other drifted down her side, stopping just as it reached the lacy edge of her pajamas. If he crossed that line, he knew there was no going back.

She was everything he remembered and more, his

impulsive experiment backfiring in spectacular fashion. It took all he had to realize it and pull away.

The moment their lips parted, Harley felt reality start to close in on him. What the hell was he doing? He was here to protect Jade and find out what had happened at the hospital. Not to manhandle her and start something up between them that he might regret. Yes, it was just a kiss, but he could feel his grip on his self-control slipping away. The way she responded, the soft noises she made... He had to put some distance between them or things were going to go too far. He rolled away, grabbed his pillow and climbed out of bed.

"Where are you going?" Jade asked breathlessly.

"To the couch."

Her face wrinkled with displeasure as she looked up at him from the bed. Everything about her beckoned him to come back. To cross the line. "It was just a kiss. You don't have to go."

Harley had been waiting for an invitation and this was it. If he could accept it. Instead, he shook his head and walked around the foot of the bed to the door. "Yes, I do."

Without looking back at her, he marched down the hallway to the living room. He wrapped himself in the blanket and curled up on the couch so he would fit. With a sigh, he closed his eyes and wished for sleep.

The universe was definitely testing him. And it could kiss his ass.

Five

That kiss was a recipe for insomnia.

Jade was a fool for letting it happen, a fool for wanting it. But she did. If she hadn't, she wouldn't have started that ridiculous conversation. She would've closed her eyes and gone to sleep, keeping her hands to herself the way she'd promised. No, instead she'd pushed him until he broke, and it was everything she'd imagined a kiss with him could be. The reward was short-lived, though, as moments later she was alone in bed with a pounding heart and a liquid center.

Once Harley left for the couch, Jade had lain there staring up at the ceiling fan and trying to figure out what the hell she was doing. She was the one who'd broken it off back then. Teasing Harley with the goods she'd once deprived him of was cruel to them both. They had no business kissing, much less doing anything else. They'd both moved on from their high school days. A physical relationship between them would be nothing more than a complication she couldn't afford, with him around 24/7 trying to protect her.

But at that moment, none of that had mattered. All she'd wanted was a kiss. A touch. To feel desired again after years of thinking she wasn't enough for a man. Lance had stopped touching her after his car accident. It had been pretty serious, resulting in back surgery that would never really fix the problem or get rid of the pain. Months later, when she'd hoped perhaps they could get back to the way things were, he'd decided the rush of popping a roxy was better. He hadn't told her that, though. He'd said he hurt, or just plain avoided the subject. He'd stayed up late, knowing she went to bed early. He'd pulled away whenever she came too close.

It might've been a stupid thing to do, but last night had felt damn good. It had made her feel like a desirable woman for the first time in a long while.

This morning, she was a *sleepy* desirable woman.

Normally she went straight to the shower, but she needed some caffeine first. Jade pulled on her chenille robe and nearly crawled from the bed to the living room, where she found Harley on the couch, already awake. He actually looked as though he was well into his day. He was fully dressed, in a pair of pressed khaki pants and a dark blue shirt, and surrounded by paperwork he was reading through. There was an empty coffee mug in front of him on the table and his blanket was folded neatly over the back of the couch. Apparently he hadn't slept much, either.

"Good morning," she said, as she moved past him into the kitchen.

"Good morning."

Jade poured herself a cup of coffee. When she turned around, Harley was standing in the doorway of the kitchen. She eyed the fully dressed man who dominated the room with his presence. "Did you not sleep at all? That couch is miserable, I told you."

"I slept enough for me. I'm usually awake by four, anyway. If I can get four or five hours a night, I'm good. I've survived on less."

Jade shook her head. "I'm jealous. If I don't get eight, I'm a zombie."

"You didn't get eight last night," he noted. "That's my fault."

"It's the sofa bed's fault." She took a sip of her coffee and tilted her head back. "You'll notice these dark circles under my eyes. That's a sure sign of my undead state."

He studied her face for a moment and shook his head. "I don't see anything. You look beautiful, as always."

"You must still be half-asleep," Jade argued. "I just stumbled out of bed, I've got crazy hair and I'm wearing a bathrobe. Nothing about that is beautiful."

"Nope. I've gone on a four-mile run, taken a shower, had coffee, read through some paperwork and cleaned my gun. I'm very much awake. You're just stubborn."

"Stubborn?" She set down her coffee in surprise.

"Yes. I'm not sure what happened between you and

Lance. I only know how it ended. But what I do know is that he didn't take the opportunity he had. If he had appreciated the gift you'd given him by being in his life, he would've cherished it. He would've told you how beautiful and smart and amazing you are. Then you would believe someone when they gave you a compliment instead of arguing with them about it. It's a shame, really."

Jade was stunned by his words. She hadn't really thought about it that way, but he was onto something. She shouldn't let Lance's influence take over her new life, too. "You're right. Let's start over. Tell me I'm beautiful again."

Harley smiled. "Now you're just fishing for compliments, but okay. You look beautiful this morning."

Jade did her best to return his smile with a genuine one of her own. "Thank you."

"See? That wasn't so hard, was it?"

"Me accepting a compliment is like you following the rules. We can do it when we're put on the spot, but it's not instinctual."

"I can follow rules," he said, with a frown lining his forehead.

That made Jade laugh out loud. "Sure you can. That's why you were always in detention."

"That was before the navy. In the military, you follow the rules or you get punished. You obey the chain of command or someone gets hurt."

"So you're saying your bad boy days are behind you?" Jade asked curiously.

A wicked grin spread across his face, one that made Jade want to melt into his arms. He leaned in and pinned her with his baby blues. "Once a bad boy, always a bad boy, Jade. That doesn't change. These days I'm just better at knowing when the punishment is worth the payoff. It usually is."

Her eyes widened as he grew closer, his gaze drifting to her lips. It was enough to make her clutch her coffee mug for dear life. If she had her hands free, who knew what she might do. Reach for him? Touch him? Bad boys certainly had their appeal. She wished they didn't. Things would be easier in her life.

"Today, I work until four," she said, abruptly changing the subject. She turned away from him, fished into the junk drawer and pulled out a spare key to the house. "I'm not sure what's on your agenda, but since you refuse to go to your hotel and sleep in a comfortable bed with room service, here's a key."

Harley reached out and plucked the object dangling from her hand. Jade noticed he did it without touching her, even after leaning in to tease her the moment before. It made her wonder if it was deliberate on his part. Touching each other seemed to lead down a path neither of them were eager to travel.

"Just so you know, I'm not staying at a hotel. I've been staying with Mom while I'm in town. It's a bit out of the way, though, so your place is more convenient. Thanks for the key. I'll be out and about today, but I will make a point of being back by the time you get home."

Jade planted her hands on her hips. He made it seem like a bogeyman was going to leap out of a cabinet at any moment. He didn't appear to be the kind to overreact, but one little letter had really set him on edge.

"You don't have to. You're being paid to research the case, not babysit me."

Harley slipped the key into his pocket and sighed. "I know what I'm being paid for. And I can have it done by four."

"Okay," Jade said. She wasn't about to argue with him. It would give her some peace of mind that he was here, she had to admit. "Anything exciting on your agenda today?"

"I think I'm going to the hospital to meet with them and go over their data. They've pulled a lot of the records from the archives for me to search through. They weren't digitized back then, unfortunately, so that means a lot of shuffling through old papers in someone's abandoned cubicle."

"Sounds like a long, boring day ahead." She held up the coffee carafe, swirling around the last inch of black brew in the bottom. "You can finish this off."

Harley just shrugged, holding out his mug for her to refill it. "It can't all be tracking bad guys and apprehending suspects. Sometimes the paperwork is the most important part. That's where the truth usually lies."

"People don't tell the truth?" she asked.

"They tell the truth as best they know it. Or as they believe it to be."

That was a cynical way of looking at things. "And what about your plans for tomorrow?"

"What's tomorrow?"

"It's my day off. That, and Sundays. Are you going to sit around and look at me all day? Or work your case?"

Harley's lips twisted into a frown. "I'll have to figure that out. I wasn't expecting you to be off during the week, but it's my fault for not asking."

"I could help you with your research," Jade suggested. She was anxious to have answers and she didn't mind doing some of the legwork.

He stiffened and shook his head briskly. "No, sorry. I can't have you around while I'm investigating. You're too close to the case. It wouldn't be right."

"Oh, so now you follow the rules. You won't break them when it benefits me? I guess it isn't worth the payoff in this scenario."

That earned her a sigh and a roll of his eyes. "I don't want any of my findings called into question, okay? I'll figure out what to do about tomorrow tomorrow," he said, taking his turn at changing the subject.

"Fine. Be that way. I've got to get ready for work." With a shake of her head, Jade took her coffee and left the room. "I'll see you this evening," she called as she walked down the hall.

After reaching her bedroom, Jade flopped back on her bed and groaned aloud. He hadn't been in her house twenty-four hours and she was already a mess. Hopefully, he was as good a detective as he was at being alluring and irritating. He'd have the answers about her birth in no time and she could get him out of her house and move on with her life. Not that she had much of one, but it was hers and she was in control of it.

She looked over at the clock and realized she had to get a start on her day. That meant a shower. And after that chat with Harley, it would be a cold one.

* * *

"Well, well, well. Mr. Jeffries didn't warn me that he was having a meeting with Mr. Tall, Dark and Handsome today."

A sassy woman with dark, curly hair greeted Harley as he approached the receptionist's desk. She was wearing a hot pink sweater and earrings just as brightly colored, although they were hidden within the complicated ringlets of her hair. She smiled widely, turning her full attention to him as he approached her.

Harley was startled by the woman's bold assessment, but he tried to smile and pass it off. She appeared to be in her late fifties, and older women especially loved to flirt with him. He usually played along to give them a little boost to their day. He'd found that being sweet to the ladies could make or break an investigation. They'd trip over themselves to help him get what he needed.

"I usually just go by Harley Dalton," he quipped.

She looked over at her computer and nodded. "Have a seat, Mr. Dalton, and Mr. Jeffries will be with you momentarily. Can I get you coffee or something?"

"No, thank you, Mrs. White," he said, reading the placard on her desk as he settled into his seat.

"Oh, it's *Ms*. White," she clarified. "Although you can just call me Tina, sugar."

Harley sat up straight in his chair and hoped that Mr. Jeffries would hurry. Because Tina meant business.

Thankfully, before long the door opened and a man he presumed was Mr. Jeffries stepped out. "Good morning. Come in, Mr. Dalton."

He got up quickly, shaking the man's hand and following him through the door. Before disappearing into the room, he gave a quick glance over his shoulder to confirm that Tina wouldn't be joining them. He got a sassy wink from her, but she stayed in her seat.

As the door closed and the man gestured him toward a guest chair, Harley took a deep breath, then said, "Thanks for seeing me this morning."

"I'm sorry it's taken me this long to sit down with you. I've been tied up with other matters, but you know how that goes. Thanks for taking this case and handling it personally. I know you grew up in the area. I read all about that kidnapping case in the news not too long ago, and when we decided we needed outside help, your company was the first to come to mind. Like any hospital, we have our share of claims and malpractice suits, but this was different. Babies don't get switched around every day, you know."

Harley just nodded and let the man talk. "Hopefully, it won't take long to find out what happened," he said eventually.

"We've set up an office for you here, just down the hallway," Jeffries explained. "I've had all the records from that time brought down from the archives and put in there for you to go through. If you need anything, just let Tina know. I've instructed her to make you comfortable and give you whatever you might need."

Harley nodded, suppressing a smirk. Jeffries's admin assistant had taken the orders to heart.

"Is there anything else I can do to help you get your investigation started?"

Harley flipped through his notes, underlining something he'd written earlier. "Who was the CEO of the hospital back then? I'd like to talk to him or her if I can."

"That was Orson Tate. A helluva guy. I'm sure he'll be happy to speak with you." Mr. Jeffries reached to his phone and pressed the intercom button. "Tina, can you please pull the contact information for Orson Tate? Mr. Dalton will need it." He released the button. "Anything else I can do to get you started?"

"Actually, I do have one last question before I go, Mr. Jeffries."

"Please, call me Weston."

"Very well. I've spoken with Ms. Nolan and it seems she's been receiving threats in the mail, trying to scare her into dropping the case. You wouldn't know anything about that, would you?"

Weston's eyes widened in surprise, but his gaze didn't flicker from Harley's. "I don't. I'm sorry to hear that. I sincerely hope you don't think anyone at St. Francis is behind the threats."

It was clear the man knew nothing about it. "Thank you for your time, Weston." Harley stood, shook his hand and headed out of the office.

As expected, Tina was waiting there with the former CEO's contact information and a wide smile. "I'll be right here if you need anything else, sugar."

He smiled back and quickly made his way down the hall to settle into his investigation. St. Francis's staff had faxed him some paperwork to review before he came to town, but the proprietary hospital and personnel files had to be reviewed in person. In the office, he found three large file boxes on the desk. He'd hoped there would be some video surveillance tapes as well, but it didn't take long for him to realize why there weren't.

A quick review of the security schematics from 1989 was revealing and unhelpful. Unfortunately, hospital security was not as good as it was now. While each floor had had cameras, the tapes filmed over themselves every twenty-four hours. If there ever was video evidence of someone switching the infants, it had been almost immediately destroyed. And that was if the cameras were even on. The hospital had been running on emergency power after the storm. Cameras weren't nearly as critical as life support equipment.

Specific security measures for the maternity floor weren't any better. The infants had had identification bands that matched them to their parents, but there were no alarms or tracking protocols in place to keep someone from leaving with a child or removing a band. It was possible that the bands got mixed up and put on the wrong babies to begin with. Or if they were correct, anyone with access to the nursery could've gone in and swapped the babies in their beds. It would've taken seconds to move them and switch their identification bracelets. During the storm, who would be focused on such a thing?

It was a good question. Who would've taken the opportunity to do something like that when people's lives were in danger? The ID bands weren't about to fall off the babies and they weren't removed for any reason until the babies were discharged with their parents. That meant it probably wasn't a mistake. Someone had done it deliberately, but why? Looking at the boxes, Harley was certain the answer was in there. He just had to know what he was looking for.

Settling in with a large coffee he got from the cafeteria, Harley dug into his work, taking detailed notes. After a few hours, his eyes were going out of focus, but he had a solid handle on the situation. At least, he had a handle on who Jade's biological parents might be. He was thankful, because there wasn't enough coffee to keep him awake for another hour of flipping through files.

Despite being paid by the hospital to find out what had happened, the moment he'd laid eyes on Jade his priorities had shifted. Yes, he wanted to find the truth and who was behind it, but for her, not for the money. The look in her eyes when she'd told him about never fitting in had nearly crushed him. He didn't know if finding her real family would give her the peace of mind or the sense of home she was searching for, but he was going to do his damnedest to try. He wasn't able to make her happy back then, but maybe he could now.

There were only five baby girls in the hospital at the time of the storm. Thankfully, the window Jade's parents had given him was narrow. Five was a manageable number.

He copied down the names, addresses and phone numbers on file—which were from the late eighties—hoping to make contact and potentially pay the families a visit. Ideally, he'd like to get DNA samples to eliminate the other girls. Although he envisioned them in his mind as infants, they weren't girls, they were grown women now. Likely with families of their own. And one of them had no idea her birth parents were out there somewhere, wondering what had become of her.

Harley got on his computer and sent the names to his right-hand man, Isaiah Fuller, at his office in DC. The odds of all those people being at their old addresses with the same phone numbers were slim. His research team could look up the families in various databases and records, and provide more current contact information. That wouldn't take long. Then he could reach out and start putting faces to the names.

By the time the weekend came to a close, he could very well be on his way to knowing who Jade's real parents were. The remaining question of why the babies had been swapped, and by whom, might take quite a bit longer to nail down. It had been thirty years and he worried that the trail had gone cold long ago. But he would get to the bottom of this. For Jade's sake.

Six

Jade wasn't used to coming home to someone, but when she pulled into her driveway, Harley's Jaguar was already there. Seeing it evoked an odd sort of feeling, a sense of home the little cottage hadn't really had before. At the same time, her little car seemed a bit dowdy beside the luxury sports car. Sort of how Jade felt beside Harley. At one time, both she and her little four-door sedan had been stylish and desirable in their own way. Now they both had a lot of miles on the engine and dings in the paint job.

And yet no matter how many different ways she'd tried to run through the scenario in her mind from the night before, Harley had been eager to give her a test drive. At least at first. Then he'd run for the living room sofa, and any chance of igniting something between them had seemed like a fantasy.

It was just as well. Sophie might think that a hookup was the best thing for Harley and her, but Jade knew better. He was like her favorite potato chip. She couldn't eat just one, or even a handful, and set them aside, sated. No, she'd keep at it until she devoured the whole bag. It was easier not to eat a single chip sometimes. Or not even keep any in the house. Unfortunately, this particular treat wouldn't leave. It was about two hundred pounds of trouble she didn't need in her life, even just for a fling.

When she went in the front door, she found the house quiet and mostly dark. She didn't think Harley had been home very long. His messenger bag and suit coat were still sitting on the armchair in the living room and a light was coming down the hallway from the bathroom. She could hear the shower running.

Tired of her stuffy work attire, Jade headed to her room, where she could change into something less itchy and more comfortable than the pale pink tweed suit she'd worn beneath her white lab coat at the pharmacy. She quickly slipped into a pair of jogging shorts and a tank top. It was winter still, but the house was warmer than usual—or she was warmer than usual—with Harley around. She followed up the change by flipping her hair back and catching the mess of white-blond strands into a high ponytail out of her face.

She was stepping into the hallway when she collided with an unexpected wall of muscle. It was Harley, wet-haired and mostly naked, coming from the bathroom. She stumbled backward from the impact and he reached out to steady her, pulling her close to him again and wrapping her in the heat of his embrace.

When she recovered and was stable on her bare feet, she found herself in quite the situation. When her gaze met his, she found his serious blue eyes watching her from beneath wet strands of hair that had fallen into his face. There was an intensity there that was different than when they kissed. It wasn't even like when he'd become incensed by her threatening letter. Harley was focused one hundred percent on her in a way that made her heart stutter and her throat go dry. He might have run off the night before, but he didn't seem to be wrestling with his attraction to her now.

Unable to take it any longer, Jade broke away from his gaze and looked down to where her palms were pressed against the damp, bare skin of his chest. She could feel the rough curls of his chest hair that had intrigued her when she'd seen him in his briefs on the collapsed sofa bed. There was also a sprinkling of scars she hadn't noticed before. Cuts, surgical scars, even what looked like a bullet wound. He hadn't mentioned much about his time in the military, but it was obvious he hadn't sat safely on an aircraft carrier, swabbing the decks.

Not that she'd ever expected him to. Harley was the kind that would jump first from an airplane. Kick down the doors of suspected terrorists. He loved the rush, which was probably why he'd made a career in this business. It was an element of his personality that had worried her just as much as a teenager as it did now. She wanted to be with someone who would come home every night, not leave her wondering if tonight was *the* night she'd get the call she dreaded.

Jade's thoughts were derailed by the stirring of Harley's desire. Her cotton shorts were slightly moist from colliding with the bath towel he had slung low around his hips. Even with the multiple layers of fabric between them, she could feel his need for her pressing against her stomach. Any questions she had about him wanting her were put to bed instantly. The bigger question now was whether she could allow herself to want him. And if so, could she manage to indulge without emotionally compromising herself? She wasn't sure.

"I'm sorry," she said at last, trying to move back and break the connection between them. Jade didn't get far. Mostly because Harley still had his arms around her waist.

"I'm not," he replied in a dead-serious tone.

Jade stiffened. She wasn't sure what to say. Was she brave enough in the moment to take what she needed? She did want Harley, even if she couldn't keep him. She wanted to feel what it was like to have someone desire her again. It was plain to her that he did. She needed to heed Sophie's advice and just go for it.

She looked into his eyes, gathering every ounce of courage and seduction she had inside her. Then she slid one palm down his chest and over the hard muscles of his stomach. She could feel him tense and quiver beneath her touch as she reached for the edge of the towel. They were both holding their breath until, with a quick flick of her finger and thumb, the white terry cloth pooled on the floor at their feet.

Harley's serious expression softened slightly as a devious smile curled his lips. "I don't think you're sorry, either," he said.

She wet her lips with her tongue and shook her head slightly. "You're right. I'm only sorry it took this long." Then she figuratively jumped in with both feet and kissed him.

The floodgates opened the minute their lips touched. All the reasons they'd had to stay away from one another went out the window as desire trumped their good sense. Jade clung to his neck, trying to draw his mouth closer to hers even as he towered over her. His hands roamed her body, reacquainting themselves with the long-denied landscape.

Jade was overwhelmed with the sensations that coursed through her. She was barely aware of their movements as Harley guided them backward into her bedroom, until she felt the mattress press into the back of her thighs.

This was really going to happen. For a moment, she almost felt eighteen again, and as if she was giving herself to Harley for the first time. A surge of nervous energy ran through her body as he slipped her tank top over her head and threw it onto her bedroom floor. She'd been so wrapped up in him back then, and the feeling was similar now. He was the bad boy, the handsome rogue who wanted her when it felt like the rest of the world didn't. There was no way her teenage self could have resisted those charms. She'd fallen head over heels.

This time was different, though. She was no enamored virgin with naive expectations about the future. She might not feel like she fitted in any more now than she did then, but Jade was a grown woman and knew that this wasn't the way to solve that problem. She was simply a woman with needs that a man like Harley could fulfill if she let him.

"Damn," he whispered in a low, gravelly voice as he looked down at her breasts. She'd always been self-conscious about them, or really, the lack of them, but he didn't seem to mind. He cupped them in his palms, sending Jade's head back as she gasped. They were small, but extremely sensitive. Her nipples turned to hard pebbles beneath his touch, aching for his mouth to taste them.

Jade eased backward onto the bed, shifting across the mattress as Harley's naked body moved forward. In an instant, he was covering every inch of her with his heated, damp skin. His desire pressed against her bare thigh as he rested on his elbows and continued to tease her nipples with his tongue until she arched her spine and pressed her hips against him.

She couldn't remember how long it had been since she'd wanted a man this badly. Had she ever? Even her attraction to Harley when they were teenagers couldn't measure up to this. They had been kids then. Now he was a man. A solid wall of man that a woman like her desperately craved.

Harley pulled away long enough to grasp the waist-band of her shorts and tug them down over her hips, along with her thin cotton panties. As they reached her ankles, she kicked them off and drew up one knee to hook around his bare thigh.

"Do you have protection?" she asked. It was a little

late for a question like that, but she hadn't exactly come home from work expecting this to happen.

"My gun is in the other room," he replied, with a deadpan expression on his face.

Jade smacked him on the shoulder. "You know full well what I mean. Condoms."

He grinned. "Yes, I do." Harley pulled away from her, obviously admiring every bare inch of her body as he revealed it. Then he crossed the hallway to the guest room, where he'd left his luggage.

Seconds later he returned with a fistful of gold foil packets. "Feeling ambitious?" she asked, as he tossed them onto the dresser beside the bed.

"I'm feeling like I've got a few years of making up to do." Harley reached for one and dropped it next to her on the mattress. "I also need to make up for the subpar lovemaking I offered you when we were teenagers. My form has improved greatly since then."

Jade smiled. She expected—even fantasized—that sex with Harley would be hot and frantic, but she was amazed to find that lying here with him was more comfortable than anything else. Laughter and desire blended together in a way she never could've expected. That was even better than some frenzied rush to the finish line. Jade was certain the frenzy would come soon enough, but it was nice to enjoy this moment, as well.

"Has it, now?" she teased.

Harley arched a brow. "Was that a challenge?"

She shrugged her shoulders and lay back against the mattress. "Make of it what you will."

He didn't answer. Instead, she felt his hand dip between her thighs and spread them apart. His focused gaze never left hers as his fingers sought out her center. She gasped as he gently brushed over her sensitive parts, teasing her by never fully touching her where she desired it the most. Then, when she couldn't stand it a moment longer, he stroked her hard and her body arched up off the bed.

Jade gasped and writhed, tensed and squirmed beneath his touch. He dipped his fingers inside her, rubbing the heel of his palm against her clit in a motion that made her every nerve ending light up. Within seconds of him stroking her that way, she could feel her long-denied release building up inside.

"So close," she said between short breaths.

"That's it," he coaxed. "Let go, baby."

Jade didn't have much choice. With another stroke of his palm, her orgasm exploded through her body. She was rocked by the intensity of it, as though the last few years without a lover had built up inside and burst from her all at once.

This was one of Harley's new moves and she approved.

Even as she lay on the bed, her whole body almost liquid, she reached out for him. Her fingers curled around the firm heat of his desire and slowly stroked him from base to tip. She didn't have a lot more experience to show off from their time apart, but she remembered how he liked to be touched.

Nothing had changed there. Within seconds of her touching him, Harley pulled away with a curse. That meant she was doing everything right. He grabbed the condom on the bed and sheathed himself.

Jade welcomed him with open arms as he covered her body with his own. They fitted together perfectly, each of her curves molding to his hard angles. When he filled her, that fitted perfectly, too. She drew her legs up, letting him go deeper, and clung to his back with sharp nails that dug into his skin the harder he thrust.

The closer he got to his undoing, the tighter he held Jade against him. His fingertips eventually slipped through the strands of her hair, grasping a fistful at the base of her scalp. The grip was gentle but firm, tugging her head back and exposing her throat to him. She whimpered, teetering on the edge of pleasure and pain, but realizing that the harder he pulled, the closer she came to losing control once again.

His teeth grazed her throat and she could feel the vibration of a growl from deep inside him. "Harder," she whispered, and it seemed to be exactly what he needed to hear.

His grip on her hair tightened, holding her perfectly still as he thrust into her with everything he had. The combination put Jade over the edge and the spasms of her orgasm brought on Harley's own release. With a loud groan, he thrust into her one last time, and it was done. He collapsed against her, his face buried in her shoulder for a moment before he rolled onto his back and away from her.

Jade let her body relax into the bed and took a deep breath. Even then, her mind was spinning. That was unexpected. The whole thing. And now that it was over, she wasn't sure what to do. Cuddle? Nap? Get up and make dinner? Thank him for the orgasms and put her clothes back on? She'd never had a fling before, so she wasn't quite sure what came next.

Without a better option, she pressed a kiss to Harley's cheek, rolled out of bed and went to take a shower. Maybe the hot water and breathing room would clear her mind and she could figure out the path forward.

If she was honest, the path would probably lead right back into bed with him.

Harley was confused.

Sex had rarely been a complicated thing in his mind. It was a physical release, a meeting of desires, nothing more. And that was what it was supposed to be with Jade. That's what he'd told himself, at least. But things always seemed to be more complex when Jade was involved. At least it was this time. He didn't recall it being like this the first time. There had been emotions involved back then. Puppy love, he supposed.

That was a long time ago. Things were different now. They were both mature and there was an unspoken understanding that this tryst had a time limit. He would conclude his investigation and go back to DC. She would find her family and move on with her new life. This temporary connection should be simple and enjoyable, without a bunch of expectations and romantic notions.

But now, it was the decided lack of emotions from Jade that bothered him.

It wasn't that she was disengaged or not attracted to

him. The opposite was true. She had blossomed into an enthusiastic and skilled lover over the years. He tried not to think too hard about where she'd learned some of the things she'd done to him the night before. It made him want to drive to the prison just so he could punch Lance in the face.

No, what bothered Harley was the wall. Jade was physically closer to him than she had ever been, but more closed off than ever before. He supposed he should be relieved that she didn't get too attached to him too quickly, but the opposite reaction was unnerving and very unlike his Jade. The girl he remembered was an emotional open book. So full of love, so trusting.

This Jade was older, harder, less willing to open up to him or anyone else, he'd wager. It wasn't something he'd done, either. It had to be Lance. That guy had taken her innocence and stomped all over it. After going through all that, perhaps she didn't have the right head space for anything beyond the physical.

Maybe despite everything, Harley was still not good enough for her. Perhaps he would do better to focus on his case than to focus on his ex. That was what he was getting paid to do, after all.

A familiar ring tone roused him from his thoughts. It was Isaiah. Harley had been expecting this call, although he hadn't been expecting it this early in the morning. Then again, Isaiah knew what hours he kept.

He reached for his phone. "This is Dalton."

"Hey, bro," he answered in a chipper voice, despite it being five in the morning.

Harley chuckled. While technically his employee,

Isaiah was more his friend than anything. He kept things sailing smoothly for him. "Good morning."

"So, I got your email about the equipment install and the list of people to run through the database. I've got good news and bad news. How do you want it?"

Harley bit back a groan. "Bad news first. Always bad news first."

"Okay. We're out of stock on a few items we need to install at the Charleston residence, so I'm afraid I won't be able to send someone down right away."

Damn it. "How long are we talking?"

"Just a few days. Maybe Monday. It depends on how quickly we can get our hands on it all."

Since Harley was staying with Jade, he supposed a delay wasn't the end of the world, but he still didn't like it. What if this had been a paying client? Or someone without a security detail to keep her safe while they waited on some video camera to be in stock? "Okay. But I want you to have a chat with inventory control. We should never be out. We should have a backup for our backups. Got it?"

"Roger that."

"And what's the good news?"

"That I have your list of addresses for all the parents and most of the daughters."

"Excellent. Email them to me."

"Already done. Check your in-box."

Harley pulled the phone from his ear and noticed the new-message alert. He opened the email and scanned through the list of names and addresses. It was incomplete, as Isaiah had mentioned. The daughter of the

Steele family wasn't there. "What about Morgan Steele? She's not on here."

"I told you I had most of the daughters. She's my exception. It's going to take a little more work for her. Morgan's last known physical address was in Charleston with her parents, but that was before she went to college. After that, all I could get was a PO box at the University of South Carolina."

Harley frowned. "I doubt she's still in college."

"Correct. School records show she graduated several years back. She's likely got nothing in her name to trace. The Steele family is rich beyond belief, with multiple houses and investment properties. I'd bet she's living in a property owned by her father's trust or beneath their corporate umbrella. She probably has corporate credit cards and offshore accounts."

"What, no driver's license?"

"She has one, but it lists the family home as her address. My research shows she works at the DC facility for the family company, so I'll probably be able to get her contact information from there. Just give me a day or two."

"Steele. Why do I know that name?" Harley asked. He'd copied down the names from the hospital files, but hadn't done any research of his own yet.

"It sounded familiar to me, too, so I started doing a little research on them. The family founded Steele Tools, man. Apparently it was started in Charleston over a hundred years ago by their great-great-grandfather. They started off selling through catalogs and now they're in every home improvement store in the country. The

Steele family is one of the wealthiest and most power-ful in South Carolina. Or dare I say, America. They've spawned their share of CEOs, but also a senator, a judge, doctors, lawyers…you name it. Morgan works for the company, as do most of the people in the family."

The longer Isaiah spoke, the more Harley's stom-ach started to ache. He'd had no idea his list of candi-dates included such a high-profile family. Swapping babies started to make a little more sense now. Well, at least why one of the families might be targeted. Once you were that well-known, you were the focus of every crazy who wanted a piece of what you had.

"I need you to find out everything you can about the Steele family, especially over the last forty years. Any little detail could be important."

"A family like that is going to be in the papers every time one of them takes a big crap."

"I don't care. I want it all. Get your guys on it. Espe-cially focus on Morgan Steele. If she's our girl, I want to know as much as I can about her. And get those parts we need for the surveillance system down here. I can't watch this house every second."

"Sir, yes, sir," Isaiah said sharply, with an edge of sarcasm. He would do it, though. Harley could always count on his operations manager to get things done. "Just one last question and I'll get right on it."

"Yeah?"

"What are you really doing down there, Harley?"

And with that, they'd just transitioned from em-ployer-employee to friends chatting on the phone. "I'm investigating a case. What do you mean, what am

I doing here?" he asked, knowing full well what his friend meant.

"I *mean*, since when does the CEO cart his ass down to Charleston for a piddly little case like this?"

"When the CEO gets tired of paper-pushing. And this isn't a piddly case, Isaiah. If this links back to the Steele family, it could become a very high-profile job."

There were a few moments of silence on the line before Isaiah responded again. "Cut the crap, man. Who is this woman? Tell me you'd still be down there if it were anyone else."

Harley couldn't, and they both knew it. He wasn't one to lie—he preferred avoiding the truth, which wasn't quite the same thing—and he wasn't going to lie to his best friend. He'd tell him. He just might not tell him everything. "She's my ex-girlfriend from back before I joined the navy."

"I knew it!" Isaiah shouted into the phone. "I knew there was more to it. So, what, you still carrying a torch for her or something?"

"Please," Harley said. "Have you seen me moon over a woman in the years you've known me?"

He was hardly the kind of guy who got wrapped up in a relationship, much less pine for someone. He honestly couldn't say that he'd had something that even looked like a relationship since he'd been out of the service. He hadn't had the time, the energy or the inclination. And even if he did, he hadn't met anyone who made him want more than just a little physical pleasure.

At least until he woke up this morning feeling used

for the first time in his life. How the tables had turned when he least expected it…

"No. You're pretty cool and collected when it comes to the ladies. Too cool, if you ask me."

"I didn't."

Isaiah chuckled into the phone. "You're a little snippier than usual this morning."

"I'm not snippy," Harley said, knowing full well that was *exactly* the word for his tone of voice. "I'm just not in the mood for you to philosophize about my love life. It's too damn early. Yes, I was curious about Jade and what had become of her. Yes, I'm trying to do her a favor by finding out what happened to her and keeping her safe in the meantime. But that's all there is to it."

"So you're not sleeping with her?"

Harley sputtered for a moment, knowing that even when he got his words together, Isaiah wouldn't believe him. "And if I were?" he asked at last.

Isaiah sighed heavily into the receiver and Harley could almost picture him with his feet propped up on the desk as he leaned back almost too far in his executive chair.

"I'd say there's way more to this story than you're letting on."

Seven

"Yes, I'd like to leave another message for Mr. Steele. Please press upon him the importance of my call. It's about his daughter, Morgan. Yes, it's Harley Dalton with Dalton Security calling again. I'm working on a case with St. Francis Hospital and it's imperative that I speak with Mr. or Mrs. Steele as soon as possible about a private matter."

Harley clicked off with more force than was necessary to terminate a call on a smartphone, and chucked it onto the dashboard of his car. There just wasn't the same satisfaction as slamming down an old landline phone. He needed some kind of outlet for his frustration. It was the sixth call he'd made to the Steele family's various numbers over the last three days and all he'd managed to reach were assistants or housekeepers. With them dodging his calls, all he could do now was slip his phone into his pocket and carry on with the last of his interviews.

He should've felt some sense of accomplishment by the time Sunday rolled around, but he didn't. He blamed Isaiah and his relationship meddling for that. All weekend, his friend's words had made him feel off-kilter for some reason, as though he had some kind of mental vertigo. It made him want to question his own justifications behind this investigation and why he was here in Charleston. He could've sent anyone; his friend was right. But Harley had told him to mind his own business and had got off the phone.

Now, days later, he didn't have a better answer. He just didn't know. And lately, he had too many other things to worry about.

Not that he hadn't made significant headway in the investigation over the last few days—he had. With the contact information he received from Isaiah, he'd called all the families, talking to some and leaving messages with others. With the local families he could reach, he'd set up appointments to meet with them at various times over the weekend. He'd been able to talk to every family but the Steeles so far. That didn't surprise him, but it did raise his suspicions about the wealthy family. Once he finished what he had on his plate for the day, he intended to follow up on them.

With his interviews keeping him away from the house, he'd had to figure out what to do with Jade. Since she didn't work that Friday or Sunday, he had to factor her into his plans. He scheduled as much as he could while she was working on Saturday, but there was only so much he could do then. In an abundance of caution she felt was unnecessary, he'd insisted that she spend Friday and Sunday afternoons with her parents. She had grumbled at first, suggested going with him—and then finally relented. With Jade's well-being taken care of for the afternoons, Harley was finally able to conduct his interviews in person.

Each family visit had gone the same way: he'd interviewed the parents, spoken with the daughters if possible, and taken DNA samples from anyone he could. He wasn't about to rely on clues like physical resemblance to the Nolans. Genetics were a funny thing, with recessive traits playing tricks on your eyes. Just because someone did or didn't look like their parents wasn't enough for Harley. He wanted the DNA report in hand to prove without a doubt that they shared enough genetic markers to be parent and child.

Though if asked off the record, Harley would admit all the families he'd met with today could be eliminated. Not a single person he saw had the large doe eyes he'd fallen for back in high school. By process of elimination, that left just the elusive Steele family. He was hoping that wouldn't be the case, but the minute Isaiah had mentioned how rich and powerful they were, Harley's instincts had told him that was the path he needed to follow. The most difficult path, of course. To the family who hadn't returned his calls. With the daughter who left barely any trace of her existence.

Even then, he'd wait for the DNA reports before he shared that information with anyone. He'd had the collection of samples overnighted to his lab, and then went to see the former head of the hospital, to talk about the facility back in the nineties.

That's where he was now—sitting in the driveway outside the mansion of former St. Francis Hospital CEO Orson Tate. He killed the engine of the Jag and walked up to the front door.

It was an impressive home, filled with all the charm a traditional Charleston home should have, but few could afford. It wasn't an historical landmark, but a new building with classic details, bordering the golf course behind it. Harley rang the doorbell and waited a few moments before Orson Tate answered. He had a full head of white hair, and was wearing bifocals and a sweater.

"Mr. Dalton?" he asked.

"Yes, sir."

"Come on in," the older man said, gesturing inside as he stepped out of the doorway.

Harley shook his hand after he closed the door behind them. "Thank you for taking the time to speak with me today, Mr. Tate."

"Oh, I've got plenty of time. I can't play golf every day. At least that's what my wife tells me. Come this way. We can chat out in the sunroom. My wife put out some tea and cookies for us."

He followed the man through the house and out a pair of French doors to a sunroom that overlooked the golf course. His prized view included a water hazard with a fountain that attracted cranes and other wildlife. Harley could see a group of golfers out on the course, laughing and playing the nearby hole.

The two of them settled into a pair of white wicker patio chairs with a platter of sweet iced tea and sugar cookies between them. Harley took out his phone to record the conversation, as he always did, and got started on their chat.

"So what's this all about, Dalton?" Tate asked as he took a sip of his tea and sat back in the cushions with a weary sigh. "Jeffries didn't tell me much on the phone, just that you would be in touch."

Harley imagined that the current CEO wanted as few people as possible to know about the situation. "Mr. Jeffries hired me to look into allegations that babies were switched at the hospital back in 1989. Specifically during Hurricane Hugo."

Orson winced and shook his head sadly. "That was a hell of a thing. Absolute chaos. I like to think we ran a pretty tight ship at St. Francis, but if something was going to go awry, that would've been the time for it. We were so close to the coast we got hit hard. It was all hands on deck. Even I was giving out water and helping nurses in triage. You know it's bad when that happens."

He could only imagine. Harley had been just a few months old at the time, with no memories of the storm, but his mother had spoken about it from time to time. Everyone in Charleston did. You didn't even have to say hurricane. It was just Hugo, like some beast had come ashore and ravished the town.

"Mr. Jeffries gave me access to all the files. There wasn't much in terms of security in place back then, at least not that survived the last thirty years. Even then, I can't help but think it would've had to have been an inside job. Perhaps one of the doctors or nurses working the floor. They were the only individuals who would've had access to the babies."

The older man nodded thoughtfully. "We considered our technology to be state of the art back then, but it's nothing compared to now. They damn near put a GPS tracker in their diapers these days. I hate to think one of our staff might have been involved in something like that, but you're right. It's that or gross incompetence, and I can't imagine how that could happen. The babies each had name bands that matched them to their parents. The bands stayed on through baths, treatments, even surgery if it was needed. You had to practically cut them off the baby's leg when they were discharged. They did not slip off. Never."

That confirmed Harley's suspicions that someone had deliberately done it. He couldn't imagine how it would happen otherwise. That meant it was time to dive into the staff's backgrounds. "I reviewed the personnel files for everyone who was working in the maternity ward during the storm." Harley reached into his bag and pulled out copies of photos taken for their hospital ID cards. He handed them over to Orson. "I don't expect you to remember every employee that worked at the hospital, but I was hoping maybe you might remember something about them that might help the investigation."

Orson flipped through the photos, studying each one thoroughly. "Dr. Parsons and Dr. Ward. Two great physicians. Never saw them lose their cool even under unimaginable stress." He turned over a photo of a nurse

next. "Karen was one of our best. Uh… Karen Yarbor-
ough, I believe. She retired from the hospital after over
forty years working labor and delivery. I remember her
well. These other two, not so much. Although…" His
voice trailed off as he studied the last photo. "This one
stands out to me, but I don't remember why. What's
her name?"

Harley glanced at the photo of the dowdy redhead.
"That's Nancy Crowley," he said, flipping through his
notes. "She worked at the hospital from 1987 to 1990,
although only for a few months in maternity. Looks as
though she left St. Francis not long after the hurricane,
judging by what I wrote down."

"Ah," the older man said, tapping the picture with
his finger. "I remember now. She didn't quit. I'm sorry
to say it, but she killed herself. There were rumors that
she had a drinking problem and some issues at home,
but I can't be sure of it now."

Harley had a hard time disguising his surprise. He
turned back to the notes and realized that her termina-
tion date was less than a week after the storm. "May I
ask what happened?"

"She threw herself off the roof of the hospital. I had
plenty of employees die during my twenty-five-year
tenure, a few even committing suicide. It's high stress
work, after all. But Nancy was the only one who did it
on hospital property. That's hard to forget. It haunted
the staff, especially the ones who found her. We had to
bring in trauma counselors to help folks work through
it. Her coworkers couldn't understand it. They said she
was always so upbeat and friendly with the staff and the

patients. If she had a drinking problem, she hid it well enough. No one suspected anything until it was too late."

Harley listened thoughtfully. It was an interesting lead to follow up with later. He'd have his team look up anything they could find on Nancy's death. The timing was too coincidental to ignore. "Did you ever hear anything else about it? Was a police investigation conducted?"

Orson nodded and handed the photos back to him. "Yeah, but it was pretty open-and-shut. The roof was restricted access. Surveillance cameras showed her going up there alone. When they spoke with her brother and her boyfriend, they all seemed pretty torn up about it. They didn't expect something like that from her, either. I guess you never can tell. Everyone has their demons."

When the alarm went off Monday morning, Jade woke up to a cold, empty bed. Harley had been there when she'd fallen asleep, but judging by the feel of the mattress beside her, he'd been awake for a while. She pulled on her robe and stumbled down the hallway to search for him.

Harley was sitting at the kitchen table, staring down at his coffee mug as though the answers to all the questions of the universe would be in there. Jade watched him curiously as she walked past him, poured her own cup of coffee and then sat at the kitchen table across from him.

"What's wrong?" she asked, skipping the morning pleasantries. He wasn't in the mood, judging by the look on his face. "Did you get any sleep?"

"Not really. I have too much to think about."

Jade understood that. When things were at their worst with Lance, she'd almost gone crazy from sleep deprivation. Every time her head touched the pillow, her brain would start spinning with worries that wouldn't let her drift off.

She hoped Harley's worries weren't about the two of them. They'd developed a comfortable, uncomplicated rhythm the last few days and had always ended up in each other's arms. She didn't want either of them overthinking that. "Hit a snag in the investigation?" she asked.

Harley looked up at her and frowned. He had been fairly close-lipped about his research so far. Jade tried to be understanding about it, but it was hard knowing he had information that might impact her life. She supposed that if it really mattered, he would tell her. There wasn't much use in telling her things before he was certain. Still, it was weird that he was going out to track down the truth about what happened to her, then coming home and engaging in idle chatter about the weather.

"You could say that," he said at last. "I've hit a roadblock I wasn't expecting."

"You've only just started. How can that be?"

"People are stubborn," Harley explained. "I've spent the entire weekend meeting with various people who might have information about what happened."

"Like who?"

"Like the couples who had daughters at St. Francis around the same time as the Nolans. Hospital staff. Anyone I can get to answer my calls, really."

Jade swallowed hard, the coffee burning in her throat. One of the people he'd spoken to could be one of her parents. It was hard to believe, but true. "Oh," was all she could manage to say. "Any luck?"

The lines in his forehead convinced her that he was conflicted about what he'd found. "Yes and no. Have you ever heard of Steele Tools?"

Jade shrugged. "Yeah. I think I have a set of their screwdrivers. Why?"

"My team has been doing a little research on them. They're a fascinating success story that started here in Charleston, actually."

He continued talking about what he'd learned so far, but Jade wasn't really listening. While the history of Steele Tools might seem fascinating to Harley, she wasn't sure why she should care. Or why it seemed to weigh so heavily on his mind. "That's all nice, but what does that have to do with the case?"

Harley pressed his lips tightly together as though reluctant to say anymore. That was too damn bad. He'd started this conversation and he was going to finish it.

"Spill, Harley."

He sighed. "I've been able to contact and basically eliminate every family that had a baby girl at St. Francis when you were born except for one. Trevor and Patricia Steele were at the hospital and they delivered a daughter during the storm. They named her Morgan."

Morgan. Jade had always liked that name. She'd personally never been a huge fan of Jade, but at least it was different. It suited her, she supposed, although she was beginning to wonder if that was the reason she liked

Morgan better than her own name. Was that the name she was supposed to have? The one she'd been given the day she was born? Somehow thinking of the name like that made it sound foreign and odd to her ears.

"The problem is I've been unable to get in contact with them. I've left messages with all their secretaries and assistants, and they haven't called me back. It's incredibly frustrating, because I know we're close to the truth."

Jade tried to process what he was telling her. If all the other families had been eliminated, that meant the Steele couple's daughter was the only real candidate to be swapped with the Nolans'. Which would mean that Jade was...

"If I'm right about this, and I think I am, you're the daughter of billionaires, Jade."

She hesitated for a moment, staring blankly at Harley. She was waiting for the punch line. The gotcha. The bazinga. Instead, he just looked at her with his large eyes as though awaiting a bigger reaction.

"Billionaires?" she said at last.

"Yes."

She slumped down into the chair, trying to process what he'd told her. Right now, it was just supposition on his part. There was no evidence, no DNA to confirm it. But even if there were, a part of her wouldn't believe it. That kind of stuff just didn't happen. "Let me guess, I'm also the crown princess of Genovia, too."

Harley flinched. "Gen-*what*? I'm serious, Jade. I think you were switched at birth and deliberately taken away from the Steeles. It all makes sense."

"Does it?" she said, her voice beginning to sound hysterical to her own ears. "It doesn't make a damn bit of sense to me."

"No, listen. Follow this… You've been unable to understand why your parents were targeted. I don't think they were the targets. I think the Steele family was the real target. Your parents and their daughter were convenient."

"Why?"

Harley sat back in his chair and sighed. "That's the piece I haven't figured out yet. A family like that would be a prime target for a kidnapping or something like that."

"Kidnapping, sure. But what do they gain from swapping me with some other baby? Nothing."

"I know. It doesn't make any sense. I don't have all the pieces yet, but I know I'm on the right track. I feel it in my gut."

"Maybe you're just hungry," she said with a dry tone.

Harley scowled at her over his coffee. Apparently her humor wasn't as welcome when he was stuck on a case. "You know, I thought you would be more interested in what I had to tell you, but you're treating it all like a joke. I mean, really, I shouldn't have said anything, but it seemed like you needed to know. It's a big discovery."

Jade came to his side and placed a gentle hand on his shoulder. "I know, and I'm sorry. Thank you for telling me. It's just a lot for me to think about. I didn't know what I expected when this whole process began, but I certainly wasn't planning on it involving rich people and kidnapping plots. I don't know what I'm supposed to do or think about the whole situation."

"You don't have to do anything. Just mull it over and let yourself get used to the idea. I don't want you to be blindsided when it all comes out and you've got reporters in your face asking you how it feels to be an instant billionaire."

She was grateful for the warning. Truly. But somehow being hit with news like that suddenly gave her more to worry about. Now she would fret, if the dull ache in her stomach was any indication.

Morgan Steele. That woman sounded powerful and in control of her life. The daughter of a wealthy family. The socialite heiress who was poised and polished to a shine. Jade was none of those things and couldn't imagine that she ever could be. It had to be a mistake. Harley was barking up the wrong tree.

Though when she looked up at him, she noticed a light of determination and seriousness in his eyes. He knew he was right. So what did that mean for her?

"You don't seem very excited by the news. I think most people would love to find out that they're secretly a member of the wealthiest family in town."

Jade supposed she wasn't most people. "It just makes me worry, Harley. I've never fit in with my family as it was, and we were raised poor. How will I possibly fit into a family that's überwealthy? I don't know how to be rich. I don't know how to be an elegant, refined person. I'm going to stand out like a sore thumb and that's the last thing I wanted. I was trying to find out where I belonged."

"I don't know what you're talking about. You're beautiful, you're smart. I could put you in a ball gown and take you to any fancy party you could name and you'd fit right in."

Jade sighed and looked down at the worn wood of her kitchen table. It was a hand-me-down from her parents, as were most of the things in the house. She hadn't had many new belongings in her life. What little she'd gotten as wedding gifts years ago were worn out or gone by now. She hadn't bothered to bring much back from Virginia when she'd packed up and left her life with Lance behind.

To find out that she really was a Steele... She couldn't even imagine what it would mean for her life, but she hoped Harley was right. She wanted more than anything to fit in somewhere. Hopefully, a nice dress and a smile would do the trick.

She doubted it.

Eight

When Jade returned home from work Monday afternoon, she found Harley where'd she left him that morning—at the kitchen table surrounded by paperwork, staring intently at his laptop. He hardly looked up when she came in, not acknowledging her presence until she dropped her purse onto the chair beside him.

"How's it going?" she asked.

"It's going." He sighed and shut his laptop. "You're home early."

Jade winced at his observation and turned to look at the clock on the microwave. "Actually, I'm home later than usual. It's almost five. You've been buried in your work for hours. Have you eaten anything today?"

Harley sat up straight in the chair and put more thought than should have been necessary into the answer. "I ate some of those shortbread cookies you had in the pantry."

She sighed. "I appreciate your dedication to the case, but you need to eat. There's nothing in the house worth cooking. Are you up for going out to dinner? You need a break from all this, I think."

"Sure." Harley stood up and stretched with a loud groan. He had to have been sitting there for hours. "I was actually thinking of taking you someplace really nice for dinner tonight."

Jade stiffened where she stood. Someplace nice? She wasn't quite sure what that meant. Or what it implied. Did he mean a date? They'd had sex. Things were casual but flirtatious between them. But nothing as traditional as a date had been mentioned before. So that probably wasn't what he meant. Or did he? She groaned internally and decided to focus on what she knew for sure.

"Really nice? Are we talking Red Lobster or... I don't even know what's nice in town. A lot changed while I was living out of state."

Harley rolled his eyes. "Actually, I thought we might take the opportunity to dip your toe into a little of the fancy lifestyle you may be facing if you're a part of the Steele family. Give you a chance to be more comfortable with that sort of thing."

So, *not* a date. Jade was both disappointed and relieved. "I think that's a little premature, but I suppose it can't hurt."

"Great. You go get ready and I'll see if I can wrangle some last-minute reservations."

Jade wandered down the hallway to her room to figure out what she was going to wear. Sorting through her closet, she eyed some choices and settled on the ever-appropriate little black dress. It was a silky fabric with lace cap sleeves and a deep V neckline that highlighted her collarbones. It had a ruched waist, giving her the appearance of an hourglass figure she didn't have, and fell right at the knee. Not too long or too short. With the right accessories and some black patent leather pumps, she hoped this dress would be suitable for any of the nicer restaurants in downtown Charleston, which she'd never visited before.

She pulled her hair back into a chignon at the base of her neck and touched up her makeup to last a few more hours. She added the pearl earrings and matching necklace her parents had given her for her wedding day—the nicest jewelry she owned—and then studied herself in the mirror.

Jade had to admit she looked lovely. Maybe as lovely as she ever had. It would probably be enough to pass at whatever restaurant Harley chose tonight. But this was just a test run. Would the woman in the mirror pass for a member of the Steele family? That was a better question.

And would it ever come to that?

When she returned to the living room, she found Harley there in a black suit with a silk, charcoal-gray shirt. He'd forgone the tie tonight and she liked it. The open collar gave just a peek of the hollow of his throat, which she was certain smelled like a mix of his cologne and the warm musk of his skin. It took everything she had to pick up her purse and not bury her face there to draw in his scent.

After seeing him around the house in more casual clothes the last few days, it was nice to see tailored and put-together Harley once again, too. He was like a chameleon, blending in to any environment. Looking at him now reminded her of the moment she'd opened the front door to find him on her porch. It was hard to believe that was only a week ago. The same butterflies took flight in her stomach when she looked at him this time, too.

He didn't seem to notice. Harley was too busy staring at her. "You look…" He cleared his throat and nodded. "You look very nice."

Jade smiled and glanced down at her ensemble. "Is this okay for where we're going?"

"Absolutely. I'm sure you'll be the most beautiful woman there tonight."

She had a hard time believing such a big compliment, but after their earlier discussion, she decided not to argue with him. He seemed to believe it, which meant it was true, at least in his eyes. "Thank you," she said.

He offered her his arm and escorted her out the door to his Jaguar.

"So where did you end up getting a reservation?" she asked as he drove out onto the highway toward downtown Charlestown.

Harley smiled, his eyes fixed on the road. "Well, I know a guy who has recently invested in a great steak house in an old converted carriage house. You're going to love it."

About twenty minutes later, they pulled up to the valet stand outside of Harrison Chophouse. While Harley handed over the keys, Jade waited patiently on the curb, reading decals on the tinted glass windows that pronounced several awards they'd won, including most romantic restaurant and top ratings from various dining and travel sites.

Inside, they found a dimly lit room made all the more intimate and warm by the dark wood paneled walls and crackling fire in the stone hearth in the center of it all. Each table had a white tablecloth, a flickering candle and a small centerpiece of fresh flowers. Most tables were occupied and a small crowd was gathered in the lobby, waiting for seats.

Harley made his way to the maître d's stand, and Jade was surprised when they were immediately escorted back to an intimate corner table. She settled into the chair across from Harley and accepted the menu that the maître d' handed her.

Her gaze had barely flicked over the selection of seafood and steaks when another man approached the table and introduced himself as the restaurant's sommelier. "May I offer you something from our extensive wine list?" he asked. "I highly recommend the 2014 Opus One, which is a lovely red blend, or the Silver Oak cabernet sauvignon."

"Do you like red wine?" Harley asked.

She nodded. "Whatever you like best," she said. In truth, she wasn't sure if she liked red wine or not. She hadn't drunk much wine in her lifetime. She occasionally had a glass of white wine at social functions, but that was about it. Especially after things went down with Lance. Somehow consuming any kind of addictive substance had made her uneasy for the first year or so. But she was willing to try whatever was appropriate for tonight. It was part of the experience, she supposed.

Harley looked over the wine list for a moment and ordered a bottle of something she couldn't pronounce. The man seemed pleased, disappearing for a few moments and returning with Harley's selection.

The sommelier went through the ritual of opening the wine and pouring a small sample for Harley to try. Once he approved, the man poured a glass for each of them and left the bottle on the table.

Jade casually picked up the wine menu and found what Harley had selected. It was a four-hundred-dollar bottle of wine, and didn't even come close to being the most expensive choice on the list.

"You'll get used to it," he said with a smile as he seemed to notice her reaction.

Jade looked at him and frowned. "Get used to what?"

"Your new life. If it turns out that you're the true Steele heiress, a lot of things are going to change. It took me a while to adjust, too, especially after spending so many years overseas. I was accustomed to living in such rough conditions that just coming back to the States was luxurious. Then once my company took off and I found I had more money than I could ever spend, it took time to adjust to a new way of looking at the world. I had always had a poor man's perspective. In some ways I still do, but I tried to broaden my horizons. If I wanted something, I could have it. I could eat at nice restaurants and wear expensive suits. I can spend more than I paid in rent money for my old apartment on a single bottle of wine. The key for me is to never take it for granted."

Jade wasn't sure if she could ever do that. "Don't you feel like an imposter?"

"Every day of my life. I thought for the longest time that people would see through it all and kick me to the curb as though I didn't belong. But it never happened. The same will happen to you, Jade. You might feel out of place, but you'll fit in soon enough. I'd say you already would fit in if you'd take a deep breath, take a sip of that ridiculously expensive wine and allow yourself to relax."

She shook her head and looked back down at the menu. "I don't know about it being that easy," she said, but forced herself to take a deep breath, anyway. "I'm not so confident that my life is going to change, Harley. Even if you get the proof you need and the Steeles turn out to be my real parents, that doesn't mean they're going to welcome me with open arms. And even if they did, I doubt they're going to give me a room in their mansion, hand me a checkbook and immediately rewrite their wills to include me. I might end up like the distant cousin that only gets invited to Christmas dinner. After all this, I'll probably live the same middle-class life I've scratched out for myself."

Jade reached for her glass and took a healthy sip. It was lovely. Better than the twelve-dollar-a-bottle stuff she was used to having from time to time, as well it should be.

It worked its magic on her quickly, however, especially on an empty stomach. The splash of cabernet warmed her and relaxed her muscles. Perhaps that was why the rich liked wine so much, she thought. It helped them deal with the stresses of their wealthy, complicated lives.

Harley looked at her across the table with exasperation in his blue eyes. "You haven't even met these people yet and you're already planning their inevitable rejection. Care to tell me why that is?"

She didn't know for sure. "I don't know what to say, Harley. I just can't buy into the fantasy. My whole life I've fought to do the right thing and make the best choices, and it always seems to fly back in my face. I don't know why this would be any different. Maybe a part of me knows that if I expect the worst, I might be pleasantly surprised for a change."

"Is that how you feel about me? About us? That if you expect all of this to end badly and it doesn't, at the very least you won't be disappointed?"

Jade narrowed her gaze at him. He was looking so handsome in his suit, even as he pressed her about unpleasant topics. She studied the lines and angles of his face for a moment as she gathered her thoughts. It was easier to focus on the broken, offset nose, the evening stubble along his jaw and the dark brown eyebrows that framed his face than on the two of them and what was going on between them.

"I don't know how you and I are going to end, Harley. But yes, there's certainly a part of me that knows better than to give too much importance to it. You're going to crack the case and go back to DC, while I stay in Charleston and work through my identity crisis. Thinking what we have is anything more than a fun indulgence to scratch that itch for old time's sake is a recipe for heartbreak, don't you think?"

He didn't answer, but studied her face intently as she spoke. Jade wasn't sure if he agreed with what she'd said or was irritated by it. Finally, he nodded and reached out to pick up his wineglass. "What shall we drink to tonight?"

Jade thought for a moment as she picked up her own. "To the future?" she suggested.

He smiled. "To the future," he replied, clinking his crystal glass gently against hers. "And being pleasantly surprised by everything it has in store for you."

"For both of us," she corrected.

They returned to a disaster area.

Harley was beyond furious as he watched Jade step gingerly through the remains of her living room in her nice dress and heels. While they were away at dinner, someone had broken in and done his best to try to scare Jade.

As she bent down with trembling hands to pick up a shattered frame containing a photograph of her family, Harley worried that perhaps whoever it was had been successful. Jade was a strong, stubborn woman, but everyone had their limits.

The cops had already come and gone, taking statements and photographs, but offering little to make Jade feel any better about her situation. As it was, the living room bore little resemblance to what they'd left behind only a few hours ago. It was the same in all the other rooms of her tiny bungalow—nothing seemed to be taken, but everything was torn apart. Overturned furniture, dumped out drawers, broken glass…even a message spray painted across her living room wall: Quit While You're Ahead.

Just looking at the sloppy red paint splattered across her beautiful little space was enough to send Harley's blood pressure skyrocketing. She'd come back to Charleston to start a new life. To rebuild after Lance destroyed everything they had together. And now, something that had happened thirty years ago was threatening this new chance. He didn't know that Jade would ever be able to live in this house alone and be comfortable. Even with all the best technology he could install.

Damn the delays. If his guys had been here days ago the way they'd planned, the house would've been rigged with cameras rolling to catch the intruder as he approached. The system would have protected the house, and more importantly, protected Jade's feelings of security. She'd argued with him that her neighborhood was safe and she didn't need all that equipment. He doubted she would argue with him about it now.

"I don't understand," Jade said, as she dropped the photograph back to the floor and sat down on the couch. "Why would someone do something like this?"

"To rattle you," Harley replied. "If this is the same person who wrote the note, and I think it is, he's escalating their threats. You haven't dropped the case, so they wanted you to know they're serious."

"But who cares?" she lamented. "Why would someone be so invested in me not finding my family? I'm no Princess Anastasia."

He shook his head and moved to sit beside her. "If we uncover the motivation, we may very well find out what happened to you as a baby and why. Whoever was involved doesn't want the truth coming out. You're just the driving force behind the investigation, and therefore, the target of their aggression. Simple as that."

"Simple as that," Jade parroted with a flat tone and dead eyes that focused on the spray-painted threat.

Harley didn't like seeing her that way. It wasn't like his Jade. She was a fighter, and this bastard had broken her. Harley's hands curled into fists in his lap as he looked around at the mess. He felt helpless, something he almost never was. He always had something he could do to correct a situation. He wanted to beat the person responsible to a pulp, or drop them into the world's worst prison, where they'd never be heard from again.

But for now, he needed to figure out what he could do to help.

As he was thinking, Jade leaned against him and laid her head on his shoulder. She wrapped her arms around his biceps and held him tightly. "I'm glad you're here," she said. "If I had come home alone to find this, I don't know what I would've done."

She was right. At least he was here with her. She wasn't going through all of this alone. He was glad he'd followed his instincts when she'd received that threatening letter. Jade hadn't been happy about him imposing on her life, but it had been the right choice.

He turned to bury his face in the white-blond strands of her hair, and breathed in the scent of her shampoo. The familiar and fruity smell helped him relax, letting the knotted muscles in his neck and shoulders unwind. He didn't need to prepare for battle. At least not tonight.

"I'm glad I was here, too. I'm going to find out who's doing this to you, Jade, and I'll make sure they can't hurt you ever again."

She didn't respond, just clung more tightly to his arm. He'd hoped that he would get a chance to hold her again tonight, but this wasn't what he'd had in mind. The mood was definitely shattered, along with most of her things.

Jade said she would call her insurance company in the morning, but he knew they would do only so much. He would phone the office and have his assistant set up a cleaning crew to get the place put back together, while his team installed the security equipment that had arrived a day too late.

But in the meantime…

"Jade, pack a bag. We're leaving."

She snapped out of her sad fog and sat up, turning to look at him with confusion furrowing her brow. "What?"

"This place isn't safe any longer. We're not staying here tonight."

"Where are we going to go?"

Harley thought about it for a moment, firming up the plans in his mind. "We're going to my mother's house."

"I don't know, Harley. That would be weird. I don't want her getting the wrong idea about us."

"She won't."

"I don't want to impose."

Harley sighed and crossed his arms over his chest. Why was everything an argument with Jade? "You won't be imposing. My mother's house is huge. I paid for it. I pay someone to clean it. If you tried hard enough, she might not even know you were there."

"We can't just get a hotel room here in town?"

"No. I was staying with her until I came here. And now, so are you."

"But…"

"No buts. The threats are getting more serious, Jade. The only way to end them is to complete the investigation. I can't do that and also protect you every minute of the day. My mother's house is an old plantation property surrounded by twelve acres of wooded wetlands. It's gated, alarmed, surveilled and completely secure. It's a damn fortress with arches and columns. That's the only place I would feel comfortable leaving you right now. I'm not even sure I want you to work for the next few days. You're too exposed to the public there."

Jade took a deep breath, and as she let it out, he could see the fight draining out of her, too. "Okay. I'll call in sick for a couple days. How much should I pack?"

He didn't want to say it out loud, but he couldn't see Jade living here again, so everything? "At least enough clothing and toiletries to get you through two or three days. We can always come back and get more if we need to."

"More than three days?"

Harley shrugged. "It all depends on my investigation. Until we know the truth, and the person responsible for this is in jail, I don't know where else you can stay. They'd just trace you to your parents' house. No one will know you're with me, or where my mother lives. She's as big of a black hole of digital data as I am. They won't be able to find her."

Jade nodded and stood up to make her way to what was left of her bedroom. It should be easy to pack, with everything strewn on the floor, but he figured it would take her a while to get things together. Before she went down the hall, she stopped and turned back to Harley.

He thought she might say something. Her eyes were overflowing with emotion, but instead of speaking, she just lunged forward and wrapped her arms around him in a ferocious hug. Jade's face was buried in his neck as she clung to him. She didn't say a word, but Harley got the message loud and clear.

He hadn't wanted it to happen this way, but he'd finally brought down the wall between the two of them. The last of Jade's fortifications had fallen and she was letting him in, at last.

And he wasn't sure what he should do next.

Nine

When Harley said he'd bought his mother a plantation, Jade had been thinking it was a metaphor for a big house, or at the very least, an exaggeration. Then the iron gates opened and his Jaguar traveled down the road that led to the Rose River Mansion and she realized he was telling the truth. It was an actual 1800s-era plantation home.

Unlike the typical White House style with two-story columns, Rose River was unique in these parts. She was no architect, but *Gothic* was the only word that came to mind, even with its traditional white wood siding and copper peaked roof. Like a cross between an old chapel, a house and a European chalet, it was so detailed that Jade figured she could stare at it for hours and see something new every time she looked. It was like something out of a novel, making her little bungalow look like a shack in comparison.

As they parked and walked up the pea gravel path to the front door, she gazed at the ancient oak trees overhead, which were dripping with Spanish moss highlighted by the moonlight. Brick steps led to a grand porch with three cusped arches and clustered piers welcoming guests inside. As they climbed the stairs to the porch, however, Jade saw modern touches of Harley in the old house. There were video cameras beneath the eaves and technologically advanced locks on the front door and windows. Knowing him, the original glass had been replaced with bulletproof panes.

Instead of using a key, Harley reached out to punch in a six-digit code, then pressed his thumb on a scanner to unlock the door. It swung open and he gestured for her to go inside ahead of him.

Jade stepped into the grand entrance hall with its two-story ceiling, sparkling chandelier and spiral staircase. She couldn't imagine living someplace like this. It was quite a leap from the tiny apartment Harley had shared with his mother back in high school. She knew he had done well for himself with his business, but this was on another level.

"Is your home in DC like this?" she asked, as she studied the marble floors and intricate moldings.

Harley shut the door and dropped their bags on the floor beside him. "Not even close," he said. "My taste runs a bit more modern. I have a three-story town house in Georgetown. It's over a hundred years old, but you wouldn't know it."

"I'm sure you gutted all the charm out of it and added all your security features in the process."

"I didn't have to," he stated with a smile. "The previous owner was a higher-up in the CIA. It was completely renovated and locked down tighter than the Vatican vaults when I bought it."

"Sounds perfect for you," she said smugly.

"Harley, is that you, dear?"

Jade turned in time to see Harley's mother come through a set of French doors to greet them. Though she certainly looked older than when they'd last met, the years had been kind to her. She paused for a moment as she gazed at the two of them in the entry, then grinned widely.

"Jade?"

"Yes, it's me, Mrs. Dalton."

The woman came forward quickly, scooping Jade into a big hug. It was just like the ones she remembered from her teen years, although now his mother smelled like Chanel No. 5 and was wearing sparkling diamond studs in her ears. She finally pulled away and studied Jade for a moment. "Lovely. Just lovely."

Then she turned to her son. "Harley Wayne Dalton, why didn't you tell me you were bringing Jade here tonight? I would've had a room prepared for her. Now the housekeeper has already gone to bed for the evening. It's past eleven."

"It was a last-minute decision, Mama. Her house was broken into and I didn't want to stay there tonight."

"Oh no, that's just awful," she said in the thick Carolina drawl Jade remembered. "Of course you're going to stay here, aren't you? Since Gabby is asleep, I'll run upstairs and get a room ready for you." She paused for a moment, looking curiously at them both with arched eyebrows. "Unless you'll just be sharing Harley's room?" she asked with a hopeful twinkle in her eyes.

"That's fine, Mama. We'll share. I told her you wouldn't go to any trouble."

Mrs. Dalton frowned in irritation, and in that moment, Jade could see she really was the female version of Harley. Her dark brown hair was pulled back, showing the silver streaks that ran through it like elegantly placed highlights. She had the same high cheekbones, the same piercing blue eyes and the same devious smile. "It's no trouble," she fussed. "I don't get company very often."

"No, really, Mrs. Dalton. Don't worry about me. At the moment, I just want to get out of these heels, find a bed and pass out on it. I'm exhausted."

"Okay," she agreed reluctantly. "Harley, why don't you show her around and take her upstairs to your room. If you need anything, you just come and get me."

Harley nodded, picked up their bags and headed toward the grand staircase. Jade followed him, taking in the artwork and decor as they climbed the curving stairs and went down the hallway.

"My room is in the west wing of the house," he explained. "We're down here to the left."

He nudged open the door with his shoulder and stepped inside. Jade followed him into the large, bright room with its king-size bed. It had a pale blue duvet that matched the paintings on the walls. Most of the furnishings were white and oversize, but fit well within the space. There was a desk and television on the wall opposite the bed.

Harley placed both bags on the bed and then flopped down onto the mattress beside them. "The closet is there—" he gestured to a door "—and the bathroom is over there." He pointed toward a second one.

Jade kicked out of her high heels and sighed in relief as her feet sank into the plush carpeting. It had been a long, stressful evening and her body was starting to feel the effects. She peeked her head into the bathroom and found a Carrara marble palace awaiting her, with a large soaking tub and a tile-and-glass shower big enough for two.

"I think I'm going to take a bath," she said.

"Enjoy," Harley answered, as he kicked off his own shoes and reached for his laptop bag. He took out his computer, and then his handgun, which he placed on the nearby nightstand. Thankfully, all his things had been in the car with them tonight. She had no doubt that her intruder would've taken or destroyed Harley's notes and files to set back the progress of the investigation.

He still seemed preoccupied and on edge, and Jade understood. While everything that happened tonight was traumatic for her, it was different for Harley. Even if he didn't see the situation as some sort of failure on his part, which it wasn't, it was more than likely going to fire him up. He was already pouring everything he had into the investigation, but with the stakes raised, he wouldn't rest until he had the answers.

Jade closed the door to the bathroom behind her and

did her best to leave her worries, and his, outside the marble oasis. She started the hot water, pouring in some rose-scented oil she found on the counter. She stripped out of her clothes and jewelry and pulled her hair up on top of her head in a messy bun before dipping in her toe and climbing into the bathtub.

She was exhausted, both emotionally and physically, and this was exactly what she wanted. Her little house offered most of the things she needed, but not a soaking tub. It made her miss the one she'd had in her house with Lance. One more thing to add to the list of things that she'd lost over the past few years.

When Jade lay back and closed her eyes, she found she couldn't relax as easily as she'd hoped. She was worried. Not about the investigation. Not really even about the break-in. Yes, there was a threat from an unknown source, but she had no doubt that Harley would do everything he could to protect her. That was actually the problem. He would do anything. That scared her.

When they'd found her home in disarray, she'd noticed something change in Harley. A switch had flipped inside him and any ideas she might have entertained about him settling into the quiet life of a CEO went out the window. He was instantly in combat mode, pushing her behind him and searching the house, pistol drawn, to make sure the culprit wasn't still there. When he was satisfied, he'd called the police and put away his weapon, but she could tell he was still wound tight.

She appreciated his efforts, but the excitement in his eyes worried her. Her bad boy from high school had always enjoyed living on the wild side. The military fed right into his need for adrenaline. His money and success might offer him fewer opportunities for adventure, but he still enjoyed the rush of danger. Jade supposed he couldn't go from jumping out of airplanes and interrogating suspected terrorists to filing paperwork, and still be fully content with his life.

She knew that much. She'd known it when she'd walked away from him all those years ago, and she knew it when she'd invited him into her bed a few days ago. That was why she'd gone into this whole situation with caution. Harley was older and wiser, but not everything had changed. The quiet, peaceful, secure life she craved was never going to be okay for a man like him.

Jade took a deep breath and tried to let the hot water and the scent of the oil relax her and chase away her anxieties. The bottom line was that keeping emotionally distant from Harley was hard, but necessary. She had enough going on in her life without dealing with the inevitable heartbreak of falling for him. Whether he ended it or she lost him in a dangerous twist of fate, she would end up alone and hurt, and she couldn't go through that again.

When the water started to go cold, she gave up on her brain winding down into relaxation and decided she needed to just go to bed. Maybe then she could get a break from her own thoughts for a while.

Wrapped in a towel, she stepped out into the bedroom and found Harley sitting at the desk with his laptop. He wasn't frowning at the screen this time, though. There was a glint of interest in his eyes that caught her attention. That was different. It made Jade wonder what information he'd managed to uncover this late, after such a long and miserable night.

"I believe I'm going to have to think outside the box with this case," he said. "If I can't get the Steele family to contact me, I'm just going to have to go directly to them."

"What do you suggest?" Jade asked, as she unzipped her bag and pulled out something to sleep in. "I can't imagine you could just stroll up to their front door or march into their offices downtown."

"Normally, you'd be right." Harley turned his laptop around to face her.

She tugged on an oversize Clemson T-shirt from her undergraduate years and walked over for a closer look. It was the website for the annual Steele Tools charity ball, scheduled for Friday night at the Steele estate.

"Isaiah just sent me the link for this, along with more background on Morgan. This is the one night of the year that you *can* stroll right up to their door and go inside, as long as you pay for a ticket. As the community outreach representative for the company, Morgan will be at that party, I have no doubt. As will the rest of the family. All I have to do is dust off my tuxedo and lay out the required donation to get that ticket."

"You're going to look suspicious going by yourself," Jade said.

If the family had been deliberately avoiding him, they probably had people on the lookout for attendees that didn't belong. She had no doubt he would look handsome, but a single man typically wouldn't go to a party like that alone. Especially a man who looked like Harley, fresh from the front lines. "You're going to need a date if you want any chance of getting in the front door."

Harley stopped and looked at her with conflict in his gaze. He knew she was right, she could tell, but he didn't like it. "I can't take you to the party," he said.

Jade couldn't hide her pout as she crossed her arms over her chest. "Why not? You said if you put me in a pretty dress you could take me anywhere."

"That's absolutely true. But you know I'm trying to not involve you in the case. I'll be there to ask questions and try to get an in with the Steeles. Is that really how you want to meet your potential family? Accidentally bumping into your birth mother in line at the bar?"

She hadn't thought about it that way, but the more she considered what he said, the less it mattered. "Actually, I think this might be better. It would take the pressure off to just be there and observe them, without this big announcement about me being their daughter hanging over my head."

"And you think you'll be able to keep your cool and not say anything? Pretend like they're nothing to you even as I try to corner Morgan into a private discussion? If her parents aren't cooperating, it's critical that I get her on board to help."

Jade nodded confidently. "I can. And even if I couldn't, you have to take me, Harley. You can't leave me by myself. You said yourself that it's too dangerous."

"I can leave you here. You're perfectly safe with my mother," he countered.

"Well, then who else are you going to drag to a black-tie party on such short notice?"

Finally, after she'd chipped away at all his excuses, he relented, although he still had a wary look in his eyes. "Okay, you're right. I don't have a lot of options here. I can't believe I'm about to say this, but Jade Nolan, will you go to the dance with me?"

Harley felt incredibly out of place in the department store. Like a bull in a china shop, he tried to stay in the corner and out of the way, but he was just too large a man in such a tiny dressing area. The dressing rooms themselves were down a narrow hall, but he was waiting just outside of them where a three-paneled mirror offered a view of your every angle whether you wanted to see it or not. The room was also had a small counter where a chic woman dressed all in black assisted the ladies and rehung outfits that they passed on. Every time a woman went in or out, he had to press into the wall so she could pass between him and the clerk.

"Do I have to be here for this?" he said loudly, making the clerk roll her eyes at him. He didn't care.

"Yes." Jade's voice drifted to him from over the wall partition. "You've generously offered to buy me a new gown, so should get some say in what I wear to the party."

Yeah, that's what she'd said as she lured him into the department store. After perusing rack after rack of beaded and silky gowns, Jade had led him to the dressing area so she could try on a few of the selections. Somehow the idea of seeing Jade model a bunch of slinky garments was better in his mind than it was in reality.

"Fine," he growled. He didn't understand why a place selling dresses that cost more than his first car couldn't have a bigger fitting room area. He should've just hired a personal shopper to handle this, but Jade had told him he was being silly. It was bad enough that he was buying her a dress, she'd said. Jade hadn't wanted to accept, but he'd insisted she needed something nice enough to blend in with the other rich partygoers. Since she didn't have anything suitable, she could choose between staying home or letting him buy her a dress.

Only then had she relented. But she wasn't going to let him go overboard. She'd insisted she would just pick out something off the rack, whatever that meant.

He sighed and crossed his arms over his chest. Hopefully, one of the dresses she'd selected would work. Harley couldn't imagine going through all this a second time at another store.

"Are you going to come out in any of them?" he asked.

"As soon as I find one worth showing you, yes."

After an eternity of waiting, he finally heard a door down the corridor unlatch, and a moment later, Jade emerged from the dressing room in a crimson beaded gown. It had a plunging square neckline that highlighted the delicious curves of her small, firm breasts and her long, graceful neck. The cap sleeves left most of her arms bare, highlighting the stark contrast between her pale skin and hair and the blood-red fabric. The beaded and sequined design crisscrossed over the dress and down to the floor, where it just barely pooled at her feet.

She looked—in a word—stunning.

Harley felt his chest tighten as he stared at her. She was every bit the elegant lady he suspected she really was. She felt like she'd never fitted in, but he was certain that was only because she hadn't grown up with the family she was meant to have. Even with her blond hair up in a clip, and her feet bare, she looked ready to walk down a grand staircase into the elegant party she was about to attend.

He would be more than proud to have her on his arm. In fact, he was more than a little worried that she'd be too beautifully conspicuous for them to attend the gala unnoticed.

And he wanted to whisk her into the dressing room and violate every rule the department store had. Being escorted out by security would be worth it if he could get his hands on her at that moment.

Clearly oblivious to his thoughts, Jade examined herself in the three-way mirror and finally looked up at him with concern wrinkling her forehead. "I'm not sure about this one," she said. "What do you think?"

"I love it," he said. And he meant it.

Jade narrowed her eyes at him suspiciously. "You're just saying that because you're tired of shopping. I could come out in a trash bag and you'd be ready to buy it."

"That's not true," Harley argued. "That's hardly a trash bag. The color is beautiful on you, and the cut is very flattering."

"This is an Elie Saab," the clerk said, as she swooped

in to help Jade make her choice. "He's right, it really does look lovely on you."

"See?" Harley challenged.

Jade just shook her head and turned to the mirror again. When he saw the back of the dress, he felt as though his lungs had turned to stone in his rib cage. He couldn't breathe as his gaze ran over the bare expanse of her skin and the low dip of the fabric. It begged him to run his fingertips down her spine.

He could envision them dancing at the ball together as she wore that dress. Her body pressed against his, Harley's palm flattened to her bare lower back. He hated dancing. Had no interest in it normally. But that dress could change his mind.

"I don't know," Jade said. He could still hear the doubt in her voice. "It's a pretty dress, but is this what I want to be wearing to meet what could be my family for the first time?"

Harley had been wondering if there was more to her indecision than just a fashion choice. They'd looked at twenty dresses before she chose a few to try on. Now it seemed as though they were closing in on the real issue. Jade would look lovely in anything she wore, but she wanted to make a good first impression.

With a sigh, he walked up behind her and pressed his palms into her shoulders. He looked at her through their reflection in the mirror with a sincere expression. "This party is just our chance to make first contact. We don't have to tell them who you are if you're nervous. But if they really are your family, Jade, they're going to love you no matter what you have on. Whether you wear this beautiful dress or the trash bag you mentioned earlier, they're not going to care, because you're amazing."

He watched in the mirror as Jade's eyes started to tear up. She nodded slightly and then blinked them away. "You really like this one?" she asked, with a more confident smile painted on her face.

"I do. I'd be happy to buy it for you. I'd also be very happy to help you take it off."

Jade turned to face him. "Well, if all goes well at the gala, you might just get that chance."

He wrapped his arms around her waist, seeking out the bare expanse of her back. Her skin was cool to his heated touch, making a chill run through his whole body at the contrast. He took a deep breath to wish away the surge of desire suddenly racing through his veins. "You mean after dangling this tempting fruit in front of my face, you're going to make me wait until after the Steeles' party to taste it?"

Her dark eyes were focused on his as another smile curled her lips. "You won't have to wait for a taste, but I'm not letting you mess up this dress before I even get a chance to wear it."

"I'll just have to get you naked then," he said. "To preserve the dress."

A loud "ahem" from the salesclerk distracted them both and severed the sexual tension building in the tiny dressing room lobby.

"This is the one," Harley insisted. "Ring it up."

Jade nodded and pulled away from his embrace. "I'll change and be right out." She gave him a sly wink before she rounded the corner and disappeared from sight.

Lord, he wanted that woman.

Harley had never experienced anything like it in the years they'd been apart. He'd met and wooed his share of beautiful women. Smart women. Strong women. Talented women. They were each appealing and alluring in their own ways, but not one of them held a candle to Jade. He was drawn to her on every level—chemical, physical...even on an emotional level. And it was dangerous. If he wasn't careful, he could give himself up to this pull she had on him.

And then what?

He wasn't sure. That wasn't his plan when he'd first kissed her. He'd wanted to overdose and get Jade out of his system. Instead, he'd become an eager and willing addict.

No, he wasn't sure what the future held for the two of them, but for the first time, he was anxious to find out.

Ten

The house was dark and quiet when they returned from the department store with Jade's new dress. She'd expected Mrs. Dalton to be in the living room, reading a book or watching television, but she was nowhere to be found.

Harley looked down at his phone as he flipped on the light in the entry hall. "She's gone to dinner and a movie with a man she met on OurTime.com," he said, reading her text aloud. "She says not to wait up for her."

Jade smiled. "Good for her."

He didn't seem to be as excited. "When she comes home, I'm getting the guy's information and running a background check on him."

"So suspicious," Jade noted, shifting the garment bag in her arms.

"Do you know how many cases we handle that deal with internet dating? Scammers, catfishers, missing women, false identities, stalkers, bigamists…too many to count. And that doesn't even take into consideration your run-of-the-mill jerks or perverts sending unsolicited dick pics."

Her eyes widened. If the idea of internet dating had appealed to her before, she was second-guessing it now. "I guess it's a good thing I haven't bothered to sign up for any of those sites yet."

"Good," Harley replied gruffly. "You don't need to be on there, anyway."

She turned toward him. "Why not? That's how people meet these days. I've been divorced for almost two years now. I didn't think I was ready to date yet, but maybe it's time. I'll have to ask your mom how it's going for her when she gets home."

A glint of jealousy flickered in Harley's blue eyes, and it was exactly what she'd hoped to see when she said those things. She wasn't really interested in online dating. What she wanted was for him to tell her why she didn't need to do it. That she wasn't single. That she didn't need a dating site because she had him. Perhaps that he cared for her on some level. But she knew he wouldn't. And it was foolish of her to even entertain such a thought.

For a moment, he looked as though he might prove her wrong. Words seemed to linger on the tip of his tongue for a moment as his square jaw flexed. "You can meet plenty of guys in real life without going through all that," he added instead. "Especially when you're wearing a dress like that one."

Jade let a smug smile curl her lips. She thought she had gotten a rise out of Harley in that dressing room. He was flirty, as always, but there had been a light of appreciation in his eyes when she stepped out in the dress that she couldn't ignore. Even if she'd hated the dress she would've bought it just for the way he looked at her while she was in it.

"Speaking of which, I'm going to go hang this up, in your bedroom. Do you want to help me?"

Harley frowned. "You need help?"

Jade looked at him with the sultriest gaze she could come up with. "Well, it is an awfully big house. I don't want to get lost. And we are here all alone…"

He caught on fast. Before she could even take a step toward the staircase, Harley had scooped her up into his arms and was carrying her across the marble hall. Jade squealed in surprise, clutching the dress high in her arms to make sure it didn't trip them in catastrophic fashion.

She buried her face in his neck as he climbed the stairs. It was soothing to breathe in the scent of his skin and think about what was coming instead of pondering how painful a fall down the stairs would be. When she finally looked up, they were at the bedroom door. He kicked it open, stepped forward and gently set her down on the edge of the bed.

"What was that all about?" she asked, now that she was safely on the ground.

"You said you needed help and didn't want to get

lost." He grinned. "I try to be as helpful as I can, especially when a lady is in distress."

Jade shook her head. "You're a show-off, is what you are." She stood and carried the dress to the closet to hang it up. "That was very Rhett Butler of you."

"You're lucky I thought to do it like that. Normally, I just throw someone over my shoulder like a sack of potatoes. That's how I've carried my fellow soldiers out of dangerous buildings and situations when they were wounded."

"Good call," she said. "Ladies don't like to be hauled around like potato sacks."

Harley came up to her and placed his hands on her waist. His fingers pressed into the flesh of her hips as he gently stroked the knit fabric of her sweater dress. "I thought that might be the case."

Jade wrapped her arms around his neck. She could feel the dress inching higher on her thighs as he gathered the material in his hands. His gaze never left hers as he reached the hem and lifted it up over her head. As Harley tossed it aside, his blue gaze dipped down to study the treasure he'd uncovered. She'd worn a black strapless bra and a matching thong to try on formals without visible straps or panty lines. Judging by the expression on his face, he approved of the undergarments.

He flattened a hand over her collarbone, then slid his palm down her chest: She wondered if he could feel her heart pounding as he hesitated for a moment, then cupped her left breast through the silky fabric. She reached behind her to unclasp the bra and let it fall to the floor. The movement elicited a groan of appreciation from Harley's lips.

"Beautiful," he whispered as he admired her body.

His palms rose to cover both breasts. The rough feel of his hands against her sensitive nipples teased them into hard peaks, and every graze across their tips sent sparks of pleasure down her spine. She could feel her body grow flush, and heat built between her thighs by the second. She was amazed at how quickly she reacted to Harley. Just a touch, a glance, a wicked smile, and her body was ready for him instantly.

He leaned down to kiss her. This time felt different, though. Maybe it was because this was their first intimate moment since the break-in. Or maybe the last few days had just changed things between them. The urgency was gone, replaced with a gentleness as he sought to savor every moment with her.

Jade leaned into him, molding herself into his embrace. She enjoyed stroking his stubbled jaw, tracing the line of his throat to his collarbone, then on to the row of buttons on his shirt.

His tongue grazed hers, drinking her in even as her fingers undid the last button. She pulled away from his kiss long enough to push the fabric over his shoulders and down to the floor.

Harley took a deep breath and undid his belt. He turned his back to her and walked over to the bed, where he slipped out of the rest of his clothes. He sat on the edge of the bed, eased back to lean against the pillows and watched her from across the room. His appreciative gaze on her body made her feel sexier than she ever had before. She'd always felt too thin, even boyish in shape with no real curves to speak of. But he looked at her like she was the sexiest thing he'd ever seen and she wanted to show off for him.

Jade started by turning her back to him, displaying the curve of her ass in the thin black G-string panties she was wearing. She reached up and pulled the pins from her hair. The twisted bun unraveled, letting the pale blond strands cascade down her bare back and shoulders. She shook it out a little, hearing his sharp intake of breath from the bed.

Then she hooked her thumbs beneath her panties and started easing them over her hips. She did it slowly, bending at the waist as they slid down her legs until she was able to kick them aside. When she turned to face him again, his hands were fisted and his jaw was tight with restraint.

"Come here," was all he said.

Jade moved to the bed, and Harley reached out for her waist and tugged her into his lap. She straddled him, looking into his big blue eyes as he again leaned back against the pillows that lined the padded leather headboard. There were so many unspoken emotions trapped there. If she gazed long enough into their depths, she wondered if she would uncover how he really felt about her. She could easily sense his desire for her. And that he cared for her. But was there more to it than just that? And if there was, would she let her heart have what she wanted this time?

Last time, she'd done what she thought was right and followed her head, not her heart. She'd taken the advice of her well-meaning friends and family, and gone after what she thought she needed in her life. Not what she wanted. Because then, as well as now, Jade wanted Harley. Not just in her bed, but in her life. She wanted to share *his* life. Share his last name. She wanted to share a future with him, even without knowing what that would entail for them.

Because she loved him. If she was honest with herself, she'd have to admit she loved Harley and always had. She had talked herself out of it, insisted it was youthful infatuation and directed herself onto the "right" path with Lance, but that had never made her a fraction as happy as she was when she was with Harley.

The realization should've made her glad. At last she knew what she wanted in her life. And yet she felt the prickle of tears. Leaning forward, she kissed him and squeezed her eyes shut to keep them from rolling down her cheeks, where Harley could see them.

He wrapped his arms around her body, pulling her tight against his chest and lifting her up just enough for him to slip inside her. She came back down at a tantalizingly slow pace, stopping for a moment to cherish the feel of him. In this moment, they were connected in a way she'd longed for. It wouldn't last forever, though, so she needed to treasure every second they shared like this.

That's how they came together. Rocking back and forth on the bed, riding every high together until her thighs burned, her center throbbed and they couldn't hold out any longer. When she came undone, it wasn't with a cry, but a soft gasp in his ear as she clung to his neck. He followed her, groaning her name in a way that a man wouldn't do unless he felt something for her.

When it was over, Harley gently rolled onto his side. Scooping Jade into his arms, he tugged her back against his chest and curled protectively around her. "Jade?" he said, in a hushed whisper from behind her.

"Yes?" she replied, her stomach suddenly tightening. He wasn't the kind for pillow talk, so whatever he wanted to say to her right now was important.

"I know you're nervous about meeting the Steeles and what it might mean for you and your future. You always worry about fitting in. But you're amazing," he said. "Don't let anyone ever do or say anything to make you feel otherwise."

It was a sweet thing to say. Something she needed to hear, for sure. But in that moment, it wasn't what she wanted to hear. It had felt like the moment. His chance to say that he wanted more with her. That he cared for her. That he loved her. But instead, she got a lovely compliment and a boost to help her through her nervousness.

She knew then that she couldn't, wouldn't, tell Harley how she felt. Not now, at least. Maybe when the case was over. Right now, it was more important that he focus on what he'd been hired to do. His mind seemed to always be centered there, anyway.

And if he packed up and headed home to DC without a backward glance, she'd be relieved to know she'd kept her mouth shut and hadn't made a fool of herself a second time.

* * *

"You know, if I wasn't seeing it with my own eyes, I wouldn't believe it."

Confused, Harley stopped short in the entryway of Jade's house. The voice he heard didn't make sense in this context. He scanned the room, stopping when he spied Isaiah installing a motion detector in the corner of the kitchen.

"What the hell are you doing here?"

"Installing the equipment you ordered. This is the last of it, actually." Isaiah climbed down from the stepladder and set the drill on the kitchen table. "The cleanup crew is on their way to straighten up the place, too."

Harley shook his head. "That's not what I mean. What are *you* doing here? This isn't your job. You're supposed to be back in DC watching over the office, not putting in cameras and sensors in Charleston."

"It seemed like a rush job, so I came down with the other guys to lend a hand."

Harley stared at his friend in disbelief. "You know better than anyone that you can't lie to me."

Isaiah grinned widely, giving up any pretense about why he was here. "Fine. But do you really think I'd pass up this chance?"

"What chance?"

"To see the great Harley Dalton in love."

"Pish!" Harley said dismissively. "You came down here for nothing, man."

Isaiah crossed his arms over his chest in defiance. "You're not the only one good at picking up when someone is lying. I've known you long enough to tell when you're full of shit. And when you've fallen hard. I wasn't sure I'd ever see the day, but it's here."

Harley didn't want to talk about this right now. Not with Isaiah or anyone else. He didn't know how he felt about Jade, not really. He cared about her. He wanted her badly. He couldn't wait to be back at her side to sweep her into his arms and kiss her again. But that wasn't love. That was just… He didn't know what the hell it was, but he certainly didn't need his best friend telling him how he felt.

"So where's the lucky lady?" Isaiah asked. "I was hoping she might be here with you."

"She's with my mother."

Isaiah's eyebrows went up. "She's met your mother?"

"We dated in high school," Harley snapped. "Of course Jade has met my mother. Besides, I had to take her somewhere when the house was broken into. Mom's house is the safest place I know of in town."

"That's the truth. The Fort Knox of South Carolina." Isaiah looked around the house. "So what's going on with this case, man? I thought it was a baby switcheroo. How'd we get to home invasion and threats?" He gestured toward the spray paint on the living room wall.

Harley followed his gaze and shook his head. He wished he knew. The house was still in shambles after the break-in. He had forced Jade out the door with a suitcase that night and hadn't let her come back. He wouldn't until it was safe. He just wasn't sure when that was going to be. He thought perhaps once the security system was in. Or once the case was solved.

Now he wasn't so sure. He felt uneasy when Jade was out of his sight.

But maybe that had more to do with Isaiah's insinuations about love than actual fear for her safety. No matter what, he would feel better when the wacko who broke in was behind bars. He hoped.

"This isn't just a case of a lazy nurse mixing up infants," Harley stated. "This was deliberate. When you called with the information about the Steele family, I was more confident of that fact than ever. Someone deliberately targeted the Steeles' baby. But I don't know why. Nothing ever came of it, best I can tell. Jade's parents went home from the hospital with the daughter they thought was theirs and continued on with their life. There's no damn point to the whole thing. And this…" He lifted his arms to gesture at the mess around them. "There's no reason for this, either. Someone is trying to intimidate her into dropping the case. They've made that clear. But I can't understand what finding out the truth would hurt."

"Unless finding out the truth could uncover the person behind the swap. It's been thirty years, but that doesn't mean they want the cops showing up on their doorstep."

"Maybe. Or maybe the Steele family knows the truth and is desperate to keep it quiet."

"Why?" Isaiah asked. "If they knew they had their own daughter taken from them, why wouldn't they want to know the truth about what happened?"

Harley shrugged. "You said they had politicians and other important people in the family. People like that are different from the rest of us. Maybe they want to avoid scandal at any cost, even if it means raising someone else's child. Or even threatening Jade to keep the story quiet."

"That's ridiculous."

"I know," Harley agreed. He didn't want to think the Steele family was behind the threats, but they certainly weren't cooperating, either. "But I can't explain why else they would ignore my calls. I've phoned both Patricia and Trevor Steele at their home and at his office. I always get housekeepers and assistants who take a message and then no one returns my calls. I have told them who I am and pressed upon them the importance of my call, but have had no response. It seems like they don't want to know the truth."

"What about their daughter, Morgan? Surely she has a vested interest in finding out what happened and meeting her real family."

"I thought the same thing. And when you got me her work information, I called there too and they told me she was out of town on business."

"What about that link I sent you to the charity gig?"

"Yes. That's our saving grace. She's obviously come to Charleston for the event. The Steeles have appearances to keep up, and that means the whole gang will gather tomorrow night at the family compound for their annual charity ball. They hold this fund-raiser and then send teams out with their tools to build housing for the less fortunate."

"They don't sound like arrogant assholes."

They didn't. And that bothered Harley more than

anything else. It was hard for him to understand why people who did so much for charity would be so heartless about their own child. It was possible they didn't realize what he was calling about, but he had mentioned Morgan and the hospital. How could they not at least return his call to see what he wanted? To just blow him off seemed out of character, given the facade they presented to the world.

"Are you going to this charity thing, then?"

"Yep. I've got my tuxedo pressed and ready to go. I intend to start up a conversation with Morgan and hopefully get to the bottom of this whole situation."

Isaiah didn't look convinced by his plan. "You're a monster of a man, dude. You've got money, sure, but you don't look like them. You're going to stand out among all those rich, stuffy people. No one is going to think you're a guest. At best, they'll think you're undercover security. You're way too conspicuous."

"That's why I'm taking a date."

"You're not taking Jade, are you?" Isaiah asked, a wary expression in his eyes.

"She insisted, and she was right. She said the same thing you did. I need a date to fit in or I won't make it past the front door, ticket or not."

"A date, yes. But Jade? There's a lot of personal crap involved there. You don't think that taking her is a bad idea? This is potentially her family she's meeting for the first time. You're there to get information. She's there to see the life she's missed out on. What if your objectives are at cross-purposes? She could panic and blow your cover. She could say or do something to get you thrown out before you can do what you went to accomplish. If it comes down to Jade or the job, what will you choose?"

"It's just a bunch of rich people mingling and writing checks so they can feel better about themselves. I can't imagine it being so dire that it would come down to me choosing between my case and Jade."

Isaiah crossed his arms over his chest and sighed. "Then you need to imagine harder."

Eleven

Whoa. *Money.*

The Steele mansion was ridiculous. It was exactly what Jade would've pictured: a typical two-story plantation home, with a long driveway that led up to it, lined by oaks dripping with Spanish moss. It was white, with massive columns that reached for the sky and huge windows flanked by black shutters. There was a line of cars out front and a crowd of people walking up the stairs to the open entrance. There were valets in dark green suits greeting the guests and taking their cars to a grass lot around the side of the property.

When they pulled up, Jade found her heart pounding so hard in her chest she could barely breathe. This was it. Harley was fairly certain that her real parents were Trevor and Patricia Steele. Pictures she'd seen on the internet had only confirmed his suspicions. Jade was no doubt a younger version of Patricia.

In a few moments, she would walk through the front door of their home and lay eyes on them in person for the very first time. She would probably be able to pick them out of a crowd. But what would they think when they saw her? She didn't know.

It was her idea to come tonight. She had sworn to Harley that she could keep her cool. Yet in the moment, she found she couldn't make herself reach for the handle to open the passenger door. It wasn't until the valet did so with a smile and offered to help her out that she started to move. Jade gathered up her small beaded clutch and stepped out of the Jaguar to face her future.

Harley came around the front of the car and took her arm. "Are you okay?" he asked.

"Why?"

"You seem a little tense."

She tried to smile and dismiss both their worries. "I'm just nervous. I'll be fine." She took a deep breath. "So, do we have a plan of action for tonight?"

"Observe. Try to talk to the family, especially Morgan, if we can. That's it. I don't intend to make a scene. I really just want to make the connection without their staff in the way. I'm certain once they realize the seriousness of the situation, they will fully cooperate."

At the top of the stairs, they stepped into the grand foyer, where they turned in their tickets and were greeted by servers with flutes of champagne. They each accepted a glass and continued toward the sound of music and laughter coming from the far side of the house.

"Nice," Jade said, after she took a sip of the champagne. It was dry, but had a sweet finish and enough bubbles to tickle her nose. "I wasn't expecting it to be so good. I could get used to this."

"It should be nice. Tickets to the party were ten thousand dollars a couple, and I'm not even sure they're serving a meal."

Jade came to a sudden stop and turned to look at Harley. There were easily a couple hundred people at this event so far. "Are you serious?"

He nodded. "They're raising money for charity and most of these people have the cash to burn and tax deductions to seek out. You're not going to build houses for the poor charging twenty bucks a head."

She nervously took another sip of her champagne and hoped the alcohol would calm her nerves. This was the life she very well could've been born to. It was a surreal thought. But not so surreal as the sight of the ballroom when they stepped through the wide French doors.

The room was huge, with gold and crystal chandeliers hanging overhead and thick velvet drapes framing each picture window. An orchestra was in the corner playing to the crowd on the dance floor, which was surrounded by dozens of round tables draped in gray and red fabric and topped with tall floral arrangements of bright red roses. Those were the Steele Company colors, of course. The sight was almost as overwhelming as the sound of music and hundreds of voices coming at them like a wave.

"Are you ready?" Harley asked.

Jade threw back the last of her champagne and set

the flute on the tray of a passing server. "As ready as I'll ever be."

Harley smiled and led her through the crowds of people to one of the tables that had empty seats. He left Jade for a moment to go to the bar and get more drinks for them. When he returned, he sat beside her for a moment, seeming to want to give her time to acclimate.

"What now?" she asked.

He scanned the room thoughtfully. To their right was a big buffet display with hot and cold appetizers and a large bar. On the other side was the dance floor, where quite a few people had gathered. "May I have this dance?" he asked.

"I'm not a very good dancer," she admitted.

"Neither am I. I just want us mingling. It'll make it easier to track down the family." Harley pushed up from his seat and offered Jade his hand. She accepted it and he led her through the maze of tables. They found a spot near the center of the dancefloor and blended in with the rest of the crowd. The music was slow and steady, allowing Harley to take Jade in his arms and rock back and forth in an easy rhythm.

Jade finally relaxed, with his hand resting warm and secure on her lower back. Things seemed easier when he touched her, somehow. It made her wonder how she was going to deal with what was to come without him.

"Have I mentioned how beautiful you look tonight?"

She gazed up at him and smiled. "Almost enough times to make me believe it."

"I know this probably isn't the right time to say this,"

he said, "but I need to get it off my chest. The music and the champagne are making me brave."

Jade stiffened in his arms. "What is it?"

"I should've fought for you," he said. "Back then. I'm sorry I didn't. I know you always feel like you aren't good enough, and I understand what it's like because I've never felt like I was good enough for you, either. That's why I didn't fight. I wanted to. I wanted to drive to Clemson, knock on your dormitory door and kiss you until you couldn't even remember Lance's name. But I thought you'd be better off without me."

She didn't know what to say. What would she have done if he'd followed his heart? How would their lives be now?

"I'm not sure what's going to happen tonight. Or next week. I'm not sure about a lot of things. But I know I don't want to make the same mistake with you twice. Jade, I…"

The song that was playing ended. That's when the band leader called the Steele family to the stage and they started to make their way to the front of the ballroom.

This was the moment Jade had been waiting for, and yet she wished she could put the whole party on pause to hear what he wanted to tell her. He looked reluctantly at the gathering and gave her a sad smile. "To be continued," he said.

Jade squeezed her eyes shut in frustration for a moment, then tried to focus on what was going on with the group gathering onstage. They were easily some of the most beautiful people she had ever seen in person. It was as though they'd all walked off the cover of a magazine. She easily recognized Trevor and Patricia from their photo. They were standing together, sharing a quiet moment of conversation. Trevor was tall and lean with graying, honey-gold hair and dark eyes. Patricia had Jade's same white-blond hair and high cheekbones. She was very slender, like Jade, and carried herself with unmistakable poise.

Their children were gathered near them. Three sons, all handsome, all spitting images of their father. It looked as though two of them might even be identical twins, although Jade couldn't be sure. Perhaps it was just their flawless tuxedos and bright smiles that made them appear so alike. Then she turned her gaze toward the woman one of the sons was speaking to, and that's when Jade realized it was none other than Morgan Steele.

Jade froze in place, taking in every feature of the dark beauty. Morgan was a marked contrast to the rest of her family, with her thick, almost black hair and green eyes. In that moment, she looked so much like Jade's mother that Jade felt a punch of jealousy to her stomach. She had always wanted to fit in, to look like the rest of her family. Morgan fit in perfectly and she didn't even know it.

And yet she fit in with the Steele family, as well. She had a different look to her, but she also had their regal carriage, their elegance and their confidence. Morgan wore her emerald gown and sparking jewelry as if they were made just for her. She would fit in anywhere she chose to and people would flock to her.

Then there was Jade. She'd felt so pretty in her dress tonight. And in an instant she might as well have worn a T-shirt and jeans to the party.

She'd come here tonight in the hopes of finding out where she belonged. In her mind, she'd thought that somehow seeing her biological family would make the pieces click together and suddenly her life would make sense. But it didn't. In that moment, she wanted nothing more than to sit around the worn kitchen table at her parents' house and play a board game with them and her brother. They had never made her feel like she was an outsider in the family. Jade was the only one who seemed to notice the differences.

They'd never said it, but it had to have hurt them to have Jade pursue her real family so doggedly. It wasn't as though they hadn't been the best parents a girl could ask for. They had been. She wouldn't trade them for the world, and she hoped they knew that.

She wanted to go and tell them that right now. To walk away from all this before she couldn't turn back.

The longer she stood watching the family mingle, the more she realized this wasn't what she wanted. This was a mistake. Someone didn't want the truth to come out, and now she wasn't so certain that she wanted the truth to come out, either. Maybe it was better to leave well enough alone.

"I'd like to welcome everyone," Trevor Steele said as he stepped forward with the microphone in his hand. "My name is Trevor Steele and I'm the current CEO of Steele Tools. This is my beautiful family." He gestured toward the others on the stage, beaming with pride as the crowd applauded. "We are all so thrilled to have you here with us tonight to make a difference for those in need. I'd like to invite my incredibly talented daughter, Morgan, the head of our community outreach program, to step up to the microphone to tell you all a little about why we've gathered here tonight and what you can do to help."

Morgan moved gracefully across the stage, accepting a kiss on the cheek from her doting father as she took the microphone. "Write a big check," she said with a grin, and the crowd laughed.

Everyone seemed to be having a good time tonight. They got to dress up, mingle with their peers and feel like they were giving back and doing something good. The room was charged with positive energy. And Jade had never wanted to get out of a place more in her life.

"Harley, I've changed my mind. I want to go home."

He stiffened, turning to her with a stunned expression on his face. "You what?" he whispered, trying not to draw attention to them while Morgan spoke onstage.

"I want to go home. I think this whole thing was a mistake. I—I don't know if this is the right thing to do."

Damn it. He knew bringing Jade was a potentially bad idea, but he couldn't say no to her. She was his weakness and now she would potentially ruin his chance to get to the Steele family. He'd barely laid eyes on them, and had come nowhere close to actually speaking to any of the Steeles. "You're just nervous," he soothed. Harley reached for her elbow and led her off the dance floor.

Once they were clear of most of the crowd listening to the speeches, he stopped and turned to her. "It's totally understandable to be anxious about something like this. This is a big deal. I won't even pretend to know how big it is for you. But running away isn't going to change the truth, Jade."

She pulled away from his hold and hugged her own waist apprehensively. "It may not change the truth, but I'm starting to think it's better this way. Things worked out the way they should've. The family seems so happy. I don't want to mess that up for them. Or hurt my own parents more than I already have. I'll call the hospital myself and tell them I'm dropping my claim against them."

"It's too late for that. Come on, Jade, think about the people who broke into your home. They were trying to stop you from finding out the truth. If you give up now, they win."

"It doesn't matter. It's been thirty years. This isn't my life and it never will be. I'd rather let it lie."

Harley squeezed his eyes shut. He wanted to shake some sense into her, although he wouldn't dare. He had to find a way to reason with her. There was no way to stop the train once it left the station. Whether she wanted it to, whether he dropped the investigation… The hospital administrators knew there was an issue now and they would get to the bottom of it.

He reached out and gripped her upper arm, feeling she might run from the ball like Cinderella if he didn't. "I can't let it lie, Jade. This is my job. A job I was hired for because of you. And I was hired to find out the truth. I'm going to do that whether you want me to anymore or not."

A flash of pain danced across Jade's pale face before she jerked herself from his grip. Her dark eyes grew glassy as she slowly shook her head in disbelief and heartache.

"Jade…" He reached out again.

"No. Don't," she argued, stepping out of his reach. "You have your priorities and I have mine. I thought I might rank higher on your list, but that was foolish of me. I wasn't Lance's priority, either. He was more interested in getting high and you're more interested in the thrill of the chase."

The crowd applauded loudly and the orchestra started playing again. They both turned to see the Steeles step down from the stage and return to mingling with their guests and donors. If Harley was going to talk to Morgan, he needed to do it soon. If he could just convince Jade to give him ten minutes… Just ten minutes could make all the difference in the world.

He turned back to her with pleading eyes. "That's not true."

She shook her head more adamantly. "We'll see about that. Go on, go be the badass who saves the day. But I'm going home, Harley. Home to my own house. I'll ask one of the valets to call a cab to pick me up." Jade spun on her heel, a blur of crimson beading, and then made a beeline for the ballroom entrance.

Harley reached out for her, about to chase her down and beg for her to wait a little bit longer. That's when he saw it. His moment. His chance.

Out of the corner of his eyes, he spied Patricia Steele setting her empty champagne flute on a nearby table. If he could pick up the glass before a waiter got to it, he could get a DNA sample and confirm his suspicions even if the family wouldn't cooperate. They'd answer the phone when the hospital's attorneys called, he was pretty sure.

He tore his gaze away from the glass for a moment to see Jade slip out of the ballroom and toward the front of the house. If he moved fast enough, he could get the glass and reach Jade before she could arrange a ride back to her house. She wouldn't be happy with him for grabbing the glass after she'd asked him to stop investigating and leave the party, but that was a risk he was willing to take. An opportunity didn't come wrapped in a bow like this very often.

Darting through the crowds of milling people, he reached the table and snatched up the flute. Holding it as though it were his own, he slipped away and headed toward the door. He looked around to make sure no one was watching, then tucked it in his coat's inner breast pocket. It would go in an evidence bag the first chance he got without a crowd of witnesses.

But first, to catch up with Jade.

This evening was not going at all the way he'd hoped. It was supposed to be a night of breakthroughs. They were supposed to connect with her family and usher in that happy reunion. He had even been on the verge of telling her how he felt about her when they were out on the dance floor.

If the speeches had come even a minute later, the

words that had been lingering on the tip of his tongue would've gotten out. He would have told Jade that he loved her. And maybe then, when the fear got to her, she would've known that he was doing this for her. Not in spite of her.

Harley made his way through the house. He paused at the registration desk near the entrance. "Did a woman in a red dress come by here just now?" he asked. If she'd hidden in the restroom instead of going outside, they wouldn't have seen her.

There were two women at the table and they both nodded. "She went out about a minute ago. She seemed upset," the older lady said with a look of disapproval.

He went past them and down the front stairs to the circular driveway, where the valets were mostly sitting idle. Jade was nowhere to be found. "Which way did the woman in red go?" he asked.

The group of men all pointed to the far side of the house. Perhaps she'd gone that way trying to get better cell phone reception.

Harley jogged to the end of the building, expecting to see her there calling for a ride. And she was. But before he could say anything, a white van pulled to a stop in front of her. The door flew open and in a blur of red, Jade was pulled inside by two men in dark clothes. The door slammed shut and the van's tires squealed loudly as it took off from the driveway and roared down the narrow lane away from the house.

Harley took off on foot after it, shouting Jade's name, as though he had a chance in hell of catching it. But as the taillights disappeared into the distance, he came to a stop. His lungs burned in his chest even as his heart ached just as fiercely. He'd promised Jade he would keep her safe. He'd promised he would solve the case quickly so she wouldn't have to live in fear of the threats any longer.

Turning on his heel, he ran back to the house, yelling for the valets to call the police and report the abduction. He couldn't take back what had just happened, but he could redeem himself in her eyes and his own by doing everything he could to bring her home safely.

She'd thought she was safe with him. He'd taken his eye off her for only a moment. A big mistake, especially after she'd asked him to leave with her.

But Jade was right. He'd chosen the job and the glory over her. He just hoped he wouldn't regret that decision for the rest of his life.

Twelve

Jade rolled around the back of the van and hit her head against the metal wall with a dull thud. At least she thought it was the wall. It was hard to tell with the blindfold over her eyes. She wasn't thinking too clearly anyway. Her head was already throbbing from the strong whiff of chloroform they'd used to disable her. They hadn't given her enough of a dose to knock her out cold—that took a few minutes and some dedication—but it did its job in disorienting her enough that they could drag her into their vehicle. Now she was dizzy, with a pounding head and a bad attitude.

"Ow!" She groaned loudly as she felt the knot rise up on her forehead and a warm trickle run down the side of her face. It was probably blood. And with her hands tied together, she was unable to stop the bumping and brace herself as the van sped around corners. She was like a rag doll back here, feeling the beading of her dress catch and snag as she slid across the unfinished floor.

Abduction aside, the thought of the beautiful gown Harley had bought her being ruined brought angry tears to her eyes.

"Slow down or we're gonna get caught," one man hissed, presumably at the driver. His voice was gravelly, like he'd smoked three packs a day for thirty years.

"If I slow down, we *will* get caught. We've got to get the hell away from the Steele mansion first. That guy is crazy enough to follow us."

"I don't see his Jaguar behind us. I think we're safe."

"You're an idiot," the second man said. His voice was deeper, but smooth as silk. "There's no such thing as safe until we've got the money in hand, the woman is back with her rich family and we're chilling on a beach in Puerto Vallarta. Then and only then will I take the first deep breath I've taken in thirty years."

Jade tried to ease back until she was leaning against the side of the van for some stability. She didn't make a peep, not wanting to interrupt her captors' conversation. She intended to memorize every word so when she got out of this mess, she could turn all of it over to Harley and the police.

Provided she actually got out of this. She didn't know what these guys wanted with her, but it couldn't be good. One of them had mentioned money, so maybe this was just about ransom. That seemed a stupid choice. Her family didn't have any money. At least, not the family who had raised her. Maybe these two knew even more about Jade than she did.

"Here's the turn," the man with the gravelly voice said.

"I know where the damn turn is. I don't need you to tell me how to drive. I've got this under control." The van slowed and went over a bump. "I learned my lesson after the last time, when your sister screwed us both."

"Screwed *us*? She's the one who died, not you."

"Yeah, well, if she was feeling so guilty that she was thinking about doing something like that, she should've turned over some crucial information first. Like which damn baby was which. We've sat on our hands for three decades because of her stupid conscience and I'm not taking that risk a second time. I want my money and I want this done."

"Do you think they'll pay for her? They don't even know who she is."

"She's their blood. They'll pay. And if not, well, maybe we go after the big guy. Did you see how long he ran after us? Like he was gonna catch the van. That dope is in love. I'm willing to bet he'll shell out whatever we ask."

Jade's breath caught in her throat. They had to be talking about Harley. She hadn't seen him outside. Had he followed her out in time to see the men take her? She hoped so. He'd chased after her. She didn't know if she could take these thug's word for it, but they seemed to think Harley was in love with her. She couldn't believe it.

They'd better hope they were wrong. If he did love her, these men better pray the cops found them first.

She heard the sound of a metal garage door going up as the van came to a stop. The vehicle inched forward and finally the engine shut off. The metal door started creaking again, likely closing this time, trapping her in whatever garage or warehouse they'd chosen to take cover from the cops.

They'd probably be headed to the back of the van to deal with her soon. Jade took a deep breath and hoped she had the strength to get through this. To see Harley and her parents again. Her real parents. The Steeles might be lovely people, but the faces she wanted to see belonged to Arthur and Carolyn Nolan.

"All right, we're here," the driver said. "It's time to make the call."

Harley marched back into the ballroom, and casting aside any pretense of being a normal guest or donor, went straight up to Trevor and Patricia Steele. "Are you behind this?" he asked, unable to keep the anger from his voice.

The couple turned to him with wide, surprised eyes. They didn't look as though people took that tone with them very often. "Are we behind what, sir?" Trevor asked, with a sharp edge to his voice.

"Someone just abducted Jade from your driveway. If you're behind this, tell me now."

"Abducted?" Patricia said, bringing a hand to her chest in dismay. "Jade who?"

"Your daughter, Jade. The one I've been trying to call you about for the last week."

They looked genuinely confused by the entire conversation. As much as he wanted to leap ahead, it seemed as though he'd have to go backward. "My name is Harley Dalton, with Dalton Security. I've been calling you both repeatedly this week about a case at St. Francis Hospital. Did you not get any of my messages?"

"No," Trevor said, looking mildly irritated, albeit not with Harley. "Although the week leading up to the gala is usually so hectic. My staff might've been remiss in passing your messages along. They tend to filter out what they deem unnecessary when we're so busy. We get a lot of calls. You're working for St. Francis Hospital, you say?"

"Yes, where your wife gave birth to a daughter during Hurricane Hugo in 1989."

"Our daughter, Morgan, is right over there." Patricia gestured to her. "I don't understand what's going on."

Harley didn't want to be the one to say this, but the sooner they all got on the same page the better. "That is not your biological child. Two of the infants in the nursery were switched during the storm. Your daughter was raised by the Nolan family, who recently uncovered the mix-up during DNA testing. The woman you know as your daughter, Morgan, is actually their daughter, Jade."

Harley watched Trevor Steele's face blanch for a moment as he absorbed the news. Before he could gauge any more of their reactions, a man ran up to the two of them with a wild-eyed expression on his face. "Mr. Steele, the police are here. They said they got a call about an abduction."

Harley was about to step in, but Trevor collected

himself and beat him to it. The CEO instantly began barking orders at everyone around him. "See them into the library, please. We will be there momentarily." He turned to his wife. "Patricia, go get Morgan and meet us in the library. I'll have the boys clear out the room. The party is over."

Harley breathed a sigh of relief that the family was taking this seriously. He watched as Patricia escorted a confused-looking Morgan out of the ballroom, while her father went in search of his sons to handle the other guests. Trevor appeared at Harley's side a moment later. "I'm sorry that we didn't get in touch with you sooner, Mr. Dalton. I will be having words with my staff once this is cleared up. Let's head over to the library. A flood of people are about to come through here once my oldest makes the announcement."

The Steeles were cool and collected in the face of drama, something that both confused and concerned Harley. It wasn't until they reached the library and sat down with the detectives that he understood why.

"This isn't our first kidnapping, Mr. Dalton, so I'm sorry if we seem unaffected by this. We've learned the hard way to save emotions for later, once what needs to be done is done."

Harley made his statement to the police, letting the family listen in anxiously as he recounted the threats, the break-in and finally Jade's abduction from the property. She and the Steeles were related; they had to be. And if the Steele family wasn't trying to keep Jade quiet, he had no leads on who the kidnappers could be.

The police were sending a crew to the house to set up

a surveillance team in case the kidnappers called in a ransom request. In the meantime, every cop in the city would be looking for a white van with South Carolina plates that started with the number 7.

"This is our fault," Patricia said, once the police stepped out and left them alone together in the library. She'd been sitting on the couch, holding a dumbfounded Morgan against her side for the last hour. Harley couldn't begin to imagine how the young woman was processing everything under circumstances like this. "It's happening again, just like with Tommy."

Trevor came around the couch and placed his hand on his wife's shoulder. "We got Tom back safe and sound, and the same will happen here. We will get Jade back, and then we will find out what happened at the hospital and why."

"So someone switched babies, then thirty years later, they kidnapped the one who's really our sister?" one of the twins asked. It was either Finn or Sawyer, Harley wasn't sure. The young man stood by the window looking confused.

"Morgan is your sister," Trevor insisted, pointing to the woman on the couch. "In every way that is important. But yes, if this man is correct, your biological sister, Jade, was taken because she was trying to find her family and someone didn't want that to happen."

Morgan stood up from the couch, her eyes red, but tearless. "I'm going upstairs," she said. She rushed from the room.

"Let her go, Patricia," Trevor said. "This is a lot for her to take in. What's important for her to know—and for all of us to impress upon her—is that she is no less a member of this family because of what happened."

Harley was pleased to hear them say that. He was equally hopeful that they would welcome Jade with that same attitude. She deserved that much, especially after he'd basically forced her into going through with it all tonight. What if he'd just taken her home instead of arguing with her? They'd be in bed, holding each other, instead of him waiting anxiously for a phone call or news from the police about Jade's whereabouts.

"I wish they would just call already," Patricia said. "The waiting is the worst part."

As though the kidnappers had heard her plea, a phone started to ring. They all expected it to be the Steeles' home phone, where the police had the lines tapped, but it was Harley's cell phone.

He didn't recognize the number, but he answered, putting it on speakerphone so everyone could listen in. "Hello?"

"Ten million dollars," a raspy male voice said. "Small, unmarked bills. Fill a black tote bag with the money and leave it in locker 17 at the bus station downtown by ten tomorrow morning. If you follow my instructions and we're able to pick up the money without police interference, I will text you the location of the woman. If the cops are waiting for us, or we get intercepted in any way, you'll never see her again."

"I want to talk to Jade," Harley insisted, but the man just laughed and hung up. As the line went dead, he felt a sense of hope rise up to battle the ache of dread in his stomach. They just wanted money. He had plenty of that. He'd happily comply with their instructions to get Jade back safely. He just had to hope that the kidnappers played by their own rules.

"Ten million is a lot to get our hands on in less than twelve hours," Trevor said.

"I know," Harley said. He'd learned early that to make money he had to keep his cash tied up in things that would continue to earn for him. Untangling that was not a quick job. "I'll have to think of something. I can easily get my hands on maybe a third of that."

"How much do we have in the safe, darling?" Patricia asked her husband.

"Four, I think. Maybe four and a half. We could get more wired over without a problem. It's morning in Switzerland, isn't it?" Trevor walked over to where Harley was standing and patted him on the back. "Between the two of us, we'll get Jade back safely. Never fear, she's one of us now. And in this family, we live by the strict motto of No Steele Left Behind."

Jade heard a noise and shot to attention on the cold steel wall she was slumped against. She wished she could pull off her blindfold and see what was happening, but it was impossible with the zip ties on her wrists and ankles.

She'd been alone for a while, but she wasn't sure how long. She'd heard the men talk about going to get the money and then they left in the van. They didn't say much to her while they kept her captive, but they left her with parting words that chilled her to the core… The next thing she saw would either be her rescuers if all went well, or the two of them before they put a bullet in her head.

If someone was here, wherever she was, she was about to find out which it would be.

"Jade!"

"Harley? Harley!" Jade heard his heavy footsteps pounding across concrete toward her. She breathed a sigh of relief at the sound of his voice and felt the tears start rolling down her cheeks. She hadn't allowed herself to panic; she didn't have that luxury. But now all her emotions were pouring out of her at once.

She felt someone drop to the ground beside her and rip off her blindfold. Her eyes struggled to adjust to the light after hours in total darkness, but she could make out Harley crouched beside her. He made quick work of the ties on her ankles and wrists, allowing the blood to flow into her extremities again.

"Oh my God, baby, I'm so glad you're okay. I'm so sorry. I never should've let you out of my sight." Harley clutched her to his chest and she happily curled up against him.

She'd spent a long night with her thoughts, reliving what had happened before and after the abduction. She knew she'd overreacted. And in this dire situation, her dangerous bad boy was the only man qualified for the job. He was up to the task, and for that, she would be eternally grateful.

"It wasn't your fault," she croaked with a hoarse, dry throat. "You saved me."

"Of course I saved you." He sat back and cupped her face in his hands. "I love you, Jade. More than you can ever imagine. I would do anything to bring you home to me."

He loved her? Jade was overwhelmed by everything going on, but she couldn't let that detail pass by unnoticed. "Did you say you loved me?" she asked.

Harley smiled. "I did. I love you, Jade Nolan. Very much. I only wish I'd gotten to tell you before all this happened. For a while last night, I thought I might not get the chance."

Jade brought her hand to his cheek. It was very stubbly, as he probably hadn't shaved or showered. He was still wearing his tuxedo, minus the bow tie. His eyes were lined with worry and he looked as exhausted as she felt. And yet he was the most beautiful thing she'd ever seen. "I love you, too, Harley."

He leaned in and pressed his lips to hers. The kiss was loaded with emotions they'd both held in. Now it all poured out at once. Love, relief, need, happiness. She pulled away from his kiss only when she had to cough. She'd been hacking most of the morning.

"I'm sorry. My throat is so dry. I haven't had anything to drink since the champagne at the party."

"I can fix that." Harley lifted a phone to his ear. "She's here. Yes, she's safe. Bring the blanket and the water."

As Jade looked up, she noticed there was a virtual crowd of people rushing over to her. She recognized the silhouettes of her parents immediately. Arthur and Carolyn swooped in, practically nudging Harley aside to hold their daughter. She had never been happier to see her family.

"Are you okay, honey?" Carolyn asked. She brushed the hair from Jade's eyes and studied the bump on her head. "You're bleeding."

"I'm fine, Mama. I'm just happy to see you."

Arthur squeezed her shoulder and smiled. "There's some other people here that are happy to see you, too." He stood and stepped aside to reveal another couple hovering nearby.

It was Trevor and Patricia Steele. They were standing awkwardly at a distance, obviously wanting to help somehow, but not wanting to intrude on her moment with Harley and her parents.

Patricia stepped forward at last, crouching down to hand Jade a bottle of water they'd brought with them. "Here you go, dear. I'm so glad you're safe. We were worried sick all night."

Those were words she wasn't expecting. A lot must have happened while she was tied up in this warehouse. "Really?"

Harley smiled and rubbed her back encouragingly. "They know everything. They even helped pay the ransom."

Trevor came up beside his wife and got down onto one knee. "No Steele Left Behind," he said with a smile. He studied her face for a moment, then shook his head in amazement. "You look almost exactly like your mother did at that age. It's uncanny."

He reached out and put a comforting hand on her shoulder. "We've got a lot to talk about, little girl, but let's get you out of here first. We have plenty of time to catch up."

Harley helped her up off the concrete floor and wrapped her in a blanket Trevor brought in with them. Jade was content to disappear into the cocoon of soft wool as they walked slowly out of the warehouse to awaiting cars. The Steeles waved to her before they piled into a black Escalade with a uniformed driver. Beside it was her father's minivan and the Jaguar, parked haphazardly as though Harley had rushed in to find her.

"Harley has to take you to the police station to get your statement and let you get checked out," Carolyn said. "You call us later and let us know you're okay."

"Yes, Mama." Carolyn kissed her on the cheek, and then let Arthur guide her over to the van.

As they pulled away, Harley helped Jade into his car, then came around his side to sit down beside her. Instead of starting the engine, he reached for her hand and held it tightly in his. "Before we go to the station, there's something I need to say. Jade… I would've done anything to get you back."

"Including paying my captors ten million dollars?" she asked. The sum seemed ridiculous, but her kidnappers were aiming high.

"In a heartbeat. I'd pay it again if I had to."

Jade looked into his blue eyes, which were glassy with tears, and felt her chest tighten with emotion. "Don't say that loud enough for those guys to hear you or they might try this again. Unless they've been… *caught*?" she asked.

Harley shook his head. "Unfortunately, no. The police were watching the bus station, but had to wait to move in until after those thugs texted your location to me. By then they were long gone, and the cops lost them in the maze of streets downtown. But we'll find them. You can count on it."

"Another exciting job for you to take on," Jade said with a rueful smile.

"I think I'm going to leave most of that to the police. The last twelve hours have provided enough excitement to last me a lifetime," Harley said. "The only rush I need is the feeling of you in my arms and the flutter of nerves in my stomach when I see you smile at me from across the room. I'd happily sit behind my desk and live a safe and secure life with you until I draw my last breath. Which hopefully will be well into my eighties or nineties."

"You really mean that?"

"I sure do. Let me prove it."

Harley reached across her to the glove compartment of the car and pulled out a small box that was instantly recognizable. He opened it and offered it to her, showcasing the sparking ring in its bed of navy velvet. It was beautiful. The center was a large princess-cut diamond set in platinum, and in the band were alternating round diamonds and dark blue sapphires. "As a navy vet, I thought perhaps some sapphires were appropriate."

"When did you have time to get an engagement ring?" she asked. After everything that had happened, it was the last thing she'd expected.

"Before the party," he said. "It was in my coat pocket the whole time. I was going to give it to you after we left the gala, but that didn't really work out."

She just stared at the ring, anxious to reach out and

slip it on her finger, yet waiting on him to ask her the all-important question first.

"Jade Nolan…last night was the worst night of my life. I wanted to marry you before all this happened, but now I truly can't imagine a day of my life without you. We've already lost over a decade and I don't want to lose a minute more. Will you do me the honor of being my wife?"

Jade smiled and leaned in to give him a kiss. There was no question this time that she would follow her heart. "Yes," she whispered against his lips. "A million times, yes."

Epilogue

Jade never thought she'd see the moment that both sets of her parents would be sitting together, enjoying a warm spring day on the top deck of the Steeles' luxury yacht, the *License to Drill*. But here they were, along with Harley, all her brothers and Morgan, to celebrate their engagement.

After weeks of working through the details, taking DNA tests and verifying the results to everyone's satisfaction, the families had come together in the first of many events. It was a bittersweet moment for Jade, to realize she would now be sharing her parents with Morgan, but seeing the tears in her mother Carolyn's eyes was worth it.

The two families were so different, and yet they were united in their desire to share Morgan and Jade, and build a relationship together. After all, they would always be tied together by the strange twist of fate that swapped their babies that day.

Jade sipped her mimosa and watched everyone with a smile on her face. Her old brother, Dean, and her new brother Finn, were deep-sea fishing. Her mothers were sharing stories about what the girls were like as babies. Her fathers were discussing the different virtues of Scotch while they stood at the bar. It had turned out better than she ever expected it to.

There were still loose ends, but she knew those would be resolved in time. Her kidnappers would be found, and maybe they would be able to find out if the thugs were involved in the original switch. They still didn't know for sure, although the conversation Jade had overheard in the van certainly made it sound like the two crimes were connected. She had relayed all the information she could remember, but knew there were details she'd forgotten in all the chaos. Despite his initial disinterest, Harley was still working that angle of the case, this time with the Steeles fully cooperating and partially funding the investigation.

It was hard to think about all that, though. It was much more pleasant to focus on her upcoming wedding to Harley, and her newly expanding family.

"I had the sweetest nurse at St. Francis," she heard her mother Carolyn say. "I've been trying to remember her name since all this started and it's been making me crazy. Did you have her? She was a redhead. Big smile. Very chatty."

"I think I do remember her," Patricia said. "I wasn't having the greatest labor and she kept talking. I wanted more than anything for her to shut up and go away. I want to say it was something like Noreen? Tracy? Nadine?"

"Nancy?" Harley interjected.

"That's it!" both women said together.

"Nancy. Thank you," Carolyn said. "That's been driving me mad."

The conversation continued, but Harley made his way across the deck to where Jade was sitting. "How did you know the name?" she asked.

"I have the personnel files from the hospital. There was a nurse named Nancy working that day. A nurse who just so happened to kill herself less than a week after you and Morgan were swapped."

Jade's sharp intake of breath was barely audible over the ocean breeze and the sound of the music playing through the deck speakers. "Do you think she was involved?"

"It had to be an inside job."

"I wish I remembered more from the night of the kidnapping. I feel like they said something important, but the whole night has blurred together. Maybe if we find more information, it will jog my memory."

"Maybe so. Let's see what we can find."

Harley didn't hesitate to pick up his phone and dial Isaiah. While it rang, he leaned in and kissed Jade hard enough to make her blush.

"Hey," he said into the phone, as he pulled away and gave her a wink that promised more, and soon. "I need you to find out everything you can about a former St. Francis labor and delivery nurse named Nancy."

* * * * *

STAR-CROSSED SCANDAL

KIMBERLEY TROUTTE

Dedicated to anyone who has
felt mistreated or invisible.

Know that you are not alone and
love is our greatest strength of all.

History of Plunder Cove

For centuries, the Harpers have masterminded shrewd business deals.

In the 1830s, cattle baron Jonas Harper purchased the land grant of Plunder Cove on the now affluent California coast. It's been said that the king of Spain dumped the rich land because pirates ruthlessly raided the cove. It is also said that no one saw a pirate ship after Jonas bought the land for a rock-bottom price paid with pieces of eight.

Harpers pass this tale on to each generation to remind their heirs that there is a pirate in each of them. Every generation is expected to increase the Harper legacy, usually through great sacrifice, as with oil tycoon RW Harper, who sent his children away ten years ago.

Now RW has asked his children to return to Plunder Cove—with conditions. He is not above bribery to get what he wants.

Harpers don't love; they pillage.

But if RW's wily plans succeed, all four Harpers, including RW, might finally find love in Plunder Cove.

One

Hot, dreamy sex.

That's what the man stepping out of the limo exuded. And pulsing music. If Nicolas Medeiros was a song, he'd be a Brazilian beat, throbbing with dance, liquid fire and lyrics a girl couldn't get out of her head.

Standing between her two brothers at the entrance to the Plunder Cove resort, Chloe Harper had a moment to drink Nicolas in while he talked on his cell phone and waited for the driver to bring his luggage out of the trunk. The long sleeves of his sharkskin-gray shirt were rolled up to reveal tanned, muscular forearms. His dark charcoal slacks accentuated his thin waist, and his suit jacket was casually slung over one shoulder. He was the adult version of the teen heartthrob Chloe Harper had fallen in love with a long time ago.

She fanned herself.

"Are you okay?" Jeff, her brother closest to her in age, wrapped his arm around her shoulder. "You look like you're about to pass out."

"Hell, you, too?" Matt, her oldest brother, grumbled as

he studied her. "This morning Julia had that same look on her face when I mentioned that Nicolas Medeiros was coming to town and staying at the resort. What's the big deal?"

"He's a big deal," Chloe whispered.

Nicky M had been a pop star legend back in the day, and now he was a huge music producer who had discovered several of the biggest names on the charts. He was a legend! More than that, he was…her Nicky M. When she was eleven years old, Chloe had kissed his poster every night before she went to sleep. He'd been her savior when no one else cared. And now her crush was striding up the walk of her family's resort with those dancing hips. And if they made a good enough impression, he'd sign a deal to do his next pop music reality show here.

As the resort's activities director, she was the one who would be showing him around. Her family had given her the task of getting his name on the dotted line.

They'd be spending a lot of time together.

She made a strange noise at the back of her throat that sounded like a closed-off squeal.

"Oh, man. You've got it bad. Maybe we should give the job to someone else," Matt teased.

"Don't you dare!" she said way too loudly. Nicky M—correct that, *Mr. Medeiros*, her *guest*, her *job*, looked up from his call.

"Relax, Chloe," Jeff said out of the corner of his mouth. "Dad wants the deal to work and so do I. Medeiros and his music production company are the next step in building the resort to its full glory. It's up to you to convince him that he needs us."

She shot Jeff a dirty look. "Is that supposed to make me relax?"

Matt laughed. "Just do your thing, sis. He's a guy. He'll love you."

She bit her lip. Oh, she'd spent many lonely nights fantasizing about being loved by Nicky M, all right, but that's not what her brother meant.

"Mr. Medeiros!" Jeff offered his hand. "Welcome to Casa Larga Resort at Plunder Cove. I'm Jeffrey Harper, the executive director of the resort and restaurant."

Nicolas put his cell phone away and the two men shook hands.

"You remember Matt, your pilot from LA," Jeff said. While Jeff ran the operations of the family's resort empire, Matt pursued his passion of flying. He offered flights to important resort guests and volunteered his skills with locals in need.

"Of course. The flight was short and sweet. You are a very good pilot." Nicolas shook hands with Matt, too.

Oh…that voice! His deep, melodious Brazilian Portuguese accent had played a part in quite a few of Chloe's fantasies. She wished he'd take off those dark sunglasses. She longed to see his eyes.

Stop it! She warned herself. She shouldn't be longing to see any of his body parts. Chloe had made a deal with herself to steer clear of men for a while and was determined to keep it. Looking was fine, but acting on her desires was out of the question.

"Dad sends his apologies for not meeting you himself. He's not feeling well," Jeff said poignantly.

That was an understatement. The last time Chloe had checked in on her father, he'd been sitting in his room with the shades drawn, fighting the downward spiral into his dark place. Her father had fought with untreated depression for decades. She'd dealt with the dangerous effects of it as a small child, before the stress led to her parents' divorce, but then she'd left the family estate with her mother. And she hadn't understood her dad's mental illness until she saw it up close. If he didn't come out of it soon, Chloe would disobey his wishes and bring a psychiatrist into the home, the rumor mill be damned. RW Harper was a powerful man and few people bucked his orders, but she was worried about him and would do whatever it took to help him.

"That is too bad. I was hoping to talk to the great RW Harper. Plus, I have questions about the contract he sent me," Nicolas said.

"He'll make time for that during your stay," Jeff said smoothly. "This is Chloe, the resort's activities director. She'll take care of all of your needs for the week."

Jeff meant *business* needs. So why did her gaze take a sudden roam across Nicolas's body. Broad shoulders, narrow waist... She forced her eyes back up to his face. He was watching her.

Her cheeks were on fire. A trickle of sweat ran down her back.

She stretched her hand out and was beyond relieved it wasn't shaking. "Welcome to Casa Larga."

"Chloe. I like that name." He lifted his dark glasses, and his gray-blue eyes locked on to hers and melted her insides. She was seriously going to pass out if she didn't figure out how to breathe around the man.

He held her hand for several long beats. A Brazilian custom or her own hand refusing to let go? Chloe removed her hand but couldn't unlock her gaze from his. She used to wonder what had happened to a boy to make his gray eyes project such a soulful expression. The man before her still had the look, but now it was mixed with mature comprehension, as if he knew exactly what she was thinking. His eyebrow lifted as if he could see the desperate desire pulsing inside her.

Oh, God, did he know what she was thinking?

Because she suddenly wanted to break all her rules for him.

Matt chuckled beside her. "Hell, guess some things are a bigger deal than I thought. I'd better go give my wife some lovin'. See you all later." Heading toward his motorcycle, he gave Chloe a thumbs-up.

Surely Matt didn't think their guest was attracted to her. Nicolas Medeiros dated supermodels and pop stars. Although she was an heiress to the great Harper fortune and a celebrity yoga teacher in her own right, she was no supermodel. She rarely wore makeup and believed in enhancing the inner natural beauty of a person through spiritual awakening. Nicolas, on the other hand, dated women who had professional makeup artists on staff.

"Right this way, Mr. Medeiros." Jeff motioned for Nicolas to step into the entryway.

Nicolas held back and gave her a look that heated her skin. "Ladies first."

Walking ahead of him, she wondered where his gaze was—on the low dip in her blouse, exposing her back, on her butt, or on the ten-foot crystal chandelier overhead?

Jeff guided their guest to the foyer, where building plans were spread out across the marble table. "The restaurant will officially open to the public at the end of the week. However, the staff is eager to serve you now. They need the practice."

"Complimentary, of course," Chloe said softly and then stepped back to let Jeff do his thing.

Nicolas's cell phone buzzed. He checked the text and shook his head before returning his attention back to them. "Sorry. Work."

She hoped to help him unplug from work during his stay. Nicolas was a big music producer, but everyone deserved a little downtime. It was her personal mission as an activities director and yoga teacher to help people learn how to live in the moment. To relax.

"Would you mind telling us about your show? It'll help me gauge what sorts of activities to prepare for the contestants," Chloe said.

"*If* we choose the Harper's resort for the show," Nicolas said. "There are three properties under consideration."

"Oh, I understand." She looked him in the eye. "I intend to help you make your decision. And choose us, of course."

"Intriguing." His lips quirked and she couldn't help but wonder what it would be like to kiss those lips for real.

"*Song of the Heart* is a reality show." His voice gave her a tiny shiver up her back. "Ten singer-songwriter contestants live together in a luxury setting, write songs and compete for a million-dollar music contract."

"I love it," she said.

"I'm very familiar with reality shows. We can help yours be a success," Jeff said as a nod to his past career as the host of *Secrets and Sheets*, a hidden camera critique of luxury hotels. "Let's look at the resort blueprints and see where the contestants would spend their time and where you could set up the camera crews. The resort will be ready for guests in eight months, but if your show needs it earlier, Harper Industries will make it work…"

As Jeff talked, Nicolas studied the plans while Chloe studied him.

He had a cropped beard and his hair was dark, thick and cut short. His shoulders were broad. Her schoolgirl crush had matured, but his gaze still had the power to turn her insides to mush.

Nicky M had always been more than a poster boy to her. She'd fancied herself a singer-songwriter once and had truly appreciated Nicky M's talent. He'd drawn a young, scared girl out of *her* dark place and lit up her imagination. He'd lifted her heart with his lovely words and beautiful melodies. She owed him more than he'd ever know.

But she didn't have any business fantasizing about Nicolas now. She wasn't hooking up with anyone until she got her own life under control. She had to learn how to love herself before she could love anyone else. Until that happened? She wasn't sleeping with any man. Not even super sexy Nicky M. She had a job to do.

Her father had tasked her with showing their guest all that Plunder Cove had to offer so that he'd agree to film his show at the new resort. Her dad's exact words were, "Don't let the man leave without signing the contract, Chloe. I'm counting on you."

She'd been desperate to please her father her entire life and had failed at every turn. A small part of her still wondered if that was why he'd banished her from Plunder Cove years ago, sending her to live with her mother after the divorce—because she wasn't good enough to be a Harper.

In the past, her parents had crushed her spirit. They'd broken her family, sent her away and taken away the music she'd loved. But she'd found her own path through yoga, and she was doing everything she could to heal herself. She'd even returned home not too long ago and reestablished a relationship with her older brothers. She was determined to prove she was worthy of her family's famous name.

She wouldn't fail at this.

How hard could it be to keep her hands and lips to herself and get a man to sign a few pieces of paper?

Even if he was the sexiest man on the planet.

Nicolas stopped listening to Jeff Harper's spiel about the building plans the moment he noticed the *gostosa* eyeing him.

The gorgeous activities director had a stunning figure.

A brown skirt molded to her hips like dark chocolate on a strawberry. Her red crepe blouse dipped low in the back and was not quite see-through but made him want to strain his vision. The long blond braid intrigued him, but it was her aquamarine eyes that really got to him. When they locked on to his, he saw golden feathers within the blue irises. Amazing and deeply magnetic.

Strange. He wasn't usually so poetic. Not anymore. "The resort will be ready in time for your show." Jeff's voice drew Nicolas's gaze away from Chloe. "We guarantee it."

Of course he'd say that. The man was a Harper. RW Harper, Jeff's father, had the reputation for being a scheming, sneaky bastard. But also a savvy one. This hotel empire would be the most luxurious one in the nation, maybe the world. That was why Nicolas was here. He was after a contract for a big beautiful property to showcase his show. Funny, in the past he would have been looking for a quiet, beautiful spot on the beach to sit and write music. He wouldn't be on the phone or in meetings making deals, no, he would have been making music. Those days were over. He'd moved from making his own songs to making stars.

"That's about it. I'd better get back to the site. I'll leave you in Chloe's capable hands." Jeff walked out the door, leaving Nicolas alone with the beauty.

She stepped closer, moving with the poise and grace of a dancer. He was fully aware of her soft curves and was intrigued by the toned muscles in her arms and back. She had an athlete's body.

"I'll show you to your room," she said.

Nicolas enjoyed the sound of her voice. It had a rich, pure tone, with a slight emotional crack in it—fragility mixed with strength. *Leather and lace.*

"As the man said." Nicolas grinned. "I am in your hands."

"I'll do my best to handle your, uh…" A pretty pink blush traveled up her neck. She cleared her throat. "…needs."

He looked forward to seeing what her best was.

She led him down the hallway, her stride matching his. "I like the concept of your show, Nicky—excuse me—*Mr. Medeiros*."

"Nicolas. I do, too. I support singer-songwriters and am looking for talent that is different, unique."

"Brilliant," she sighed. "Helping young artists is exactly what I thought you'd do when you got old." She covered her mouth. Her pretty eyes were wide. "I mean, you're not old now, just, you know, mature. Handsome."

"Thanks." She was a tongue-tied and adorable fan. He was used to woman falling over themselves around him, but he wanted Chloe to relax and treat him like a regular guy. He smiled. "People gave me a hand when I got started. I work hard to give back to the industry."

They passed a grand hall. Soft music played in the background. When they walked under one of the largest chandeliers he'd ever seen, the fractured light cast dancing stars across the tiled floors. Enchanting, yet hard to compare to the brilliance in Chloe's blue eyes. She led the way up a winding stairway, her beaded sandals snapping with each step. He noticed her toenail polish. Purple. His favorite color. His gaze traveled from those beautiful feet up to her toned legs.

Santa Mãe, she had a great figure. He wouldn't mind spending time with this beauty, nothing serious, of course, just short-term, hot sex.

"You've such a lyrical gift for storytelling. Those contestants are lucky to have an amazing songwriter like you to mentor them," she said.

He *used* to have the gift, but the muse had left him without any good stories to tell. Now he made money, not poetry. He was okay with that, and if he sometimes missed songwriting, he just reminded himself of how far he'd come. His success was worth the price of any small dissatisfactions. He would never go hungry again. But why tell her all that?

Instead he said, "Thank you."

Did she know how he'd been discovered? Most of the tabloids had reported some version of the truth. None knew all the nightmarish details about why he'd spent every moment from age ten to this day supporting his mother and four sisters. Singing was the only thing he had been able to do to repay his bottomless debt. Every penny he'd made went to his family. Until he'd had more than any of them would ever need.

And yet somehow it never felt like enough.

Still his *mãe* loved it when he sang and he loved to make her smile. "Your songs are made of stardust, Nicky," his mother had said as her tiny cracked fingers hand-washed clothes for other families. "A blessing from the saints!"

An American music manager had seen him perform for tourists on Ipanema Beach and promised to make him a star. He'd been sixteen then, full of drive and blind trust. He'd allowed the manager to record him, and the first song hit all the charts. Nicky M was a sudden sensation. He flew to California on the back of that one song, trusting that riches were right around the corner. He'd planned to buy his family a home and get them out of the slums. *Mãe* wouldn't have to work so hard and his sisters could focus on school.

It was a poor-boy success story. The tabloids loved it.

But they hadn't printed the whole truth. How could they? Some secrets were too shameful to tell.

The manager he'd trusted siphoned money from Nicolas's bank accounts until there had been nothing left. Only months after leaving home, he'd been sixteen, scared and alone in a country where he barely spoke the language. There was no money to send home. He didn't have enough funds for an airline ticket. His mother and young sisters had been forced to find extra jobs cleaning rich people's homes to survive. They all went hungry.

The experience had hardened him.

It was the first of many painful disappointments. The industry battered him and taught him the most important lessons of his life: people lie, steal and use one another to get what they want.

It had taken cunning, luck and persistence to move from a pop star to the music producer who called the shots.

Nicolas trusted no one but himself. He worked his ass off to stay at the top. In those early years, lyrics had swelled up from deep within him, and music pulsed through his bloodstream. He had the natural ability to create eternal truths that people loved to listen to. He didn't have to work at writing music. It just happened, like breathing. The press had called him "the greatest Latin songwriter of our time."

But songwriting had become music production, the business, and star-making. He'd exchanged lyrics for the constant buzz of his phone, the high of making millions on others' stories.

And then…the music stopped.

The stardust had blown away, and the silence was like a death. He didn't have time to grieve the loss. Instead he spent every waking moment looking for the next star. He'd found fame, money, women—a lifestyle most people could only imagine.

There was no joy in it. But he told himself joy didn't make millions.

"Mr. Medeiros, we're going to be together a lot this week…" He wanted to imagine the breathiness in her voice wasn't solely from walking up the stairs. "I feel, um, I should tell you something."

He leaned closer. "Chloe has a secret?"

Her blue eyes shimmered. "I had a tiny crush on you when I was a girl."

Every now and then his past came in handy, especially when a beautiful woman seemed to appreciate his talent. Or, at least, the talent he used to have. Maybe this sexy blonde with the long braid and "kiss me" lips still remembered who he used to be.

They were on the landing on the top floor.

He pressed his hand to his heart, pretending to be wounded. "Only tiny? Not a man-size crush?"

"Honestly, it was more than tiny." She chuckled. He loved the richness of the sound. "I named my iguana after you. Little Nicky M."

He cocked his eyebrow. "Was he a handsome lizard?"

"Very. A red iguana with pretty eyes. Almost as amazing as yours."

Perhaps she would be his beautiful distraction for a few days. He needed a break and sleeping with a sexy fan would help him feel like himself, not the high-powered producer, for a while.

"We are going to get along fine, Chloe. Remind me to thank RW." It was a stroke of genius to send Chloe his way. But if Harper thought a sexy woman would drive Nicolas wild enough to instantly sign a contract, the man was wrong.

Nicolas could be as ruthless as RW when it came to the music business.

"Oh, no. My father can't know!"

Father? "You are a Harper, too?"

"Yes. I thought you knew. Didn't I say so? Sorry. I got a little excited when we met." She bit her lip. "Way too excited. Even now I'm having trouble—" she fanned herself "—getting my words out. Which is exactly why my father might not want me to work with you. If he knew about my huge..." Her gaze dipped toward Nicolas's crotch and bounced back up to his eyes again. Her cheeks flushed. "Uh, infatuation. When I was *younger*."

He spoke, his words low. "It will be our secret, then."

"I'll be completely professional with you—I promise." She crossed her heart, which had the effect of drawing his gaze to her chest.

"*Que pena.* Are you sure there's not any infatuation left?" Stepping closer, he looked into her eyes and pinched the air with his thumb and forefinger. "A flicker?"

Her breath hitched. She tried to play it straight, but her full lips seemed to want to turn up of their own accord. He liked the dimples in her cheeks. They reminded him of sideways smiles, and he had the urge to caress one of them with the back of his hand.

She blinked, clearly flustered. "A flicker, sure, but I want you to trust that I'll be..."

"Professional?" he finished for her.

"Yes." Her voice cracked. The way her gaze locked on to his told him she was into him, even if she didn't want to admit it.

He noticed they'd stopped in front of a door. "Is this my room?"

"Yes." She took a key ring out of her pocket, unlocked a door and held it for him to step inside. "Mine is just down the hall. Let me know if there is anything you need."

When he passed her, he inhaled the coconut scent of her shampoo. Did she taste as good as she smelled?

She licked her bottom lip as if she'd heard his thoughts.

The suite had a large sitting room, wet bar, overstuffed leather couch, full-size desk and large patio.

"There is something I need," he said circling back to her. He could hear her swallow. "Name it."

Leaning against the door frame, he crossed his arms. "A date for dinner tonight. Will you be mine?"

Her breath came out in a rush. "Me?"

He was thoroughly intrigued by the blush traveling up her neck. What was she thinking? Whatever it was, he liked it. He usually avoided starstruck fans, but she was too tempting for his usual caution.

"Yes, *gata*, you."

She blinked. "Did you call me a cat?" Her voice was barely a whisper.

"*Gata* is a term of endearment in Brazil. *Gatinha*, as well, which means kitty. Would you prefer I say *sexy*?"

"*Gata*," she tried the word on for size. "I like it."

Her gaze dropped to his mouth. Pure heat flashed between them.

He wanted to kiss her. Tasting a stranger was nothing new for him. Women still threw themselves at him. Wild hookups came with the territory as a musician. As a producer, he still had his pick of women, though he was careful not to mix business with pleasure. He enjoyed sex. But as he'd gotten older, he started to think he was missing something—a real life with deep, loving relationships.

But he wasn't the picket fence, loving wife and two kids in the yard kind of a guy. He'd left Hollywood for Plunder Cove because of the show and because he had a rather public breakup with a supermodel. It was better for him to stick with short-and-sweet-while-it-lasted flings. A pretty blonde fan might be exactly what he needed right now.

"Seven o'clock?" he pressed.

Her lips parted but no words came out. Some emotion he couldn't read passed over her face. Worry? Sadness?

Droga. Was she going to decline?

"Say yes, Chloe."

"Nicolas, there's something I should tell you…" she began in a tone that did not bode well for him.

His phone rang. *"Merda,"* he cursed. "Sorry. Give me a moment to take this."

To his disappointment, Chloe used the phone distraction as her chance to walk away from him. For some reason, that hurt.

Just before his door closed, she said the word he desperately needed to hear.

"Yes."

Two

Contrary to what he'd led his daughter to believe, RW was not going to stay curled up in a dark room all day.

His chest hurt and the pain behind his eyeballs was excruciating, but he wasn't staying in bed. Not today. He waited until Chloe went down to greet their guest before sneaking out the back to take care of business.

His daughter had a job to do and so did he.

Even if his children didn't know it.

Shielding his eyes from the California sunshine, he strode across the patio and took a seat across from the first woman he'd ever loved—Claire Harper. It had been ten years since she'd walked out on him, taking their daughter with her. She'd arrived back in Plunder Cove for Jeffrey's wedding two months ago, and for some damned reason she was still here. He'd invited her for a late lunch today to get to the bottom of what she wanted.

"Claire, you do not age," he said.

She smiled at the compliment, but the fine lines around her eyes and lips hardly creased. Her forehead was smoother than he remembered. Ah, so that's where some of the millions he'd sent her had gone.

A flash of Angel, the woman he loved now, entered his mind. He preferred a real lady who came with wrinkles and flaws. A woman who could accept his flaws, as well.

Dealing with Claire was the first step in bringing Angel back to him.

"And you seem—" she studied him "—healthy."

He wasn't. Not yet. Still, he was much better than he'd been when he had lived with Claire.

"I'm impressed with this place. Our son did all this?" Claire motioned to the restaurant.

Where they sat under the eaves, it was easy to see that the amazing wood-and-glass structure resembled a pirate ship. It was an architectural masterpiece that was sure to grace the pages of magazines for years to come.

"That boy has come alive with this resort and restaurant project. I'm so proud of him."

A waiter arrived carrying one plate of pasta that he sat down in front of Claire.

"I went ahead and ordered my lunch. Wasn't sure you'd show," Claire said.

"I'm here, Claire. This is my home."

The waiter nervously stood by him. "Sorry to interrupt. Would you like anything, Mr. Harper?"

"Just a glass of water. Thanks."

The waiter quickly walked away.

"Water? Not bourbon and Wagyu steak?" Claire wound the fettuccine carbonara around her spoon and took a bite. As she chewed, her face tried to screw up into her old expression of disgust, but her forehead refused to budge. "The sauce is horrid."

"Impossible. Our chef is acknowledged as a top chef on both coasts."

Tentatively, she licked the sauce on her spoon. "It's spoiled!" She scrubbed her cloth napkin over her tongue.

A satisfied smile crept over his lips, for he knew what Michele had done. God, he loved his daughter-in-law. "I wouldn't eat the rest of that."

Claire swigged her pinot to cleanse her palate only to find a tiny bandage at the bottom of the glass. The look of horror on her face made his entire year.

RW threw his head back and roared with laughter. For the first time in…hell, he couldn't remember when…tears of laughter streamed down his face.

Indignantly, Claire stood. "It's not funny. Do you see what's in my glass? The health department will shut Jeffrey's restaurant down for this sort of negligence. I'm going to have a talk with the chef."

"Sit down," he ordered, wiping his eyes. "The chef is Jeffrey's wife."

She sat slowly. "My daughter-in-law did this to me? Why?"

RW shrugged. "She heard about the time you locked Jeffrey in the shed, Claire. Expect a night getting close and personal with your toilet bowl."

"She wouldn't poison me." Claire pushed her plate away just in case. "The shed thing wasn't my fault. The servants were supposed to let him out."

"That's crap. It was your fault and mine, too. I was so wrapped up in my own personal hell that I couldn't see what was happening in yours. Our kids deserved better parents than us, Claire. You deserved a better man. I'm sorry."

She cocked her head. "I've never heard you apologize before. Or laugh like you just did. You've changed."

"I'm working on it."

"I can see that. Don't change too much." Her gaze traveled over his tanned, muscular arms. "You're a good-looking man. Strong, rich, sexy. You're fine the way you are."

"You don't know me anymore."

"What do you mean? I married you and had your three children. I know you."

"I'm not the man you married. You left that guy for dead a decade ago. With good reason. I'm not an angry, despicable sap anymore. I… I woke up."

"You woke up? What does that mean?"

How could he explain it? He'd suffered from depression for most of his life. Deep down he'd known he needed help, but his parents had said that Harpers didn't have *those* problems. Claire must've known he was ill too, but she pretended the despair that overtook him—sometimes so debilitating that he locked himself in a dark room for days—was normal behavior.

She'd put up with the way he treated people. He'd been an ass, not because he wanted to be, but because he didn't know how to interact, to connect, when he hurt so much. Hell, running a multibillion-dollar company was far easier than connecting on a deeper level with the people he loved.

He'd closed off his feelings to survive. The only emotion that seeped out occasionally? Anger. Matt had been the only one who stood up to him, taking the rage that RW fought to control, shielding the rest of the family from RW's outbursts. His son shouldn't have had to live that way. None of them should've.

After a while, RW had reached a breaking point. Why take his next breath when no one cared if he did? His kids hated him. Claire wished him dead—that's what she screamed at him more than once—and he didn't care anymore. Ten years ago, he'd sent the kids away so he couldn't hurt them anymore and he quit life.

Or he tried to.

By some miracle he never deserved, a beautiful woman rescued him. She'd said he had a mental illness. If the wound had been in his leg, would he have let it fester and rot without treatment? she'd asked. No. So why be ashamed of the pain in his psyche?

Gentle, kind and strong, Angel became his therapist as he started the arduous process of healing his mind. Feelings, like colors of the sunset and sweetness on a tropical breeze, flooded his senses. He wanted to survive. No, more than that—he wanted to be happy.

Angel told him happiness was achievable if he followed her three rules: *seek redemption, make amends, forgive yourself.* The first two were going to take a lifetime to achieve, since he'd hurt so many people. He didn't deserve forgiveness.

But even though he was undeserving, he sought redemption anyway.

And he fell in love with Angel.

For the first time in his life, he had a purpose.

He woke up.

Claire would never understand. She turned her light brown eyes on him and twirled a platinum-blond curl around her finger. "Things weren't always bad between us."

"They weren't good enough. I know the difference now. I don't intend to ever settle again. How about you? Don't you want to feel joy? Happiness? Love?"

It was her turn to laugh, but there was more spite than humor in it. "What has gotten into you? You really think a guy like you can fall in love? When will you have time for it?"

His mood darkened. "Why are you here?"

"I want what's mine." She leaned over the table. Her stature was fiercely determined, but something else, too.

Desperation. "The kids are back and you are better. Plunder Cove is where we all belong. Together."

He leaned over, too. "No. Go home, Claire. I've found someone else and I'm going to marry her, if she'll accept me."

He didn't tell her that he had no idea where Angel was at the moment.

"Polygamy is a crime, sweetheart," she said with a wicked smile. "Or have you forgotten? I didn't sign your divorce papers."

"Damn it, Claire! Enough. Sign the divorce papers, take your money, hop on that broom of yours and fly back to Santa Monica."

"Now, *that's* the man I remember." Crossing her arms, she sat back. She seemed rooted to the chair and was decidedly not leaving.

"This is my home," he said, "passed down from my family. Mine. Understand me? Be happy with the money I've given you the last ten years and get on with your life. Leave me the hell alone."

Without yelling or throwing anything, RW got up and walked away. He was surprised at how steady and sure of himself he felt.

He picked up his cell phone. "Robert, bring the Bugatti around to the side. It's time to go."

Claire would eventually sign those papers. He had no doubt. He needed to move on to the next item on his agenda.

He was sneaking off to a quiet town on the coast, far away from prying eyes. If all went as planned, he'd be back before his kids knew he'd left Plunder Cove. If they realized he'd overstated the extent of his illness this morning to sneak out, he'd have some explaining to do.

He couldn't drag his children into the danger surrounding Angel. He was expendable. Hell, he was living on borrowed time already. But the woman who'd saved his life needed him to save hers.

She'd been running from a Colombian gang of murderers and drug dealers for years, barely staying one step ahead of them. She'd been hiding in his home under an assumed name all this time. But when the gang came to his home, searching for her a few months ago, Angel fled to protect him.

She thought she'd be able to hide from the gang, from him, but he had resources she couldn't imagine.

Enough was enough. He'd do whatever he could to force Cuchillo and his gang to their knees and bring Angel home.

Even if it meant sacrificing himself as bait.

Three

Chloe was about to combust or squeal or any number of things that would not be the least bit professional. Instead she quickly went down to the restaurant to talk to her sister-in-law.

She found Michele in the kitchen, her arms coated with flour as she kneaded pasta dough.

"You're here!" Chloe said.

"Where else would I be? Oh! How's it going with Mr. Dreamy Eyes?" Michele asked with a smile.

"He's so handsome…and that voice, the accent, oh, my God. He turns me to mush." Chloe closed her eyes and took a deep breath. "Complete idiotic mush. Mind if I pace a little? I grumble better when I'm moving."

"Grumble? Why aren't you ecstatic? You get to spend all week with him."

"It's not him—it's me."

"Have at it." Michele motioned to the floor. "Just don't slam anything around. I've got cake rising in the oven."

"I'm not my mother. I don't slam things." Chloe paced quietly, making sure not to stomp.

"Hey, speaking of the wicked witch…" Michele glanced

over her shoulder and lowered her voice. "I messed with her a little earlier—not bad, just enough to teach her she's not welcome in my restaurant, *our* restaurant. She doesn't get a free pass after what she did to Jeff."

Chloe blinked. "Mom's still in Plunder Cove?"

Michele whispered, "Yeah. She met your dad for a late lunch. Weird, huh?"

Weird didn't begin to describe it. "Did she throw dishes, wine bottles? Did my dad toss her out?"

Goodness, if her parents started fighting while Nicolas was here, the deal for the show would be off.

"Not at all. They talked quietly. Civilly. Then your dad left before she did."

In the Harper household, civil parents didn't make sense. What were they up to? Chloe stopped walking in circles at the counter, where Michele was pounding the dough. "Can I do that?"

"You want to knead my dough?"

"Can I beat it a little, too?"

"Sure." Michele stepped back. "Wash up and you can knead away. Want to tell me why you want to punch dough?"

Chloe dried her hands and began kneading. "The guy who inspired me to play the guitar is upstairs. In my house. Nicky M! And holy moly, he looks so good. I can't even begin to describe how well his butt fills out those slacks. But I'm representing the resort in this deal. I shouldn't be thinking about his anatomy!"

"But you are." Michele smiled wickedly.

Well, yeah. "You'd think I'd use this opportunity to—I don't know—ask him how he comes up with his perfect rhythm. Or ask about the inspiration behind his lyrics in 'Baby, Come After Me.' I have this amazing chance to learn about lyrics and music from a master. Instead of asking intelligent questions, I could barely put more than two sentences together. What's the matter with me?

"You have a right to be flustered. It's Nicky M."

There was that. Her crush aside, he'd been her inspiration for continuing to sing and play the guitar in her off time. Her parents had made it clear that being a singer wasn't her true calling, but it made her happy. Nicky M had given her that.

"I don't get starstruck. I got over that nonsense working at my yoga studio in Hollywood. Directors, big-name stars, models—they're just people. I dated enough of those guys to know that they're just looking for happiness and love like the rest of us. And quite a few of them are..." *As broken as I am.* She kneaded that dough until her hands hurt. "Lost. Hollywood ruins people. Star power doesn't have any effect on me."

"But Mr. Dreamy Eyes does?"

"Oh, gosh, yes." Chloe pressed a hand to her heart, leaving a handprint of flour on her blouse. "Maybe his eyes have hypnotized me. Yep. That's my story and I'm sticking to it."

Michele handed her a glass of wine, which Chloe waved off. "Wait, no alcohol either? I get giving up meat, but no wine? That's just...uh-uh. No way."

Chloe shrugged. "I'm trying to live better. Clean. Healthy." *Trying to learn to love myself.*

"I totally get it about Nicky M. If Gordon Ramsay came to hang out in my kitchen for a week, I'd probably accidentally cut off my hand or set the place on fire. Nicky M is yummy. Stop beating yourself up. You'll be fine once you relax."

Chloe poured herself a glass of water and took a long sip. "How do I relax? I can barely look at him without losing all rational sense."

"Hmm. That's an interesting dilemma since it's up to you to get him to sign the contract for filming his show here. I handle the food, and Jeff can only do so much. You have to sell it."

"Super. More pressure. You're not helping, Michele."

Michele smiled. "Sorry. Maybe you just need to find a way to work out your nerves. I cook when I'm stressed or, you know, have my way with your brother."

Chloe scrunched up her nose at that comment, even though she was thrilled Michele and Jeff were so deeply in love. That's all she ever wanted for her brothers, their happiness. She was working on her father's happiness next. RW and Angel were good together, even if Dad hadn't figured it out yet.

"Hey, that's it." Michele snapped her fingers and a puff of flour rose into the air. "You should kiss Nicky M and get that nervousness out of your system. That's what I did the first time I cooked for your brother."

"Right. Just walk up and kiss a legend." What if his kisses didn't compare to her fantasy? Or worse. What if they were better? She'd be ruined for life.

"I don't mean assault the guy. Do what feels right for both of you. Jeff said Nicky M seemed to be into you."

Chloe's jaw dropped. "When did he notice *that*?"

Michele shrugged. "Men can feel the vibe, too."

Chloe shook her head. "Nicolas just got out of that train wreck of a relationship with supermodel Lila what's-her-name. He's not ready for anything else. And if I misread the situation…" It would be a disaster. She'd fail at getting the contract, fail at finally doing something right for her family. "Nope, nope, nope. Kissing Nicolas is not a good idea."

Michele cocked her head. "Or what if you're not misreading the situation? What if you're judging your feelings and his perfectly? It could be a really great thing, Chloe. I'm all for following your dreams. If I hadn't gone for mine, I wouldn't be here right now. You don't always get a second chance to make your dreams come true."

"I can't. I shouldn't. No, definitely not." Chloe could hear the disappointment in her own voice.

She needed to get this deal, for herself and for her family. But more than that, she'd meant it when she'd sworn off men. She'd spent too much time losing herself in men, in dating, in sex. She needed time to find herself, especially now that she was back in Plunder Cove.

Yet part of her knew that Michele was right. There weren't always second chances to live in the moment. And a big part of her really, *really*, wanted to indulge in this moment with Nicolas.

That flicker of attraction he'd talked about? It was a raging wildfire inside her.

"And yet you want to," Michele said, reading what Chloe wasn't saying.

"Well, *yeah*."

Michele laughed. "Then if you get the opportunity and he's into it, go for it. When was the last time you got hot and heavy anyway?"

"Hot and heavy?"

"You know. Being with a man you want to shave your legs for."

"Let me think…" Chloe squeezed the dough in her fist. Should she tell her sister-in-law why she'd stopped dating? Would Michele understand?

"If you have to think that hard, it's been too long," Michele said with a laugh.

"I'm not, uh, dating right now. To find spiritual happiness, I need to find myself first. Loving who I am will help me find true love."

With her hand on her hip, Michele blew her bangs out of her eyes. "Seriously? No men? At all?"

"Something has to change," Chloe said quietly. She'd spent her life wishing someone, anyone, would love her. She'd been kicked out of the mansion when she was fourteen years old. Living with her mother had been difficult, to say the least. She hadn't heard from her brothers or father until recently, and her heart was still aching with desperation to keep them all close.

Michele's face softened. "Your life is changing. You're here, you're part of the family. You aren't alone anymore, Chloe."

Chloe's eyes welled. "I don't want to lose my family again."

"You won't, hon. I understand trying to better yourself—I do—but you're going to let your spiritual journey keep you from the man of your dreams? What if *he* is the love you should be with and you let him slip through your hands? And aren't you always the one saying you should appreciate every moment in life? You might not get this chance again."

Chloe chewed her lip. There was that. "I'm nothing like the women he usually dates."

"So? Maybe he wants a change, too."

"Nicky, uh, *Nicolas* did ask me to join him for dinner. A business dinner. If I thought he'd be into me—"

"You'd go for it?" Michele nudged her with her shoulder. "Do it!"

Should Chloe put her spiritual quest on hold so she could live out a fantasy? "Maybe."

Michele rolled her eyes. "You Harpers are so darn stubborn. Just go with your passions, Chloe. Let yourself breathe."

Chloe grinned. Michele had used one of the mantras

Chloe had become famous for when teaching yoga to the stars. "You're a Harper now, too," she told her sister-in-law.

"And Jeff would tell you that I can be pretty stubborn myself. Use the strength you have and trust yourself."

Trust herself with a man she'd fantasized about her whole life? And at the same time not mess up the contract her dad wanted her to secure? Her family was depending on her to get this right.

The whole situation sounded dangerous.

But more than anything, she wanted to breathe.

She kissed Michele's cheek. "Thanks for the pep talk. See you at seven. Make sure everything is perfect for dinner."

"Nice. Thanks for stressing *me* out now," Michele grumbled.

Chloe just waved as she left to find the man of her dreams.

Nicolas finished up his fifth phone call in the last few hours. He took out his laptop and checked his emails. He pressed the ache between his eyes. There were 120 music videos from potential candidates waiting for him that had been sent to him by his assistant, who had already waded through thousands of applicants. Putting on his headphones, he sat on the bed and viewed five of them. One kid was a standout, but the others were not even close. He put those four into the Do Not Call Back folder. Only 115 more to wade through.

This was a grueling process. He hated to shatter dreams, but only ten could be chosen for the show, and they had to be the best of the best. Rolling the tension out of his tight neck and shoulders, he stood and popped his spine. It had been a long day.

He cast his gaze longingly at the guitar he'd brought with him just in case the music returned to him. Nothing. It sat silently challenging him to write and play something worthwhile. Instead he went to the full refrigerator in the kitchen, grabbed a beer, and went out onto his private patio for fresh air. The penthouse suite that Harper had put him in was full of amenities. He had everything he could ask for except a warm woman in his bed. He didn't sleep alone very often, especially not in a hotel room. He'd have to rectify that situation.

He sipped his beer and enjoyed the view from his balcony. The sinking sun had painted the sky in golden strokes. Warm breezes danced in the palm trees on the beach and lifted tiny white peaks on the Pacific. His gaze meandered back from the sea, up the grassy pastures and settled on a garden below his window.

The last rays of the sun lit a figure moving in the garden. He'd recognize that blond braid anywhere.

Chloe.

She wore tight purple-and-white-floral pants and a white T-shirt. Her clothes accentuated her awe-inspiring figure.

Was she dancing? He sipped his beer and watched. No, stretching. But nothing like the hamstring stretches he did before and after his runs. This was fluid, intense and beautiful. She was like a panther—flexible and strong. When she bent over and pressed her hands on the ground, her sweet ass pointed straight at him. The sight stirred him up.

Exhausted to erect in twenty seconds. A new personal record.

The only sound he could hear was a mocking bird, the waves and the whisper of the wind through the trees. Still, she moved to her own beat, her internal rhythm, and became the personification of a melody. Something deep inside him pulsed, too.

Chloe lifted her long arms over her head and sat on an invisible chair. Nice, strong glutes. He doubted he would be able to hold a pose like that for so long. She rose up and went into a graceful lunge, one arm stretched in front, the other behind her. Straight lines like a warrior goddess. Bendy as a wet reed. She reached, squatted and arched her back. Even though she didn't know he was watching, Chloe seemed to be a woman on a single mission to drive him wild.

Every move and every hold was like a dance. Like sex. Who knew yoga could be so hot?

Before that moment he hadn't had the slightest interest in yoga because Tony Ricci, his former agent-turned-best-friend, had warned him against it. Tony'd had a bad experience with a yoga studio in LA. Supposedly the instructor was a man-eater.

Tony would probably tell Nicolas to stay away from Chloe too and keep his head on the show and his hands to himself. Most likely Tony would pull up a clip of Lila dumping Nicolas on camera. Nicolas didn't need any reminders.

Lila had used him, like so many others had, as a ladder to her success. He'd thought for a while that she'd be the one to fill the missing piece in his life. Lila was gorgeous, fun, sexy and had a pretty nice singing voice, too. Not amazing, but nice. He'd pulled all the connections he had to get his girlfriend the singing contract she'd asked for. How had she repaid him? By breaking up with him in front of tabloid cameras.

Lila didn't love him, but she adored his former drummer, Billy See. The two were engaged to be married and chose national television as the way to break the news. His buddy and girlfriend were off making music together.

And Nicolas was left alone, in silence.

Merda.

He watched Chloe reach for the sky.

Maybe Chloe was the music he needed to feel whole for a night.

Four

Family was the most important thing in the world to Chloe. She'd lost her father and brothers once, when her father had sent them all away, and she'd sworn then that she'd do anything to get them back. By some miracle, they were all in Plunder Cove together again, working toward one goal—to make the Casa Larga Resort a success.

Jeff and Matt and their new brides had all given up their careers to come to Plunder Cove. The local town was invested in the new venture, too. Getting Nicolas to agree to Dad's plan was the next step in sealing everyone's future, and it was up to her to get it done.

She needed to wow him, which was about the place and had nothing to do with what she felt about him. Nothing. No matter how much his sexy Brazilian accent melted her, a Harper heiress did not throw herself at guests.

If she'd met Nicolas a year ago, she would've agreed to his dinner proposal without even questioning it and might have angled in for more already. In those days she'd been a serial-dater, a man-addict. At least that's what her mother had called her.

To that ridiculous statement, Chloe had rolled her eyes and replied, "That's a sexist comment, Mom. Men hit on me all the time at the yoga studio. Why shouldn't I say yes sometimes? It's not like I'm sleeping with all of them. Just having a little fun."

Besides, dancing, dinner and going to the movies kept Chloe from being home by herself. She'd been having a good time until the day she started crying over her morning matcha green tea because she was bitterly empty and alone. Though she'd glossed over it, she had never really recovered from her emotionally challenging childhood, and she still longed for stability and someone to love her.

Unable to shake the depression, she'd flown to Rishikesh, India, to her old yoga masters for a spiritual tune-up. She was surprised when they told her that her chakras were blocked. How had that happened? She was a yoga instructor who helped her students tap into the vibration from the centers in their own bodies, and yet hers was clearly not functioning properly. The chakra most damaged was her sacral chakra—the center for her emotions, creativity and sexuality.

Men were her shields for her loneliness and bandages to her wounded heart. When she was with a man, she didn't have time to sit quietly with herself and work through the abuse she'd lived through as a child. She used guys to keep from feeling and experiencing her own life. If she didn't correct the problem, her teachers told her, she would lose herself.

Oh, God. Mom was right.

The best way to fix the problem was to stop dating altogether until she was happy with who she was. "Go work on Chloe," her teachers had said. "Find her, love her and allow the light of the universe to open up for her."

Far easier said than done. She'd been on a self-discovery

journey for over a year now and still wasn't satisfied with who she was. Coming to Plunder Cove was both helping—since she got to be with her family again—and dredging up past heartaches…because she got to be with her family again. It was a gut-twisting journey, each day full of baby steps forward and slinks backward.

Would she ever truly be happy? She had a terrifying feeling she'd never be a good girlfriend, let alone a wife or mother until she figured it out. She'd stood hip-deep in the holy waters of the Ganges and swore to herself that she would be a better person before she gave herself to anyone else.

For the first time since that day, keeping her promise was tough.

Remembering the casually sexy grin Nicolas gave her as he leaned against the door frame made her fan herself again. A year and a half ago she might've kissed Nicolas right then to steal back a little of her lost innocence. Today she knew she couldn't use him like that. He was the poster boy of her childhood dreams, but he was also a real man with real feelings—not a drug to ease her heartaches. Plus, he was going through his own issues after a public breakup with Lila what's-her-name. Why complicate things for both of them?

But oh, man, how that handsome Nicolas made her want to backslide straight into his arms.

Chloe shaved her legs.

There was a soft rap on his door at seven o'clock on the dot.

"*Boa noite*, Chloe," Nicolas said as he opened it.

She pressed her hand to her chest and sighed. "That never gets old. You could talk Portuguese to me all day. I wouldn't understand, but I do love to hear it."

He grinned and filed that tidbit away for a later time.

Chloe's hair was in a bun, with a few loose golden waves framing her face. She wore no makeup except lip gloss. The look was perfect. He preferred kissing skin over caked-on powder. He longed to see if the light pink gloss coating her lips was flavored.

"Are you ready?" Chloe asked, her voice breathy again.

She stood before him in a pale sleeveless blue dress with a deep V-neckline. A gold chain dipped into the valley between her breasts. Those toned arms that had recently held her body in a perfect plank glowed as if they'd been soaped and moisturized. In order to quell the urge to run his hands over her skin, he shoved his hands into his pockets.

"I am. You look gorgeous."

Her gaze took a nice stroll down his body and back up. "You do, too."

He liked the sound of that.

"Do I need a jacket for the restaurant?" He was wearing his tan slacks and black short-sleeve shirt.

She shook her head. "No, but you might want to bring one in case it gets chilly. I was hoping we could take an evening stroll. There are a few things I would love for you to see at night."

He cocked his eyebrow. What did Miss Chloe want to show him? "I'm all yours."

The blush crept up her neck and her lips parted. No sound came out.

He held out his arm. "Shall we?"

She hesitated for a split second and then hooked her arm with his. "Absolutely."

They went outside and down a winding torchlit path. The night air was cooling off quickly and the breeze danced in Chloe's hair. He tucked one of the loose strands behind her ear.

His touch seemed to give her a shiver. *File that away, too.*

"We're here," she said softly.

He could smell steak coming from inside, but the wood-and-glass two-story building didn't look like any restaurant he'd ever seen. "It's shaped like a…ship?"

"A pirate ship. Do you know the history of Plunder Cove?" She led him inside. "This property used to be a Spanish adobe on a land grant purchased back in the 1800s." She paused. "By the pirate Harpers."

He opened the glass door for her. "RW's ancestors were pirates?"

"That's the legend."

He knew all about legends. Truth and lies were told to keep the stories alive and certain men on top of the heap. What were Chloe's legends? He longed to hear them all.

A hostess called out, "Welcome, Mr. Medeiros. We're happy to have you here. Your table is ready."

They sat in a private alcove next to the window. The ocean view was expansive. It would be a great place to sit and watch the sun come up, especially after a night of lovemaking.

They ordered—him the Wagyu steak and lobster, her something vegetarian.

He made a face. "You don't eat meat?"

"Fish occasionally. Eggs sometimes."

He shook his head. "No idea how you live that way."

"It's a choice that's right for me."

A bottle of wine and a basket of fresh, steaming bread arrived.

"I saw you doing yoga in the garden," he said. "You looked…" He offered the basket of bread to her while searching for the right adjective. *Super hot* didn't seem quite appropriate from a guy who was spying on her while she stretched. "Flexible."

"Do you practice yoga? I teach a class in the garden tomorrow morning, as the sun comes up. You could join us." Interest lifted the notes in her voice.

"Me?" he chuckled. "Ah, no."

He took a sip of his wine. It was the best pinot he'd ever tasted.

"I could show you a few things, help ease that tension in your shoulders." She motioned toward him with her bread roll. "And your jaw. If you don't mind me saying so, it looks like you chew nails."

She could see he was tense from across the table? "No nails. Just a lot going on." He forced his shoulders to relax as he drank his wine.

"I know," she said softly.

He looked up from his glass. *Droga.* He'd been thinking about all the work he still had to do for the show, but the wisdom in those blue eyes and a soft, sympathetic expression made him believe she was thinking about his public love life. Or the explosion of it. Had she read all the damning details about his breakup? What a way to ruin the mood.

"How long have you been doing yoga?" he asked, changing the subject.

"Since I was fourteen. It saved my life."

He frowned. "Yoga?" He'd always heard it was some sort of mumbo-jumbo thing. At least that's what Tony had told him after he'd gotten dumped by a yoga instructor.

"Growing up as a Harper was hard. Very hard." She sucked in a breath and blew it out with force. "Past history. I won't bore you with the details."

He was surprised by the tears welling in her eyes. He reached out and touched her hand. "You can tell me about it. I'm a good listener." He wasn't—not always—but tonight he wanted to hear her story.

Her gaze met his. A large tear dropped off her lashes.

"Maybe later…or never. Probably never." She shrugged. "Why ruin this moment with Nicky M?" She curled her hand around his and squeezed. Electric currents passed between their hands, and for a moment they just looked at one another.

"Nicolas," he corrected. "I'm not that teenager anymore. Sometimes it feels like I never was."

"I understand that. We all grow up, right? And move on."

"Sometimes there is no other option." He told himself the life he had now—wealthier than he could have imagined, the provider for his family—was enough. What did it matter that the poetry in his life was gone?

The waiter brought the appetizers, and Chloe pulled her hand away from his. A chill settled over him. Nicolas looked around to see if a window had been opened. No air moved in the restaurant. The absence of Chloe's warm skin on his had produced the chill. He'd never had such a reaction from holding a woman's hand before.

"I had to grow up and figure out some way to take control of my life. As a kid, I had no control of anything. I went with my mother to India. She hated it, but I found spiritual peace. Meditation and practicing yoga were worlds away from the lessons I'd learned in Hollywood. Polar opposites, in fact."

That surprised him. "You lived in Hollywood? Why have we not met before?"

She laughed. "We travel in different circles, Nicolas."

He really liked the sound of her laughter. "We need to rectify that situation immediately."

She sipped her glass of water. He noticed she hadn't touched the wine he'd poured for her. "I moved here because I couldn't stand the fakeness. The superficiality."

"Ah, you were an actress. Hollywood can be brutal for people starting out in the film industry."

"Good guess, but me, an actress?" She snorted. "Perform in front of cameras? Are you crazy? Well, yeah, I guess you are, Mr. Singer. I was a private yoga instructor with ten students at a time at most. No cameras. No squealing fans."

It was his turn to laugh. "I might have squealed when you did some of those stretches. You are very good. How do you move your body like that?"

"Practice. I can teach you some of those stretches."

"What would it take to convince you to go back to Hollywood?" he surprised himself by asking. Even more startling? He meant it. He wanted to see Chloe in her element, lifting that sweet backside in the air again. "I might want to try yoga. If you'd be my teacher."

"That place nearly destroyed me." There was a flash of something like pain in her eyes. "It crushed my spirit."

"That surprises me. You seem strong, calm, normal."

"I've been working on it. Coming home to be with my family was exactly what I needed. I won't go back to LA."

He'd be lying if he said he wasn't disappointed. "If I've learned one thing in the music industry, it is to never say never."

The entrées arrived. His steak cut like butter, and their conversation was smooth and flowing. Nicolas enjoyed the dinner even more as Chloe relaxed. It was fun when she was starstruck and tongue-tied around him, but this was better—spending the evening with an intelligent, insightful date.

"My spinach raviolis are sinfully good," Chloe said. "One of the things I've learned from my yoga practice— take your time to enjoy all the good things in life. Moment by moment."

She took a bite of her pasta and closed her eyes to savor the taste. Her bottom lip was wet with the light lemon-and-olive-oil sauce. The tip of her pink tongue touched the corner of her mouth, slowly getting every last drop. His fork stopped midair. He enjoyed Italian food, but he'd never been so turned on by seeing a woman eat raviolis. Pasta had never made him hard before.

Slowly she opened her eyes. Her cheeks pinked. Did she see the sexual hunger in his expression?

"You try it," she said softly, giving him a bite of her ravioli. "Close your eyes and describe what you taste."

"I'd rather watch you. You are sexy when you eat. Makes me think of how your lips would taste right now." His voice was low and sounded dirty. Chloe was turning him into a voyeur. He liked it.

Her response wasn't verbal. Her eyes widened and the pupils went dark. Slowly she inhaled through parted lips. He watched her beautiful breasts rise and fall. He liked that, too.

"Careful, Nicolas, or you'll make me break a promise to myself." Her cheeks seemed heated.

"What promise?"

Her gaze bore into his. "To keep my hands and lips off you."

"How can I convince you to break that promise? Over and over again."

Her mouth opened but the waiter stepped up to the table, interrupting the moment. "More water?"

"Yes, please," Chloe's voice was hoarse. He imagined her saying that to him, later in his room. Maybe she'd drop the *please* and add his name. Maybe she wouldn't say anything when she grabbed him and bruised his lips.

As the waiter poured water for both of them, Chloe downed half the glass, cleared her throat and changed the topic. "I've planned a few adventures to help you get to know Plunder Cove. Is there anything special you'd like to do while you are here?"

Nicolas couldn't keep his lips from twitching. The only special adventure he'd like to do was sitting across the table from him. And he'd like to do more than one thing with her. He had never met anyone quite like Chloe—pretty, genuine, unique, and he'd already seen how flexible she was. His imagination heated up.

He waited for the waiter to leave and then he leaned forward and said nice and low, "I'm sure you and I can figure something out."

"Nicolas…"

"Yes, sexy?"

She bit her lip. Her right hand curled in, gripping the tablecloth and releasing. Was that how she gripped the sheets during sex? Yes, she was on the same page. She made a strange sound in the back of her throat and choked. Then she grabbed her wineglass and drank it dry.

"More?" He held up the bottle.

She coughed one more time. "Sorry. I never expected to hear my teenage dream call me that. It's a little overwhelming."

"Sexy?" He poured. "I'm just a man. And you are a very desirable woman. Two people who can make one another very happy."

"It's not that simple. I'm on the job and you are—" she let out breath "—you are my Nicky M."

He smiled. He liked the way she wanted to possess him. "I can be yours tonight, in the flesh. Let me make all your dreams come true. Say yes."

She toyed with her wineglass, her blue eyes capturing the candlelight. "And how would you know what all my dreams are?"

"Easy. You will whisper them to me. One by one. I'll make them happen."

She chuckled. "Do those lines work with supermodels?"

He lifted his palms. "*Claro*. Practice makes perfect, just like yoga."

"Man, oh, man. I'd better change the subject before I get myself into trouble."

"Trouble can be fun."

"Not when you're running away from it. I've spent years trying to clean up the mess in my life. And I'm still…not there yet."

There it was again—the flash of pain in her eyes.

He frowned. What had happened to her? He knew all about messes. His life was littered with them. Instead of fixing them, he usually left them behind as fast as he could. Some things were just too big to change. But for the first time in a long time, he wanted to help someone who wasn't in the industry. A real person with regular problems. And kissable lips.

"Is there anything I can do to help?"

She cocked her head, studying him, and then she shook her head. "As lovely as that sounds…no, I've fallen into that trap before and it just makes things tougher. I learned the hard way that I let men be my crutches, but at some point I have to do the work and heal my own wounds. This is on me. I have to fix me by myself."

"Wounds?" The waiter showed up again before he could get Chloe to explain. "Hey, *homem*. Can I pay you to take a hike and leave us alone for a while?"

The waiter blinked. "Uh, sorry. I didn't mean to interrupt. The chef would like you to try her signature dessert. Two spoons?" Between them, the waiter placed a decadent tower of tiramisu drizzled with dark bitter chocolate and sweet caramel. He then left the table quickly.

Chloe whispered. "It's the chef's better-than-sex tiramisu."

"Better than sex?" Nicolas shook his head. "You have been with the wrong men."

"No argument there," Chloe said.

File that information away, too.

He was already strategically planning where he would lick her and exactly where he'd suck. At the moment he didn't care about his reasons for being at this resort. He wanted to ease Chloe's wounds, or at least try. He was going in.

Five

His gaze caused a blast of heat to melt her insides.

She shouldn't be thinking about his body on hers. No man was supposed to be under her sheets until she fulfilled her promise to herself. Her gaze traveled across his shirt, and before she could stop herself, she was imagining releasing each button. She hadn't felt like this in a long time, maybe never. Her body pulsed with need. Usually, she could stay away from a gorgeous guy, but Nicolas was different. She had a feeling that his lips were better than a delicious dessert and she wanted, needed, a taste.

"All right, Mr. Hot Stuff." She took his spoon, scooped up a large bite and swirled it around in the chocolaty sauce. "Now close your eyes and open your mouth."

His lips quirked. "I like a bossy woman who wants to feed me a sex dessert."

Her heart was pounding way too hard when he opened his mouth. He peeked at her through those dark lashes.

"All the way closed," she ordered. Her hand was not exactly steady when she touched his tongue with the treat. "Don't just taste. Feel. Listen. Take everything in. Savor the moment."

Chewing, he tipped his head back and moaned with pleasure. Wow, she felt that between her own legs. Resisting him was going to be the hardest test on her self-journey yet. Each minute with him made her want to indulge in him and forget for a moment about the promises she'd made.

"I taste chocolate, cinnamon, mascarpone cheese. Espresso, I think. And some spices I cannot quite recognize. As for what I hear…" He tilted his head, listening. "I can hear you breathing, your heart beating strong in your beautiful chest. There. You shifted in your chair, pressing your legs together. You are thinking about all those dreams you want me to make come true."

She gulped. How did he know *that*?

He opened his eyes. So damned cocky. And something else… Hopeful?

"Might be the case with all those supermodels you've dated, but I was thinking about taking a bite of that tiramisu." Her hoarse voice gave her away. She shifted in her chair again, trying, as he'd said, to quell the ache.

"Admit it, Chloe. Say you want me more than any dessert."

Oh, heck, yeah.

And that was the moment she decided to say yes.

When would she get the chance to kiss Nicky M if she didn't go for it now? When would she feel a desire like this again? Since she'd never felt anything like it before, she refused to let it pass her by. She might have used all of those other men to forget her own problems, but none of them had ever made her feel like this.

She dragged her finger through the chocolate sauce. "I like sweet-and-sticky things." She licked it off her finger. "About the promise…"

"Yeah?"

"If you really meant it…that you want me…"

"I did. I do."

She chewed her lip. "I'm considering breaking my promise. For tonight."

He grinned. "Best news I've heard all year." He pushed his chair out and helped her with hers. He curled her arm under his. "Come. Let's get out of here."

Chloe was shaking when he led her outside, pulling her along the torchlit path toward the garden. A lot had changed in a few short minutes. Her head was spinning. Was she really doing this? Could she have one hot, unforgettable night with her fantasy man?

She swallowed hard.

As if sensing her nerves, he stopped walking and faced her. His warm hands cupped her cheeks. She could feel the calluses. Those amazing, talented fingers were now setting her skin on fire.

"Do you want me, *minha gatinha*?" he asked, his expression sincere. "You can say no. There won't be any hard feelings."

She swayed, melting from his heat. Want flooded her senses. The walls she'd carefully erected to insulate herself from her past crumbled beneath her desire for this man.

She rose up on her toes and kissed Nicolas Medeiros on his beautiful lips.

When he returned the kiss, his full lips were far more delicious than she'd ever imagined. She got lost in the taste of him, the heat pulsing through her, the pure bliss.

"Wow." She sighed.

He rubbed her cheek with the pad of his thumb. "Indeed, far better than tiramisu." He angled in for another.

Her heart was pounding and every cell in her body was begging for another kiss. It took all the willpower she could muster to put her hand on his chest and not rip open the buttons. She held him at arm's length. She couldn't afford to be kissing such an important *guest* here, where Dad or his staff could see her. "Let's go somewhere. A secret place."

"Ah." He leaned in close like he'd done when they were on the stairs. "I like Chloe's secrets."

She took his arm and led him through the back of the garden, past the fountain and under the low-hanging wisteria. As they passed, he reached up and plucked a purple flower and held it to his nose.

"*Santa Mãe*, that smells almost as good as you do."

He'd been smelling her? She was in deep trouble here. She was already craving another taste of his lips. She had the feeling that once she let herself truly enjoy him, she would be lost. Could she throw away all the work she'd done over the last year, improving herself, for one quick fling?

She shouldn't. She knew it.

But in this moment, she wanted to indulge in Nicolas and deal with the consequences later.

"This is it. Over here." She pulled him through a small opening between the hedges. "Be careful that the branches don't tear your clothes."

When they slipped out the other side, they were in one of Chloe's special spots—a small grassy meadow on the edge of the bluffs overlooking the Pacific Ocean. There were no clouds to block the legion of twinkling stars above them. The moon was a spotlight on the midnight blue sea. A breeze rolled across the water, lifting the tips of the waves and blowing the salty fragrance their way.

"I was thinking this spot would be good for the show. You could film a few of the contestants here, especially at sunset. It's an inspirational place. A good songwriting place."

He whistled soft and low. "What a view. The shape of the bay reminds me of the moon when it is barely a fingernail-slice in the sky."

God, his imagery was amazing. That's what she'd loved the most about his lyrics. "That's where the Harper pirates boldly dragged off all their booty. It's where we modern-day pirates boldly strip off..." She stopped herself. "We swim at night. The phosphorescence in the water is really amazing if you've never experienced it."

"Maybe later. When was the last time you brought a guy to this secret spot?"

She chuckled. "Never. It's been years since I've been here. I was always alone."

"Years?"

"Yeah. When my parents split up, Mom and I were kicked out of the mansion. But I used to come here all the time to escape the yelling inside. No one knew I was here. It's peaceful."

"Sounds like you had a tough childhood." He wrapped his arms around her like a blanket to shield the bad memories and tugged her back against his chest.

"I did. Sometimes I felt so alone and helpless."

He understood those feelings.

"You were the one who saved me," she said.

He tipped his head so he could see the side of her face. "How so?"

"When my parents screamed at each other and did terrible things, your music was there for me. I feel like I've known you my whole life—you just didn't know me."

"I wish I had known you then. I would've done my best to make you smile." He rubbed her shoulder. "My younger self would have tried to sneak a kiss or two then, too."

"My teenage self would've passed out if Nicky M's lips had touched hers."

"How about now?" He turned her in his arms and kissed her on the lips.

"Yep, the world is spinning. More, please." She wrapped

her hands around his neck and pulled his lips to hers. He deepened the kiss and she felt like she was flying up and off the cliff. He shifted his stance so he could hold her tight to him. She relished the feel of him against her—his hard chest, muscular thighs and...*oh*. He was very hard everywhere.

She sucked in a breath.

"Chloe," he whispered into her ear, making shivers roll up her spine and into her scalp. "It's your call. We can go back to my room and make love all night. The rest of the world be damned." He pressed his lips against the shell of her ear. "No stress. No strings."

She sighed. "This won't have any impact on the contract or the show, right? Just one fun night."

He studied her for a long beat. "A fun, *sexy* night."

She held out her hand. "Deal."

He took her hand, turned it up and nibbled on the palm. Then he kissed a few fingers and sucked her thumb into his mouth as if she was the sweetest thing he'd ever tasted.

"Deal."

She was in way over her head.

Six

He kissed her hard to seal their arrangement. Then he took her hand and led her back inside the mansion. No one was in the hallway. They were alone.

"Want anything to drink?" she asked. "I can get something from the cellar."

"Got any *cachaça*?"

"I don't know what that is."

"Most Americans don't. It's similar to rum and is used to make *caipirinha*, one of my favorite Brazilian drinks. How about bourbon, whiskey, tequila?"

She led him to a lounge chair. "Here. Sit and I'll go see what I can find."

"Wait." He hooked her wrist and pulled her closer. "Don't go."

The look she gave him spoke in sexy volumes. Passion darkened her light eyes and set the golden feathers aflame. She sucked in her bottom lip as if she could already feel his mouth on hers. She wanted him to kiss her. That made two of them.

He pulled her close. Hanging on, his hands around her waist, he dove in. She tasted better than *cachaça*. Chloe did not hold back. She ran her hands behind his neck, through his hair, and fastened his lips to hers. When he felt the pressure of her tongue against his lips, he opened up and let her in. She made an exquisite sound of pleasure. His tongue pushed hers back and he tasted as much as he could. Still, he couldn't get his fill.

He pressed her against the wall, caging her with his arms, wishing he could take her right there. He didn't want to think about what this meant or when it would end. He needed to feel. To drive both of them higher until her moans of delight became the music he couldn't create, let it fill his silent brain. He was desperate for release and peace.

With his eyes on hers, he slowly ran one hand over her throat, collarbone and chest until he found her breast. He cupped it through her clothes, enjoying the weight of it in his hand. God, she was perfect.

"I want you naked," he growled.

She was breathing fast. Her hands were on his ass. "Feeling is mutual."

They kissed and groped each other in the hallway like teenagers so hot for each other that they couldn't move toward his room. Or hers. He sucked her bottom lip and she cried out in his mouth.

There was a noise from down the hall and Chloe ripped her lips away from his. Her eyes were wild. "Oh, God. Is it my dad? He can't know about us. Come on, let's go."

She dragged him to his room, unlocked the door with her universal key and pulled him inside. He barely had a chance to register how badly she really didn't want her father to know about them. Her lips were on his throat and she was sighing in that way that made him hot. He didn't care who knew what at this point.

"Nicolas." Her lips moved against the cord of his neck. "There's something you should know."

"Another secret?"

"Sort of. It's more an admission. It's been a long time since I dated anyone. I'm probably rusty and not as practiced as the women you usually date. I'm especially not like your last supermodel. At all. I don't want you to be disappointed."

He ran his hand down her cheek. It was so damned soft. "My supermodel?"

"Tell me the truth." She tipped her head up and her eyes shimmered in the moonlight pouring through the window. Her gaze poured over his face, searching for…what? He hadn't lied to her. Did she think he would? "Do you want to sleep with me as a rebound? It's okay if you do, I understand revenge sex, or trying to forget her or…whatever this is. I just… I want to know."

Making love to this gorgeous woman would go a long way toward helping him block out what Lila and Billy had done to him. They'd destroyed his trust and friendship. He would never trust like that again. He'd been burned enough.

But none of that had anything to do with Chloe.

"I'm over Lila."

"Thank God." She let out a breath she'd been holding. "She was horrible. You deserve so much better. I'd never do what she did to you."

"Good." He nuzzled her neck. He wouldn't let anyone do that to him again. He was no fool. "I want you, Chloe. You're special, different, refreshingly honest. I don't care if you are rusty. I promise we will have a good time enjoying each other."

"You want me. Just as I am?"

"Hell, yes."

She hesitated and he wondered, not for the first time, why she had made that promise to herself not to touch him.

And then she kissed him again and whispered against his lips, "Good."

He cupped her jaw. "Now my turn. I'm worried you'll be disappointed with me. I'm under a lot of pressure to live up to your fantasy."

She smiled and his heart did a funny, fluttering beat. "So, we're both under pressure, huh? What in the world are we going to do to release it?" She pressed her hand to the bulge in his pants.

"Careful, *mulher.*" His voice was husky. "Keep breaking your promise like that and you're going to get into a whole lot of trouble."

Her eyes were hooded. "That's the plan. I'm going to get into as much trouble as I can tonight. Over and over. No regrets."

He was glad they were on the same page.

Nicolas didn't have female friends. With the exception of a few brief relationships, he mostly had quick hookups, which might last for a long weekend. If she didn't want to spend the night with him, he'd just as soon leave Plunder Cove and send someone else in his place to scope out the resort for the show. An entire week of sexual frustration was not part of the job description.

"I want you, Nicolas. Just as you are," she said as she ran her hands down his back.

He dove his hands into her hair and devoured her lips.

She unbuttoned his shirt. Her soft hands dipping inside the opening. "Please, I need to touch you."

He had no problem with that. He pulled the shirt off his shoulders and she inhaled in awe. If that didn't do his ego good, nothing would.

He stood before her, willing to go at whatever speed she needed or wanted. Her gaze traveled over him as if memorizing every inch of his skin. He couldn't remember anyone looking at him like that. She pressed her palms to his chest and slowly, tentatively touched his skin.

"So warm, muscular. My fantasies don't compare to this."

He grinned. "You can touch me all you want, *gata*."

"What happened here?" She fingered an old scar near his collarbone.

"Surfing accident when I was a kid."

Her eyes met his. "You surf? I didn't know that. I used to surf a lot."

"Me, too. I don't have much time for it anymore."

"Plunder Cove doesn't typically get big waves, but we can bodysurf while you're here."

"Naked?" he asked.

She looked up to see if he was kidding. He wasn't, if she was game. Her smile was wicked. "As long as no one sees us."

No one in general, or her family? She was a grown woman. Why was she so concerned about her family judging her? Or was she mostly worried about what they'd think if she was with him? He'd get to the bottom of it. Later.

Her fingers trailed over a rib and continued to trace his abs. "You are so beautiful. I can't believe I'm really touching you. It seems like a dream."

He tipped her chin up to look into her eyes. "You are the beautiful one, Chloe."

She pressed her lips to his chest in one long, intense kiss. She breathed in the smell of his skin, exhaling pleasure. No one had ever done that to him before.

Wrapping one arm around his back, she flattened the other hand over his heart as if trying to connect to the rapid beat. Wet, delicious kisses peppered his skin. She savored the taste of him as if he was her tiramisu. It was incredibly hot. He'd never been so turned on while keeping his pants and on. Chloe was amazingly sexy and hadn't taken anything off, which he wanted to fix immediately. She said she was rusty, but obviously knew her way around a man's body. He liked this slow, intense pace, but it was getting harder and harder to keep his racing hormones in check. He wanted to kiss her badly.

She lightly dragged her nails down his back. Goose bumps danced across his skin, rejoicing at her touch. When her hand cupped his ass, while her lips trailed wet kisses across his chest, he couldn't keep himself in check any longer.

"Chloe," he growled. "I want you naked." He pulled her to him, grabbed her ass and lifted her off the floor. "Now." He carried her to his bedroom.

He set her feet down next to his bed and sat on the mattress to watch her undress.

With her gaze on his, she unzipped her dress and let it drop to the floor. Her light blue bra and panties matched the dress and looked amazing on her skin. But he wanted them on the floor, too. Yesterday.

When she stepped out of her panties, he sucked in a breath. She was lean and sleek, with a narrow waist, taut core muscles and perfect breasts from years of practicing yoga. Nothing phony; no corrections needed.

"You are so damned beautiful." He rose to his feet, kicked his pants and briefs off and wrapped his arms around her. *"Linda,"* he mumbled with a kiss to her neck.

He ran his hand down her shoulder, her breast, her belly, her side and stopped on her amazing butt. All the while, her gaze was locked on his, her pupils dilated.

He sat back down on the bed and pulled her closer, pressing her legs wider until they were straddling his lap. He cupped her and ran his finger through her folds. "Tell me what you want, Chloe."

She gasped and closed her eyes. "You."

"Look at me."

Her eyes flew open.

"I'm no fantasy. Say what you want."

"You. To put that amazing mouth on me."

He grinned. He held on to her backside and placed a kiss right where she wanted it.

"Oh, God." She swayed.

"I've got you," he said before kissing her again. She squirmed in his arms. He licked and she started breathing heavily. He licked a few more times and she was panting. She sounded close. He really wanted to slow this down so she could savor every second, but he couldn't. He was close, too. He sucked.

She yelled out and collapsed into his arms.

He picked her up and laid her down on the bed.

"Don't move. I'll be right back." He went to grab a condom.

"Move?" she laughed. "With what bones?"

He put the condom on the pillow and stretched out beside her. She ran her hand over his chest, down his belly and gripped him.

"Mine," she said. "For tonight." She scooted down and put her mouth on him. Warm, wet heat engulfed him. She did something with her tongue that made him see stars. It was too good, too much.

"Hell, Chloe, I need to be inside you."

She took the condom, put it on him and then climbed on top. She was so wet. So hot. She rode him hard, fast. As if desperate for release. But he didn't want this to end yet.

He gripped her hips and slowed her down. It was his turn to savor every moment. He sat up so he could reach her lips. He kissed her as he went deep, and pulled back slowly. He could feel her muscles tightening, hanging on, loving him on the inside, as he devoured her mouth. He wanted to touch her everywhere at once. To please her in every way.

Deep dive, slow retreat.

Her hips rocked with him, a perfect slow dance. Intensely intimate.

He went even slower this time. She moaned and bit her lip as he pulled back. The expression of pleasure on her face sent a shock wave to his balls. They were both panting now. She cupped his jaw and licked his lips, her hair draping his face, her blue eyes locked on to his. Emotions, raw and pure, flooded her expression. He'd never seen anything sexier. Had never been this connected with a woman.

Deep dive, slow retreat.

Her lips parted and a breathy moan came out. He felt it deep in his chest. This wasn't his style, this slow-motion, deeply connected love. It was emotional somehow in ways he couldn't quite figure out, but he liked it. He liked her. He wanted their night to be as good for her as it was for him. More than that. He didn't want it to end. For a few moments he could let himself hear the music in his soul. Feel that he deserved that look of awe on her face.

He rubbed her back, hips and smooth legs.

Deeper…

She moaned and gripped his shoulder. Waves of searing heat rolled through him. He held her hips and encouraged her to pick up the pace. And she rode him faster, faster, throwing her head back and arching her spine. His vision was filled with stars. He couldn't hang on much longer. She cried out and he joined her as they both sailed away in ecstasy.

Seven

Nicolas tucked Chloe in close, his arm around her so he could touch her in as many places as possible as she slept. She was out like a light, softly snoring, completely satiated. He went to sleep with a smile on his face.

The dream started up quickly.

He was on a stage, getting ready to sing, but he didn't have a song. The audience booed him, calling him a loser. It was a repeat performance dream that he had at least once a month, only this time something was different. He wasn't alone. Chloe stood beside him with her hand in his.

She kissed him on the cheek and said, "Don't listen to them, Nicky. Be better."

He blinked at her. How?

She nodded at him like he knew the answer.

For her, he picked up his guitar and started to play. A wild melody poured out of him that was strong enough to vanquish the crowds and push back the despair. It was as brilliant and pure as Chloe's blue eyes, as intricately wound as her long braid.

The music was so real that his eyes opened. He wondered for a split second where he was. *Not my bed. Harper's home.*

He didn't linger on the thought, because he had to hurry and grab his guitar. He could still hear the chords of the melody, feel it pulsing through his blood. He got up quietly so as not to wake Chloe, took his guitar into the other room of his suite and closed the door behind him.

The first notes sprang from his fingers. He played the chords of the song from his dreams over and over again, trying to remember the rest. He couldn't quite grasp it. Still, he knew he was smiling as he strummed because miracles like this didn't happen to him anymore. He was flying. Joyful. For the first time in years, he was riffing on a new song that no one had heard before.

Chloe had opened a door inside him that had been bolted shut for too long. How had she done it? He'd only slept with her once, and yet he was dreaming about her. That never happened to him. She had touched him, maybe deeper than anyone ever had, and she had flipped one of his recurring nightmares into a song with real potential.

He played the chords again, faster, with more heart. The sound was unique and fresh. It reminded him of hope. Truth. Redemption.

Chloe.

It was early, probably around five o'clock in the morning, and Chloe was awake and gazing at Nicolas's face. God, he was gorgeous when he slept.

A stream of moonlight came through the window and highlighted a lock of his hair that had fallen across his forehead. How she longed to brush it off his brow, but she didn't dare move for fear she'd wake him. She stayed perfectly still and soaked him in. His jaw was relaxed. The stress lines above his nose were gone and his full lips parted slightly as he breathed in and out. The best part was that his arm was still wrapped around her as if he wanted to keep her. If he really did, she'd never move again. But that was crazy thinking. It was a one-night stand—nothing more. And she was the luckiest girl on the planet. The night had been magical. But it was only temporary because she needed to find herself.

Nicolas had kept his end of the bargain and loved her like she was special, important. He took her to heights she hadn't reached in a long time—maybe never before. She'd let herself go, while cherishing every moment. He was amazing. It was all a glorious memory to keep and replay like a movie or a song whenever she got lonely.

Like right now.

Even in his bed, while touching him, smelling his clean skin, studying his face like it was the last time, she felt bereft. Her heart beat was a solemn drumming in her chest. She knew herself well enough to know that the single night of bliss was going to come with consequences.

Because already she longed for more kisses and touching. More Nicolas.

There is no more.

She blinked hard on the burning sensation behind her eyes. Last night was a fantasy, pure and simple. Now he had to go back to being a guest at the resort, and it was time for her to be professional. To continue in her quest to find something that would last longer than just one night. Their secret deal was done. If she stuck around for the morning hellos, she'd only embarrass herself by wanting what she couldn't have. Best to get gone before any of the blubbering or begging started.

She slipped out of bed and tiptoed out the door. She made it to her own room without a single tear dropping and went to the bathroom to clean up. Somehow, she was going to pretend she hadn't had the best sex of her life with the man of her dreams. She would go teach her yoga class at 6:00 a.m. and act like nothing had happened between them. Like the world hadn't just tilted on its axis while she was in his arms.

For all she knew, nothing extraordinary had happened for him. Maybe it was just another Tuesday with some woman he'd forget by Friday.

She couldn't let that bother her. She wouldn't. She'd known going in that it was nothing more than a no-strings night. Now it was her job to show Nicolas around Plunder Cove and get him to fall in love with the place. Falling for her wasn't part of the plan. Her family depended on her. She could do this. Somehow.

After she got out of the shower, she found a note on her bed from her dad. It was early and Dad had already stopped by? That couldn't be good.

"I want to talk to you," was all it said.

Crapitty-crap-crap. Did he know she'd spent the night with Nicolas? Was he going to think worse of her? Be angry? Tell her to go back to LA? Once she was ready to face the answer to those questions, Chloe knocked on the door to her father's study. Her palms were sweating.

"Enter," her father's voice called out from inside.

"Hey, Dad. Are you okay? It's early."

She stepped inside his library and immediately felt like the eleven-year-old girl who'd lost control of her bike and crashed into the Lamborghini, leaving an ugly scrape on the sports car.

RW Harper sat at his massive desk. He was writing on a large yellow tablet that he turned over when she stepped inside the room. She saw columns and notes as if he was weighing a pros and cons list.

"I can't sleep. Come in, sweetheart. There is something I want to talk to you about."

"Yeah, I know, Dad. It just sort of happened. I won't do it again. I promise."

He looked at her over his reading glasses. "This is about your mother. You need to convince her to leave Plunder Cove. She might listen to you. I want her gone before Angel comes home."

This wasn't about spending an outrageously hot night with a man she was supposed to be wooing as a Harper representative? Relief rushed into her limbs. "Oh! You've heard from Angel. When is she coming back?"

Her dad's face was solemn. "No, I haven't heard from her, but I'm making arrangements to bring her back. I need her, Chloe. I'll do everything in my power to make her safe here."

"That's good, Dad. She should be here with you. You guys are great together."

"It's all her. She makes me a better man."

The conviction in his voice helped to cement her theory—Dad was falling in love with Angel. Did he know it yet? She studied him. He seemed thin, and his face showed signs of fatigue, but he wasn't as gray as he had been. His cheeks were slightly pink, like hers got when she was energized or embarrassed. More than that, she noticed an intensity to him. He wasn't depressed. His gaze was just as piercing as always. And that yellow notepad he had been writing on, the one he didn't want her to read, intrigued her.

Whatever he was planning must have something to do with how he was going to bring Angel home.

What was he up to?

"Your mother can't be hanging around here, Chloe. She needs to go back to Los Angeles."

"I'll talk to her, Dad, but you know Mom."

"Unfortunately, I do."

Claire Harper was a force to be reckoned with—a woman who did what she wanted and made life hell if you tried to stop her. Chloe wasn't sure why her mother hadn't left yet. Perhaps Mom wanted to see Jeff finish the resort. She was extremely proud of Jeff's accomplishments. Chloe crossed her fingers and hoped that was the reason Claire was still in Plunder Cove, and not anything more sinister.

"I'll try."

"Please, do what you can. I need Angel," RW said.

Please? RW Harper did not use that word very often. "I will." Chloe kissed his cheek. "Is there anything else I can do for you?"

"Just one, Chloe. Be careful," he said. He looked her in the eye and she saw a swirl of emotions. She was used to anger, disgust and intolerance on RW Harper's face, because during her childhood, that was all she'd seen. Since Angel had come into his life, though, Chloe had been surprised by how expressive her father's eyes could be. Her father was a different man than the one who'd broken her heart as a child. His transformation was strange and amazing all at once.

"I am, Dad. I won't let you down."

Eight

Nicolas reached for her before he opened his eyes. His bed was empty. She'd left him before the sun came up? Women didn't usually run away from his bed so quickly. He usually walked them out and had his driver take them home. This was…unusual.

What did you expect, homem? *It was a one-night stand. You shook on it.*

Strangely, he felt sad about their deal. It was what he'd wanted last night, and yet he wasn't happy about it in the foggy haze of morning. The way Chloe made love—no, not made…*savored* love was inspiring. He'd never been with a woman who had touched him like she had. Would a second night be the same way? Did he have the right to ask her to extend their arrangement?

Probably not. She'd been clear about not wanting her family to know about their attraction. He was going to have to act like Chloe Harper had not gotten under his skin.

Since he was awake and frustrated, he got out his laptop and immersed himself in his job. Like any other day.

After an hour of critiquing show contestants, Nicolas

stretched his arms over his head and stood up. He needed a break. The singer-songwriters were all starting to blend together. Why couldn't these kids write something unique? Something that grabbed his heart, or gut, and wouldn't let go?

Perhaps it was because none of the artists had really lived yet. Storytelling required backstory, angst, a broken heart and devastating loss. He sighed. He'd had all of those things in spades by the time he was eleven. He didn't actually wish any of it on another kid.

Stretching his neck, he stepped out onto the balcony. The sun had just come up and the landscape was peaceful. He took in a deep breath and instead of inhaling the sweet smell of flowers or grass, he picked up a fragrance that reminded him of his childhood in Brazil—the sea. He longed to go for a swim.

Naked. With Chloe.

Down below, he saw her. She had a small class of about seven women, all stretching and reaching toward the sun. None of the seven women did the poses as well as Chloe. Nor looked as hot. He put his bathing suit on, determined to convince her to join him for an early-morning swim after her workout. Maybe once they got to the shore, they could strip their suits off.

He continued working until he heard her door close down the hall. Draping a towel around his neck, he knocked at her room. The pounding heartbeat in his chest surprised him. He felt like a teenager again, throwing rocks at his first girlfriend's window. The strangeness of the situation did not get past him. He was years and many girlfriends away from his first girl. Chloe was a sexy hookup—nothing more. And yet...his heart raced to see her again.

Chloe must have seen him through the peephole because

her cheeks were already pink when she opened the door. Her face looked sparkly clean, as she wore no makeup. Her hair was in one long braid draped over her shoulder. Her pale blue tank top and yoga pants clung to every curve. He had to stop looking. His swim trunks were getting tighter by the moment.

"I'm not here to cause trouble," he said quickly.

Her gaze took a quick trip down his mostly naked body and popped back up again to his face. "As long as you're not here to cause trouble."

He couldn't help but smile. Discreetly, he wiped his damp palms on his towel. Chloe had quite an effect on him. He had to get a grip.

"The sun is shining, the sky is crystal blue and the water is wet. Come bodysurfing with me," he said.

She smiled and his pulse stilled. His chest warmed. How did she do that?

"Now?"

He shrugged. "Unless you have something else planned for us." He was hopeful their plans might involve dropping those yoga clothes to the floor.

"We were going to start with breakfast. Do you want to hit the waves first?"

He leaned against her door frame, crossed his arms casually and asked. "What's for breakfast?"

She swallowed loudly, as if she'd read his mind. He wanted to taste Chloe again. He could skip eggs and bacon and kiss her all morning instead.

"Whatever you're hungry for?" Her voice cracked.

He pushed off the door frame and moved closer. She smelled so good. "In that case I'm craving more of last night. You left before the sun came up. Why?"

Her eyes widened. "We had a deal. One night only."

To hell with that. He wanted heat, pressure...her. He caressed her cheek and marveled again at how soft her skin was. "I got robbed. Make it up to me." He took her hand in his and rubbed her palm. He'd promise her anything if she'd agree.

Her beautiful lips parted into a shocked O-shape. "We agreed—it was a casual, one-time thing."

It was supposed to be, but there was nothing casual about last night. Chloe had given him something special—herself. People didn't usually do that during hookups. They always kept something under a mask, protected, reserved. Chloe hadn't held anything back. She'd touched him as if they'd been lovers for years. No, better. As if they'd been *in love* for years. He had never experienced anything like it and he wanted more, needed more.

"Is that what you want? To put last night behind us?" his mouth asked, but his body was already humming with the ache to pull her into his arms. He was a little stunned by his growing need for her. She wasn't his usual type. Chloe was sincere, earthy, real. He'd never been with anyone like her.

She blinked. "I don't understand. You still want me?"

"Hell, yes." It came out as a growl. "Chloe, last night was one of the best I've ever—"

She grabbed the towel around his neck and pulled him close. He forgot what he was going to say when her lips melded to his. She was such a fantastic kisser. His tongue probed her sweet mouth, tasting minty toothpaste. His hands roamed over her skin as he tried to reacquaint himself with her curves and lean muscles. Heat engulfed him and he was instantly hard.

She pulled her lips away long enough to whisper, "Come inside." She guided him into her room and closed the door behind him.

He pressed her up against the wall. Lifting one of her legs, he wrapped it around him. She was so damned flexible. Gripping her hips, he moved her into the perfect position and kissed her hard. A hungry growl rumbled at the back of his throat.

She cupped his face with her hands and kissed as good as she got. She was hungry, too. He kissed her neck and peeled her tank top off her shoulders. Her bra beneath the tank was lacy and black, beautiful.

"*Beleza.*" He kissed her soft skin from her collarbone down into her cleavage, and unlatched the bra, freeing two exquisite breasts. Not large, not small, but simply perfect. He cupped one while kissing the other.

Chloe moaned with pleasure. "More."

He sucked.

She arched her back and tipped her head back, breathing fast.

"Like that?" he asked.

She bit her lip and nodded.

"Say it, *gatinha.*"

"More, Nicolas. Give me more." She pressed down against his erection, rolling her hips.

He liked that.

They moved together. Flying, dancing, a perfect melody of a sexy song. He took the other nipple into his mouth, playing with it, licking, teasing.

She gripped his head, holding him in place. He reached his hand into her yoga pants and was pleased to find her not wearing underwear. He cupped her and pressed his finger inside her wetness.

"Oh…feels so…oh…" She didn't finish the sentence. She rocked against his hand. Beautiful, wild and sexy beyond words.

He sucked her nipple while she rode him. Chloe cried out, coming undone. So unbelievably beautiful. He pulled her lips back to his and savored them.

"So? Can we extend our deal? Stay another night with me. The whole night this time."

She pressed her forehead to his and opened her eyes. "I swore to keep my hands off you. Now look at what I've done." She was playing it light, but there was a hint of something else in her voice... Sadness?

"Why did you make that promise?" He sat on her love seat and pulled her into his lap, curious.

She played with his hair. "I'm trying to focus on making myself a better person before I lose myself in someone else."

"You seem pretty great to me."

Her bottom lip quivered. "I'm not great. You don't know what it's like to be a Harper. I've never been loved, Nicolas. Not ever. By anyone. I want what other people have, just once—to feel loved. Like I deserve it."

He was going to still that lip after she answered the next question. "Your family didn't love you?"

"My father sent us all away and I had no contact with any of them except my mother. And my mother...well, she doesn't show love."

He pressed a gentle kiss to both of her lips. "You deserve love, *gata*. You've had a run of bad luck. That's all. You don't need to change who you are for anyone."

She pressed her hand to his chest. Connecting with his heartbeat again. "You're amazing, Nicolas. I'm glad I got to know you."

He held out his hand. "Do we have another deal? I will prove to you that you are special the way you are. If things work out, we will have a whole week together. I promise that you are a better person than you believe you are. Let me show you how wonderful you are."

"And then? After the week is done?"

"I go back to Los Angeles and get ready for the show."

"Alone, again?" She petted his cheek. "Don't you want more in your life? I want so much for my life and relationships."

"Relationships don't last. All I want is here and now—you naked and me deep inside you." He was still hard and aching to feel her under him, or over him—he didn't care. He'd take her any way she'd let him.

She ran her finger over his bottom lip. "I want that, too. But I want the feeling to last. I've never had a long-term loving relationship, or anything real. At this time in my life, I need to set the bar to that level. Real love that lasts. Don't you want someone who—" her gaze was intense and sincere "—fills your dark spots?"

He thought he'd wanted that…once. He'd failed then and would fail again. He wasn't cut out to be anyone's lasting relationship. Even knowing he couldn't be that for Chloe, he wanted her for this short time.

"Long-lasting doesn't work for me. People take what they want and then everyone leaves…" He paused. "I will make you happy for the week, but I'm not your forever-after man, *gata*. I don't know how to be that guy."

Her gaze bored into his with such anguish and conflict that his heart melted, but he held his ground. He wouldn't lie to her. The next step would be up to her.

"Decide what you want, Chloe, and I'll give it to you. No questions, no pressure." He lifted her off his lap. "I'm going to take a quick shower and then we can meet for breakfast. Bodysurfing will have to come later. I'm starved."

Nine

Nicolas Medeiros wants me?

She would have thought she was dreaming, except she was still jelly-legged from his wicked touch. The man had a way of making her come like no one else. A reckless, wanton ache between her legs made her want to race down the hall and be with Nicolas again. But something he said kept her feet rooted to her silk carpet.

Everyone leaves.

She knew exactly how that felt. How much of his sentiment related to his recent breakup? Chloe didn't know, but she'd never been one of those people who got what they needed and then walked away.

She wished she could be the one to show him what a long-term relationship looked like. Funny. She'd never had any sort of relationship herself, and maybe she still wasn't ready for one, but she knew she could love someone forever if she had the chance. That's why finding herself before dating anyone else had been so important to her.

But that was before Nicolas.

She could try to explain this belief in love to him, but he'd have to decide that he wanted it for himself.

She cared about him. She didn't want to be on his list of users and leavers. Staying away from him would be the best thing for both of them, no matter how fantastic his lips felt on her skin or what his hot gaze did to her insides.

But staying away was impossible, both personally and professionally.

How would she get her job done if she couldn't work with him? Nicolas was her job, the only assignment her family had given her. What would Dad say if she told him she couldn't do what he'd asked because she wanted Nicolas Medeiros more than any contract?

She groaned. What was she going to do?

Wait. What was that?

She opened her door, peeked her head into the hallway, and listened.

Music. Nicolas wasn't in the shower; he was riffing on his guitar in his room. The sound was both haunting and passionate.

Just like Nicolas.

Chloe's cell phone rang on her nightstand. She closed her door and saw Michele's caller ID on the screen as she answered.

"You'd better get down here," Michele whispered. "Your mother is expecting me to feed her breakfast. Demanding, really. Please say I can kick her out on her skinny butt."

"No! Do not throw her out or she'll make a huge scene. I don't want Nicolas to see Mom's antics."

"Dreamy Eyes is not with you?" Michele asked coyly.

Sadly, no. "Tell Mom I'm coming. Get her a Bloody Mary and do not make small talk with her. Repeat—do not engage."

"Sounds like a crocodile," Michele mumbled before she hung up.

Chloe hastily changed into a white dress and hustled down to find her mother sitting at the same table where Chloe and Nicolas had sat the night before. It had the best view in the place. There was some light cloud cover over the water, but other than that it looked like it was going to be a gorgeous day.

"Chloe, darling. So glad you could join me for breakfast," Mom said. She kissed Chloe's cheek and whispered, "The chef is quite obnoxious. Don't know what Jeff sees in her."

"She's actually quite lovely." Chloe sat across from her mother. "What are you doing here, Mom?"

"I can't come have breakfast with my daughter?" Claire pouted.

"Sure. I could've met you somewhere, like say, Santa Monica? They have lots of nice restaurants on the Breakwater."

Claire sipped her Bloody Mary. "I was hoping I might run into your father. Can you call him? Ask him to join us?"

Chloe's jaw dropped. "You *want* Dad to join us. Why?"

"You and your thousand questions." Claire shook her head. "I might have missed your father. A little."

Chloe sat back in her chair. "How much alcohol is in that glass?"

"Hardly any." Claire fluffed her hair. "RW is more handsome than I remembered. When he's not yelling, or brooding, he has a nice smile."

Nope, nope, just no. "You can't still love Dad!"

"I never stopped. The anger and hatred just blocked the good stuff. Time has made me realize that we could be good together. Passionate. Funny."

This was all shades of wrong. "Mother, do you hear yourself? How many years did you tell me how bad things were? How horrible my father was? How you wished you'd never met him."

Claire shrugged. "That was then—this is now. There's a lot at stake here, Chloe. I think we should try again, your father and me. We are older now, more mature. We can make it work."

What sort of hell is this?

As Chloe tried to make sense of her mother's words and why she would be saying them, Nicolas came strolling up the path in white shorts. His blue-gray polo shirt made his eyes look amazing. Her gaze took a happy trip over those glorious muscular arms, chest and beautiful legs, and suddenly she couldn't think straight. When he waved at her and gave her a sizzling smile, she could barely breathe.

"Who is that handsome young man?" her mother asked.

My Nicky M.

Chloe shook her head and drank her water. He wasn't hers. At least not for longer than this week.

Do not come in here, she tried to telegraph to him. Her mother would ruin everything.

He cocked his head, as if studying Chloe's body language through the window. When her mother wasn't looking, Chloe mouthed *sorry* and held up a finger. She tried to convey that she'd be just a minute, but who knew with Mom? It could be an hour that felt like a year.

Frowning, he turned and walked in the other direction.

"Oh, darn. He was easy on the eyes. I was hoping he'd come in and join us," Claire said.

Over my dead body. "Um, Mom, I need to get back to work. Are you okay here by yourself?"

"You can't stay for breakfast with your mother? Fine. Go. But ask your father to come down first."

Chloe couldn't fathom how she'd been put in this position. Claire was not good for her father, especially since she'd seen him change after being with Angel.

What was she supposed to do here?

"He's probably busy, Mom."

"When is he not busy? Call him. He'd hang up on me, but he'll listen to you."

Chloe dialed her dad's number, trying to figure out what to say when he picked up.

"Hi, sweetheart. What is it?" Dad answered.

"Um, Mom's here and wondering if you'd like to join her for breakfast."

"No can do. I'm on my way to a business deal."

Surprised that he didn't yell or laugh at the idea, she frowned. "I didn't know you had a meeting today."

There was a long pause.

"I do. An important one. Might be the last I ever have."

What did *that* mean? She hoped it meant he was retiring, but in his current emotional state, she worried Dad might be in trouble. "You haven't been feeling—" she suddenly realized her mother was listening and chose her words carefully "—well. Maybe you should take Jeff with you."

"Not today, Chloe. I've got to do this thing on my own. Which reminds me—I left an envelope for you in my study with a set of keys to the F1. Maybe you should drive Nicolas around, give him a tour of Plunder Cove."

She almost swallowed her tongue. "That's crazy, Dad. You told me to stay away from the F1. If I remember correctly, you said I'd be grounded for life if I went within ten feet of it."

"You were eleven, Chloe. And you'd just crashed your bike into the Lambo. Forgive me for being a little cautious. You're all grown up now. I want you to have it."

Her mouth fell open. "Wait. You're giving it to me?"

"Sure. The color and class remind me of you. It suits you."

Chloe fought the tears since her mother was watching. "That's an amazing gift."

"You are an amazing daughter. Stay sweet. Take care of yourself and your brothers. And tell your mother to go home."

"But what are you doing—?"

The line went dead.

A heavy dose of foreboding settled in her chest.

What was Dad up to?

Ten

Chloe had asked Michele to send a tray of food to Nicolas and to keep him away from the restaurant. Well, away from Claire Harper.

Chloe stayed with her mother as long as she possibly could and then left to go find Nicolas.

He was sitting on a lounge chair by the pool. His long legs were stretched out and he had tucked his left arm behind his head. He looked relaxed and so beautiful that her heart swelled. He had his laptop out and headphones on. Coming up behind him, she could see he was watching a music video. It looked like an audition, which meant he was working on this gorgeous day when she really wanted to *play with him*.

She bit her lip.

No, she meant *show him around Plunder Cove*.

She stepped into his sunlight. "Please tell me you are relaxing and enjoying the day."

"Senti sua falta, linda." He moved his glasses down To look at her. "That means 'I missed you, beauty.'" Those gray eyes, that smile, the Portuguese…yep, she couldn't get enough of him.

She pressed her legs together discreetly. "I'm sorry I couldn't join you for breakfast. I was dealing with a crisis." She took a deep breath. "My mother dropped in unexpectedly for my brother's wedding two months ago and never left. But now she's saying she wants to get back together with my dad."

"I could tell it was a tense moment."

"Really? I was trying so hard to scream only on the inside."

He smiled at that. "I read your body."

The ache grew when he left off the word *language*.

"She's gone now. But she'll be back. Hopefully we'll be out of here by then. I'd like to take you on an adventure to introduce you to the area. Is this a good time?"

He closed the laptop. "It's always a good time to have an adventure with you."

"Great." Her voice cracked.

She swallowed hard and reminded herself that her focus was on doing her job today—as a Harper heiress and promoter of the Plunder Cove Resort. She was *absolutely not* going on a date with Nicolas.

Sleeping with him was one thing. But she was not asking for more. At least not during the day.

When the sun went down, she'd see what adventures were in store for her.

He moved the laptop to a drink table and placed the plate of half-eaten food on the table closest to her. Scooting a little, making room on his lounge chair, he opened his arms to her. "Join me. Tell me about this crisis."

No one could see them out here by the private pool. She nestled in under his arm and put her head on his chest. She inhaled. Why did he always have to smell so good?

"Did you have a good relationship with your parents?" she asked.

Nicolas let out a breath. "My father drowned when I was a kid. Fishing accident. My mother never got over it. She suffered from alcoholism, poor nutrition and extreme poverty. It was up to me to take care of her and my four sisters." He'd said the words flatly, as if they didn't sting, but his voice was strained.

She looked up and saw anguish on his face. "Oh, Nicolas. I didn't know."

"My agent kept the bad news out of the media. No one wants to hear why a kid is poor and singing on the street corners, just that he rose up and became famous."

She rubbed his arm, drawing her nails slowly across his skin. "That's why you work so hard."

"I had to. Otherwise my sisters would have starved. They all went to school and are happy and healthy. I'm proud of them. Mom is doing well, too. She got herself dried out and remarried."

She hugged him. "You did so much for your family, Nicolas. Isn't it your turn to live a little? You don't have to keep working so hard. They are grown and on their own. You should give yourself permission to relax. Take a real, nonworking vacation once in a while."

"Can't. Success is a moving target. If you take your eye off it, even for a moment, it all slips away from you. Besides, I don't know how to vacation. But how did this become about me? Tell me about your mom. You looked like you were the one chewing nails when you were sitting by her. Why?"

"Where to begin? My parents used to fight. A lot. Their words and violence hurt the entire family. It got worse and worse. I could feel the end coming, you know, like a ticking time bomb sitting in the center of the dining room table."

She shuddered and he wrapped his arms around her tighter.

"When the explosion finally happened, my family blew apart. Mom and I were forced out of the house. My brothers were sent away, too. All of us in different directions—shards in the wind. It was terrible. I missed my father and brothers so much. Mom stayed in her room all day, cursing my dad and drinking. I was alone. Broken. No one cared about me. I mostly raised myself." She made a noise of disgust. "Poor little rich girl, right? What you must think of me, complaining about my life when yours was so hard."

He tipped her chin up and melted her with those amazing eyes. "Hey, they're all idiots. You deserved to be a happy kid. So did I, but sometimes life doesn't turn out that way. What you do with the hand you are dealt is the key. Look at how well you turned out."

Chloe didn't usually talk about her painful past. Nicolas was an amazing, sympathetic listener. It was surprising how well they were connecting. Chloe scooped a strawberry off Nicolas's plate and fed it to him. "I used to blame my Mom, but I'm sure my mom was lonely when we were banished from Plunder Cove. She'd never been without a man to support her—first her father and then mine. She went a little bonkers. That's the only reason why a pampered woman who'd never practiced yoga in her life would've read a brochure about a resort in Rishikesh, India, and decided it would be the perfect getaway." She chuckled. "You should've seen her once we got there. She didn't expect that the resort would be rustic, that there would be bugs or poor people or no room service."

He laughed. "Sounds like she read the wrong brochure."

"Or she'd lost her mind. I'm not sure what she sought, but all she found in India was dirt, hunger and a waste of time. In her typical way, Mom demanded her money back."

"Did they return her money?" he asked.

Did he know he was rubbing her arm in slow, sensual circles?

"Most of it. The teachers there don't care about money. They provide tools to assist people on their paths toward spiritual enlightenment. The only thing Mom found in the end was that she hated India. Her fourteen-year-old daughter, on the other hand, found the meaning of life."

He pulled back to look at her. "Really?"

"I was young and my spirit was desperate to be healed. I took to yoga like my first breath. I've always been athletic and flexible, and was able to bend my body into any pose they gave me. They taught me to let go of the past and live in the moment. For the first time in my life, I started to love myself when no one else did. I felt lighter, stronger. Free. India put my feet on a path to happiness."

His smile was warm, genuine. "Maybe you can teach me some of that lighter, free happiness. Unless it requires some sort of twisted pose no one should do."

"No poses. I would love to share what my teachers told me."

He nodded. "I'm a skeptic, but I'll listen."

"Listening is the start. My teachers told me I cannot kill the past, so I might as well make it my friend." She made her voice mimic the old sage she'd loved the most. "Is it not better to sup with an old friend than to have to battle him night after night?"

He laughed. "That's a good imitation."

"I thought it was lousy advice." She shook her head. "I'd rather have wiped out big chunks of my childhood so it would stop hurting. Surely, I thought, there's a meditation or yoga pose for that!"

"Is there?" Nicolas asked. "I'd give that pose a try."

"Apparently not." Now he played with her fingers as she talked. "They taught me to think of the past as grains of sand on the wind—each one forming us, shaping us but not hurting us anymore. The past is gone and the future doesn't exist at all. There is only this moment." She tapped his chest. "And all you have to do during that moment is breathe."

"Just breathe?" Nicolas asked, capturing her hand against his chest. "Is this the advice that drives you to become better?"

"Sounds easy, huh? Maybe for someone dedicated to a spiritual life. For a regular person, it's hard. But the advice reminds me to be present in the here and now."

"Hmm. I guess that's not total mumbo jumbo. As long as it makes you happy."

"I'm working on it. I do think I can help you to be free and happy, too."

He swallowed. "I don't know how to find real happiness, *gata*."

"Neither do I. But what I am trying to do might get us there. Isn't it about time we both try to figure it out?"

They looked at each other for a long moment.

Nicolas finally broke the silence. "What do you want me to say?"

"Say what you feel. That we are worth the effort. That you deserve to be happy."

"It sounds like a lot of effort. But I do want to be happy."

"Good. I think you will like what I have in mind. But first we need to make a pact."

He lifted his eyebrow. "Another deal? If it extends our night, I'm all ears."

"I like your idea of extending our night, but I want to propose another option."

He ran his thumb over her breast. "I'm intrigued. Go on."

She sucked in a breath. It was now or never.

"Remember how you told me that you could prove I am special the way I am?"

He pressed a kiss to her ear, and thrilling waves rolled through her. His deep voice whispered, "My offer was to love you so well that you'd know how special you are."

"I'll accept your challenge if you let me try to prove that you, Nicolas Medeiros, know more about love than you give yourself credit for. I believe you are long-lasting material."

"What?" He flinched.

She rushed on. "I don't mean you have to fall in love with me, or stay with me long-term—I'm not sure *I'm* ready for that. I just think you *could* find yourself loving someone, believing in love. You could have a real, deep relationship... with someone, someday."

He let out a soft breath. "Long-term is not in my makeup, Chloe. I tried. It always ends up a colossal failure. I don't want to hurt you. Or anyone."

"I'm a big girl and I want to do this for you. Give us the week. Let yourself truly feel...free. Enjoy each moment and see where it takes you. Just try."

He closed his eyes. "What if we spend the week together, and at the end it's simply...over. I will go back to LA. What then?"

She kissed his hand. "Then it is what it is. But you and I will have tried. I think it is important for us both to reach for happiness. We might actually find it. What do you think?"

He opened his eyes. She struggled to read the expression swirling in them.

"And all we have to do is..."

"Touch, feel, enjoy each moment together, honestly, fully. Let ourselves be in the present and see what happens. Just breathe. We can find something meaningful for once, together. I know we can."

"I'll get to make love to you whenever I want?" He grinned and pulled her on top of him.

She looked around, made sure her two brothers and father were nowhere in sight. "Mmm-hmm." She kissed him, sinking into his hard body. "As long as there are no Harpers around."

He wrapped his arms around her and kissed the breath out of her lungs. She could feel his heat, waves rolling off his body dancing with hers. She was flying again. She wanted to rip his clothes off right there, in plain sight of any Harper who happened to come swim in the private pool.

He pulled back and studied her face. "You are the most unusual woman I've ever been with. I want you, Chloe. I'll take you any way I can. I'll try to be in the present and breathe and feel—whatever that means. You, *gata*, have a deal." He gripped her butt as he said it.

And sealed the deal by kissing her nipple through her shirt.

Eleven

When they finally came up for air, Chloe said. "Are you ready for our first work adventure?"

"Every moment is an adventure with you."

She scooted away, feeling weak and giddy. He had a way of stealing all the energy from her cells and electrifying her nerves.

He rose and she got another whiff of his body soap. It made her mouth water. "Let me put my computer in the room, and I will be ready."

"And your cell phone."

A crease formed above those gorgeous eyes. "What?"

"Leave your cell phone, wallet and all your gadgets in the room. I want to untether you from the outside world for a few hours."

"I do not go anywhere without my phone."

She nodded. "I get that. Trust me. It'll be good for you. Those emails, texts and calls will be waiting for you when you get back."

He put his hand on her shoulder. "You'll have to keep me really busy to distract me from the outside world."

She knew she was smiling, but couldn't help herself. "I'll do my best. Let's go," she said.

"Not yet." He spun her around and pressed his lips to hers one more time. Then he tucked a loose strand of hair behind her ear and said, "I don't leave my cell behind."

"I know but—"

He pressed his finger to her lips. "You are making a new man out of me already."

"Meet me in the front. Your adventure awaits." She rose up on her toes, nibbled his chin and then left him to watch her walk away.

Nicolas couldn't stop smiling. He'd made a connection with Chloe, and that didn't come easy with him. She was different and surprising. He had no idea how to live in the present, but he was willing to give the experiment a try for a week. Breathing with Chloe. Hell, as long as they were both naked and he could put his lips all over her soft body, then sign him up. After that? He'd go back to LA. Chloe was amazing but she wasn't going to prove that he was long-lasting material. He wished she could, but he knew it wasn't in him. He'd never be that guy, because he didn't know how to really love anyone other than his family. He never had.

His mind knew all of this. His body, though, seemed to have a language of its own. When Chloe Harper was near, his fingertips were drawn to her skin, his nose had a heightened awareness of the intoxicating scent of her shampoo and the soap on her body, and his lips longed to taste hers. Loving every inch of Chloe's naked body was a reoccurring theme in his brain.

He waited out front as she'd asked and heard an engine purring in the distance. He sucked in a breath when a volcano-orange McLaren F1 pulled up next to him. It was one of the hottest cars he'd ever seen, especially when the doors bat-winged open to reveal Chloe sitting in the front seat, wearing a white dress and a sexy grin.

"Ready, handsome?" she asked.

Santa Mãe. It was going to be a rock-hard day. "This is a McLaren F1 Longtail. Is it even street legal?"

"Yes?" She shrugged. "Probably. I guess so. Most likely."

"Seems legit to me." He climbed in. "You've driven a race car before?"

"Sure. My brothers and I played racing video games all the time when I was a kid. How hard can it be?" She winked at him. "Don't worry. I'll be safe."

The doors closed and he took a long look at the woman in the driver's seat. "It suits you."

She grinned and the look on her face was a mix of excitement and wonder. That suited her, too. If he could get her to look like that in his arms, he would be a happy man.

"That's what he said, too."

He frowned. "Who?"

"My dad when he gave it to me this morning. Let's take this baby out on the open road and see if you're both right."

She pressed the gas and roared down the drive.

Chloe was giddy. Again.

Taking the curves on an empty backcountry road in her very own race car? Having Nicolas in the passenger seat, eyeing her as if she was a tasty treat? Never in a million years could she have imagined this day. The heck with being professional; she wanted to enjoy the moment. She squealed her delight.

Nicolas laughed. "You are so damned beautiful. A natural-born race car driver. You should get some time on a race track and open her up."

She side-eyed him. "Really?"

He grinned. "It's clear to me, *gata*—you have a need for speed."

She didn't respond. He was correct. Part of her wanted to pull the car over in a lookout spot and grab Nicolas and kiss him like she'd never kissed anyone. Her fingers itched to touch him everywhere.

She added pressure to the gas pedal. The engine purred and she could feel the rumble in her core. She slowed the car and cast Nicolas a glance. "Wow, that felt good."

"You look good." Nicolas's voice was deep, sexy. "Maybe we should pull over. I've never kissed a race car driver before and I want to. Right now."

Excitement raced through her veins. "Mmm. That can be arranged. Let's stop in Pueblicito." Slowly she drove down the main street, while Nicolas took in the small town.

"I've never heard of Pueblicito and yet it looks like it's been here a long time," he said.

"It's probably too small to show up on most maps, but you're right—it has been here since the 1800s. The town started out as a working ranch for my family."

"The pirate Harpers went into ranching?"

"No, the next generations went into cattle and became the land-baron Harpers. It's not a great chapter in my family history." She grimaced. Several chapters in her history were less than stellar. "People have lived in this town all their lives. Several generations back, their descendants were brought here from Mexico to work in the house, fields, pastures or on the range for the Harpers. Those poor people were not always treated well by my ancestors. My father is changing all that." She parked in front of Juanita's Café and Market.

"Your father." He looked puzzled. "RW Harper is upgrading this town, too?"

"In a big way. He is paying the residents of Pueblicito a

percentage of all money made on the new resort and restaurant. That is apparently the reason he is going into the resort business to begin with—to give back to the residents in this town and correct past mistakes. Expect to see Pueblicito on the map in a few years."

He cocked his head. "Interesting. It's hard to imagine RW as a charitable guy. I always heard he was a cutthroat businessman. One that shouldn't be trusted."

She laughed. "You aren't wrong. I was skeptical, too. Since I've been home, I am awestruck by how much he has changed from the father I knew growing up. He seems to be making amends and coming through on his promises. It gives me hope that people can change." She opened the doors. "Come on. I can't wait for you to try the dulces here."

They stepped out of the car and were quickly surrounded by a group of young boys ogling her car.

"Aunt Chloe!" her nine-year-old nephew, Henry, came running over. "No way! Grandpa let you drive the F1?"

She smiled and gave Henry a hug. "Even better. He gave it to me."

Henry's face fell. "Is Grandpa okay?"

Henry knew how much RW loved his cars. The kid and his grandpa were remarkably close. The whole family was worried about RW since Angel had disappeared.

"Yep. He's fine." She hoped. "Let me introduce you to my friend. This is—"

"Nicky M!" Julia, Henry's mother, rushed out of the café, letting loose a string of Spanish words as she came. Chloe didn't understand half of it until Julia switched back to a flood of English words. "Holy Madre, I can't believe you're here. I have every record you ever made. Every one. I have watched all your music videos dozens of times. More! Maybe hundreds of times. This is, I mean, I can't even…" She looked at Chloe. "Oh, my gosh, it's Nicky M!"

Chloe laughed. "Yes, I know. Nicolas, this is my sister-in-law, Julia. She's Matt's wife."

"Con mucho gusto," he said in Spanish, not Portuguese, as he shook Julia's hand. "Matt? He is the pilot?"

"Yes."

Chloe elbowed her. "The crowd is growing. Let's go inside."

Julia blinked dreamily and then seemed to mentally shake herself. "Pardon my manners. Of course. Come in. I'll make you two something yummy to eat."

"You're cooking? That's new. Oh, wait." Chloe held up her finger. "Henry?" Chloe called to the boy peeking in the windows of her new car.

Henry held up both hands and took a step back. "I didn't touch it, I swear."

"No, that's fine. If you and your friends are careful, I'll let you sit in my car."

The boys hooted and hollered. "Thanks, Aunt Chloe. We'll be careful," Henry promised.

"Wow. I wish I had an aunt like you when I was a boy," Nicolas whispered as they walked through the glass doors. He put his hand on her back, causing a shiver of delight to roll up her spine.

"I have only one nephew and I reserve the right to spoil him rotten." Chloe inhaled deeply. The sights and smells of the Mexican market never disappointed.

Julia led them to a table in the café. "What would you do with another nephew? Or maybe a niece?"

It was then that Chloe noticed the sparkle in Julia's eye.

"Julia! Really?" Wrapping her arms around her sister-in-law, Chloe gently squeezed. "I am so happy for you. Does Henry know?"

"Not yet. Matt and I are going to spill the beans tonight,

after he returns from his flying exercises for the Forestry Service."

"*Parabéns* to you and Matt," Nicolas said. "That is very exciting."

"Nicky M, you could write a song about the excitement in my life. The love of my life returned from the dead, I found my lost mother and now…" The tears welling in her eyes did not dim Julia's radiant smile. "Another baby." She swiped at her wet cheeks. "Stupid hormones."

"Aww. I am so happy for you and Matt. Henry, too. He's going to be a great big brother if he is anything like mine." Chloe kissed Julia's cheek.

"Sit, please. Let me make you lunch," Julia said.

"You've taken over Juanita's while your mom is gone?" Chloe asked.

"Yeah. Has your dad heard from her?" Julia's cheeks were suddenly pale. "I'm so worried."

"Sorry, no." Chloe didn't want to mention the mysterious meeting her dad ran off to this morning. No need to get Julia's hopes up if the meeting had nothing to do with Angel.

Julia sighed. "Let me know if you do, okay? I'm dying to tell her about the new grandbaby. Hopefully that'll convince her to stay here. Now that I finally have a family, I want them all to stay put."

"I get it," Chloe said.

"Family is everything," Nicolas said softly. "I wish my mother would come to California to live, but she refuses to leave Brazil."

"That is rough. I lived most of my life without knowing my mom and dad. It sucked," Julia said.

"Hey, you two should come and hang out with us at the bonfire tonight. Matt invited some of his friends. Jeff and

Michele will be there. You could bring your guitar, Chloe. Maybe we can all show Nicky M how talented we are."

"You play the guitar?" Nicolas's eyes were on her.

Chloe could feel her cheeks getting hot. "I try. Just don't ask me to sing, because I don't do that in public."

He leaned into her and lifted his brow. "What would it take to get you to sing for me in private?"

"Um…"

Julia cleared her throat.

"What do you say, Chloe?" Nicolas pulled her into his arms. "Be my date to the bonfire party?"

"Aww. You two make a great couple," Julia said as she walked away to make lunch.

Blood whooshed in Chloe's ears. "But my brothers will be there."

"And?" He laced his fingers with hers. "What are you afraid of?"

She rubbed her thumb on the top of his hand but couldn't look him in the eye. "Messing this whole thing up. With you. With them. Dad. The world." She half chuckled, or at least made a sound that she hoped sounded like a casual laugh. "Yep, that's about it."

"You think if they see us together they'd assume…what? That you are sleeping with me to win the contract?" The tone in his voice! She'd hurt him.

She looked up. "No! Well, maybe. I want them to believe in me. I can't lose my family again."

Tears fell. She couldn't stop them.

"Maybe we can do something else tonight? Just the two of us?"

He leaned forward and looked deeply into her eyes. "I would like to do something else with you before the bonfire party. And after." That grin of his made her wet. "But this is my part of the bargain, proving that you are worthy.

And fantastic just the way you are. Look at what you have done already. Not only are you doing your job, convincing me that this place is great for the show, but you are changing me. You've converted a workaholic cell phone addict into someone who can breathe in the present moment and try to become a long-term guy. All in two days! You are a strong force of nature, who I believe can do anything she sets her mind to. If anyone doesn't see how amazing you are, they are the ones messing up. Please say yes and go with me to the bonfire, Chloe. Seize the moment with me."

When he looked at her like that, she would agree to anything. And the thought of before and after was rolling through her brain like a forest fire.

"Nicolas…" she began, her voice thick with need. God, she wanted *before* and *after*. Not to mention tomorrow and next year.

Even though Nicolas was not that guy.

His gaze was on her lips. "Say it, Chloe."

But he was the guy she wanted. Right. Now.

"Yes," she said. "Oh, God, yes."

Nicolas reached across the table, put his hands on Chloe's wet cheeks and captured her lips. His tongue licked until she opened up and let him set her world on fire. She had never been kissed like that before, especially not at a little table in a small café with people watching. She didn't care about any of her surroundings. Her senses were hypersensitive to him—his touch, sounds, smell, taste. Nicolas was sucking her bottom lip and lighting up every cell in her body.

Life had never felt so good.

Before had already begun.

Twelve

Nicolas had been with a lot of women. He wouldn't apologize for that fact. Some were great lovers, and others helped his career. But most were crutches he leaned on while he limped through his lonely life. And some, like Lila, had tried to destroy him.

Not one of them was like the woman he was kissing in the Mexican café.

Chloe had…something he couldn't quite name. In the music industry he might have called it the It Factor. Still, that seemed shallow when trying to describe the depths of Chloe Harper. What she had went way beyond her brilliant shine, the way she drove a race car, her laughter, the softness of her lips or the wisdom and kindness in her eyes. Whatever it was, it lived within Chloe, a place he was not good enough to touch or understand. She was simply beautiful.

Far too good for him.

Tonight, he'd go to the bonfire and prove that he was a man who deserved the It Girl.

Julia arrived with a tray full of food. "*Machaca, sopes*, soft tacos, rice and beans."

Chloe pulled her lips away and sat back in her chair. Her cheeks were pink, her braid a little messy and her eyes hooded. Love-drunk was a good look on her.

Nicolas helped distribute the food. "*Obrigado*. Smells good, Julia."

Julia shook her head, giggling. "Nicky M just spoke Portuguese to me. This day keeps getting better."

"I know, right?" Chloe smiled. "That accent is amazing."

Julia left them alone again.

"If I spoke Portuguese to you, would you sing?"

She snorted. "That would be a cruel thing to do to you. But you might convince me to play my guitar…" Her eyes widened. Something over his shoulder caught her attention. "Did you see that man?"

He turned and looked. "Where?"

"Behind the counter. A bald man with tattoos. There. He's staring at you."

"I'm used to people recognizing me. It's one of the hazards of the job. Eat. It's okay. It is nice that you are trying to protect me, but paparazzi is everywhere. Hang around with me long enough and you get used to people staring." For the first time he actually envisioned what it would be like if she was with him in LA.

"I guess I could get used to it. I was worried that the man was spying on us for…well, for another reason." She twisted her napkin between her hands. "I think my dad has kicked a hornet's nest."

He cocked his head. "Meaning?"

She shrugged but fear sparked in her eyes. "My father left today for some secret meeting that he refused to tell me about. On his way out of town, he gave me one of his prized cars. I'm worried about him."

"Why? What is the hornet's nest?"

"Harper business, I guess." She shrugged but he could tell she knew more than she was saying.

"Maybe your father just went for a drive to buy a new F1."

She nodded. "Maybe."

He wanted to ease the tension in her shoulders and make her smile again. "Let's go for a swim."

There it was. The light returned to her eyes and a sexy smile lifted the corners of her lips. "Naked?"

He leaned closer until their noses were almost touching and stroked her leg under the table. "*Mulher*, you read my mind."

"How about we save that for tonight? I have another secret place I'd like to take you to now."

"I'm in your hands."

Julia brought them a bag of candies and reminded them to come to the bonfire. Chloe hugged her and paid, and they left the café. Nicolas wrapped his arm around Chloe as they walked out of Juanita's. His eyes scanned the perimeter, watching for any sign of paparazzi. For the first time in his life, he was the bodyguard protecting the star.

It felt good. He could get used to taking care of a woman like Chloe Harper.

After shooing the little boys away from her car, she and Nicolas climbed in. Putting the pedal to the metal and zooming onto the beach to naked bodysurf was oh, so tempting. Still, she had to slow her revving sex drive the heck down and at least try to salvage the job she was supposed to be doing for her family.

Before she started the car, she said, "There are a few places I'd like you to see."

Leaning over, he moved the dress strap off her shoulder and drew free-form designs on her bare skin with his finger. "I agree wholeheartedly. There are more than a few places I would like to see. Touch. Lick."

Her skin danced in anticipation. She started the car, the rumble adding to her shivers.

Driving down the main street, Chloe gave him the tour of the small town of Pueblicito. "I bet you could film this town as a backdrop for your show. Like you said, it looks old and historical. I envision some of your candidates walking down this street, describing the inspiration for their songs, or maybe talking about their hometowns."

He nodded. "You have a good eye. But I must remind you that it is not a done deal yet. We haven't chosen Plunder Cove as the venue for the show. There are two other locations still to consider."

"I understand."

"I am willing to let you try to convince me, though." She caught the lift of his eyebrow. "More than willing."

His words set off all sorts of warning bells. She pulled the F1 over to the side of the road. "This is what I worry about. If my family thought I threw myself at you just for the contract…" She shook her head. "That's not me. At all. I hope you know that I care about you. I would never sleep with a man for a job or a promotion or…a contract."

"Chloe." He cupped her cheek. "I was joking."

She swallowed hard. "You were?"

"Of course. I've known enough women and men who would sleep with anyone for a career move. You are not one of them."

Satisfied with his answer, she started the car again.

Thirteen

Chloe drove Nicolas to some of her favorite spots in Plunder Cove, all the while highlighting how the contestants of the show could be filmed in each one. Normally she would take guests to the beach or on one of the boats up the coast, or maybe they'd take out the Jet Skis. Right now, she wanted to do something different with Nicolas, so she took him in the opposite direction—to the mountains.

She parked near the stables. "Let's get out and walk. I don't have the right shoes on, but it's okay. There is a short hike up to one of the most beautiful views in the area, called Lover's Point. Your contestants will love it."

He took her hand in his and they walked up the horse trail and got lost in the Monterey pine forest. When they got to the top, they sat on a large boulder and gazed out across the forest. The green valley below spread like a velvety carpet that ran all the way to the deep blue ocean. A red-tailed hawk cried as it circled overhead. The gentle breeze carried a fragrant mix of pine and sea.

"Wow. I can't even remember the last time I was up here. I forgot how beautiful it was," she said.

"I wish I had my cell phone."

She frowned. It made her sad that he was so connected to his technology that he couldn't enjoy a peaceful moment in nature without his phone. "You probably wouldn't get reception up here anyway."

"No," he captured her chin between his thumb and finger. "I wanted to take a picture of you. This light, the look on your face when you gaze out there... You are beautiful, Chloe."

"Thank you for giving me a chance to be with you, Nicolas. I feel so blessed." She kissed him sweetly, gently pouring all her hope and desire for them into that kiss.

He pulled back and looked at her. Raw amazement lit his features as if he understood the weight of the kiss. The meaning.

"I am awestruck by you," he said.

That melted her through and through. She turned her back on the view and pressed herself into Nicolas. He was caught between a rock and a needy woman. She ran her hands behind his neck while she devoured his lips with kisses that were no longer sweet.

He cupped her butt through the white dress, while his tongue probed her mouth. She was moaning already. His lips pulled away and found the sweet spot on her neck. The electric bolt shot straight through her spine to her toes. Her legs threatened to buckle.

She wanted to feel his skin and quickly began unbuttoning his shirt.

He stilled her hands. "If we keep going like this, I am going to take you here. And it won't be slow. Is that what you want?"

Her head was flying. "Please," she begged. "I need to touch you."

She got his shirt open and ran her fingers over his chest.

He made a guttural groan and ran his hand up her thigh and under her dress. Finding the edge of her panties, he pulled them down. She sucked in a breath and his mouth was instantly on hers. His kisses made her crazy with want, especially with his hand stroking between her legs.

"Chloe," he said in between kisses.

"Hmm?"

"We have a…situation."

That hand was still driving her wild. Fingers dipping in, rubbing, pressing. She tipped her head to the blue sky. "Situation?"

Against her neck, he mumbled. "Someone convinced me to leave my wallet behind. I have no condoms with me."

"Oh." She moved away from his wicked hand and tried to reign in her desire. "Well, we could go back to your room."

"Later. Right now I want to touch you. Make you feel good. But I can't do it with you looking at me like that. I am too close."

She touched the large bump in his pants. "I could—"

"No. This is for you. Let me do this. Turn around. Hands on the boulder."

She did as she was told. He unzipped her dress slowly, following the zipper down with kisses peppered against her skin. Delight and anticipation rolled through her. Her palms pressed the boulder and she spread her legs a little for balance.

He took her dress off. She was standing on the mountain, wearing only a bra and sandals. A cool breeze blew from the ocean, and the sun warmed her shoulders. Her body was a live wire of anticipation. She waited to see what Nicolas was going to do next.

"Don't move," he said.

One of his warm hands were on her hip. She heard him rustling behind her. Squatting?

He kissed the back of her knee and she jerked.

"You moved," he said. "I'm in a precarious spot. I don't want to fall down the hill today."

"Sorry." She pressed herself harder into the boulder.

He kissed her there again and she didn't knock him off the mountain. "Better." He kissed her inner thigh and she twitched. She was hypersensitive and loving it.

"God, Nicolas. Your kisses are electrifying me."

"Is that a good thing?"

"So good. More, please."

He kissed her bare bottom and she was suddenly panting. He rose, standing behind her. She could feel his pants against her bare legs. Moving her braid away, he nibbled on her shoulder blade, making his way to her neck. One hand wrapped around her belly, holding her to him. The other...

"Oh, yes," she moaned when his hand cupped her. One finger dipped inside her—moving in and out—while his palm exquisitely pressed her nub.

He nibbled on her neck and his fingers did magical, wonderful things inside her. "Come for me, baby."

She let go. The waves rolled over and over her, higher and higher, as if they'd never end.

"*Minha paixão*, you are gorgeous," he said into her ear.

Minha paixão? She'd look up that expression later. As she started to come down, one warning bell rang out through her love-hazed brain. *I'm in trouble here.*

Her eyes were shut. She could feel his breath on her skin, hear his deep voice rolling through her, smell his manly, delicious scent, feel her body floating with pleasure. She was fully present.

Fully, wholly...his.

She sensed he was trying to go with the flow, but he

wasn't there yet. And at the end of the week, he would be going back to LA. What was she going to do about that?

"Wow." She put her dress back on. "I've never experienced anything like that."

She wrapped her arms around him and petted his bare chest. Memorizing his warm skin and muscles as her fingers stroked every inch. She kissed his chest, collarbones and that dip between his pecs.

He wrapped his arms around her and kissed the top of her head. Neither one of them spoke.

She held him like that for several long moments and pretended that he would always be hers.

Something had happened between them on the mountain.

Nicolas felt it with blinding intensity. It started with that sweet, gentle kiss. He had never been kissed quite like that before. And then when she came for him with such wild trust...*wow* was the word.

Nicolas felt closer to Chloe than he had felt to any woman in years. Maybe in his whole life.

What was it about Chloe Harper?

"I have to work today," he said softly. "Just a few hours." He also needed a cold shower and a few moments alone to figure things out. It was all new to him.

She was getting to him in ways he had never experienced. It was exhilarating and worrisome all at once. He was usually in better charge of his emotions and the situation. When he was with Chloe, control was far from his reach.

He'd held her on the top of that mountain and realized that he truly wanted the pure, deep, all-in type of relationship that she was offering.

But something whispered from the broken hole inside his being, *You will screw it up, Nicolas. You always do.*

And it would hurt worse than what Lila had done to him. He knew this instinctually because he hadn't given all of himself to Lila. He'd always held something back. For Chloe, he'd have to give everything.

Was he capable of such a sacrifice?

He honestly didn't know the answer, but he sure as hell better figure it out before he dove any deeper with the woman in his arms.

"Perhaps we should head down now," he said.

"Of course."

She pulled back and the breeze chilled his skin through his open shirt. He would be lying if he said he wasn't a little disappointed when she left his arms.

As they walked back down the hill to the car, she talked almost nonstop about different scenes she could picture in the show. It was nervous chatter, as if he'd knocked her off her feet, too. He wasn't the only one with emotions soaring over the mountain.

And then she surprised him again by dangling the car keys in front of his face.

"Want to drive?" she asked.

"You'll let me drive your race car down the mountain?"

She nodded. She trusted him.

He whooped, scooped her up in his arms and swung her around in a circle. *"Cada momento que passa eu me apaixono mais por você."*

Laughing, she said, "Is that a yes?"

Chloe had dropped Nicolas off at the front of the mansion and circled back to park the car in the garage. Very, very carefully she pulled in next to the Ferrari and cut the engine. She was alone in her car when she pulled out her cell phone and translated as best as she could what Nicolas had said to her in Portuguese.

With each passing moment, I fall more for you.

She pressed her hand to her heart. Did he mean it? She hoped he did and yet it scared her because she was falling fast for him. Too fast. She knew she should enjoy every moment, should feel it all, savor her time with Nicolas and not think about the future.

She wished she could answer the burning question: *If I truly embrace the moment, how can I protect my heart from the hurt at the end?*

Chloe wasn't a teenager anymore. Or a fool. She knew Nicolas's track record with women; heck, she knew her own lousy record. The odds weren't in their favor to have a loving and successful relationship.

But she wanted to try.

"We deserve to be happy," she said to the universe. "Please give us a break."

Determined to fight for what she wanted, she went into the house. First, she checked in on her father. He hadn't returned yet and none of the workers in the house knew where he was. She was still worried about him, but she knew he could handle himself. And he'd ask for help if he needed it. He'd changed so much.

Passing by Nicolas's room, she put her hand on his door for just a moment, but did not disturb him. Music played inside, which probably meant he was working. It was a good time to stretch some of the angst out of her muscles before the bonfire party.

She put on her yoga pants and T-shirt, and took her mat outside.

Fourteen

Nicolas was having a tough time focusing on music videos. He'd had to play the last one three times because his mind kept wandering back to a particular blonde *gatinha* and her "kiss me" lips. It was suddenly too warm in his room to work or even think straight. He put on a pair of shorts and went out to the patio in the hopes of catching a breeze. What he caught instead was an eyeful. His girl was sexy stretching again.

To hell with work. He slipped on his running shoes and went out to join her.

Her sweet backside was high in the air when he approached, and it was all he could do not to put his hand on her firm glutes.

He leaned against a tree, crossed his arms and said, "Don't mind me. I love to watch you do that."

"Why just watch?" She broke his heart by dropping to her knees and effectively moving her sweet *bunda* from his reach. "I can show you some yoga moves." She stretched up, opening her chest, arching her back. "Are you finished with your work for today?"

He was now. She was so damned sexy.

"What do I need to do?"

When he sat on her mat, she put her hands on his shoulders and massaged. "Relax. Be open to the experience, let lightness fill your chakras."

He shook his head. "I have no idea what that is, but I am open to the experience of you touching me." And he liked the pretty pink flush that was spreading across her chest.

She had him sit cross-legged. "Close your eyes. Breathe lightness all the way to the bottom of your belly. Hold it. Release all the pain from your past in a deep exhale. Slowly. Good. Breathe in light, let out fears." Over and over he did as she told him. With his eyes still closed, she massaged his jaw, starting at his ear all the way down to his chin—slow, sensual pressure.

"I am releasing the stress in your jaw. Keep breathing," she said.

"It feels good," he said. He wanted that pressure all over his body.

When she was done with his jaw, she placed a light kiss on his lips. "Okay, now we practice yoga. First stretch up. Inhale, filling your lungs." She lifted her arms and chest high. "And exhale while swan diving toward the mat and let yourself hang in a forward fold."

He did as he was told three times. "Piece of cake."

"Yeah, you've got this. Okay, the next pose is called Downward Dog. Let me show you how to do it."

She pressed her hands and bare feet into the grass next to the mat, and her cute ass was pointed toward him. It was his favorite pose. *Muito gostosa.*

"You try," she said.

He did his best but was sure his pose didn't look sexy.

"Close. But…" She stood up. "Mind if I put my hands on your, um…?"

He grinned. "Please. Touch my *um* all you want."

She coughed. "*Hips*. That's what I meant to say."

Coming up behind him, she wrapped her hands around his hip bones and gave them a gentle tug. "Pull your hips back to right about here. Tailbone toward the sky."

Her words were businesslike, but that husky tone was driving him wild. He wished he could see her face instead of staring down at the mat. Her hands held him in place, and his tailbone wasn't the only body part reaching for the sky. If only she would bring her hands forward a bit.

"Perfect." She released him and the coldness rushed in. It happened every time she removed her hands from his skin. Getting down beside him, she did the dog pose, too.

"Now we are going to lower ourselves down to a plank position. Sort of like the start of a push-up. Just hold it," she said. "Good. That's it, except lower your butt a little."

He did. "Like this?"

"Too much. I'll show you." She stood up and straddled him. And then she put both hands on his glutes. Only she didn't just lower his body to the correct position. She rubbed his butt for a long beat, as if enjoying the bunching of his muscles under his cotton shorts.

Why did his friend Tony say he hated yoga?

"This dog likes that," he said.

"Oh! I'm… That's not… I didn't mean to…" Surprise made her voice rise, and the warmth from her hand was gone. Still in a plank position with her straddling him, he felt her moving away before he saw her go.

"Wait," he growled.

He turned over, reached up, grabbed her wrist and pulled her on top of him. Her body on his was perfect. He kissed her like the hungry dog he was.

Her hands gripped his shoulders. She kissed him back, just as greedily. Her legs were on top of his, and her breasts were against his chest. He could feel the pounding of her heartbeat. And the blessed heat between her legs. Her braid dangled by his face. He wrapped the braid around his hand and gave it a gentle tug, exposing her neck.

"I like this pose the best," he whispered against her neck. He cupped her butt with the other hand and pressed her down harder against his aching erection.

She moaned and ground herself against him.

He was close to coming already, if she made that sound again or moved, even a little, it would be difficult to stop himself. Normally he had better control, but with Chloe control went out the window.

Releasing her braid, he ran his hands up her shirt, going on a relentless search to touch as much soft skin as possible. He unhooked her bra from the back and continued forward until he had one of her breasts in hand.

She inhaled. Her eyes wide. "We shouldn't..."

But she didn't get up, didn't release his shoulders. He watched her swallow. Her eyes locked on to his. It seemed like a storm was brewing inside her deep blue irises. The golden feathers were taking flight.

What was she thinking?

"Not here," she said. Her pink tongue swiped across her bottom lip. "Your room or mine?"

"Wherever you want me."

"Everywhere. When I'm with you, touching you, I want more. Crave more. You are all I think about. Please take me to your room and...." She bit her lip. "I want to make you feel good like you did for me."

He ran his hand over her breast. "The licking? Kissing? Sucking?"

"Oh, God, yes." She rolled off him and his body felt bereft.

He stood up, feeling lighter than he had in years. Was that his chakras he was feeling or desire? Didn't know. Barely cared. All he could think about was Chloe.

"Leave the mat," she said. "And hurry."

Fifteen

RW sat in an unmarked car, outside the house where he hoped to save the woman he loved.

The man who had been chasing Angel all these years was inside. RW felt alive and filled up with white-hot… redemption. He would keep Cuchillo away from Angel once and for all.

The plan he'd begun with Angel's help was working. Matt and Jeff were finally happy with women who loved them. With Nicolas in Plunder Cove, Chloe was going to be happy, too. His children had each other; the people of Pueblicito had the resort.

Saving Angel by ending Cuchillo would be RW's last great act.

"Is the wire working?" RW asked, pressing it to his chest to make sure it was still there.

The detective who'd helped RW get to this point checked the system. "Yeah, don't touch it. We're good to go."

RW opened the car door and stepped out. Quietly he walked across the street and toward the house. But as a car approached, RW stepped behind a tall juniper bush.

The car door opened and a woman stepped out. She

stood for a long moment, staring at the gate and waiting for…what? She looked around nervously, as if sensing that she was being watched. And when her face turned toward the juniper bush, RW's heart nearly fell out of his chest. Even though it was dark as he peeked through the bushes, he was sure. He'd recognize her beautiful face anywhere.

Angel.

He was so stunned that he didn't move. He didn't yell. His brain was exploding with questions, the foremost being—what in the hell was she doing here?

Squaring her shoulders, she quickly walked toward the gate. She was going in.

No, damn it, no.

RW rushed out of the bushes, toward Angel. He had to stop her before Cuchillo saw her. He'd throw his body over hers, promise Cuchillo the world, anything to protect her. Before he could get to her, the door opened.

Angel went inside. Willingly.

RW moved close to an open window. He needed to plan carefully. He couldn't see, only hear. His heart was pounding in his ears.

"I never thought I'd see you again, *Ladronita*," a man's voice said. "Missed me? Search her."

"She's clean, Cuchillo," a woman said.

"Smart girl. Why are you here?" Cuchillo asked.

"To ask you to stop chasing after me. No more threats. Don't kill anyone else because of me."

"Kill anyone? You've been watching too much television, *mujer*. We are a good group of people. You know that."

She laughed. It wasn't the joyful sound RW enjoyed hearing. This was a sound of disgust. "I am not wearing a wire, Cuchillo. There have never been lies between us. Why start now?"

"No lies, then. You know what I am going to say."

More silence. RW could imagine the dipping of her head in acknowledgment. She did know. She'd told RW what Cuchillo would say and do if he ever caught up with her. That dire promise had been why RW had plotted and planned to get to this point.

"I plucked you off the street and brought you into the family, into my home. You became an extremely skilled thief, *Ladronita*, truly brilliant. And yet I never would've believed you could steal from me. You robbed me of the only things I care about. Family. Legacy. You don't steal those things, *mujer*. Give them back."

"I can't do that, Cuchillo," she said.

There was silence in the room. RW held his breath as he thought of the family Cuchillo referenced—Matt's wife, Julia. Angel's daughter. The one she'd fled with and hid to protect. Angel had sacrificed so much for Julia, for RW.

He would do the same for her, even if it meant fighting his way in to give her a chance to escape.

"You stole *from me*!" Cuchillo roared. "My own flesh and blood. My only child. Bring me my little girl."

"She is a grown woman who makes her own decisions," Angel said in a voice that was surprisingly calm. RW admired her courage so damned much. "I could ask her if she wants to meet you. At a public place of our choosing, hers and mine. You will stop looking for us after that."

"Interesting proposition. I will agree to let her go, if she chooses." Cuchillo went on, "But you, *Ladronita*? You are another *cosita linda*. You must pay for your crimes against me. Against our family."

RW searched the bushes for a rock or heavy stick. Quietly he crept along the building.

"I never talked. You know that," Angel said.

Cuchillo growled, "You did talk because old-man Harper knows. His private eye talked, *mujer*. People always do."

There on the ground, RW found what he was looking for. Not a rock, but a hammer. RW picked it up.

"Please, Cuchillo, let it go. RW doesn't know much, I swear," she said.

I know enough.

"Get ready, Cuchillo," RW whispered, readying the hammer.

"To pay off your crimes, you go back to your rich old man and give me something of his—equal value plus ten years' of interest—and I will let you go."

"Steal from RW?" Angel's voice cracked. "I can't. I won't."

"Fine. Then you pay, here and now. And I'll find my baby girl without you."

"No!" her voice exploded through the room. "Don't try to contact her, Cuchillo. Leave her alone."

"I will do what I want. She is my flesh and blood," he barked.

When Angel cried out in pain, RW saw red and moved toward the door.

"Okay. I'll do it," Angel whimpered.

Wait. RW stopped. *She's going to do what?*

"I'll… I'll steal from RW. Just let me talk to my daughter first. Give her a chance to make up her own mind and meet you on her own terms. It'll be better for her…and for you."

"Fine. We have a deal. Do not break it, *mujer.*"

RW lowered the hammer and backed away into the shadows. Why had she gone back to Cuchillo? Why didn't she trust that RW could protect her?

Angel, his beautiful Angel, the woman he was willing to risk his life for was finally coming home.

To rob him.

Sixteen

Chloe was in Nicolas's room. Both of them were in Nicolas's favorite state—naked.

"Oh, my." She smiled at all the manly beauty before her. *"Quão lindo."*

"It turns me on when you speak Portuguese." He crawled on top of her. His dreamy blue eyes locked with hers. "More, please."

She ran her hands through his hair. *"Obrigado. Cachaça. Rio de Janeiro."*

"Ay, *gata*. What you do to me. You must learn this one." His lips hovered over hers. *"Me beije."*

"What does it mean?"

"Kiss me."

"Me beije," she said softly.

His lips were on hers and his gaze never wavered. Her heart raced and yet everything else slowed down.

"But it's my turn to make you feel good." She pushed him over on his bed and had her way with him. It was her desire to kiss him from toe to head, but she got distracted by his glorious midsection and lingered until he cried out.

Feeling powerful and complete, she kissed his belly.

"Come up here." He took her by her arms and pulled her to him. His expression resembled awe. How could that be? He'd been with many beautiful women in his life. She was no supermodel. No actress. No famous singer. She was simply Chloe Harper.

He kissed her slowly, deeply. She saw so much emotion on his handsome face. She'd had fantastic sex in her life and had been with a few handsome, sexy men, but never, never had she been kissed like this. Until Nicolas. He kissed her like she was a goddess. It brought tears to her eyes.

One of his hands went around her waist and roamed over her back, caressing, pressing, loving. He gripped her butt and pressed her to him.

"Minha linda."

She understood that phrase. *My beauty.* Still didn't quite believe the words, but liked hearing them. She clung to him, naked, with both arms and legs around him, and pretended that she was his. For now. This was the best moment of her life and it might not last.

Tears burned hot in her eyes again. She didn't dare voice her fears.

Oh, my God, this is what love feels like? Why does it hurt so much?

"Are you okay?"

"Sorry I'm so emotional. I'm loving this."

He grinned. "Me, too. I'm ready." He slipped on the condom and entered her.

"Yes. Deeper," she said.

He obliged and went in deeper, harder, thrust after thrust. It was driving her wild. She bucked under him, taking him in, matching his speed, giving back in turn. It was no slow, deliberate dance, but more of a frenzied pounding of drums in the midst of a firestorm. Could a desperate woman burn up from so much heat? And still he needed more. Deeper. Faster.

They moved together—one breath, one heart, a driving insatiable thirst for release. She was close, so close. Gripping him with everything she had, she held on, wanting it all to last.

She felt him start to shudder and let herself go. She joined him as they shot up and over the sun. He collapsed on top on her.

Emotions, so powerful that she couldn't sort them out, rolled over her. Tears wet her cheeks.

"Chloe?" He sat up. "Did I hurt you?"

Yes. No. Her heart had shattered, for she knew, really knew that she had fallen hard for him. She wanted to keep him.

Forever.

"I'm fine," she lied and rushed to get up and hide in the bathroom until her tears stopped and she could get control of herself.

"Wait." He jumped up off the bed and stood before her in all his naked glory. "Tell me. What's wrong?"

"Nothing. That's just it." She lifted her chin and looked him in the eyes. "You are insanely perfect. It's me. I want too much and am afraid I can't have what I need."

"What does that mean?"

She chewed her lip. The tears threatening to rain down and ruin everything. "I don't want it to end, Nicolas."

He gave her a smoldering look and ran his finger down her chest. "Who says it has to end? I was just getting started."

"But it will end. You're going back to LA."

There was something there—in his eyes, the turn of his lips—that she wished she hadn't seen. She'd wounded him.

"Don't give up on me, Chloe." His voice was choked

with emotion, too. "I'm working on giving you…us…wha we both need."

She swallowed but the lump in her throat wouldn' budge. He shook his head. "Am I doing this wrong, sweet heart? Tell me what you want."

The tears came. "You, Nicolas. I want you. I always have."

"So take me, Chloe." He wrapped his arms around her "I'm here."

She ran her hands around his neck and kissed him, pour ing all her mixed-up emotions into that kiss. Taking his comfort. His passion. Needing so much to believe this wa real.

He pulled her back to the bed and she kissed him jus like she wanted. Soft, deep, real.

And he flipped her over on her back. "Now I'm taking what I want."

The kissing and licking started at her jawline. When h got to her chin, he nibbled. "Mmm, honey."

She laughed. The tears were gone. "I don't taste like honey."

"You are right. You taste better." He kissed her neck and waves of desire rolled through her.

Oh, wow. How did he do that?

He dipped his tongue in her ear and she almost lost her mind. He sucked her earlobe and whispered, "You know what I want?"

To torture me with desire? "What?"

"To make you come again. At least two more times."

She sucked in a breath, her heart thundering in her chest. "Is that so?"

"Just relax."

Hard to do when he was kissing her breasts again.

"I am going to take my time here. Go real slow." His tongue circled her erect nipple.

"You don't have to go too slow."

"My turn to call the shots, *gata*. I've got a lot of licking and sucking to do. And a whole lot of honey to dip my tongue into." He lifted his eyebrow and burned her with his sexy grin. "I do this thing. I've been thinking about showing you how it feels all day. Can I show you now?"

Holy moly. "You do a thing? With your tongue?"

"Lie back and see."

She lay back and quickly learned that Nicolas had a wicked, wicked tongue. She closed her eyes and let the man of her dreams kiss her worries away.

Seventeen

Chloe asked Robert, her dad's driver, to drop her and Nicolas off at the beach. She had her guitar and a beach blanket for them to sit on.

"Can I carry that?" Nicolas pointed to the guitar.

"Sure. Thanks."

It gave her a happy little zing when he linked his fingers with her free hand as they walked toward the bonfire. He gave her hand a reassuring squeeze. She side-eyed him to make sure he was comfortable with the idea of hanging out with her family tonight. He seemed fine—jaw relaxed, shoulders not climbing up to his earlobes, a soft smile lifted his lips. She probably looked the same. It had been a long time since she had felt so good. He'd loved all the stress out of her limbs.

"Aunt Chloe! You're late." Henry ran toward them. "We're making s'mores."

"Yum." She smiled at her nephew. "My favorite."

"Hey, Fish made it," Matt called out.

"Fish?" Nicolas asked.

"It's my nickname. I used to spend hours and hours in

the ocean, chasing after these two—bodysurfing, swimming to the buoys and doing handstands in the water." She leaned closer and whispered. "We'll swim later."

"Finally," Jeff said, to which Michele playfully slapped his arm.

Chloe blushed. "Yeah, uh, sorry we're late."

Matt was watching her with a strange look on his face. Concern? "You missed my friends from my Forestry volunteer work. They had to go. We still have some of the tritip and I think there are some Santa Maria beans left, but the rest is gone."

"They all ate like it was their last meal," Julia said.

"I tried to get them to wait, but…" Jeff raised both hands.

Did Jeff give her a weird look, too? They were both worried about her. Protective. Huh. She did not expect that. At least their expressions didn't seem to be judgmental. Maybe Nicolas had been right all along when he thought her brothers wouldn't judge her for having a boyfriend. Her heart squeezed.

Boyfriend? Was that what Nicolas was?

In an attempt to not look any of her family members in the eyes while she sorted out all the crazy thoughts in her head, she spread the blanket down on the sand. The blush was already warming her neck and cheeks.

"My fault," Nicolas said. "Chloe was showing me her yoga moves."

"I bet she was," Michele mumbled.

Julia fake-coughed.

Could they all tell she'd been having wicked sex with the man of her dreams?

"Henry, how about you make me a s'more?" Chloe changed the direction of the conversation. "Nice and toasty."

"Sure thing, Aunt Chloe!" Little Henry hustled off to stake a marshmallow for her.

"You brought your guitar. Are you going to sing for us, sis?" Matt elbowed her.

She snorted. "Right. Nicolas doesn't want his ears to bleed."

"Come on, you're good. You used to sing a lot," Matt said.

"Yeah, all the time. Day and night, everywhere. Seriously annoying, but I liked your voice," Jeff said.

What were her brothers trying to do to her? She stopped singing long ago because her Dad told her to stop the noise when she was small. She had craved love and needed attention and had been devastated when her dad had shut her up. Her heart had broken and her voice went silent. She never sang in public again. And she for sure would not sing in front of Nicolas now. "Uh-uh. You two are nuts. Maybe Nicolas will channel his younger self and treat us with a song, though. I can strum along, or he can use my guitar."

Nicolas rubbed her shoulder. "I would like to hear you sing. No judgments."

As much as she loved him rubbing her skin… "My brothers are joking around. Ignore them. Let's eat. I'm starved."

They all got comfortable around the campfire. Michele sat in front of Jeff on a blanket, leaning against him. He played with her hair. Julia sat behind Matt, rubbing his neck and shoulders, while their son squatted next to them in marshmallow-roasting bliss. It was the picture of a happy extended family. Chloe's heart melted. She'd wanted to be a part of this scene for so long that she'd almost given up hope that it would ever happen. And yet here she was. It made her happy that her brothers had both found true love.

"Shall we?" She motioned for Nicolas to sit down on the blanket she'd brought. She sat beside him. Shoulder to shoulder. Touching but not nearly enough in her book. His body heat was lifting the hairs of her arm, and his manly fragrance was making her achy again.

Gosh, she was always in a state of want around this man.

She had to focus on something other than her insane desire to push him back on the blanket and have her way with him. "Hungry?" she asked.

"Starved." He gave her a lazy, sexy glance. "For something as sweet as honey."

She swallowed loudly, remembering how he'd tasted her as if she was the best dessert he'd ever had. Bumping him with her elbow, she whispered. "Later."

"Promise?"

She nodded. Her imagination was already getting ahead of her.

He took her hand and said far too loudly. "Okay, then. I'm going to hold you to me."

Everyone stopped talking. All eyes were on her.

"The expression is *hold you to it*," Jeff corrected him.

Nicolas lifted his shoulders casually and looked her in the eye. "Not the way I do it."

Chloe sputtered. "Tri-tip! Can we eat now, Matt?"

They ate their share of barbecue meat and beans, and had their fill of s'mores while Matt shared some of the search and rescue stories that he'd assisted on with the Forestry team. Matt didn't need to work because he was the heir to the Harper family fortune but he volunteered as a pilot for the forestry service because her loved rescuing people who were in trouble or lost. He'd always loved flying. His little boy hung on every word, but Chloe could see that his eyes were getting heavier and heavier. It was late for him. Finally, Henry curled up next to his mom and fell asleep.

When the conversation hit a lull, Nicolas picked up the guitar.

Her teenage, fan-girl self silently squealed. Her mature self politely clapped to cheer on her man and then promptly had heart palpitations. Was he really her man? It was crazy and so sweet at the same time. But mostly crazy. Her emotions were a hot mess.

"Are you going to sing 'Baby, Come After Me'?" Michele asked.

"And are you going to dance?" Julia pressed her hands to her heart. "I used to love watching you dance."

"Hey, I thought you loved watching me dance," Matt grumbled.

"I do, *amor*. But Nicky M was…" Julia fanned herself and didn't finish the sentence.

Everyone chuckled. Chloe knew exactly what Julia meant, but suddenly didn't want him dancing for anyone but her. She truly had lost her mind. "No, we will not make him dance."

"I'd dance with you," he said to her.

"How about Saturday night at the restaurant opening?" Michele said. "We'll have a small orchestra and you all can show off your moves. Maybe my hubby will spin me around the floor."

"Jeff?" Chloe laughed. "I hope you have steel-toed shoes."

"Hey! I'm not a ballroom champ like Matt, but I'm not a bad dancer," Jeff complained. To Michele, he said, "I'll spin you like you've never been spun."

"Promises, promises." Michele winked at Chloe. They had a running joke that Jeff would make any excuse not to dance. He wasn't bad; he was just such a perfectionist that he hated that he wasn't great at it. Apparently, a little healthy competition was going to get him out there.

Nicolas had a wistful look on his face as he watched the family discussions. Did he miss his own family? She rubbed his arm.

"Nicolas, as much as I loved your big hit, my favorite song was that soft one. What was it called? 'Meu Doce Amor'?" Michele asked. "Will you play that one?"

My Sweet Love. Chloe sighed. "I love that one, too. I learned to play the guitar to that song."

"Yeah, no duh. She strummed that song a million times until I heard it in my sleep. My sister taught herself." There was a fierce pride in Jeff's tone. "She's amazing like that."

"Stubborn and determined. It runs in the Harper blood," Matt added.

"No duh," Julia laughed.

"From now on, when I sing it, I will think of you," Nicolas said to Chloe.

She pressed her hand to her chest like Julia had done earlier. "That's the nicest thing anyone has ever said to me."

"Come." He motioned for her to sit in front of him. "You play. I'll sing."

She sat cross-legged and picked up the guitar. She could not lie—the thought of playing the song in front of Nicolas made her hands tremble. Casually, as if it was the most natural thing in the world, he put one hand on her thigh. The zing shot through her body.

"Relax. Breathe in light, let out fears," he whispered in her ear. "You've got this."

Repeating her yoga mantra back to her word for word? Could he be any more perfect? She smiled at him. "Piece of cake."

She strummed and he sang the melody next to her. To her. His voice was deeper than it used to be, richer, sexier. She didn't need to focus on the chords, for her fingers knew how to play this one by heart. Instead she turned to watch him.

The way he looked at her when he sang…

His gaze was sizzling hot—as if he meant the words. The lyrics about everlasting love and forever promises caressed her skin like soft rose petals. For years she had wanted to believe that this song he wrote was nothing but pure truth. That it was possible for her to fall in love with someone who wouldn't send her away. But the truth she knew up until today proved the song to be nothing but a fairy tale. She had stopped playing it a long time ago because it broke her heart. No one loved her like the lyrics promised. There wasn't a person in her life who hadn't abandoned her.

When Nicolas got to the last line, he sang it softly and straight to her. "My love, my sweet love, forever mine."

She stopped playing. The tears welled in her eyes. For a long beat they stared at each other in silence, as if they were the only two people on the beach, next to a crackling fire.

And then her family clapped.

"You were great." His voice was thick with emotion. "I have performed that song many times, but never like that. What you do to me, *gata*." He wiped the tear off her cheek with his thumb. "Come." He stood and offered his hand to her. Sexy desire hooded his eyes. To the others, he said, "Thank you for a nice evening."

She blinked and let him pull her to her feet. "We're leaving?"

His thumb made slow circles on the palm of her hand. "*After* is about to begin."

"Wait!" Jeff rose to his feet, too. "I need to speak to you, Nicolas."

"Now?" Chloe asked.

"Yes, now. I'll take Nicolas back to his room and Matt, you bring Chloe back."

Nicolas's eyes narrowed.

"What is this about, Jeff?" Chloe asked.

Matt rose, too. "I need to talk to you about something important, Fish. Sorry, man." He shook hands with Nicolas. "Family matters."

Dad. Her heart pounded. Why didn't they say so earlier? Was that why her brothers had looked so worried?

"I understand. See you later, Chloe." Nicolas placed a gentle kiss on her cheek.

"You better. I can't wait for after."

When Jeff's car pulled out of the lot, she turned to Matt and her sisters-in-law. "Spill it. What's going on?"

"It's your father, Chloe," Michele said.

"I think it has something to do with my mom, too," Julia added.

"My sources say he's been talking to the FBI to try to help Angel, to stop that gang she used to be involved in. Stupid. He should stay out of it."

"He loves her, Matt," Chloe said. "He'll do what he has to do to save her."

"He's not in the right frame of mind and shouldn't be driving himself anywhere."

"Driving himself?" Chloe asked. RW Harper didn't put his hands on a steering wheel. He had drivers for that.

"The Bugatti is not in the garage. No one has any clue where he went. Dad's gone missing."

Eighteen

Nicolas rode back to Casa Larga from the bonfire with a very quiet Jeffrey Harper. Chloe had taught him to notice body language, and her brother had the telltale signs of tension. Something was on the man's mind.

Harper parked the car in front and turned off the engine. "Chloe is a very special lady."

No question there. "Yes, she is."

"No, I don't think you understand. She is important, beautiful, fragile. Chloe means the world to me and I will do everything to protect her."

Nicolas crossed his arms. This aggressive-brother act was nothing new. He'd had to deal with posturing before. It came with the territory of dating lots of women.

"Duly noted."

Jeff shook his head. "I know your type. Hell, I was your type. You can date anyone you want. Women drop from the sky, right into your lap."

Nicolas laughed. "Not exactly."

"But it's easy for you to make a woman's head spin. Especially Chloe's. She has been in love with you for most of her life."

Nicolas swallowed hard. Being a fan was not the same as love.

"She had it rough, man. Really rough." Jeff went on. "Some people should never have kids, and our parents were the worst. Chloe was always so eager to please, so sensitive. She loves people deeply and gives her whole heart away even when she gets nothing in return. She took care of me when I needed her. She'd stand outside my door and belt out her silly little songs. Until my dad shut her up." Jeff cussed under his breath. "Bastard ruined her, broke her free spirit. Matt and I protected her as much as we could, but then we were sent away and Chloe was left behind with that nasty woman we call *Mother*. It's a wonder she survived."

"*Droga.* She said her childhood was hard. I didn't understand how bad it was."

"I'm telling you this so you don't mess it up, Medeiros. Chloe means more to me than your business. More than the restaurant or my reputation. She's more family to me than my parents ever were."

"I understand."

"Again, I don't think you do. She cares for you—I can see that—probably too much already. It's not you—it's her. Part of her has been starving for love and attention her whole life and yet she has nothing to show for it. She'll pour her soul and heart into making this…*thing* between you into a real relationship because that's what she desperately wants. She deserves to have a man who will love her and cherish her for keeps."

Nicolas swallowed hard. The question was, did he deserve her?

"Let's cut to the chase." Jeff leaned in close. "Chloe is all that matters. Hurt her, and my brother and I will destroy you."

"I don't want to hurt her," Nicolas growled.

"But you will, right? It's what you do."

Nicolas didn't answer. They both knew the truth.

"Walk away now, Medeiros. I'll tell her you had an emergency back in Los Angeles and had to go. Matt will fly you back tonight."

Nicolas got out of the car but he didn't walk away yet. He leaned through the window and said, "No matter what happens, you need to do better by your sister. All you Harpers do."

Jeff frowned. "Me? What did I do?"

"You let her believe that she is not worthy of this job, of your love, of being a Harper—all of it. You better square that with her, or you will be hearing from me." Sure, he was growling, but he had the right. The Harpers had hurt Chloe and should feel pain for that.

Jeff's eyes widened. "She thinks that? Hell, Medeiros, she's the best of all of us."

"Then tell her, Harper. Prove it to her. Make her understand one-hundred-and-fifty percent that she is wanted here."

Jeff shook his head. "She is wanted. She's my family."

"I'm not the one you need to convince."

"All right. I'll make sure she knows how important she is to me, to our family. Your conscience is clear. But can you promise me that you are the best man for my sister?"

He breathed in and then out. It didn't help. He was still Nicolas Medeiros. "No. I can't do that."

Jeff shook his head. "Then walk away. It's the kind thing to do."

Was it the kind thing to do? Was he being selfish in seeing what could come out of this intense chemistry he had with Chloe?

Yes.

Jeff Harper knew the truth—Nicolas sang about forever relationships but he had no idea how to make one last.

He didn't say another word. He stomped to his room and plopped down on the couch.

Merda. What was the right thing to do? He wanted Chloe Harper more than he'd wanted anyone in a long time. And a week would not be enough.

He thought back over all of the pretty faces in his past and realized that Jeff was right—Chloe was special. No one had come closer to being someone who could genuinely complete his life. She was the real deal, a woman who could be a forever girl, but could he be a forever man?

Chloe thought he had the right stuff for a long-lasting relationship, but he wasn't so sure he was capable of the kind of commitment she deserved.

He couldn't change who he was, even if part of him, a big part, wanted to. He'd always be the poor, desperate boy struggling to support his family and make the world love him. He worked like the devil to keep the demons of poverty away but that meant making everyone else in his life a second or third priority. Finding space in his life to be fully present with Chloe in a real loving relationship, long-term? No, he couldn't see how to do it.

Jeff Harper was right. He should walk now.

So why wouldn't his legs move?

His cell rang. He looked around the room and remembered he'd left it inside the drawer in the bedroom because Chloe had asked him to. It was just another sign that the woman was getting to him. When had he ever left his phone behind for anyone? And yet he hadn't thought about answering emails or taking calls all day.

"Yeah?" he answered.

"I've been texting all day. I thought you'd died for real

this time," Tony, his former agent, complained. "Are you okay?"

"Never better. I disconnected for the day."

"Jeez, Nic. You've got to tell me when you are taking a break from reality. Just about gave me a coronary."

"You need to exercise more and eat less. So…what's up?"

"I was just checking in on you. Your office is driving me nuts. You apparently disconnected from their calls, too."

"I did. Everyone deserves a vacation, Tony."

"Don't bite my head off—I'm just the messenger. So… how's the Harper property?"

Nicolas thought about all the beautiful spots Chloe had shown him. His favorites were the ones where he got a taste of her lips to sweeten the view. *Deus*, she had been so beautiful standing on that ledge, looking out to sea. Like a goddess.

"Amazing. I'm going to sign the contract. The place is perfect for the show."

"You don't want to see the other two locations first?"

"No. I've seen everything I want and it's here." She was here. "And I may be staying a few more days to enjoy the area. It's a beautiful place for yoga."

There was a beat of silence. "Ah, no. Tell me this isn't about another woman. Is she the one teaching you yoga, making you sign the contract?"

Nicolas didn't say a word.

"Jeez, Nic. Lila is still out there smearing your name and you're getting it on with a stranger? What's the matter with you, man?"

She was no stranger. They'd only known each other for a few days, but he knew Chloe. It seemed like he'd known her forever.

"This lady is special, Tony. Nothing like Lila. She's genuine and sweet. Kind and thoughtful. She's one of a kind."

"Yeah, sure she is. They all are when they want something from you." Tony let out a sharp breath. "When are you going to grow up?"

That hurt. "I am trying to be a better man here."

"Really? 'Breathing in light and exhaling fears' and all that crap?"

Nicolas's heart skipped a beat. "What did you say?"

"Yoga brainwashing. Did you forget that I was taken in by a yoga instructor once? A real babe. I thought I loved her." Tony snorted in disgust. "After I talked up her studio, sent some real big hitters her way, she dumped me like a sack of trash. She was a cold, callous man-eater."

Tony had complained about this yoga instructor before, but he'd been in love? It didn't seem possible. Tony dated; he didn't settle down. The women at Nicolas's music label complained that Tony hit on them all the time and were more than a little pleased when he'd been spurned by someone outside the music industry. They had, in fact, cheered about it.

Tony was still fuming about the yoga instructor. "The blue-eyed babe had my number. What a great actor she was."

A strange foreboding poked Nicolas in the solar plexus. "What was her name?"

"Chloe Harper."

His heart all but stopped. *No, no, no. Tony had loved Chloe?*

He heard Chloe's voice in his memory. *I moved here because I couldn't stand the fakeness. The superficiality. I'm striving for deeper relationships now.*

Was that true, or was she an actress after all? She'd supposedly used Tony to advance her yoga studio. Had she used Nicolas to get him to sign her father's contract? Had she taken him like she'd taken Tony?

If so, it was his own damn fault. He'd let his guard down and trusted her.

"Are you listening to me, Nicky? Don't sign your life away. And stop sleeping with every woman who comes along."

The line went as dead as his pretty dreams.

Chloe woke with a start. Was that a slamming door?

She pulled her robe on and opened her own bedroom door. A package fell at her feet. She looked down the hall but was alone. Why hadn't Nicolas come to her room?

She turned the package over and saw a note.

Chloe,
Something came up. I had to go back to LA. I will call you.
NM
PS You did a great job making me fall in love with the place.

She opened the envelope and found her dad's contract. Signed. Nicolas agreed to having the show at Plunder Cove. She'd fulfilled her job. Dad was going to be proud of her for once.

She should be happy, but something told her that the "thing" that came up was all wrong.

Nineteen

Nicolas had rented a car to drive back to LA. The long drive gave him time to think.

Tony had been in love with Chloe, which didn't surprise him in the least. Chloe was easy to love. But what had she felt for Tony?

Was Chloe a con artist? The conniving man-eater Tony said she was?

No, Nicolas couldn't believe it. Her lips, her sexy body, hadn't lied when Nicolas touched her. She'd let herself go with him, completely, wholly. He knew who Chloe Harper was at the core. She was a caring, real, wounded woman who was working on becoming her best self. She had risen above her lousy childhood and had helped others through her yoga and kindness.

She'd tried to help him rise above his lousy childhood, too. She hadn't failed. Her process was working. When he'd tried to live in the moment and to feel as intensely as she did, he learned to just…breathe.

While he was with her, he forgot about everything that had hurt him, everything that had led him to work way too hard and lose the music he'd once loved. It was an amazing thing to let some of the suffering go and to kick the heavy baggage he'd been carrying for twenty years to the side. In doing so, he'd connected with Chloe like he'd never connected with anyone. He was completely alive for the first time in his life. Sensations, colors, feelings, everything was beautiful when he was with her.

But it wasn't enough, was it?

He cared for her, was attracted to her, to everything about her. But love? He had no idea what true love was. How could he give something to her that was beyond his comprehension? It ripped him up when she'd cried after they'd made love the last time. Had she known the truth then—that he would never be the guy she hoped he'd become? Possibly.

It broke his heart that he wasn't a better guy. He wasn't good enough for Chloe Harper and never would be.

He knew who he was.

A man who'd done very little to help humanity. One who had performed no real acts of kindness. He'd dated lots of women but hadn't loved any of them. He wasn't a father. He had few real friends. If he'd learned anything the last few days, he finally understood that he needed to do better with his life. *Be* better.

Jeffrey Harper was right. Nicolas didn't deserve Chloe. Not now anyway. If he could work on himself, like she had worked on herself, maybe he could become the man he was supposed to be. A better man. In her search for deeper relationships, she had changed. He could, too.

Maybe.

Somehow.

He didn't expect her to wait for him. She should move on and find a man who was already worthy of her. She should grow the family she cared about so much. Chloe deserved that and more.

He drove on in the night, heading toward his dark, large home in Beverly Hills, feeling lonelier than he ever had in his life.

His cell phone buzzed with a text coming in. His heart sped up, hoping it was Chloe, but his mind wondered what he'd say if it was. He didn't have the courage to say good-bye to her yet, because a large part of him didn't want to let her go. As he came to a stoplight, the image that appeared on his screen was not the one he wanted to see.

Lila.

He didn't answer it. He didn't care why she was calling. He felt exactly nothing.

Driving through the night, he realized that he'd dodged a bullet as far as Lila was concerned.

His cell phone beeped again, and the screen lit up with Lila's text.

I made a huge mistake. I need you, Nicky. Call me. Please.

He shook his head and turned on the radio, catching the end of a song he loved. He'd produced it two years ago and it still made him smile. He hadn't been the singer or songwriter, but he knew in his heart that it wouldn't still be on the radio two years later if he hadn't been the producer. He let himself absorb the good feelings and enjoy them. Breathing it in. It had been a long time since he'd felt pride in his work. There was only one word to describe what had changed him.

Chloe.

"I'm living in the moment, sweetheart," he said softly. "Wish you were here."

When the song ended, the DJ's voice came on. "Our

thoughts and prayers go out to Billy See. We all hope he gets better quickly."

Nicolas gripped the steering wheel. What happened to his drummer, his friend? Ex-friend.

He pulled off the freeway, picked up his cell phone and listened to Lila's voice mail.

"Hey, Nicky. I know you don't want to talk to me. I get it." She made a sound that reminded him of air squeaking out of a balloon. "I screwed up with you, with Billy. I'm so sorry." She was crying. "Billy and I had an argument and he got on his motorcycle… Oh, God. He hit a tree, Nicky. He's in the ICU, Cedars-Sinai. I can't… I don't have anyone… Please come."

He didn't hesitate. He texted back.

I'm about two hours out. Hang on. I'm coming.

When Nicolas didn't call the next day, Chloe got worried. She went to the hotel construction site to see Jeff. He was behind the workmen's tape, talking to the foreman.

"Jeff, can I talk to you?" she called to her brother.

He lifted his finger and came out to see her. "What's up?"

"Have you heard from Nicolas?"

"Uh. Nope."

"He left in such a hurry. What did you tell him?"

"Me?" He had his guilty face on. "Great work, by the way. I'm glad he signed the contract. The show is really going to help us with publicity."

"I'm glad he chose our resort, too. But now he's gone and I have a feeling by the pinkness creeping up into your earlobes that you know why. Spill it, Jeffrey Davis."

"Ouch. My middle name, too? That sounds serious."

She crossed her arms.

"I know his type, Chloe. He's a player. You don't want a guy like him."

Oh, yes, she did. More than anything. "What did you say to him exactly?"

"That you are special and deserve a man who will love and cherish you for keeps. You are important to me, Chloe. To Matt and Dad, too."

She pressed her hand to her chest. "Wow, Jeff. That was really sweet." And it sounded suspicious. "Nicolas told you to say that, didn't he?"

"Doesn't mean it's not true. Seriously, Chloe, I love you. We all do. You are the glue in this family that makes it all stick together."

Tears filled her eyes. "Thank you. I think I knew that, but I guess I needed to hear it out loud. You are a sweet brother." She hugged him.

He patted her back. "Yeah, really sweet. Keep that thought."

She looked up at him. "What else did you tell him?"

He rubbed the back of his neck, a typical nervous Jeff move. "After Nicolas and I had our little come-to-truth moment, I, uh, threatened to destroy him if he hurt you. You know, the usual brotherly love stuff."

"You wouldn't destroy him."

"Of course I would. If he hurt you, there would be nothing left of him. Matt feels the same way." Jeff paused. "Okay, fine. I might have told him he should leave, too."

A boulder dropped into her belly. "What? No, Jeff, you didn't!" She gave him a shove.

"Hey!"

"Why did you do that? I'm an adult. I can make my own choices with men. What is the matter with you?"

"Just listen to me for a second. What I said was just a shot across the bow, a warning. Guys get this stuff. Brothers have to say things like that to protect their little sisters. Everyone knows it."

She frowned. "Not me. No one has ever stood up for me like that before." Both Nicolas and Jeff had tried to protect her and yet here she was. Alone. "I don't understand. For the first time in my life, I *had* a boyfriend I really care about and now he is gone. Explain it to me."

"I'm sorry, sis. I really am, but he doesn't deserve you. That's why Medeiros left. You are far too good for him. He knows it. I know it. You should see it, too. I suggested that if he couldn't do right by you, then he should leave immediately. It was the right thing to do. The kind thing."

She paced in front of him, her sandals kicking up dirt. "You had no right to do that, Jeff!"

"I was trying to protect you and look out for your feelings."

She threw her hands up. "I wish people would stop looking out for my feelings and just let me feel them! I'm getting him back."

"Don't call him, Chloe. Guys hate that."

"You are not the boss of me," she said, just as she used to do when she was a kid.

She stomped back to the house, determined to dial Nicolas's number as she went.

And she was ignoring how much she worried that Jeff was right.

But when she unlocked her phone, the morning news popped up and she saw an image of Nicolas with his arm wrapped tightly around Lila. The supermodel had her head nuzzled into his chest, like she belonged there. His other hand was lifted as if to shield her and block the photographer's shot.

No, that...can't be!

Chloe stared at her phone, not quite understanding what

she was seeing, or not wanting to. The news media was wrong, that's all. They had to be using an old digital image from when Nicolas and Lila were a couple. She peered closely, studying Nicolas. He was still wearing the clothes he'd had on last night at their bonfire date. Chloe's heart beat so hard, she worried it would explode. She ripped her gaze from his gorgeous, sad eyes and read the first words of the article.

Nicky M comforts Lila as Billy See remains in critical condition after his motorcycle slammed into a tree...

Suddenly, she knew what "thing" kept Nicolas from her bed last night. Her chest shuddered on her inhale as she tried not to cry. She understood why Nicolas would be in the hospital, waiting to see if his friend—well, ex-friend— would pull through, but did he have to be holding Lila like that after what she did to him?

More importantly, would he let Lila go?

Chloe's heart thudded through a dread that felt as thick as quicksand.

Had she just lost her boyfriend to his ex-lover?

Twenty

It was midmorning when RW got home. He didn't speak to anyone. He went straight into his den, opened his safe and pulled out a leather satchel.

"There you are," Claire said behind him. "We've all been looking for you, RW. Matthew was about to send out the Forestry's search-and-rescue team."

RW hid the satchel behind his back. "A man should be able to take a drive once in a while, Claire."

"Don't snap at me. I'm just saying I was worried. Are you okay?" She came closer.

He was shocked by the compassion on her face. When was the last time she'd looked at him with any feeling other than rage or disappointment? It set him back a step.

"Yeah. I'm fine. Just had business to take care of. No one should've worried." Acting casual, he strode to the desk and put the satchel inside the drawer.

"That's what family does, RW."

Family. He would do anything for the people he loved. And everything. He'd lost sight of that when he was with Claire, or maybe he just hadn't gotten it then.

He got it now.

"Why are you still here, Claire?"

She crossed her arms, looking so much like Chloe that it was uncanny. "I told you. I'm not leaving."

"Really? Why not? You don't belong here." Another voice said behind them. RW's heart leaped at the sound.

"Angel." He pushed past Claire and had Angel in his arms before anyone said another word. He cupped her cheek and kissed her lips softly. "You came back."

"Let me see you." She ran her hands through his hair, as if drinking him in. A radiant smile lit up her face. Hell, he'd missed that smile, so much that he wanted her here no matter what kind of deals she'd made with Cuchillo.

"Who do you think you are?" Claire was suddenly standing behind them, poking Angel in the shoulder. "Aren't you the help?"

"Claire!" RW growled. "No, she's not the help."

For a moment he'd actually forgotten Claire was still in the room. He warned himself to tread lightly with Claire because she had the power to steal from RW the one thing he wanted most—Angel as his wife.

"Mom, what are you doing in here?" Chloe rushed in behind her mother. "Angel! You're back."

"Hi, sweet girl," Angel said to Chloe. "It's good to see you."

RW was surrounded by all of the women who had been important in his life. Right now, he just wanted one.

"Chloe, please take your mother outside. Or go to the restaurant. I will be meet you both later."

"Um, sure. Mom, let's go," Chloe gently took her mother's arm.

"I'm not a child that can be hushed and sent away. I asked you a question, Angel, or is it Juanita?" she asked, referencing the time Angel had spent running a café in

Pueblicito under an assumed name when she was hiding from Cuchillo. "What are you doing in RW's room?" Claire demanded.

"Shouldn't I be asking you that question?" Angel faced Claire and trembled with rage. "I've spent years trying to repair the damage you've done, lady. Why don't you crawl back under the rock you came from and leave RW alone?"

Claire looked shocked. "How dare you speak to me that way. I belong here more than you do. Tell her, RW."

"Claire! That's enough," RW barked. Putting his hand on Angel's shoulder, he said softly, "Angel, darling, we need to talk."

"Talk about her? No, we do not." Angel lifted her chin and focused her rage on Claire. "You hurt him and left him when he needed you the most. You hurt your kids, too. Who does that? And now you're back to what? Take what you can from the family who is finally starting to live again? What sort of beast are you?"

"You don't know how it was," Claire yelled at her. "He wasn't like he is now. He was terrible."

"Mom! This is not a good idea. Please let it go," Chloe pleaded.

RW hated that his daughter had to see any of this. Hadn't he and Claire done enough damage to their kids?

"She's right." RW stepped between Angel and Claire. "I was terrible. No one should have had to put up with me back then. I didn't know how to stop the downward spiral. How to fix *me*. I'm sorry, Claire. I hope you will eventually forgive what I did to us. And Chloe, I swear I will spend the rest of my life making it up to you for ruining your childhood. I'm sorry, sweetheart."

Claire opened her mouth but no words came out. Chloe blinked as if she'd fallen through a hole like Alice in *Alice's Adventures in Wonderland*, which he used to read to her.

He faced Angel, cupping her cheek in his warm, large hand. "I'm not that man anymore. I have changed because of you, Angel. You changed everything. Please don't leave again. I can't stand life without you."

"Oh, RW. I missed you so much." Angel turned her head and kissed his palm. "There's something I must tell you."

"I know. There's something I must tell you, too. Will you excuse us?" He then ushered his wife and daughter out the door.

"But—" Claire began.

"Later, Claire." He closed the door softly in his wife's face.

RW tugged Angel against his chest and wrapped his arms around her. He kissed her deeply, treasuring her lips, her breath, the way she fit perfectly in his arms.

He'd missed her so much, it hurt. Kissing her now— knowing that she might not stay after he told her the truth— hurt, too. And yet he couldn't stop kissing her any more than he could stop his heart from beating. She was his drink, his drug, his life. After several long delicious minutes of reacquainting himself with her wonderful lips, he led her to the couch and sat next to her.

"Why is she here?" Angel asked.

He exhaled heavily. "She's my wife, Angel."

She blinked, cocked her head and studied his face. "You mean, she *was* your wife."

"Hell, in my mind everything about that woman is past tense, but legally..." He rubbed her soft skin. "She's still Mrs. Harper."

"You mean you're still married?" It physically hurt him when she scooted out of reach. Her posture was tense like she was about to bolt again.

"Not in my mind, no. I sent her the divorce papers long

ago. I actually thought she'd signed them, but I didn't follow up. It seems stupid now, but that's the truth."

She chewed her lip. "You haven't been together for years. Why didn't she sign the papers?"

He closed the gap between them and pulled her legs into his lap. "She could have. It was obvious we were never going to be husband and wife again. Especially with how things ended between us. I'm not sure exactly why she hasn't signed. She continues to draw a healthy monthly income from our combined shares and never had to work a day in her life. That wouldn't change with a divorce."

Angel just shook her head. "And yet you and your children work very hard."

"I'll get her to sign the divorce papers. She must see that there is nothing more for her here. I'll explain it to her again. If I pay her enough money, she'll sign. I know she will." He pressed his forehead to hers. "Anyone with two eyes can see that I am in love with you."

"Oh, RW." Her eyes misted.

He got down on one knee. "Marry me, Angel. Please."

Her voice cracked as she insisted that he rise. "You're too good for me, RW. I'm not worthy of your love." She covered her mouth as if to keep the sadness inside. Softly she said, "You have no idea why I'm here."

He took her hand and held it to his chest. "You came back and that's all that matters."

She let out a deep breath. "I had to."

"Because Cuchillo sent you."

She went pale. "How? Why would you say that?"

"I know you went to see him. He could have killed you."

"I went to protect you, to protect Julia. And everyone here. I begged him to stop following me. I want to have a life, too, RW." She looked him in the eye. "A life with you."

He sucked in a breath. She was the only thing he wanted. "Marry me."

"I can't. Cuchillo will kill you if he knows how much I…" She bit her lip. "I just can't."

"How much you *what*?"

Her bottom lip trembled and it took all his strength not to kiss it still. "How much I love you, RW. With all my heart. You are the only man I have ever loved."

He pulled her into his lap and kissed her like he'd never kissed anyone. He poured his heartbreak, joy, fears, life and love into that kiss. He never wanted to stop.

She was the one who pulled away.

"Don't you see? Cuchillo won't let us be happy together. He will kill you just to spite me. I can't lose you, RW. That's why I've stayed away for so long. I'm afraid of what he will do to the people I love."

"First off, you can't lose me. You are a part of my heart, the oxygen in my blood, my every thought and everything I do. I'm not really me without you." He kissed her temple. "Second off, Cuchillo will leave you alone once you give him what he asked for."

She frowned. "How do you know about that?"

"I was there. I heard his demands."

"RW! You went to see Cuchillo? How could you put yourself at risk like that? He could have killed you."

"For the same reason you went. To make it safe for you to live without fear. And I know why you came back—to rob me."

She stood up. "No. I told him that, but I won't take anything from you, RW. I can't."

"You are partially right. The only thing you can take from me is my undying love and devotion. I expect you to take as much of that as you can handle. In regards to what Cuchillo wants…" He rose and went to the desk drawer and pulled out the satchel. "I'm fully prepared to *give* you what you need. Here. These are stock options that should be more than enough to take to the bastard and call it square."

"No." She pushed the satchel toward him. "I need only you, RW. I don't need your money. I'm nothing like Claire."

"I know that, sweetheart. But you have to pay that bastard, or we'll never be free of him."

"I may have another way. Please sit by me. I have a story to tell."

He sat but his heart was pounding. If she didn't take his money, Cuchillo would always be lurking in the shadows, keeping them apart.

"I told you a little bit about my past, but I want you to hear everything. You need to know who you want to marry and what I did."

Her face was stricken with worry. Did she think he'd change his mind? He knew who Angel was. The past didn't matter to him. He linked his fingers with hers and held on.

"I ran away from home when I was thirteen. My parents had passed and I didn't like my sisters bossing me around. I thought I was tough enough to live on the streets without any family." She shook her head. "I didn't have a clue. My nickname was *Ladronita*, Little Thief. I took food and clothing only, to feed myself and other runaway kids. It was all about survival. Then Cuchillo saw me and invited me into his gang. He taught me how to become a better thief. I was a member of his family then, his girl."

She looked into RW's eyes as if expecting condemnation. She'd find none there. "You have nothing to be ashamed of. You were a child who was used and mistreated by adults."

She nodded. "Still, I knew better. I thought I had it all under control, until I saw with my own eyes what Cuchillo was capable of. He was no hero, no father figure. He was an evil man." She shuddered. "I didn't want to raise my baby in that world. I ran away when I was several months pregnant."

Her hands trembled in his. "I took Cuchillo's baby from him, to protect her and myself. But that was not all I took." She dug around in her purse and pulled out a long jewel-encrusted knife.

"Whoa. What is that?" RW asked.

"Cuchillo's treasured legacy." She turned it around so he could get a good look. "His grandfather gave it to him in Colombia. It was symbolically important because the man who wielded the ancient blade was supposed to hold the family's power in his hand. The legend told through the generations is that the blade was taken from a pirate who dared to attack the family's ship."

He took the knife from her and studied it in the light. "It looks like it might have come from Spain. I have gold coins, doubloons, from the 1500s that resemble the gold used in this knife. The jewels embedded in the hilt are worth a fortune, too, each one. But—" he looked at Angel "—some of the jewels are missing."

"I know." She was pale again. Her voice was soft, her eyes full of fear. "I took a ruby and an emerald out years ago and hocked them to buy the café in Pueblicito. And then to pay for Julia's college education, even though she didn't know the money came from me. It was the only way I knew how to pay for everything."

His heart went as cold as ice. "If Cuchillo finds out you did this to his family's heirloom—"

"He'll kill me, RW. For that alone. But also for stealing his daughter. And once the news spreads, his grandfather will send someone to kill him. That's why Cuchillo is so desperate to get the jeweled knife back."

Silence filled the room.

RW's mind started spinning with ways to fix this mess.

She put her hand on his arm. "That's why I had to come here. Not to rob you, but to ask for a loan to buy the jewels back. The new owners will sell once I tell them the history. No one in their right mind would steal from Cuchillo's grandfather. Except me, of course." Her lips actually quirked with self-deprecating humor. At a time like this? God, she was amazing. "Once I return the knife to Cuchillo—and allow him to meet Julia—then maybe, hopefully, he'll leave us all alone."

RW hated the idea of her dealing with that killer again. "That's a big gamble, Angel."

She sighed. "What choice do I have?"

"Let me think on it. For now, you're staying with me," he growled.

"That's not necessary."

"Oh, babe, it's necessary. I have big plans for you tonight." He hadn't forgotten that she'd said she loved him. He'd been waiting years to hear those words from someone who meant them.

Tipping her chin up, he gazed into her beautiful, expressive face and swore to himself that he'd make her smile again. "Plus, I haven't heard an answer to my proposal."

"I'm not giving you a yes until I know for sure that Cuchillo is not going to come after us."

"I'll figure that out. For now, let me make you happy."

"You do, RW. You always do." She wrapped her hand around his neck and pulled his lips to hers.

Twenty-One

Nicolas and Lila were in the waiting room, desperate for a doctor, nurse or anyone to come out and give them Billy's status after his operation. Nicolas got up and bought two cups of coffee.

"Here. Drink."

Lila took one from him with a shaky hand. "It feels like forever."

"Yeah. If someone doesn't come out soon, I'll go see what's going on."

He sat across from her. "How are you holding up?"

She threw her hands in the air. "I'm dying here. Oh, Nicky, the last thing I said to him was…terrible."

He didn't ask, didn't want to know. She'd said terrible things about him, too. Lila was volatile and her mouth could get the best of her. "Billy knows you care about him. Just let it go."

She sipped her coffee, thinking. After a long moment, Lila pushed her hair out of her eyes. "I must look a fright."

Even with little sleep and maximum stress, she was supermodel beautiful. But he'd learned that he preferred a genuine beauty. One that got more and more appealing every second he was with her. He'd seen a true beauty and held her in his arms.

My Chloe.

"You look fine, Lila. Besides, who cares? You're in the ICU waiting room, not on a catwalk. Give yourself a break."

"Wow. You've never said anything like that to me before. You're…different," she said. "Calmer. More—I don't know—centered."

He grinned. "Yes. I am."

She tipped her head and waited for him to say more. He didn't. It felt wrong to talk about Chloe with his ex. Besides, he wasn't sure how to explain all the ways that she'd changed him.

"Well, whatever you are taking or doing, keep it up. Calmer looks good on you." She leaned forward. "I'm glad you're here, Nicky. I wouldn't have blamed you if you had told me to take a hike. What I said about you during that television interview… I didn't mean it."

"Words are powerful. Important. They mean things, Lila."

And so do lyrics.

Suddenly he understood why writing music was so important to him. Why he'd pushed it aside for so long. Words touched people, connected them, made the listener feel emotions, life. He'd been trying to hide from all of that, from all of the pain he'd felt as a child.

Chloe *had* changed him.

Now he wanted to feel everything. With her.

"I know. I'm going to try to be better. I promise," Lila said.

Better.

The word clicked in his brain and linked up with the familiar tune that played frequently in his head. It was the melody that had come to him in a nightmare in which Chloe had stood shoulder to shoulder with him as he faced his fears. It was the first nightmare in which he wasn't alone. The melody was intriguing, pulsing, vibrant—just like Chloe.

My Pirate Girl.

The title came to him like a flash of light, sending a tingle of hope up his spinal cord.

"Merda!" he said. It was perfect.

"What is it?" Lila asked.

"Nothing," he said. He wasn't ready to share the only song he'd titled in years. And he didn't want to push too hard to find the lyrics. He was afraid they might not come, so instead he said, "I've got some work to do. Mind if I do it while we wait?" he pointed toward his laptop.

She lifted her palms up. "No, of course not. I know you must have tons of work. Go for it."

He grabbed his computer and checked his email.

He had one from RW Harper. His heart pounded as he opened it. Was Chloe all right?

"Nicolas, I am excited about the prospect of producing your show on my property. I have one more caveat that I believe will benefit us both. Please return to Plunder Cove so that I can show you a gem that will make you a very wealthy man."

Nicolas stared at the screen. Leave it to RW Harper to try to negotiate another deal after the first one was done. *Sorry, Harper, but that's a big no.* If he returned to Plunder Cove, he wouldn't be able to keep his hands off Chloe. And he'd hurt her. Again. He couldn't do it. It was better for her that she believed he didn't miss her "kiss me" lips, better if she went on with her life.

As he needed to do. Someday.

He still had several contestants to listen to for the show,

so he put his earphones on, but what he played was Chloe's last voice mail. She'd left several and had hung up without a message a few times, too. He hadn't returned any of her calls. He couldn't because he was too weak. If he spoke to her, he'd hop in his car and drive up the coast to Plunder Cove. He would ruin her grand plan for a good life. It was better to not call and let her get over him.

"Hey. It's me." She sounded tired. "I won't call again because I know you won't return it. I get it. You've moved on. If Lila makes you happy, then… I'm happy. I only want the best for you." She paused. "I'm going to miss you." She made a sound that resembled a forced laugh that got clogged in her throat. "We were good for each other. I truly believe that. Because of you, I know what I am capable of feeling. But, uh, I'm not going to talk about that, because this call is awkward enough. Just…find love, okay? You deserve it. Goodbye, Nicolas."

His chest felt tight. His mind rolled with sadness because he knew he'd hurt her, even though he'd tried not to.

He'd left the only chance he had at finding love, because he was scared he'd ruin it. He hadn't called Chloe back, because he was a *burro*. He wanted the best for her, too, and Nicolas Medeiros obviously wasn't it. Not even close.

Adeus, Chloe.

He closed his eyes and envisioned Chloe Harper one last time. It was sweet torture. He could smell her fragrance, taste her honey, her lips, her sweet skin. Her voice was the music in his head. Her words, the lyrics. Her intensity, sincerity, depth, realness, kindness and goodness all poured over him. He imagined her swimming naked in the moonlight, the phosphorescence glowing around her slender figure, and wished that just once he could have bodysurfed the Pacific with her. He pictured her dancing in his arms and let her music play in his head. He was overwhelmed with feelings. He opened his eyes.

He opened his notes file, but instead of typing lyrics on a page, he let his fingers pour out all the emotions he felt about Chloe. He could barely type fast enough to keep up with the upbeat melody dancing in his brain. When he was done, he stared at the screen in utter surprise. On his computer monitor was the first song he'd written in more than a decade.

And it was good! No, not good. The song was great because it sounded like Chloe.

His heart pounded hard, for he knew, really knew, that this was a hit. This was the one he couldn't find in all the years that had come before Chloe. But more than that, he had laid out the truth in black-and-white, for even a *burro* to see.

"What just happened?" Lila asked him.

He took his headphones off. "What?"

"I was watching you work and the look on your face! I've never seen that expression on anyone. What are you watching on your computer?"

He swallowed. "A guy in love."

Before he had to say anything more, a doctor walked up to Lila. "Mr. See is out of surgery and asking for you."

Lila rose to her feet. "Billy is okay?"

"Yes. He's going to need time to recover and some rehab, but he is out of danger," the doctor said.

"Oh, my God. Thank you!" She kissed the doctor on the cheek and blew an air kiss toward Nicolas. "My man is going to be okay."

"Go to him. Tell him I hope he feels better fast," Nicolas said. "And to take care of you."

"Thank you." Lila almost ran down the hall.

Nicolas smiled. "Goodbye, Lila." He didn't think he'd

ever see her or Billy again. He was at peace with that. He hadn't loved Lila. Or anyone before his short but sweet visit to Plunder Cove. He could appreciate the difference between lust and love now.

He grabbed his stuff, jumped to his feet and rushed out of the hospital. He had a long drive ahead of him. He hoped he wasn't too late to prove that he was, in fact, long-lasting material.

Twenty-Two

RW invited Claire to meet him at the gazebo. It was a spot they used to share for quiet moments away from the kids and staff. RW recalled the times they would meet here at sunset to talk, drink cocktails and—when they'd been on happier terms—have a romantic moment.

It was a lifetime ago. And he was a different man.

"Our old place," Claire said as she climbed the steps.

"Come. Join me." He made room for her on the bench. "There is something serious I need to discuss with you."

"Let me guess. Angel, right? Is this—" she waved her hand "—*thing* with her really all that serious?"

"You have no idea." He watched her take a seat next to him—two married strangers. "I've been trying to figure out why you didn't sign the divorce papers. We haven't been any sort of married couple for years. Why do you still want to be tied to me? Is it all about the money?"

She blinked fast like she might cry. This was new. He'd seen Claire rage, scream, throw things at his head, but he couldn't remember ever seeing Claire shed a tear.

"I know you don't want me. Except for our early years,

when the kids were babies, no one has ever wanted or needed me."

He reached for her hand and took it. "That's not true."

She lifted her chin but did not pull her hand away. "It is. I admit I'm not the easiest person to be with. But you and the kids—you're my family. The only one I have. Without you, I'm simply—" she lifted her shoulders and dropped them heavily "—me."

He chuckled softly. "There has never been anything simple about you, Claire. And for the record, I am not the easiest to be with either. I know, huge news flash."

She tried not to smile but didn't succeed. "You are funnier now, too. Why did I miss out on all the good stuff?"

"Because we were wrong for each other. It took Angel coming into my life for me to see that. For me to want to seek redemption and happiness. I want all of that for you, too."

She wagged her finger at him. "You just want me to sign the divorce papers. Nice try but I will not sign over my family to that...that...woman."

He sat back, finally getting it. Claire needed the same thing he did—loved ones, people who understood and took care of one another. Family. It all made sense now.

"No matter what happens, you are still the mother of my children. No one can take that away from you. You'll still be a part of this family. I swear that to you, Claire. You are part of me, part of them. You don't need to be Mrs. Harper to be one of us."

She blinked and the tears fell. "Really?"

"Yes, really."

She dabbed at her eyes. "You'll invite me to the weddings? Baby showers? Birthdays?"

His kids were going to kill him. "Sure."

She nodded slowly, letting his words sink in.

He glanced around, making sure they were really alone, and then he told her about Cuchillo and about how he planned to take the man down. She sat quietly but her eyes were wide and her body rigid. He couldn't read her expression.

"So, this is where you step up and prove you care more about our children than you do money, Claire."

"Our children have always come first!"

"No, not always."

She wiped her cheek. "I've been a lousy mom, but I swear I want the chance to change. I love them."

"Good. Because my plan means giving up a lot of money to protect our family—stock options that are worth quite a lot now."

He'd bought the stock as the precursor to a hostile take-over. But the takeover hadn't happened, because Angel had mellowed him. How would the shareholders respond when they found out a Colombian gang owned 15 percent of the company?

"You're just going to give him the shares?" Claire asked.

"As payment. He must sign a restraining order to not come within a hundred miles of any of us again."

She glanced over his shoulder. "Including Angel?"

"Especially Angel. I want her to live without fear." RW would give Cuchillo more money than the man had ever dreamed of, but only with a signed contract and no more threats. If he saw even a shadow that reminded him of Cuchillo, he'd make sure Cuchillo's grandfather received a very broken knife.

RW let out a deep breath. "But you are still my wife. And half owner of all of my assets. You have a say here. Do I have your consent to protect our children and grandson?"

She was silent for only a beat. "Of course, you do. I'm still their mother."

RW started to step away.

"Wait!" She wrestled her wedding ring off her finger. "Here." She put it in his palm. "I'll sign your papers. And you can sweeten the pot with this. It's worth—"

"I know how much it's worth, Claire." He took the ring, remembering the night he'd slipped it on her finger. "Thank you."

He had a family to protect.

Twenty-Three

Chloe stripped down to her swimsuit and went for a swim in the ocean. She hoped the salt water would wash away her tears.

God, she missed Nicolas. He and his not-so-ex-girlfriend had popped up all over the internet. Some in the media said they had married in the hospital while Billy was in a coma. Others were reporting that Lila was carrying Nicky's baby already. Chloe didn't believe the reports—not really—but something was going on with Lila, because he hadn't called. The speculation, combined with the silence, was brutal.

She swam hard, her arms and legs driving her further out to sea until a sound made her lift her head from the water. She flipped over on her back and listened. Someone was calling her name. On the shore a figure waved at her. Her heartbeat sped up. Wiping the salt water out of her eyes, she squinted and realized it wasn't the man she wanted so desperately to see. It was a woman. Chloe reversed her direction and headed for the shore.

As she got closer, she realized the woman was her mother. *What now?* She kept swimming, focusing on keeping her strokes long, equal, breathing on both sides. She lifted her head again and saw that her mother wasn't alone on the beach.

Uh-oh. Angel stood beside her mom, close, nearly shoulder to shoulder.

Chloe kicked harder to head off the explosion that was about to happen on the sand. She lifted her head again and saw Julia and Michele walking toward the other two women. There was some sort of party going on and they all seemed to be waiting for her to get out of the water. Her mother lifted a towel for Chloe.

"Uh, what's going on?" Chloe said as she quickly wrapped up.

"It's your dad—" Angel began.

"And Matt and Jeff," Julia added.

Chloe's gaze swung from face to face. All the women were worried. "You guys are freaking me out. What happened?"

Her mother was the one who answered. "RW went to make a deal with Cuchillo, and the boys insisted on going with him."

"Oh, no. Didn't anyone stop them?" Chloe asked.

"They have to do this or the danger will never end." Claire's gaze was on Angel. "We're Harpers. And we take care of our own. We won't stand for a threat to any of us. Angel, you are one of us."

"*Dios mio.* Thank you." Angel reached out and pulled Claire into her arms. The two women hugged.

Chloe's jaw dropped. She looked at Julia and Michele, and they were just as flabbergasted as she was. How did this happen?

"My heart is not going to beat properly until they return. Let's go to the bar," Michele said.

"Cuchillo!" RW called out.

He was back at the compound, not hiding in the bushes.

He saw men on the roof and suspected they were armed. He knew he was a sitting duck and hoped that Cuchillo would prove good to his word about meeting him to negotiate. "Have your men stand down."

"Baja tus armas," a deep voice commanded from inside. "How do I know you have my family's legacy?"

"You'll have to trust me, just as I will trust you," RW said. He kept coming but motioned for his sons to stay behind him. "I will keep it safe unless you cross me."

"You have the payment with you?" Cuchillo asked.

RW lifted a satchel for all to see. "It's all here."

"Open the door," Cuchillo commanded.

A floodlight momentarily blinded RW while he was frisked. He knew he was clean. Matt and Jeff followed behind him.

"All right, Harper. Come on in. Welcome to my home. I'm sure it is nothing like your mansion."

RW didn't spend much time checking out the scenery. His eyes were pinned to the muscular middle-aged man puffed up before him and staring him down with dark, menacing eyes. "Cuchillo."

"I've got to hand it to you, Harper. Not many men would have the *cajones* to come here. Not sure if you are brave or stupid."

RW stared right back, unflinching. "Call me determined. Now, sign the restraining order and you can take the money, and Angel's debts will be paid in full. But I'll be watching. If I see even a hint that you or your gang is within a hundred miles of my family, you will pay. I've wiped out competitors far greater than you."

Cuchillo grinned. "I can see why she likes you, Harper. I will agree to your deal but I want one more thing. I want my daughter."

RW mentally begged Matt to stand down. He knew Matt

would never put Julia in danger, not even to meet the father she'd never known. "Your daughter is not part of this bargain. She is safe and happy where she is. You need to let her be. Trust me. I know a thing or two about screwing up a person's life. I'm a father who has made mistakes, too. And I am working night and day to fix them. Redemption. Forgiveness. Striving to make things better for my family. That's what makes a man worthy to be called a father. You wouldn't understand."

"I understand family," Cuchillo snarled. "I want to know my daughter. Is that so wrong?"

"Is this the sort of life you want for her?" RW waved his hand around. "You're selfish."

Cuchillo didn't respond with words, but his dark eyes flashed with anger. RW had touched a nerve with the insult. Good, he was going to grind that nerve under his heel and make the man feel the truth. "A father takes care of his daughter and works to give her more than what he has. It should always be about her. A better life, a better world, far more love and kindness, for her. Not you. Her. Don't you want to be a good dad?"

RW had hurt his children in so many ways. He'd nearly broken them, but thank God his sons and daughter were Harpers. They were stronger than he was. They were survivors, fighters, lovers.

"How would I know how to be a good dad?" Cuchillo huffed, rising to his feet. "Angel took that chance away from me."

"She did what was best for your child. Saving her from a life of crime and fear. Angel raised your daughter in a place filled with love and friends. She grew up strong but not fearful. Cherished. Wouldn't you have wanted that for her?"

Cuchillo's eyes narrowed. "You know my daughter."

RW wouldn't lie. "I love her like a daughter. She is a

part of my family now. Protected. So, do we have a deal, or will it be a war?"

RW saw what he hoped he'd see—Cuchillo blinked. He seemed to be thinking of his daughter instead of himself for once. "*Sí*. We have a deal."

As RW handed his enemy the satchel, he noticed Cuchillo's body language. Despair. RW knew how that felt.

"Let's rock and roll, Dad," Matt said.

"In a minute," RW said. "I have something else for Cuchillo."

RW raised his arm and chucked a silver object. Cuchillo caught it just as his men picked up their guns.

Cuchillo studied the object. "A phone?"

"It's a burn phone. If your daughter wants to talk to you, she can. You won't be able to trace its location."

Surprise lit up Cuchillo's features. "Why did you do this?"

"Because I know how it feels. Sometimes you want to hear your kid's voice to make sure she's safe. Happy."

Cuchillo nodded, his eyes watery. "You take care of my girl."

He nodded. "Remember our deal. Don't cross me."

He turned his back on the guns and forced his legs to walk steadily to the car. Once they got inside, Matt floored it. No one said a word or even inhaled for a few seconds.

"Hey, Dad?" Matt said, his voice soft.

"Yeah?" RW stared at the road ahead of them.

"That was seriously badass."

"Dad, you were amazing back there," Jeff agreed.

RW looked at both of his boys and grinned. "Your old man still has it in him, huh?" Then he touched both of their shoulders. "Thanks for the backup, boys. Let's go home. Our ladies are waiting for us."

Twenty-Four

It was the night of the grand opening of the restaurant. Chloe was excited for Jeff and Michele, and thrilled that Angel and Dad were attending together. Chloe's mother was there, too. Things were as they should be.

Almost.

Nicolas was supposed to be here with her—dancing, eating and loving the night away. He hadn't returned her calls or texts. She'd resigned herself to the belief that she'd never hear from him again. It broke her heart. Just when she decided to put herself out there again, the man of her dreams decided she wasn't worth the effort. It hurt.

But she had discovered what she needed to know about herself. She'd learned that she could fall in love, quickly, deeply if she let herself feel. If she appreciated every moment as it came and didn't worry too much about the future she could love herself, and build a good life with a man.

Nicolas had shown her she was worthy of love, even if he couldn't be the man to provide it. For that realization, she was grateful. It was time to retire her promise to stay away from men and start dating again. Maybe, eventually, she'd even fall in love.

She put on her favorite cinnamon-red gown and her velvet-and-crystal stilettos. Generally, she was more comfortable in yoga pants and a T-shirt, but every now and then she really enjoyed wearing a ball gown and four-inch heels. Instead of pulling her hair up into a twist or into braids, she left her hair down. The curls that usually annoyed her, or got in the way while she was working, were loose about her face.

The restaurant looked fantastic. Torches lit up every pathway. A line of cars was coming up the drive and a band was already playing in the great hall. Jeff's camera crew from his old show were filming for commercials. Chloe smiled. They were doing this. Patrons were going to see how wonderful Michele's food was, enjoy Jeff's brilliant architectural designs and get a sneak peek of the new resort they all were creating. Finally.

"Wow, you look beautiful." Jeff kissed her cheek at the entrance.

"Don't sound so surprised. I can wear something other than yoga pants sometimes." She nudged him in the ribs. "You look handsome yourself. Tuxedos always look fabulous on Harper men."

Matt joined them and snagged a basket of steaming bread and a dipping sauce as a server passed by. "Huge crowd. You ready to do our thing?"

"No. Not ever. I can't believe my dumb brothers roped me into this!"

"Us? It was Dad. He was the one who thought the singing Harper trio would add to the 'family image' of the place," Jeff said.

She held out her trembling hand. "I'm shaking already."

"Maybe you're hungry. Want a roll before we go on?" Matt offered her the bread basket.

"No, thanks. I'm too nervous to eat." She pressed her belly. "Hope I don't get sick up there."

"You won't. Breathe in light, exhale your fears," Jeff joked.

She slugged him.

Matt shook her shoulder. "Come on, it'll be fun. You only have to play your guitar in the first one."

"First?" Her eyes went wide. "There's more than one?"

"Maybe."

Jeff and Matt both laughed and dragged her up onstage, in front of the crowd. She was shaking all over. How had Nicolas ever done this?

RW picked up the mic. "Welcome, everyone. We are honored that so many of you came out to celebrate the grand opening of Plunder Cove with us. You are all in for a treat. Our chef, Michele Harper, is world-renowned and my personal favorite. She is busy right now, but later I will bring her out for a round of well-deserved applause." People applauded anyway. "Jeff here has done an amazing job getting the restaurant up and running in such a short time. The hotel is coming along well, too. Please check out the plans before you leave. This place is my home. It has been in the family for centuries, and now I want to share it with you all. My kids—Matt, Jeff and Chloe—have prepared a little something for you. Relax, eat and enjoy."

Nicolas walked into the restaurant as RW introduced Chloe and her brothers.

Nicolas stood off to the side of the crowd behind the Harper's table. Angel, Julia and little Henry were seated and preparing for the show. He looked at the small stage and his heart did a weird stumbling race in his chest when he saw her. She looked amazing in that red dress.

But something was wrong. She seemed pale and she struggled a bit to take the guitar out of the case.

"Come on, *amor*. You've got this," he said softly.

Angel turned her head. She'd heard him.

Up onstage, Matt took the mic. "In case you were wondering where all the pirates went, this is a little ditty about a pirate who turns forty far too late to enjoy the bounty. It's Dad's favorite song."

RW gave them a thumbs-up and went back to the family table. On the way, his eyes locked with Nicolas's. The man's smile was wise, as if he knew something Nicolas couldn't fathom. Nicolas dipped his head in acknowledgment and turned his focus back to the stage.

Matt sang the first part of the ballad. His voice wasn't bad. Jeff sang the next section. He too had a nice singing voice. When the two sang together, the song was actually good. Chloe played the guitar like a champ and sang the backup softly. She didn't have a mic, so no one could hear her. Nicolas smiled. She didn't have a thing to worry about.

When the song ended, the crowd roared with applause. Chloe blinked and a crooked grin covered her face. She seemed relieved to have the job done. Nicolas whistled.

"Encore! Encore!" The crowd chanted.

Jeff took the mic. "We do have one more, if we can convince my sister to sing the song she wrote for me when we were kids. How about it, Chloe?"

The crowd chanted her name. All the color drained from Chloe's face. She stared into the audience like an animal caught in the fast lane on the freeway.

"Look at me," Nicolas said.

Even though she couldn't hear him, her gaze swung

over the crowd. She swallowed hard and picked up the guitar again.

Jeff situated the mic in front of her and motioned to the crowd to quiet down.

There was a painfully long moment when Chloe didn't move, didn't make a sound. Nicolas knew all about public humiliation and didn't want her to suffer through it. He could rescue her by offering to sing the new song he wrote. He'd wanted to give it to Chloe in private, but this would work, too. He started to go, but RW put a hand on his shoulder, stilling him.

And Chloe started to play.

The first chords on her guitar were simple, childlike, but when she opened her mouth and sang, it was as if Nicolas heard light and sunshine. Hope. Her voice was sweet with a crackle of rasp. He'd never heard anything quite so pure. So unique. His mouth was open when he turned to look at RW.

"Her voice is amazing, isn't it?" RW said.

Amazing wasn't the word. He'd never heard anything like it. He listened with awe as Chloe sang to him, through him. She touched him, lifted him to heights he'd never experienced. He'd never been transported like this with his clothes on. The lyrics weren't bad either. Holy hell, she'd written them as a child?

When the song ended, the crowd roared. Nicolas was almost too stunned to move. RW rose to his feet and Nicolas snapped out of his trance, or whatever the hell she'd put him in, and applauded, too.

RW pulled him away from the table and into a quieter alcove. "What do you think? Can you get your label to sign her?"

Nicolas blinked. He still felt off balance, stunned by Chloe's singing voice. "What?"

"Sign her. Give her a music contract. Whatever you call it. Just give her the break that she needs."

Realization dawned. "*Chloe* is the gem you wanted me to see?"

"Of course. Why else would I have requested you come to stay for a week? I wanted you to see how great she is."

Nicolas should have felt used and betrayed; instead he felt…thankful. "You arranged this whole thing…for me to produce your daughter's music?"

"Hell, yeah, son. I owe my little girl. It's my fault she isn't out on tour and at the top of the music charts right now. She used to sing all the time, nonstop. It was her greatest joy. But I got tired of the noise—can you believe that? My beautiful little girl with her heavenly voice. It's my fault. My sins knew no bounds. I'm trying to fix it. All of it. Please help me make amends to my little girl."

Nicolas couldn't stop his lips from rising. Harper was a sneaky bastard, but he also loved his daughter. Chloe was going to be so happy when she knew the truth. "Have you told her any of this?"

"Not yet. I'm steeling myself for how she's going to take it." RW ran his hand through his hair, nervously. "But it doesn't matter if she hates me for this setup I arranged with you because a father gives his children what they need."

"What they need," Nicolas said. Was he what Chloe needed? *Deus*, he hoped she thought so after he had been avoiding her for days.

RW went on, "For Matt, it was the family I took away and all the planes he can fly, for Jeff it was a chance to build the best resort ever and the chef of his dreams, and now it is Chloe's turn. I want to give her what she needs and that is you, Nicolas."

Nicolas was stunned. It sounded like RW meant she needed Nicolas as a man and a music producer. "Just to be clear, Chloe didn't know you had her work with me so that I could make her a famous singer?"

RW snorted. "Son, do you know anything about women? Of course not. But I have to tell you that I didn't expect you to fall in love with her."

Nicolas shook his head. "Why the hell not? Are you insane? She's perfect, amazing and gorgeous. She's…" He couldn't think of enough words to truly describe her. "She's Chloe. And let me tell you something, Mr. Harper. You hurt her again, with even one hint that she is less than absolutely perfect in any way, and you will have me to deal with. Got it?"

The man actually smiled. "Go tell her that, son."

His heart hit the tiles. "I don't deserve her. I hurt her. She can do so much better."

RW chuckled. "As my grandson, Henry, says, 'no doy.' But if you don't try to make it up to her, you'll never know, will you?"

"Know what?"

"What it feels like to be alive." He turned to Angel. "Dance with me, my love."

"Dad looks like he's having fun dancing with Angel. Hell must be loaded with ice cubes," Matt said.

Chloe snorted. "I've got to see that."

She rose up on her tiptoes to see over the crowd but it was no good. The place was packed. She went around the edge of the great hall and sure enough, RW Harper was slow dancing with Angel. The two of them looked like they were the only people on the planet.

"Way to go, Dad," she said to herself.

"Can I have this dance," a voice said behind her, sending delicious shivers up her back.

Chloe was too afraid to turn around and yet she was incapable of stopping herself.

"Nicolas!"

"*Droga*, you look so good, *gata*."

He did, too. Harper men weren't the only ones who looked great in a tuxedo.

His gaze warmed her down to her toes. "Wow. Your hair is down." He lifted a stray curl off her cheek. "So beautiful."

She sucked in a breath and found her words. "You're here."

"Yes, *gata*."

"I didn't think I'd ever see you again. You didn't return my calls."

His gaze temporarily dropped to his feet. Embarrassed? And then his dreamy eyes met hers. "I was involved with a situation…"

"A situation." She swallowed hard. "I know. I read about Billy See. Is he okay?"

"He's going to be. He's got a lot of physical therapy in his future but he got lucky. Not many people hit a tree on their motorcycles and survive."

"That's good." She wanted to ask about Lila, but didn't want to hear about her.

"There's another reason I didn't call."

"Oh?" Her heart was pounding. *Don't say Lila.*

"I had something to tell you and thought I should do it in person." The fact that he seemed nervous scared her more than anything else. She braced herself for bad news.

"You are a special lady, Chloe. In such a short period of time, you changed me. I would never have believed it could be done." He caressed her cheek slowly. "I am so grateful."

She could hear the *but* coming. She sucked in a breath. "It's okay, Nicolas. You don't have to do this. I get it. You didn't have to drive all the way back here to say goodbye. I've done the 'it's not you, it's me' speech enough times to know what comes next."

"Like with Tony?"

She frowned. "Tony?"

"Tony Ricci. My friend who used to be my agent. Did you love him?"

"No, I didn't. I tried, but…he was someone who made me feel okay for a while, until I realized I was lonelier with him than when I was alone. Does that make sense?"

"Yes. It does. More than I'd like to admit."

"So, that's why you came back. To ask me about Tony? Sorry I hurt him. I just didn't know how to love anyone… then."

"Then?"

Her mind was spinning. "Nicolas, why are you here?"

"I don't care that Tony loved you. I'm just glad you don't love him." He wrapped one of her loose hairs around his finger and leaned in. "There's so much I want to tell you, but I can't think straight with you so close. Please, *gata*, dance with me. I have been dying to touch you. Let's dance first, talk later."

She offered her hand and when his fingers sealed around hers, her whole body sighed. It felt good to touch him. Like home.

She led him to the center of the dance floor, next to her dad, and next to Matt and Julia.

"Hey, look. It's Mr. Fast Hips. Can't wait to see what you've got, bro," Matt said just as he spun Julia under his arm.

"I showed him the music video and now he's trying to out-dance a seventeen-year-old boy," Julia explained. "Don't challenge him to a salsa dance-off, or this pregnant lady will have to sit down."

Chloe laughed. "My brother and Julia are the resident king and queen of the dance floor."

Nicolas nodded to both of them but put his hands on her. "The only queen I see is you. *Deus*, I missed you."

He held her close, his cheek to hers. They swayed softly to the beat. Everyone else in the room disappeared. His breathing in her ear both set her aflame and calmed her nerves. She was fully aware of every place his body touched hers.

There was that feeling again. *Home.*

"I heard you sing," he said.

Her cheeks heated. "Oh, God. Really? I'm so embarrassed. Sorry you had to hear that."

He tipped her chin up and looked her in the eye. "You have no idea how good you are, do you?"

She snorted. "Right."

"Chloe, this is no joke. I could make you a star."

She pressed her head to his chest. "I don't need to be a star, Nicolas." *I just need you.*

She had no idea why Nicolas was here or if he was staying. But she knew how to cherish the moment now.

She loved dancing with him. The way he looked into her eyes was enough. When he pressed his hand against her lower back, drawing her closer, she could feel how hard he was. She held him, determined to live in the moment for as long as it lasted.

He stopped moving and simply held her. It made her heart break and swell at the same time.

"Chloe." He didn't say her name; he growled it. She felt the vibration throughout her body. His lips were soft fire, burning, soothing, making her head spin. She fought against the desire pulsing within her. The heat, the need.

"I didn't think I'd see you again. I thought you moved on. Went back to your old life," she said.

"I'm here, *meu amor*." There. She could see the tightness in his jaw, his shoulders. He was nervous again.

She swallowed the lump in her throat. "Why did you come back?"

Those dreamy eyes were full of emotion. "It has nothing at all to do with your father."

She blinked. "What?"

He shook his head. "That's another story. This is about us. I'm sorry I left and didn't call. But I didn't move on." He rubbed her arm, lifting chill bumps of delight across her skin. "I think you're stuck with me. You changed me, made me realize I want long-term. There's no going back. I want a meaningful life. I want real. More than anything in the world, I want you. You are the hole in my life that I couldn't fill." He pressed his forehead to hers. "Until I found you."

"Oh, Nicolas. You are what I've been missing, too. I was devastated when I thought I'd lost you."

"You can't lose me, because I love you, Chloe Harper." His grin slid sideways. "I've never said that to anyone before." As soft as a whisper, he said it again. "I love you." Pressing his lips to her temple, he whispered, "*Minha paixão. Always. My Chloe. Minha vida.*"

She didn't recognize the Portuguese words, but they sounded like a prayer and felt like love. "I love you, too."

"I hurt you when I left. I'm sorry. I won't do it again. Give me a chance to make it up to you." The smoldering look he gave her sent a series of electric waves through her body.

"How do you plan on doing that?"

He grinned. "I do this thing with my mouth…"

Epilogue

Nicolas leaned over and kissed her cheek. "You've got this. Just look at me when we sing and it will be easy."

They were sitting on a makeshift stage by the altar in the only church in Pueblicito. The place was completely packed and it felt like every person she'd ever known was staring at her, waiting for her to perform.

"Easy?" She squeaked. "What if I mess up my father's wedding?"

"That guy?" He pointed toward her dad, who was standing at the front of the church. "Look at him. He won't even hear us."

He was right. Dad had the biggest smile on his face as he rocked back and forth on his heels, waiting for Angel to come down the aisle. He couldn't stand still. Like a kid waiting to go to Disneyland. Matt and Jeff stood beside him in their matching tuxedos, patting him on the back and grinning like two fools. How could she be nervous at a time like this? Her family was together and happy. Even Mom. Claire, who was sitting right up front so she could get a good view, waved her kerchief. Chloe waved back.

They were all here because of her dad. Because Angel had convinced him to *seek redemption, make amends and forgive himself.*

In fact, RW's plans had worked for everyone. In the end he got his family back, and each one of them had found love.

Chloe let her gaze fall over her extended family. Julia's baby bump was showing now. Chloe couldn't wait to throw the baby shower. Henry was at the back of the church, excited to do his bit as the ring bearer. Michele actually sat next to Claire. The two of them seemed to have buried the hatchet, and Claire sang her praises about the best chef on the West Coast. Her mother seemed content now that she was welcomed back into the family. Her two brothers were happy in their jobs and lives. Everything was perfect except…

"Ready?" Nicolas asked her.

"No. Never. Not in a million years," Chloe said. She was never going to be comfortable singing in front of crowds. The recording studio, okay, but on a stage? No way.

"One and two and three…" Nicolas started strumming his guitar and she quickly joined him. His voice lifted over the crowd, richer and deeper than ever. She couldn't believe that he'd written a song for her, about her. Currently it was sitting at number three on the charts. She had no doubt it would hit number one. It was amazing. When he sang the haunting, emotional ballad about being lost at sea and going down for the last time, her chest squeezed. He was on his last breath, lost in darkness, when the pirate girl plucked him from the deep and taught him about light and love.

My Pirate Girl.

Chloe sang the chorus, which ended with, "I'm here. Just breathe. Just breathe."

They finished the song together, gazing into each other's eyes. The look he gave her made it hard to catch her own breath.

"I love you, Chloe."

"I love you, Nicolas." She leaned over and kissed him.

Applause erupted in the church. Chloe blinked, remembering where she was.

Lightness and love flowed through her. Her sacral chakra was wide-open, just like her heart. Nicolas had healed her, made her feel better about who she was and let her sing. He was a dream come true.

No, better. He was hers.

* * * * *

COMING SOON!

We really hope you enjoyed reading this book. If you're looking for more romance, be sure to head to the shops when new books are available on

Thursday 13th June

LET'S TALK
Romance

For exclusive extracts, competitions
and special offers, find us online:

f facebook.com/millsandboon

𝕏 @MillsandBoon

◎ @MillsandBoonUK

Get in touch on 01413 063232

For all the latest titles coming soon, visit
millsandboon.co.uk/nextmonth

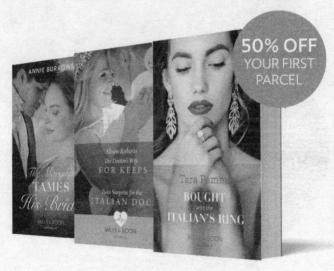